DEEP DIVE

DOUG HORNIG

DEEP DIVE

THE MYSTERIOUS PRESS

New York • London • Tokyo

Doug
Hornig

This is a work of fiction. Any real-life organizations or institutions mentioned herein are not intended to be accurate portrayals of their actual counterparts. All characters are fictitious and any resemblance to persons living or dead is coincidental.

 The Mysterious Press, 129 West 56th Street, New York, N.Y. 10019

Printed in the United States of America
First Printing: April 1988
10 9 8 7 6 5 4 3 2 1

Library of Congress Cataloging-in-Publication Data

Hornig, Doug.
  Deep dive / Doug Hornig.
    p. cm.
  ISBN 0-89296-257-7
  I. Title.
PS3558.068785D4   1988

FOR DEREK—
with the hope that in his day reading
will still be considered a worthwhile activity.

CHAPTER
1

"**I** don't see what's so god-damn funny," I muttered as I struggled to right myself. It was April Fools' Day and I felt like the Lord's original fool.

I'd been sitting on a rock, grappling with the wetsuit bottom, trying to jam my legs down into it. It was an experience not unlike attempting to pull a pair of old blue jeans over a butt that's outgrown them. I'd lost my balance and fallen over. With legs half in and half out of rubber pants, it wasn't so easy to get back up. Patricia Ryan thought that was hilarious.

I squinted up at her. "I hope you're real happy you got me into this," I said.

"Loren," she said between giggles, "I'm sorry, but I can't help it. You look so much like . . . like a turtle, that . . ." And she began to laugh helplessly again.

"Thanks a lot," I muttered. "And you think she might offer to help a friend up, right? But noooo . . ."

It *was* all her fault, too. I had never in my life considered taking up scuba diving. Not once. I mean, I used to watch *Sea Hunt* and Jacques Cousteau when I was a kid, and I thought it was neat and all that. But after I became an adult, it never seemed like something ordinary people did. Crazy guys, maybe, like the pair of Navy frogmen I'd met when I was in the service, two certifiable loonies. But me?

In addition to which I live in Charlottesville, smack in the middle of the Commonwealth of Virginia. The ocean is a day's drive away. It wouldn't have occurred to me that there were a whole lot of scuba divers in my hometown. Or that I might someday become one of them.

Lately, however, my life had taken some strange turns. Strangest of all was that I'd suddenly become rich. Not seriously rich, like Robert Redford or Ronald Reagan's former staff members. But rich by my modest standards. Over the years, I'd become accustomed to just getting by. That's all most private investigators ever do. My idea of a good month was not having to choose between the rent and the utilities.

Then, six months earlier, I'd been hired by a large corporation to help them beat a lawsuit. When the case was over, they dropped fifty thousand dollars into my lap. To me, fifty grand is rich.

Of course, I wouldn't end up with the whole stack. Uncle Sam would take a fat bite out of it come the middle of April. And Patricia had some residual medical bills. She'd done some lengthy hospital time as the result of an accidental involvement in one of my nastier cases. I'd paid what her insurance didn't cover.

Still, when all accounts were settled, I'd wind up with a weightier pocket than I'd ever had. I intended to put some of the money aside, sure. But as for the rest, I had every intention of enjoying myself to the fullest.

It was an odd, giddy feeling. Until the cash ran out, here I was: free to do whatever I wanted to do, to indulge the most bizarre of whims.

Like taking up scuba diving. That, of course, was not my idea. It was Patricia's. She'd gone through some changes, too. She'd spent a month of her life in a coma, clinging to whatever fragile thread holds the fabric together.

She regained consciousness in October. Since then, she had been living with a heightened awareness that any moment may be our last. She'd always been a high-energy person, which is one of the many reasons I fell in love with her. And now it was as if she'd turned her inner fire up yet another couple of notches.

She wanted to try everything.

One quiet evening, we'd been reading the paper when she announced, "They're starting a new scuba diving class. Let's take it."

"Patricia," I said, "it's the middle of winter."

"Doesn't matter, Loren," she said. "It says right here, classes begin next week. Come on."

I didn't much like the idea then and I still didn't like it much as I fought with my wetsuit after ten weeks of flippering around in a swimming pool with a half dozen other would-be dolphins.

"Up we go now," Patricia said.

I grumbled about it, but took Patricia's outstretched hand and maneuvered myself onto my rock. She was already suited up, of course, and I had a long look at her as she turned her back on me. Seeing her like this was one of the few bright spots of the day. It's an oddity of diving that, while men took thoroughly ridiculous in wetsuits, women look sexy as all hell.

We were forced to wear the miserable things because, despite it being only the first day of April, we were going to dive. In fact, we were going to make the final dive of the class, the deep dive. We'd done our pool sessions, learning the techniques and the equipment. The previous week we'd done our shallow open water dive. Now, if we successfully completed the deep dive, we'd become certified scuba divers.

Hot damn. What that meant was that I'd get a little blue plastic card that would proclaim my certification to whoever might be interested—for instance, someone who wanted to rent me equipment so that I could dive on my own. They'd have to have a lot of blind faith to be waiting for that day.

The site of our dive was an abandoned soapstone quarry in Nelson County, about twenty-five miles south of Charlottesville. It was a small quarry, a couple of acres at best. The water was over a hundred feet deep, though we wouldn't be going to the bottom. There were shelves and ledges all the way down. Our instructor wanted us to descend to about eighty feet, swim a few circuits, and then come back up. Visibility wouldn't be terribly good. Quarries are murky in the best of times, and what with a group of novice divers stirring up the silt, this wouldn't be one of those times. If we were lucky we might see some bass. More likely we'd only see each other.

The day was crisp and clear. Temperature around sixty. Forsythia and cherries in bloom, peach trees beginning to bud out. A nice early spring day in central Virginia. Water temperature, however, was a hair under fifty. That'll kill you in a very short time. Hence the wetsuit.

Speaking of which, I finally got mine on. It was a one-piece, called a Farmer John because it's somewhat like the kind of overalls you'd expect to see in a local barnyard. The reason it's such a pain is that it must fit you like skin, so that it can hold a small layer of body-heated water snug up to you. Otherwise, you freeze.

Once you get your legs in the rest is relatively easy. I pushed my arms through and pulled the big zipper that runs all the way up the front. The rubber booties went on next, then the hood, which tucks under the Farmer John. Fully suited, your arms hang slightly away from your sides and you walk like a robot. The whole wardrobe is done in basic black.

"Mr. Vader, I presume," Patricia said into my ear, with a little tongue added as a teaser.

"Very funny," I said. But what I really wanted was to rub against her second skin for a while.

"How we doing?" Steve asked.

Steve Furniss was the diving instructor. He was a cheerful, skinny guy in his mid-forties. He'd been diving since before the equipment was any good. He had some stories.

"Fine," I said. "Don't I look it?"

Steve smiled and adjusted my hood for me. I thought I'd had it properly tucked in, but I hadn't. He patted my shoulder when he finished.

"You two will be diving with me," he said. "We'll go first. Matt—" indicating his assistant, a hulking kid in his early twenties "—will take the next two. Then we surface, you guys exit and the next two come in with me again. There should never be more than six of us down there. Let's stick together, stay with the group you're supposed to be with. If you get separated . . . ?"

"Look around for thirty seconds," Patricia said, "then come up."

"Right. I'm gonna take you down to eighty. If we get a little deeper, it's okay. Don't worry. We won't be down long enough for anyone to even come close to the bends. Hand signals?"

We quickly reviewed the signals for emergency situations. Patricia and I had them down pat.

"You all drink your tea this morning?" Steve asked.

We laughed. Steve had told us that one of the traditional ways to keep warm is to drink a lot beforehand, then pee in your wetsuit once you're submerged. I didn't know whether to believe him, though it didn't matter. On my shallow dive, I'd found that the cold and the constant motion had made my bladder as tight as a snare drum. But when I got out of the water . . . well, this week I'd skipped the tea.

"What else?" Steve said.

"I don't know if I ever asked you this," I said, "but what if you, ah, get sick underwater?" I'd made the mistake of going out for an inelegant Mexican meal the night before. It was still sitting precariously.

"Just what are you expecting to find down there?" Steve asked.

I shrugged as best I could in my straitjacket.

"Well, it's not a bad question, actually. And the answer is, puke through your mouthpiece. Whatever you do, don't take it out of your mouth. You start gasping without your mouthpiece and you'll drown before you know it."

"Loren, you're not . . . nervous, are you?" Patricia said. She said it like a dare.

"Our fearless private eye?" Steve said.

"All right, guys," I said. "I am *not* nervous. And I am not playing detective today. I'm having fun, aren't I?" I gave Patricia a look. "If there's anything in that quarry more dangerous than a largemouth bass, I'm going to be very upset with you, Furniss."

Steve held up his hand. "Nothing," he said. "I guarantee it. Just remember what I've taught you and you'll do fine. Now, you about ready?"

We nodded.

"Okay, get the rest of your equipment together and come on down to the water. Let's do it."

He went over to the van he hauled his gear around in. Patricia and I fetched our masks, snorkels, fins and gloves, then joined Furniss at the van.

Now came the heavy stuff. Item by item, we checked it out and put it on.

The tank itself was an aluminum eighty-pounder, filled with air to three thousand pounds per square inch. I fitted the first stage of my regulator to the tank. The first stage delivers the air to you at reduced pressure, in case you don't want your lungs to explode.

That air is routed down a hose to the second stage of the regulator, the mouthpiece, which reduces pressure a little more. You suck and air flows into your mouth at a comfortable rate. You breathe out and stale air is expelled through vents in the bottom of the mouthpiece.

I slipped the tank into its backpack and tightened the straps that secure it in place. The modern backpack is an integral part of something called the buoyancy compensator, or B.C., an inflatable vest that wraps around your upper torso and fastens in the front. When you put the B.C. on, you shoulder tank and backpack as well.

Steve finished with Patricia and helped me into mine.

The next step is to activate the power inflator hose. This hose, like the one that delivers your breathing air, feeds off the first stage of the regulator, and it plugs into a little black plastic gizmo.

There are two buttons on the gizmo, and a small mouthpiece. One button lets air flow directly from the tank to the B.C. The other allows you to manually inflate the B.C., or to deflate it by raising the exhaust hose up over your head. In an emergency, if you remember, you can also use the small mouthpiece to breathe whatever air remains in the B.C. That feature just could save your life.

The primary function of the B.C. is to stabilize you under water. After your weight belt pulls you below the surface, you simply let air in and out of the B.C. until you achieve the near-weightlessness you want. This, plus its potential as a life-saving device, makes the B.C. one of your most important pieces of equipment. Yet most people have never seen one. In the movies and on TV, divers just strap their tanks right to their backs. Why? Because B.C.'s are not "photogenic," meaning that you can't see a woman's curves when she's got her B.C. on. I love Hollywood.

I now felt like I was twice my normal size and half again my normal weight. When I moved, it was like a drunk duck. I looked for Patricia. She was already at the water's edge, doing final gear-up with Steve. I waddled over and joined them on a large flat rock.

"Gonna dive today, are you, Swift?" she said.

I was unamused. I've always had what I consider a healthy distrust of mechanical devices, especially where my own hide is involved. Patricia's one of those people who rarely thinks about things like her personal welfare.

I spit in my face mask, to keep it from fogging up later, rinsed it in the water, and clamped it to my face. Next I pulled the flippers over my booties. And then, finally, I put on my insulated gloves. These have to come last or you'd be too clumsy to do anything else. I clamped my teeth over the regulator mouthpiece and took a few practice breaths. The air was cold and noticeably dry, but the thing was working fine.

"All ready?" Steve asked.

Both Patricia and I gave him a thumb-and-forefinger circle, the universal indication that everything is okay.

"Then let's go," he said.

The quarry had straight sides, so it was impossible to walk in. One by one, we rolled backwards off the edge. Just like Lloyd Bridges in the grainy, black-and-white sea hunts of my childhood. We had inflated our B.C.'s beforehand, so that we floated when we first hit the water. You want to do that until you get over the initial cold shock and the wetsuit begins to work.

I bobbed in the water. It was a strange feeling, floating there, as if I'd been suddenly dropped into a new version of the world. My vision was highly restricted, I couldn't hear much but the sound of my own breathing, I was touching only the cold and the wet. Up, down, and sideways no longer meant the same thing. I thought about Lloyd Bridges again. Then about my childhood. Then I realized that *Jeff* Bridges is pushing middle age. And then my diving partners were trying to get my attention.

We all shared thumb-and-forefinger circles again, and Steve followed by turning his thumb down, the signal to descend. Patricia and I glanced at each other. This was it. We raised the plastic gizmos above our heads and punched our exhaust buttons.

The air rushed out of our B.C.'s, and down we went.

I sank slowly and steadily. I kept reminding myself: breathe through the mouth, remain calm, don't ever hold your breath. At ten feet there was a rock shelf where we'd agreed to rendezvous. When I reached it, I stopped my descent with my flippers. Then I used the power inflator to let air back into my B.C., a little at a time. With some trial and error I was able to stabilize my buoyancy.

For all practical purposes, I was now weightless. It's the one aspect of diving that I found I enjoyed. After all, the only other way to have the experience would be to study TM or sign up for the first passenger-carrying space shuttle. This was cheaper than the one and less of a wait than the other.

With barely negative buoyancy, you can do anything a bird can do, only not as fast.

Steve and Patricia were waiting for me. Had I not known who they were, I'd never have recognized them except by the individuality of their equipment. Being underwater distorts everything. Objects appear closer and bigger than they are. The light, especially in a quarry, is poor. Water pressure compresses and flattens flesh. And colors wash out, more so the deeper you go. My diving companions' faces were a ghastly bluish-white. I doubt I'll ever get used to that. The resemblance to a corpse is too close.

They were, of course, not corpses. I could tell because they were moving around, seemingly impatient for me to arrive and get stabilized. What the hurry was I didn't know. There wasn't anything of great interest in this quarry. All we were going to do was go deep, swim around a little in the gloom, and come back up. To annoy them I took my time, ignoring them while I tested my buoyancy with a few barrel rolls and lazy somersaults. I had no driving desire to get down to eighty feet in order to see a lot of rocks that looked the same as they did up here.

I stopped fooling around. The three of us exchanged "okay" signals. Steve turned and began swimming downward. Patricia followed him and I followed her.

We swam in a spiral, descending slowly as we circled the quarry. Every once in a while I had to pinch my nose and blow through it, in order to equalize the pressure in my ears with the increasing pressure of the water. If you don't do this you rupture your eardrums, which can be painful.

The deeper we went, the harder it was to see. There had been some heavy rain four days earlier; runoff had deposited a lot of silt in the quarry, and much of it was still suspended in the water. Visibility was poor, ten or fifteen feet at most.

I tried to stay nearly abreast of Patricia. You don't want to get too far out of your buddy's field of vision. It's a real job to have to locate someone, and there's not the sense of the presence of another person that you normally have. The space directly overhead is a particular blind spot. I could hover a foot above you for half an hour and you'd never guess I was there.

There was relatively little life. Algae builds up during the summer and dies off in winter. As the quarry measures seasons, April Fool's Day is still winter. I didn't see any bass.

The sides of the quarry dropped down and shelved, pushing us gently toward the middle. There were also numerous rockslides and random slabs of stone, cracks and crannies and miniature caves. It seemed like Patricia wanted to poke her head into every crevice. I stayed with her, but these didn't interest me much. There wasn't anything in them.

After a while, Steve stopped and turned to face us. He indicated that we were to join him. We swam over. He pointed to his depth gauge. We were at eighty feet. The bottom of the quarry was still lost in the murk.

Steve checked our pressure gauges to make sure our air supply looked good, then motioned us to follow him. We began our circuits of the quarry at depth.

For the first five minutes, nothing happened.

I was fussing with my weightbelt. I had cinched it tight at the surface. But as we'd gone deeper, the spongy wetsuit had compressed and now the belt threatened to slide down over my hips. It was a struggle. The gloves were awkward and inside them my fingers were beginning to go a little numb. Plus I was trying to keep my buddies, who appeared to be having no equipment problems, in sight at all times.

Then, suddenly, Patricia turned my way. She pointed down and to the right. I looked, but didn't see anything. I shook my head. She moved her hand more vigorously, stabbing with her forefinger as if working a touch-tone phone. I stared into the gloom, looking for a giant bass shape or something. And I still didn't see it.

Finally she jackknifed her body and began to flipper downward. I didn't like this. We weren't supposed to go deeper than eighty. I wondered if she'd contracted a little case of rapture of the deep, a giddy sensation caused by excess nitrogen in the blood. The condition causes you to do irrational things. I looked around for Steve. He'd disappeared in the sludge and was now presumably looking around for us. Sweat began to accumulate between my skin and the wetsuit.

Patricia was now at the edge of my range of vision. She'd gone down about another ten feet and was occupied with a massive rockslide or something in the middle of it. I made my decision. We'd had it pounded into us in class, over and over: in an emergency, or an unusual situation, you stick by your buddy. I went down after her.

She was pulling on something, bringing it toward her, hand over hand. I couldn't see what it was until I was nearly on top of her. It was a length of braided steel cable. Now I could see a long loop of it, laying against the boulders beneath her. She continued pulling, and then she had the device in her hand.

I stared at it for a moment without comprehension. The metal was shiny. It hadn't been underwater for long. There were a couple of levers and some gears, the steel cable slipped through there and was clamped down, and. . . . Of course. It was a come-along. A small, hand-held winch that you worked with the levers. Cautious drivers carried them in their trunks. You could move a surprising amount of weight with them. You could, by yourself, haul your car up out of a ditch.

I looked around me. No car.

Patricia stared at the come-along, then at me. I shrugged. Somebody had dropped the thing in the quarry. So what? I pointed at my depth gauge and gave her a thumb-up signal. We shouldn't be down this deep.

She ignored me. I think that she's intrigued by an unanswered question even more than I am. She let go of the come-along. It fell back onto the rocks, making a dull sound, muted by the water.

I tried to take Patricia's arm, but she pulled away from me.

She hovered in place over the rockslide, turning her head slowly, peering hard into the shifting twilight of close to a hundred feet of water. I began to sweat more heavily. At a hundred feet, your margin of safety with regard to the bends is only a bit more than half what it is at eighty. I didn't feel like cutting it close on the first deep dive of my life.

Patricia still didn't respond to my signals. She'd stopped turning her head. She was staring intently at something.

Cautiously, she flippered over to whatever it was she'd spotted. There was nothing else to do, so I followed. She stopped and pointed, and now even I could see.

There, five feet from us, wedged between the rocks, in full diving gear, was a human body.

CHAPTER
2

Two weeks later, Patricia and I were drinking after-breakfast coffee and reading the Sunday morning paper. We were at my place, a small apartment in the basement of a fifty-year-old frame house built into the side of a hill in the Belmont section of Charlottesville. We'd had a nice night. We nearly always had nice nights.

The paper had gotten us into a chat about politics, as newspapers will. We have sort of a running argument going. I'm not very political. My basic feeling is that politicians are all scoundrels, out to separate us from our money any way they can. So why bother to vote?

I like to point out that over the past twenty-five years (about the span of my political awareness), the only difference between the parties has been that the Democrats have consistently brought us ineptitude while the Republicans have with equal consistency delivered scandal.

We got Kennedy botching the Bay of Pigs. LBJ dragging us into Vietnam, then dropping out when he realized what a terrible mistake he'd made and couldn't figure out how to fix it. Carter bumbling his way through just about everything.

And on the other side, Nixon and his gang of thugs, the likes of which we never thought we'd see again. Until Reagan came along and effortlessly topped him. Somehow, the Great Communicator has managed to preside over so many scandals, has had such a mind-boggling number of his high officials either indicted, fired, or forced to resign in disgrace, that by comparison Tricky Dick looks like a model executive and an impeccable judge of character.

(Where Friendly Jerry Ford fits in I'm not sure, except that he's already the least remembered president since Millard Fillmore.)

Patricia's still a believer, though. She always votes, chooses among the candidates for each office, pulls the *yes* or *no* lever on every question. She feels we have the best system there is and that using it is the only way to change things for the better.

The end result is that we acknowledge each other's points of view and have agreed to disagree, without getting all bent out of shape about it.

In the middle of our discussion my landlady, Mrs. Detweiler, had appeared to tell me that she was lowering the rent again. Mrs. D. is a flinty old lady in her mid-eighties who's been a Socialist all her adult life and fought hard in the labor wars of the Thirties. The older she gets, the more she lowers my rent. I think it's her intention to exit this life with the same number of possessions she had when she arrived.

In the meantime, she works tirelessly to upgrade my political consciousness, even though she must realize by now that I'm a very unlikely convert. Too self-centered, she would say.

On this Sunday, my landlady had treated us to some lively speculations about the evil designs of a Saudi-American consortium that was gobbling up land in central Virginia. She made us laugh even as she was driving her points home. When she'd gone, the sense of her presence lingered a while.

Neither Patricia nor I had given much thought to the body we'd discovered in the quarry. It had turned out to be the earthly remains of one Eric Vessey, a Charlottesville realtor in his early thirties. A stranger to us. Obviously enough, he'd drowned.

We'd answered the routine questions put to us by the

Nelson County Sheriff's Department. They'd filled in some forms and let us go and we hadn't heard from them again.

It had been a shock, but not a terrible one. I'd seen dead people before. Lots of them in Nam, and a few since I returned to civilian life. And then, I'd faced the real possibility of my own death, in the person of an enraged two-hundred-and-eighty-pound madman. After that, my shock threshold went way up.

I was reading the local news section of the paper, our own *Daily Press*. Of late, a lot of ink had been devoted to the subject of AIDS.

"They're announcing this week whether the kid has to leave," I said.

Patricia looked up from the feature section. "Huh?" she said. "What kid?"

"The one with AIDS. In that private school."

It had been discovered that one of the children in Albemarle County's most exclusive (and expensive) "alterna-tive" school had AIDS. The liberal yuppie parents of the other students had immediately discovered the limits of their liberalism and had petitioned the school's administrators to have the unlucky kid given the boot. It looked like they were going to win.

"Well," Patricia said, "I don't know. Maybe they should."

"It's not contagious," I said.

"They don't really know that."

"It just seems to me that you've always got one bunch of people turning another bunch into outcasts. You and me because we're not married. Some poor six-year-old because he's got AIDS. It grinds my teeth, I can't help it."

"I know what you're saying, Loren. And I agree with you up to a point. But what if *your* kid was going to school with somebody who had it?"

"I'd tough it out," I said without a lot of conviction.

"Would you? Well, I wouldn't. If it was my child, I just couldn't take the chance."

She looked at me as if to say, *You'd better agree with me on this.* We'd never discussed the possibility of having children. I'd never discussed it with anyone but my ex-wife, and then only long enough for her to declare that she had more important things to do with her life than be a mother. But Patricia had a strong maternal side. She protected her own.

Fiercely. She'd cared for a younger brother who was paralyzed in a car accident, until he'd become self-supporting. I had no doubt that someday she'd want to have a baby. When she did, you wouldn't want to cross her in anything concerned with its welfare.

I looked back at her as the silence between us drew out. A difference in political orientation was one thing. This was another. I didn't fancy turning a relatively peaceful Sunday morning into a clash over something that didn't directly affect us. All I was feeling was sorry for the poor kid who had got stuck with AIDS and, as if that weren't enough, would have to grow up surrounded by the kind of hysteria that would make sure he never had any friends. It was a rotten thing to happen to you when you were six. Or any other age.

I licked my lips. "Yeah, well . . . ," I said, just to break the silence. I really have no idea what I was going to say after that, but fortunately I didn't have to find out. The phone rang.

"I'll get it," I said quickly, and I stepped over to my desk.

"Mr. Swift?"

A female voice. High-pitched, slightly unpleasant. I didn't recognize it, but I'd have known it was a business call anyway. No one but a client ever calls me "Mister." Usually I'm contacted through my answering service, the number listed in the Yellow Pages under "Investigators." But if somebody has a job and wants me on a Sunday, fine. My home number's in the book.

"Yes," I said.

"My name is Morgan Vessey."

She paused. "Are you . . . ?" I began. It wasn't a particularly common name.

"He was my brother," she said. "I'd like to talk to you."

"I don't think there's much I could tell you, Ms. Vessey. I didn't know your brother. All I did was . . . find him. I'm sorry."

"Please." The high-pitched voice was firm. She wasn't begging. "I believe I'd like to hire you."

"What for?"

"Could we meet at your office, Mr. Swift? I'd prefer to discuss this in person."

I thought for a moment. Curiosity fought with disinterest and won.

"All right," I said. "When?"

"Are you free now?"

I chuckled. I like people who get to the point.

"Sure, why not?" I said.

I gave her directions to my house. I would have met her at the office, except that I've never had one. Cash-flow problems. This means that my desk and files and so on are in my living room. It's no more crowded than an average broom closet, but I usually try to go to my clients rather than have them come to me, just in case they'd be put off by the collection of late-1960's rock concert posters I've got hanging on the walls.

On the other hand, I don't like to leave my Sunday morning coffee for something that will probably turn out to be nothing. So I invited Morgan Vessey over.

I returned to the table. "Client?" Patricia asked.

"Maybe," I said. "Sister of the guy you found in the quarry."

"Oh. What does she want?"

I shrugged. "Beats me. I told her to come on out and we'd talk about it."

"You want me to leave?" she asked.

"Nah, unless you want to. Be good experience for you."

Patricia smiled. She's a legal secretary by trade and was working on getting her investigator's license. Supposedly because she'd then be more valuable to the lawyer she works for, an old family friend. But I suspected there was more to it than that. If Charlottesville was ever going to get a lady P.I., she had bottomless green eyes and auburn hair and she was sitting across from me.

I had very mixed feelings about her nosing about my profession, but I kept them mostly to myself. I'd long since learned that if I wanted to keep this woman I had to accept that she was going to follow her own particular path. I wanted to keep this woman.

"Okay," she said. "I am sort of involved, after all." She gave me a playfully mischievous look.

"You behave yourself," I said.

A half-hour later, Morgan Vessey arrived. She was a petite woman with a blond pageboy haircut, in her early thirties, about as I would have pictured her from her voice. She had a small head, with a pointy nose, chin, and ears. She showed tiny, sharp-looking teeth when she smiled, which was not often. If she hadn't had the squeaky voice, there was the remote possibility you might have met her and not thought of a mouse.

She examined my framed posters, lingering awhile in front of one advertising the Jefferson Airplane live at the Fillmore. It was a riot of swirling Dayglo colors.

"Poster art," she said to me. "Odd to find them . . . here."

"Everyone has their obsessions," I said. "One of mine is the music of my wasted youth."

"As gone as cave paintings," she said, gesturing at the posters. "A matter of vision. You can't reproduce what you can no longer see."

"Uh huh." Patricia came into the room. "Ah, this is my friend Patricia Ryan. Morgan Vessey."

The two women shook hands. Vessey eyed Patricia rather coolly, I thought.

"Actually, she's more than a friend," I added. "Patricia's a colleague. A paralegal. She's bound by the same disclosure laws. Whatever you want to talk about, she can hear."

Morgan Vessey nodded, though I didn't think she was crazy about the idea. I had the distinct impression that she was the kind of woman for whom all other women are simply rivals for some vague life prize. Then she looked from Patricia back to me. Her eyes were pale blue.

Suddenly, my head twitched. Sharply. I couldn't swear that she'd done it to me, but that's the way it came across. It unnerved me. I felt strongly that it would not be a good thing to be on the wrong side of this woman. For that matter, I wouldn't want to be on her right side, either. Though she wasn't attractive in any sense that I'd use the word, there was a real live wire inside her. There'd be men who were compelled to grab hold of it.

For a moment, there was a strange tension-filled silence. I relieved it by offering coffee to my visitor. She declined, so I gathered some chairs together and we all sat down to business. Patricia looked as if there was something going on that she didn't know about, but wished she did.

"Now, Ms. Vessey," I said.

"Please call me Morgan," she said. I agreed and she agreed to call me Swift. Patricia didn't say anything.

"What can I do for you, Morgan?" I asked.

"I want you to find out who killed my brother."

She said it as if stating a simple, known fact.

"Ah, killed?" I said.

"Murdered, if you prefer."

"The sheriff's office investigated," Patricia said. "They ruled it an accidental drowning, didn't they?"

"That's correct," Vessey said. "But they're wrong."

"How do you know that?" I asked.

"I know."

"Look, Morgan," I said, "from what I understand, your brother was wearing an empty air tank. Now I haven't been diving that long, but I do know that there are deaths every year. Drownings. And by far the most common cause is running out of air. People run out of air and they panic. Despite all of their training, they do the wrong things and they drown. It happens all the time."

"Eric's death was not an accident."

"He was diving alone," Patricia said. "He had no air in his tank. There were no signs of anything . . . unusual."

"What signs would there be?" Vessey said.

"Drugs in his bloodstream," I said. "Or some indication of a struggle underwater. Tears in the wetsuit, abrasions, a hole in the air hose, something like that. Now I haven't seen the actual report, but if there'd been anything the case would still be open, you can be sure of it."

She shook her head. "No. There wouldn't be anything to find. You couldn't have known Eric was down there by looking at the surface of the quarry, could you? The answer is somewhere else."

I now felt certain that this was going to be a waste of time. "All right," I said, "how do you *know* your brother was murdered? What evidence do you have, and why haven't you taken it to the sheriff?"

"It's not what you'd call 'evidence.' But it's proof all the same. Eric was my twin brother, Swift. There was a connection between us that most people can't possibly understand. One always knew what was happening to the other. Especially where threats to our personal safety were concerned."

"You felt what happened to him?" Patricia said.

She was interested now. She was fascinated by things that couldn't be explained.

Vessey shook her head. "I dreamed it," she said.

"Loren's had some premonitory dreams, too," Patricia said.

It was true. I'd had some strange dreams that tied into cases I was working on. One in particular, where I dreamed a sequence of events that had not yet occurred. When it eventually did, it follwed the format of the dream quite closely. I don't really want to know how such things work.

"This wasn't a premonition," Vessey said. "I dreamed it the night that he died, the night before you found him. I was there with him. We were always together that way. Eric was lying on some rocks under the water, a pile of them. I knew that he was dead and I screamed in my sleep and woke up. I can still see him as I saw him then. Lying on those rocks. With his air hose lying next to him. There were bubbles coming from it. He wasn't out of air, Swift."

There was a lengthy pause. None of us seemed to know quite what to say until Vessey added, "I want to hire you, Swift."

I thought about it. I didn't need the money, and I was having a lot of fun for one of the very few times in my life. On the one hand, this case *could* prove to be one of my most unusual. On the other, it could just as easily be an extremely boring wild goose chase. I glanced briefly at Patricia. She turned down the corners of her mouth slightly and raised one eyebrow, an expression which meant something like, *I don't know, sounds kinda interesting to me.*

And I thought: *Lady, if I go along with everything that sounds interesting to you, I'll be waking up in a cold sweat at three in the morning for the rest of my life.*

I looked back at Morgan Vessey.

"No offense," I said, "but can you afford me?"

"What do you charge?"

I gauged her resources as best I could and tried, "A hundred and fifty a day, if I work full-time. Plus expenses. If I can't get it done in a week, I probably can't get it done."

She eyed me intently. She didn't do the little trick she'd done before, but she didn't have to.

"Make it two hundred," she said without inflection. "With a bonus of five thousand if you find the bastard."

I gave it another moment's thought, then said, "All right, I'll see what I can do. The two hundred is fine, but *no* on the incentive clause. If it meant another five grand, I'd probably hand you a murderer whether there was one or not."

She cocked her head and gave me a very faint smile.

"Am I hiring an honest man?" she said.

"I like to think so."

"Well, that'll be a novelty. When can you start?"

"As soon as we sign the papers."

I got a standard contract from my desk and explained to her how I work. We signed our names.

"The clock begins ticking," I said as I opened my little spiral notebook.

"Good," she said. "Now, what do you need to know?"

"Tell me about your brother. He was a realtor?"

She nodded. "Real estate speculator would be more accurate," she said. "Buy low, sell high. This is a good area for it."

"He make some enemies?"

She doled out one of her smiles. "At least a few hundred. Eric was very good at what he did. He made a lot of money. You don't do that in real estate without making some enemies."

"Anyone come immediately to mind?" I asked.

She shook her head. "He didn't share much of that with me."

"Do you know what he was working on when he died? Some big project, maybe?"

"I don't know," she said.

"How about his personal life? Was he married?"

"No."

"Any problems that you know of? Drinking, drugs, gambling, bad company?"

"I don't know anything about my brother's personal life." She didn't say it defensively, just as a matter of fact.

"I thought you were so close," I said.

"We were psychically close, Swift. That doesn't mean we saw much of each other. We didn't have to." Again a seemingly simple statement of fact.

"You don't know any of his friends? His romantic interests?"

"No, I'm afraid not. Though I don't think Eric had many
friends. He had a . . . difficult personality."

"How do you mean?"

She touched her fingers under her chin as she thought
about her answer. It was impossible to tell whether she was
preparing to be evasive or whether she was just trying to be
accurate. She was an extremely difficult woman to read.

"I mean that people didn't take to him," she said finally.
"Not . . . readily."

"Why was that?"

"My brother never tried to be, I guess 'personable' is the
word. He thought it was a waste of time. So he didn't
cultivate people's friendships. He didn't *stroke* them, you
know? That's what most people want. Plus he was ambitious
and in a highly competitive field. And he had an intimidating physical presence. His manner, the way he carried his
body. He was very psychic, and people could feel that. It
scared them. I think he probably spent a lot of his life by
himself."

"He sounds like a hard case," I said.

She looked at me as if reading my mind. "Perhaps," she
said. "Though you could just as easily say that he was a
completely self-reliant person who preferred not to owe
anything to anybody. That was once a cultural ideal."

"The lone cowboy."

She gave me a half-smile. "If you want to know more
about my brother, there is one place you might try. The
Jordan Institute."

That rang a bell, but I couldn't place it. "Why do I know
that name?" I asked.

"They own the land that the quarry's on."

"Oh, yeah. I remember seeing the sign. What is it?"

"They do psychic research there. They did some testing on
my brother."

"Why would he get involved in something like that?"

She shrugged. "Knowing Eric, he probably thought he
could develop the ability to predict the stock market. I'm
sure he wasn't that interested in the advancement of science.
But mostly, he tried it because I asked him to."

"They tested you too?" I said.

"A few times. But I don't do well in the laboratory. It's all too cold and sterile for me. My gifts are more concerned with . . . human interaction."

Yeah, I thought, I know.

"All right," I said, wondering what else might be useful. "How long had he been diving?" I tried.

"About three years, I think."

"Was he good?"

She looked perplexed for the first time. "How would I know that?"

"Well, did he do it a lot?"

"Not a lot. He took a couple of vacations where he did some diving. One of those Caribbean islands."

"He was competent, then."

"I don't know that much about the sport, but I would guess so," she said. "It was important to Eric to succeed at whatever he did. He didn't care what other people thought, but he liked to live up to his own high standards."

"The Caribbean trips, did he take them with a diving buddy?"

"He went alone, I believe."

"Do you know why he was diving in the quarry?" I asked.

"If I knew that," she said, looking at me without resentment, "I probably wouldn't have needed you."

"Divers are trained never to dive alone, you realize. Yet your brother was diving alone, and at night, as well. That seems kind of strange."

"Yes, it does."

"Do you think it suggests that he might not have wanted anyone to know what he was doing?"

"Maybe," she said. "But I told you, he liked to keep his own company. And he wouldn't have given much of a damn for someone else's safety regulations."

"Well, he *was* doing *something*. Assuming that the come-along we found near his body belonged to him. Was it his?"

"I don't know."

"Do you have any theories as to what he was using it for?"

"No."

I was tiring. "You have any thoughts, Patricia?" I said.

"Well," Patricia said, "it seems unlikely to me that he was in that quarry alone at night for no particular reason. Especially with the come-along there. It would appear that he was looking for something. Something that was so massive he'd need a come-along to dislodge it. But then, if whatever it was was *that* heavy, how was he going to get it to the surface? He didn't have a winch up there. It's odd.

"Then there's the fact that he hid his car in the trees, so that we never saw it the next morning. That strongly suggests to me that he wanted to keep whatever he was doing a secret.

"So it might be useful to know what he was up to. And then again, it might not. Because even if we found out what he was doing, even if it was something illegal, for instance, we're still faced with the fact that it looks like a completely accidental drowning. The conditions were hazardous. It's very possible that Ms. Vessey's brother lost track of his air supply and it cost him his life."

"Except that it didn't happen that way," Vessey said.

Patricia shrugged. There was a brief pause, then I asked if there was anything else I should know.

"I don't think so," Vessey said.

"Okay." I told my client I thought I had enough to begin. I then warned her that if I came across any evidence of criminal activity I'd have to turn it over to the police. She said, "Of course." I also set a schedule for reporting back to her as the investigation progressed.

"And I'd like to search your brother's house," I said. "With your permission."

"Stop by tomorrow and I'll give you a key," she said. "Will that be all right?"

"Fine. Where do I find you?"

"Ah, of course." She opened her purse, pulled out a card and handed it to me. "Same address and phone as I gave you for the contract," she went on. "I work at home. Just call ahead, I'm usually around. If I'm not there, I have an answering machine."

The card read:

MORGAN VESSEY, ART & COLLECTIBLES
By Appointment Only.

And it gave her address and phone number.

I turned the card over in my hand. There was nothing on the back. I slipped it into my shirt pocket. It lay there like a carefully guarded secret.

"It'll probably be late afternoon," I said.

"That's fine."

"Good. Now, I'm afraid I have to say one more thing. I believe there are some peculiarities about your brother's death. But even so, it's going to be awfully difficult to find any hard evidence to support your dream. You realize that."

"Yes," she said.

"I don't want you to be too disappointed if I come up empty. It's the most likely thing."

She nodded. "You have a reputation, Swift. I trust that you'll do your best." She paused, glancing around at my posters. "A failure of vision," she said.

We shook hands all around and Morgan Vessey walked out of the apartment.

"Whew," Patricia said when she'd gone. "I don't care much for that one, Loren."

"There is something about her, isn't there?"

"I don't know if it's psychic power or what, but I wouldn't get too close if I were you. Not unless you're wearing rubber gloves."

"You know I'm a careful man," I said, wiggling my fingers at her.

CHAPTER
3

The quarry where Eric Vessey's body had been found was in Nelson County, so that was the place to go first.

Nelson is a dirt-poor area which lies nose-to-butt with Albemarle County, one of the nation's wealthiest. Albemarle enfolds the city of Charlottesville, home of a famous university, thirteen movie theaters, four or five shopping malls, the ghosts of Thomas Jefferson and Sally his favorite slave, and several tens of thousands of real live people including, lately, half a dozen private investigators, an occupation I formerly had all to myself. Sometimes it seems as if our population doubles every couple of years, or whenever they publish a new edition of *The Hundred Best Places in America to Live*. With more people come more problems, and more competitors for my turf. I've survived. Partly because there's been enough business to go around, but primarily because a handful of my cases have generated three dimestore novels' worth of free publicity.

Charlottesville, which used to be a sleepy Southern college town, has become a mini-version of any big city. We've got racial violence and shady land scams and bag ladies and enough cocaine to build a six-inch powder base on the slopes of Aspen. People moan as the town becomes an unrecognizable twisted sister of the place it once was. Many of the same people are raking in the bread with both hands. In the end, greed will out. It always does.

Someday, Charlottesville will be merely the most remote suburb of Washington. The six-thirty train to D.C. will be jammed with commuters. Those who can afford it will make the hop by plane or chopper. Townhouses and condos will spread across the cornfields and horse farms.

Fortunately, that day still seems a long way off. We who live in central Virginia are aware that change is coming, and more rapidly than it can be prevented. But we're also aware that we're living on an exceedingly beautiful patch of God's green earth, and we're enjoying it while we can.

Nelson County is particularly scenic, if you like mountains. Some six hundred and fifty square miles with only about twelve thousand residents, mainly because nearly all of the land is straight up and down. Tucked among the mountains are hundreds of inhabited hollows, many of them home to the same families that have tended the harsh, stony land since Jefferson and Sally were living flesh. Down the centers of the hollows run shallow, unpolluted streams, the poster-perfect image of peaceful bygone country days. Yet some have seen those innocent streams rise, in times of heavy rain, and sweep whole communities into oblivion.

The morning after I met Morgan Vessey, I got into Clementine, my battered orange '72 VW, and drove to Nelson County. It was a warm sunny day and I was feeling good. Patricia and I were happy with each other. The trees were flowering all over, peaches and dogwoods and redbuds. And I was earning my keep by playing sleuth, something I'd probably do for free if I had a sugar mama to pay the rent.

Lovingston, the Nelson County seat, is a half-hour south of Charlottesville. It's a small, unpretentious town. The county buildings, except for the stately nineteenth-century courthouse, are simple frame or cinderblock.

The sheriff's digs are in a dingy basement that smells of too much unvented cigarette smoke and too few applications of Lysol. The man himself is named Floyd Davis. He's a former deputy who didn't really want to be sheriff, but agreed to fill out the term of his predecessor, Faber Jakes, who was killed on the job. I happened to be very close by when the life leaked out of Jakes's body, but that's another story.

Floyd Davis, the lame duck for another six months, was a genial, corpulent man. He had short gray hair and the ruddy complexion of a frequent visitor to the bottle. His belly spilled over his waistband like the froth from an overfilled beer glass. We'd met briefly in the aftermath of the tangled case that had killed Jakes and his senior deputy. He remembered.

"Swift," Davis said, "I hope you ain't brung trouble like the last time." His manner was pleasant enough, but there was a wariness underneath, a desire not to get involved with anything too complicated. Jakes had been tough as a four-dollar steak. This man was soft; I wouldn't want to have to count on him in a crisis.

"I don't believe so, Sheriff," I said. "One of those in a lifetime is plenty, don't you think?"

"Surely."

"Actually, it's about the fella drowned up in that quarry a couple of weeks ago."

Davis relaxed visibly. "The skin diver," he said.

"Uh huh."

"Well, I don't believe much gonna come of that. Man drowned hisself. Anybody starts shooting over that, be a big surprise to me."

"Me, too. But there's always someone who wants to know exactly what happened, good thing for me. It's what keeps me out of the rain and some Bud in the fridge. Sounds crazy, but I got a client thinks it might not've been an accident."

He shook his head slowly. "And who might that be?" he asked.

I smiled politely.

"Okay, okay," he said.

"Would you mind talking abut the case?"

"I don't see why not. Like you say, there ain't nothing to it. Hang on."

He left the room. A few minutes later he returned with a manila folder that wasn't exactly bulging with its contents. Some modern-day cop shops have lots of fancy desktop computers; others have overstuffed filing cabinets with dented sides. You can't kick a computer when you blow a fuse.

Davis put on a pair of Ben Franklin reading glasses and opened the folder.

"Eric Vessey," he said. "What'd you want to know?"

I took out my spiral notebook. "Cause of death was drowning," I said.

"Yup. The man's air tank was empty. When it run out, he sucked water, probably tried to make it back up, but couldn't. It's over ninety foot deep where they found him. Ah, where *you* found him." The edge of wariness returned to his voice.

"Yeah, I found him," I said. "Me and my diving partners. But that doesn't have anything to do with this investigation. Just a coincidence." I smiled a delightfully disarming smile.

"Right. You find dead bodies a lot, Swift."

"Business I'm in. Like you. Now, time of death was . . . ?"

"Round about midnight. In there somewheres. They couldn't be exactly sure."

"The night before the body was discovered."

"That's right."

"There weren't any signs of a struggle?"

"Not as we could tell. You think there might've been somebody down there with him?" He asked it as if he'd never considered the possibility.

"Could be," I said. "But if he'd struggled with someone, there'd probably be signs. A tear in his wetsuit, or a mangled air hose, something like that. I understand Vessey was a strong guy. It doesn't figure he'd let someone kill him underwater without putting up a fight."

"Well, we didn't find nothing. We had a diving shop to check out his gear. Everything was normal."

"Did anyone search the quarry?" I asked.

"Uh huh. We hired a guy from Charlottesville." He peered at his report. "Name of Steven Furniss."

"Okay, I know him."

"He dived down in there a couple of times for us. Wasn't nothing to find. Some of them underwater flares. Burnt up. That's about it."

"Flares," I said. "You know, he had dive lights, too. When we found him. One on a lanyard around his wrist, and another one attached to the top of his face mask. Plus there was that come-along lying near his body. And the fact he hid his car in the woods. What do you make of all that?"

Davis shrugged. "Beats me," he said. "Maybe he liked moving rocks around in the dark. Maybe he was fixing a place to hide a half a ton of drugs. Maybe any damn thing. I don't see as it makes much difference. Whatever he was doing down there, that wasn't what killed him. What killed him was he got careless."

He said it with finality. It suddenly struck me as mighty peculiar that I was sitting here with this man, asking all these questions, because of some woman's crazy dream. But what the hell, as long as she was paying for the ride. I smiled.

"Something funny?" Davis asked.

"Nah," I said, "just thinking of somebody."

"So . . . as near as we can figure, all the man did in my territory was drown. If you come across any kind of illegal activity, I'd want to know about it. But I expect the Albemarle police would want to know about it more. That's where this Vessey lived."

Davis thought it was somebody else's business. I wasn't surprised. But it meant that he hadn't pushed his investigation too hard.

"All right," I said. "What about the scene? You find anything around the quarry? In or around his car?"

"Nothing didn't belong," he said. "This is what was in the car."

He handed me a list and I looked it over. It was all commonplace stuff. Some clothes for when he came out of the water. His wallet, a little money, keys. From the glove compartment, some maps and a bottle opener and the registration and miscellaneous papers. Nothing in the trunk but the spare tire and a few tools. I returned the list.

"You still got his stuff?" I asked.

"Yeah. Until the verdict is official, which oughtta be next week. Then we release it to the next of kin."

"Could I see it?"

He hesitated. For a moment, the wheels turning inside his head were as obvious as if they'd been right there on the desk, making gnashing sounds.

Then he said, "Ah, why the hell not?"

He buzzed one of his deputies and asked that the box with

Vessey's belongings be brought to him. He'd made his decision: if there was anything screwy about Vessey's death, it'd be just as easy to let me do the legwork on it. Which made sense, from his point of view. If I found something, he could share the credit. If I didn't, which was more likely, he would have saved himself a lot of time and trouble.

"Anything else unusual, Sheriff?" I asked. "Marks on the body, anything like that?"

"Well, there is that," he said with some reluctance. "The man had been in a fight."

"Oh?"

"Yeah. His face was cut up a little. Some bruises. But the coroner's sure it all happened at least twelve hours before he went in the quarry. It didn't have nothing to do with the drowning, we know that."

"Not directly, you mean."

"Have it your way," he muttered.

"You find out who beat him up?"

"No, we didn't. I expect it was somebody back up to home."

"You know, Sheriff, it sounds to me like there's a lot of strange things about this accident," I said.

"Swift," he said with exaggerated weariness, "I got a very limited budget in this department and we got our hands full with our own drunk fights and wife beatings and stabbings and whatnot. I don't have the manpower to spend a deal of time poking into the lives of everyone who dies in my county, especially if they ain't even residents. Now this Vessey may of been the king of crime up in the city, but I don't give a good crap. He drowned accidentally down here and there's *no evidence* to show that he didn't. You find some, you bring it to me and I'll do whatever needs to be done. Okay?"

"Okay." Acting Sheriff Davis might be ineffectual, but that didn't mean I ought to get on his wrong side.

A deputy entered the office carrying a cardboard box. He set it down on the floor near the sheriff and me.

"The last remains of Eric Vessey," Davis said, gesturing at the box. "Help yourself." He pushed the Vessey folder aside and busied himself with something else.

There was a large table in the corner, behind the sheriff's

desk. It was cluttered, but there'd be enough room if I moved things aside a little. I picked up the box.

"May I?" I asked, tilting my head at the table.

Davis nodded and I walked over and made myself a work space. Slowly, I emptied the box and studied its contents. From time to time I made notes.

I checked the clothes first. They were unremarkable. There was a pair of khaki work pants with a few spots of old paint on them. A long-sleeved, plaid flannel shirt. A navy blue sweater. Underwear and socks. Some nylon-and-leather running shoes. The only touch of class was a highly polished, oval silver belt buckle with the *End of the Trail* scene engraved on it. Essentially, the clothes told me nothing I didn't know.

At the bottom of the box were two large manila clasp envelopes. One was marked "Pockets." I opened it and shook its contents onto the table.

There was an ordinary key ring. Seventy-six cents in change. A linen handkerchief. A small folding knife. A crumpled package of Marlboros with two cigarettes left in it. A disposable lighter. And a slim leather billfold.

The billfold had plastic windows containing an American Express card, a MasterCard, Vessey's driver's license, and a tiny calendar for the year. There was a slot into which were stuffed half a dozen business cards, ivory with blue lettering: *Eric Vessey, Real Estate of Distinction*, with a single telephone number. Two twenty-dollar bills and a five. And that was it. I put the stuff back in the envelope and opened the other one, marked "Glove Compartment."

Inside were a number of maps. Virginia, the city of Charlottesville, all of the surrounding counties, Washington, D.C., North Carolina, and West Virginia. There was a bottle opener and a full pack of matches. There were some maintenance bills for the car (a recent model Saab Turbo), its registration card, and one pink State Inspection checklist. And a small notebook with the words "Gas Log" written on it. I opened the notebook. There were neat columns for odometer reading, number of gallons, price, and MPG. Vessey probably kept it for income tax deductions. The Saab didn't get great mileage.

I thumbed the pages. The entries soon stopped and the

rest of the book was blank, except for the next-to-last page.
There, what looked like the same hand had printed this:

O NW Quad

10 N

DuE Edge

85 D

X X

It meant nothing to me. I started to ask Davis, but then
stopped. He might not have even noticed this page. More
likely, he'd seen it and ignored it. Either way, there was no
point in bringing it up. Under cover of a cough, I tore the
page out of Vessey's notebook and slipped it into my own.

That was all that was in the envelope. I replaced the
contents and put it back into the box.

"Finished," I said to the reluctant sheriff.

"Find anything?" he asked without interest.

"Nope. You're right, there's nothing. Well, I guess I'll get
going."

Before I left, I had Davis describe for me where they had
found Eric Vessey's car. Then I said, "Okay, Sheriff, thanks
for your help."

"No problem," he said. "You turn anything up, you let me
know, hear?"

CHAPTER
4

On my way back to Charlottesville, I decided to stop off at the quarry. It was more or less on the way. Though I hardly expected to find anything, there was no reason not to have a look around. If I was ever going to bring this case to a conclusion (meaning, a conclusion different from the one most people had already come to), then there was only one approach. Try to find what Eric Vessey was up to the last few days of his life and hope that indicated why someone might have wanted him dead. The quarry represented his end, my starting point.

I went a half dozen miles up U.S. 29, then turned east. The gentle foothills of the Blue Ridge rose and fell around me. Five miles later I turned north on a narrow state road. I hadn't been on it since my last dive. This time, I paid more attention.

It was an area of widely spaced houses, woods, and the occasional small farm. Many of the houses had crumbling chimneys, tar shingle siding, and front porches that sagged in the middle. Yards contained discarded refrigerators and washing machines, rusting swing sets that hadn't felt a kid's bottom in years, Chevys and Plymouths up on blocks, their innards long since raided for parts. There were one or two relatively new brick ramblers with clean lawns. Commuters to the high-paying jobs in Charlottesville, or local people who'd found a way to make a good living off the others.

Three miles down the road I passed a sign on the left that said "Jordan Institute." The sign was wood, with the name burned into it. Simple. Easy to pass by if you weren't looking for it. It marked an asphalt driveway that disappeared into the woods. I went another quarter-mile and found the one-lane dirt track. I turned in.

The quarry was deserted. It lay in a clearing about three acres around. The land adjacent to it was littered with boulders and stones and chips of rock. Nothing much grew there. The underlying soil was likely so abused that it'd be a long time before anything ever would.

Beyond the cleared area was some scrubby growth indicating a zone that had formerly been open and was now being slowly reclaimed by the forest. Beyond that was only dense woods.

I stopped Clementine on some hard-packed dirt that was used as a parking area by divers, and probably summertime swimmers and amorous teenagers, and got out. It was very quiet. The noisy creatures of June and July were still in hiding, there were no hunters or fishermen around, no one was out prospecting for the tail ends of gold deposits that can still be found here and there in the hills. It was an eerie silence, the kind you only encounter in places that've been abandoned. Especially places where there would formerly have been the continuous rumble of heavy equipment.

Nelson County, I'd read somewhere, sits on top of one of the largest veins of soapstone in the world. At one time, taking it from the ground was big business here. But with a decline in demand most of the quarries had closed down. Many, like this one, were now filled with water.

I wondered how many people had died on this spot. Considering the working conditions when the quarry had been operating, chances were there had been a few—men whose bodies were crushed as they slaved in the sun for whatever meager paycheck they could get. And Eric Vessey, why had he died here? He certainly must have been playing for bigger stakes than the vanished workers.

I did some deep breathing and opened myself to whatever vibrations might still be hanging in the air. Nothing came to me, as usual. It looked like none of Morgan's psychic abilities had rubbed off.

So I went about things in a more traditional way. I walked around the perimeter of the quarry, searching for anything the sheriff's department might have overlooked. It was rough going. Outside of the parking area, there was only the stone. I had to climb over and around great slabs of rock, had to be careful not to slip on the loose chippings and fracture an ankle. When I reached the spot where the body had been brought up, I got down and crawled.

There was only what I might have expected to find. There was the rock and the dirt, and a few tiny green attempts at growth, and four thick, rusty iron posts marking some forgotten boundaries. There were crumpled cigarette packs, empty cans and bottles, a couple of condoms, three plastic milk jugs wired together, the remains of a fire within a ring of stones, and a few heavy logs dragged near the water to sit on. Nothing that obviously connected to the late Eric Vessey.

When I'd made a circuit of the quarry, I walked into the scrub until I located the spot where the sheriff said the man's car had been parked. It wasn't hard to find. There'd been no rain since the day Eric bought the farm, and the place was well scuffed up. You could easily see that something had happened there, like some kind of search and maybe a Saab being hauled away. I inspected the area on my hands and knees, but it was no-go. So many people had come stomping through, it'd be impossible to determine whose cigarette butt this was, who left those tire tracks, who discarded the half-empty can of Pepsi Free. Not to mention that it'd probably be useless information, anyway. I quit.

I'd had to take a look, I told myself as I returned to my VW. I stood by the car for one last moment, fixing the scene in my head, associating it with all the details I'd observed today and on the day of the deep dive, in case there was some little thing that'd jar loose an important insight later on. Then I left.

I drove the quarter-mile back down the road and turned in at the sign for the Institute. Morgan Vessey had said they knew her brother here. Maybe they knew something that I could use.

The drive was narrow and curving. I followed it to a gravel parking area marked for "Visitors and Guests." The road continued on, past a sign marked "Deliveries Only," and disappeared into the woods. I stopped the VW and got out. There were only two other cars in the area, both late-model American sedans. The air was still and peaceful, more like fall than spring. The loudest sound was the gravel beneath my feet, crackling like popped knuckles.

Ahead of me was a post with a small wooden hand mounted on it, forefinger extended. I went in the direction indicated, down a gravel path and through a dense pine thicket. On the other side, in a cleared area of several acres, was the Jordan Institute.

The main building was a very long, massive two-story structure built of fieldstone. It looked like a hunting lodge that was intended to host everyone in the county who wanted to go out the first day of the season. Flanking the lodge were a number of lower, smaller buildings, some of wood and some also of stone, connected to one another by walkways of raked gravel. The Institute's lawns were well-tended.

In front of the main building there was a collection of ornamental shrubs whose names I couldn't imagine wanting to know. There was a skinny elderly man working among them, spreading fresh mulch around. He was dressed all in white. White tennis shoes, baggy white drawstring pants, a loose white cotton peasant's shirt, and a white sombrero. He was working slowly, with an economy of movement that looked very efficient.

As I approached, the man turned to look at me. His front side continued the mono-color theme. He had fine white hair hanging like cobwebs from somewhere under his sombrero. It reached nearly to his shoulders. His beard was white and wispy, like that of an aged Oriental sage. The peasant's shirt was a pullover, with a deep V neck that displayed a tangle of white chest hairs.

The man's skin was the leathery dark brown of someone who spends a lot of time in the sun. His hands were deeply furrowed, with prominent veins, but they appeared quite nimble. There were perhaps eight ounces of excess fat on his frame. Except for his eyes, he looked like the archetypal

Mexican gardener who's spent his entire adult life tending an estate in Beverly Hills.

His eyes were pale blue, the kind that seem always amused with, if not actually mocking, whatever they're looking at.

I crunched up the path and the gardener gave me a slight bow.

"Hello," I said. "I wonder if you could direct me to the office, or someplace I might find whoever's in charge. I'm looking for some information about one of your, one of the Institute's, ah, subjects."

The gardener bowed again, deeply. "It is my pleasure to serve you," he said.

When it didn't look like anything else was coming, I said, "Thank you. But actually, what I'd like is the director's office, wherever people go when they . . . first come to the Institute."

Another bow. "I am your servant," he said. "Would you care to see our gardens?"

By now, I wasn't sure the old boy spoke all that much English. "The office," I said, trying to describe an important room with my hands. "Where would I go to . . . register?" I smiled and made scribbling motions.

He cocked his head at me, that inner amusement peeking out through his eyes. "The ornamental pears are very nice just now," he said. "As I'm sure you know."

I started to move away from him. As I did, one of the doors in the main building opened and a woman came out.

She was a big woman in her middle forties. Tall and broad, stout but not overweight. Strong-looking. Her straight dark hair was cut short. There were probably times when she was mistaken for a man.

When she got closer, I noted that she had dark eyes set off by long, thick lashes, and was wearing the minimum of makeup necessary to smooth the lines in her face. She was dressed in a trim, ankle-length gray skirt and matching jacket. Each step she took seemed to have its own unique purpose.

"Excuse me," I said to her. "I'm looking for the office."

She stopped. "Are you interested in one of our courses?" she asked. Her eyes never left mine. In contrast to the gardener, hers were highly inquisitive rather than amused.

"Actually, no," I said. I took out my wallet and selected from among my cards. I gave her one that featured my real name, described my trade as "Paralegal Investigations" and associated me with a Charlottesville law firm for which I sometimes do legwork. It wasn't that much of a misrepresentation. I feel like the card gives me a slight touch of legitimacy that I might not have otherwise. Besides, when people see a lawyer's name they inevitably (and justifiably) assume that trouble is on the way. That can be useful.

The woman looked at the front of the card, then looked at the back. There wasn't anything on the back. She didn't seem overly impressed. When she looked at me again, she asked the obvious question without speaking.

I cleared my throat. "I'm just after some information," I said. "About one of your . . . I don't know what to call him. He participated in some experiments. Is 'subject' the right word?"

"'Research associate' would be fine," she said.

"Right. One of your research associates. Eric Vessey. The man who drowned in the quarry here. There are some . . . questions about his death."

There was a pause, during which the earlier inquisitive expression departed her face. Then she said, very businesslike, "I see. All right, Mr. Swift. Please come with me. My name is Paula Slate. I'm the Operations Manager here at the Institute."

I told her I was pleased to meet her and we shook hands. Her grip was firm without suggesting that she was as strong as I was, which she might well have been.

"I'll speak with you later, Grover," she said to the gardener.

"Certainly, Dr. Slate," he said.

She turned and led me into the hunting lodge. The room we entered had a lot of windows, some comfortable furniture and floor-to-ceiling shelves crammed with books. There was a couch and on the couch was a boy of eleven or twelve, propped up on pillows, with a wool blanket around him. He had dark, tousled hair with a cowlick sticking up in back. He wore tortoise-shell glasses and was reading a paperback book. It was a crime novel with one of those lurid covers that suggests that the only thing mystery writers think about is sex. Paula Slate favored the boy with a warm smile as we passed.

"Hi," I said to him.

He gave me a long, examining look, at the end of which some kind of recognition lit up his face.

"Hel-*lo*," he said with a big grin.

I followed Dr. Slate.

"Dr. Jordan's grandnephew," she said over her shoulder. "He tells me he has the flu but personally I think it's just spring fever. He'd rather be here than school anyway." She shrugged. "Probably learns more here."

Beyond the front room was a short corridor which ended at a set of glass doors with heavy glass handles. *Jordan Institute for Psychic Research* was lettered in black on one of the doors. On the other was the single word *Welcome*.

The doors opened onto a spacious, carpeted area containing several easy chairs and a low coffee table littered with magazines like *Omni*, *Scientific American*, and *National Geographic*. There was a chest-high counter running three-quarters the width of the room. It resembled the check-in at a motel. Beyond it was a space that looked like any business office. Couple of desks, filing cabinets, Xerox machine. A young woman sat at one of the desks, doing something on a personal computer. She looked up at us, then back at her work.

I followed Dr. Slate around the counter, to a door in the far wall. It was a thick oak door and it had a brass nameplate on it, engraved with her name. She opened the door for me and we went into her office. The door closed by itself.

It was a nice wood-paneled office. She sat behind her teak desk and I sat in a soft leather chair. The psychic research business appeared to be a lucrative one.

"You understand that the Jordan Institute bears no responsibility for Eric Vessey's death," she said. "We open the quarry to qualified diving classes. Anyone else using it is doing so without our permission and entirely at his or her own risk. It is so posted, as you are probably aware."

I nodded that I was. "I'm not here to try and implicate the Institute," I said.

"Very well. Then why *are* you here?" She folded her hands on the desktop. She continued to look me in the eye. It would become disconcerting if I let it, but I'm pretty accomplished at that particular game. I relaxed and allowed her to look right through me.

I found that I was not warming up to the Institute's Operations Manager. But then, I've traditionally had trouble with people in her profession—that is, psychologists, psychiatrists, and whoever else gets lumped in with what has come to be called the "human potential movement." It probably began when I failed Psych 101 during my disastrous one-semester stay at the University of Virginia. My professor was a pompous ass and I told him so and he flunked me.

He may have been a particularly lousy role model on which to base my assumptions about people in this line. That's what I thought at first. Then, as I met a few more like him, I decided that he might have been more typical than not. There's just something about these people. It's the way they look at you, like you're a *specimen* of something. Or like they know some special secrets of the universe that you don't and never will. Maybe that's how they keep from running screaming into the night.

Anyway, the prim and no doubt highly efficient Dr. Slate had that same slightly condescending air about her. I felt like I was regarded as one of the less interesting specimens that had swum under her microscope lately. I didn't care.

"My client—" I began.

"Who shall remain nameless," she said with a very small smile.

"—who shall remain nameless, is interested in the manner of Mr. Vessey's death."

"That's simple enough. He made a foolishly risky night dive by himself and he drowned." She shrugged. "What else is there to say?"

"I don't know. But I'm being paid to find out if there is anything. There are certain . . . oddities involved."

"Such as?"

"They wouldn't interest you," I said casually, looking for some sign that she was anxious to know what I knew. She didn't appear to be, but then she had the professional mask firmly in place. I wondered if I ought to try to dislodge it.

"Just a few things about his life that don't add up," I went on. "They make me want to know what kind of person he was, and what he was up to those last days. Why he was diving alone in your quarry the night he died."

"People do things for any number of irrational reasons," Slate said.

"Vessey was an irrational person?"

"Not especially, no. But the forces that drive us all, they're never accessible to the rational mind, not even in those of us who study them most closely. Eric Vessey would more likely have done an irrational thing for what he thought was a very rational reason."

"You knew him well?" I said quickly.

A fleeting smile dented her mask. "Somewhat," she said neutrally.

It was the kind of conversational exchange that can make or break you as an investigator. As yet I had very little idea how to proceed with this rather insubstantial case. Here was someone who had personally known the deceased. How well she knew him might be of use to me or it might not. But it's a question that should be asked.

Then you have to decide what the answer means. People give all sorts of answers to questions like this, for all sorts of reasons. The real value may end up being less in what is said than how it is said. That's where I earn my money.

In this particular instance, there was that unexpected fleeting smile. It didn't quite go with the tone of the answer. I wasn't prepared to guess what that meant just yet, so I filed it away for future reference. No point in getting ahead of myself. There would be time to pursue whatever needed pursuing.

"What did you think of him?" I asked casually.

She leaned back in her chair, once again most professional. "Do you know what the Jordan Institute is, Mr. Swift?" she asked.

I shrugged. "Psychic research," I said. "ESP, telepathy, guessing cards, and that sort of thing?"

"I assure you that the card-guessing phase is long past. Those games were important in their time, but . . . well, the research that we do is infinitely more sophisticated now. Our labs here are fully computerized, of course. Perhaps you'd like to see them at some point. We could even test your abilities, if you like."

"Ah, we'll see."

"In any case, we've been here for thirty years, which makes us the second oldest facility in the country. Only the Parapsych Lab at Duke is older. At first, the Institute wasn't much more than Dr. Jordan himself. He bought this old place and built us up from scratch. He's quite a remarkable man, but then you will have formed your own impressions, of course."

"What do you mean?"

"I mean that people generally form strong impressions on meeting him."

"Well, I'd like to," I said. "But I don't believe I've met him yet."

"Of course you have," she said with just a trace of annoyance. "You were talking to him a few minutes ago. Over by the shrubbery."

"That was Dr. Jordan?"

"Ah," she said, amusement replacing the annoyance, "I see. He played with you, did he?"

"I thought he was the gardener."

She nodded. "He does that. Plays with people's expectations. He can often tell the extent of their psychic ability after talking with them for two minutes. It's uncanny. I've never known him to be dead wrong."

"Well I'll be damned," I said.

"You never *would* have guessed either. Unless he'd wanted you to. He knows more about the human mind than almost anyone in the country. I sometimes think of him as a shapeshifter. He is simply whatever he chooses to be. No more and no less." She fixed me with the analytical stare again. "But then, that is true of us all, isn't it?"

"I don't know. My job is to get behind people's masks. I like to think I have some small talent in that area."

There was amusement in her eyes. I wasn't sure at whose expense.

"And what of those," she said, "behind whose masks there is . . . nothing at all?"

"Like Eric Vessey?"

She laughed out loud. "Whyever do you say that?"

I shrugged. "He's the reason I'm here."

"No, your 'client' is the reason you're here."

She said it with a straight face, but I was sure she had no real interest in making me a more literal person. She obviously enjoyed trying to punch my buttons. Probably did the same kind of thing with everyone, to see what responses she'd provoke. Not unlike the way I operated. But if she intended to exasperate me, she'd succeed about the time the Red Sox won their next World Series.

"You were telling me what you thought of our late friend," I said.

"Ah yes," she said. "We got a bit sidetracked, didn't we? Well, I didn't really know him all that well. From a professional point of view, he was a real treasure, and we'll miss him a lot. Very psychic, completely able to perform under laboratory conditions. That's not always the case, you know."

I nodded as if I did. "How'd you find out about him?"

"His sister brought him here. Morgan. They were twins, of course. She had heard about us and come out to be tested. She's nearly as psychic as he . . . as he was, but unfortunately she just freezes up in the lab. So she brought him out. I don't think he wanted to come, really, but they were very close and she asked him to and so he did it. We had several sessions with him, with some notable results, but after a while he did drift away from us. There wasn't that much here to keep him coming back. He was a very . . . pragmatic man."

"Odd," I said. "I guess I think of psychics as being more, I don't know, otherworldly."

"Quite the contrary. They're more often very down-to-earth. Eric certainly was."

"How so?"

"He was a very successful businessman. As I'm sure you already know. He liked making money, and he was good at it."

"Ruthless?"

She paused. "I wouldn't make that kind of judgment," she said carefully.

Interesting. I hadn't specified whether I was asking about personal or vocational ruthlessness. The pause suggested that the question had some particular meaning for her.

"How well *did* you know Vessey?" I asked.

She smiled with what I think was for her considerable warmth. "I'm beginning to feel like a suspect," she said.

"Sorry. Just trying for the facts, Ma'am."

There was a lengthy pause, then she said, "It's a difficult question to answer, Mr. Swift. In the way one normally considers such things, I knew him very little. That is to say, socially. Yet I knew quite a bit about his psyche, through our experiments here. And that's a very intimate way of knowing. Professionally—in terms of *his* profession—I knew him not at all."

"Would you be willing to talk about the experiments?"

"No. We have our own rules of confidentiality, just as you do."

"He *is* dead," I tried.

"Sorry. It'd be a very bad precedent to set."

"Okay. He have any enemies that you knew of?"

"Mr. Swift," she said coolly, "may I ask what it is that you are looking for? Are you suggesting that Eric died by violence?"

I noted that she called him by his first name.

"I told you at the start that we think his death was peculiar," I said.

"It may be peculiar that he was diving alone in our quarry at night. But there's nothing peculiar about how he died. He stayed down too long. He ran out of air. His equipment was thoroughly examined by a disinterested third party. There weren't any malfunctions. He was simply careless, and it cost him his life."

"You seem well informed about the incident."

"Of course," she said testily. "It did happen on our property. The Institute needs to be aware of any potential liability on its part. And there *isn't* any. Now, is there anything else you wanted to know? I do have business to attend to."

"Vessey's enemies?"

"I'm sure I don't know if Eric Vessey had any enemies." She stood up. "May we call it a day?"

I got up too, and extended my hand. As she took it, I said, "Thank you, Dr. Slate. You've been *most* helpful."

I watched her carefully. For just an instant the question appeared in her eyes—*in what way?*—and then it was gone.

"Don't bother to see me out," I said. "I can find the door."

As I retraced my steps I thought about the Institute's Manager of Operations. She was a highly intelligent woman. No doubt good at her job. Well versed in the devious ways of the human psyche. Pretty tough, I would imagine. But an amateur when it came to being on the other side of the investigative table. The intangibles I'd come away with added up to a fair certainty that she'd known Eric Vessey better than she chose to let on. Or that she knew more *about* him than she'd be expected to.

Either way, all it was was food for thought at some later point. Right now, my job was to convince myself that the circumstances of Vessey's death were more complicated than they appeared, and I was a long, long way from there.

Outside, the venerable founder was still futzing around with the shrubbery. I snuck up behind him.

"Dr. Jordan, I presume," I said.

He wasn't the least bit startled. He turned and gave me one of those little bows.

"As we discussed," he said, "the ornamental pears are quite nice just now."

"Thanks," I said, "but it isn't really your gardens that brought me here."

"The garden has much to teach. All it asks is that we learn to listen."

I was beginning to feel like one of Peter Sellers's foils in the movie *Being There*. It was impossible to know what to make of this old man. On the surface he seemed a simple fool, and yet there was that lively intelligence showing behind his eyes.

"I'm sure," I said. "But I don't think the man I'm interested in was much for plants."

"Yes, of course, you're Detective Swift."

"How do you know me?"

"You showed your card to Dr. Slate, didn't you?"

"But you couldn't have seen— Are you saying you're psy—"

He was chuckling.

"Oh, all right," I said. "The joke's on me, right?"

"I don't know," he said. "Perhaps the joke's on all of us. At my age one begins to think so. But you must realize that you are something of a public person, Mr. Swift."

It was true. More than one of my cases had caused my picture to be prominently displayed in the local daily paper. "Yeah," I said. "I guess I am beyond the point where I can pretend to be someone I'm not."

"That depends on why and with whom. Artifice has its place. Life would be a lot less entertaining without it."

"I like a good movie, too. So what did you think of Eric Vessey?"

"A complex man. But dead. Why would you be interested in him?"

He'd fielded the question without any hint that it had raised his defenses. My quick take was that either the deceased had meant less to him than to Dr. Slate, or that he ranked several grades of clever higher than she. Or both. I decided to answer his question with a question.

"The dead never interest you?"

He smiled. "Not in the way that you mean, no. Although the psyche always interests me."

"What about his psyche then?"

"Interesting," he said. "I'm not a psychoanalyst, but I would have been amused to see what an analyst had to say about him. He was psychically gifted, as I'm sure Dr. Slate told you. Reasonably intelligent, as these things are measured. But there was something driving him, some buried secret that he had never fully integrated with the balance of his life. Something. . . ." He spread his furrowed hands and cocked his head at me. "He's connected with you in some way. What is it?"

I thought about it for just a moment, then made the decision as if it were somehow being made for me.

"I have a client," I said, "who thinks Eric Vessey's death may not have been accidental. What do *you* think?"

"A staged accident? Possible. Or were you rather thinking of a suicide?"

"I don't know. I never really considered that. Was Vessey a suicidal type?"

"We're all suicidal types. And increasingly so."

"C'mon, Dr. Jordan. That's a cop-out."

He shrugged. "Eric Vessey's physical form is dead," he said. "As yours will be soon and mine will be sooner. We all commit death against ourselves. The circumstances matter very little."

"They do to me in this case."

"Because you're making money from it." He laughed.

"What do you think his secret was?" I asked.

"I have no idea."

"Then how do you know he had one?"

"Tell me yours first."

The old man was getting me more than a little twisted around. I paused to generate some internal calm. One of investigation's first maxims: If you're agitated you'll probably miss what you're after, or you'll misinterpret what you do get.

"What do you mean?" I said evenly.

"You are a detective," he said. "You spend your time unraveling mysteries. What is it that compels you to do that?"

He looked me straight in the eye and suddenly I had the oddest feeling, as if it were very important that I tell the absolute truth. Unfortunately, I didn't have a clue to what the truth might be. I started to say something, but found I was tongue-tied.

He smiled and placed a hand gently on my arm. "I don't know," he said in a near-perfect imitation of what my own voice would have sounded like had I been able to speak. I laughed, feeling a good bit looser.

"You're very good at this," I said.

He gave me one of his little bows. "Larry Bird shoots five thousand baskets a day during the off-season," he said. "I do something similar."

That made me laugh some more. He pantomimed an off-balance jump shot.

"But it's only parlor tricks," he said. "My little illusion. Larry Bird's sleight-of-hand is not him, as mine has no bearing on the true value of what we do here. Perhaps you'd like to learn more about us."

"I don't know," I said. "I'm not much for psychic stuff and all that."

And why did I feel a little unsure of myself? It was no lie. When it comes to the world, I'm strictly a prove-it-to-me man. If something can't be verified by one of the senses, then I'm highly doubtful of its existence.

"Oh?" he said. "But you have premonitory dreams."

He stated it simply, as fact. It startled me at first. Then I recognized the old fortune-teller's scam: tell them something that's apt to be true. *Everyone* thinks they've had premonitory dreams, at one time or another. It doesn't require extrasensory perception to divine that, it just sounds good.

On the other hand, I did have some peculiar feelings about my dreams. There were those that had helped me piece together the facts of a case. A fascinating phenomenon, with what would likely prove a simple explanation. My unconscious mind was just doing what my conscious couldn't quite hack.

And then something jumped out at me. On Sunday morning, Patricia had told Morgan Vessey that I'd had premonitory dreams. Maybe Jordan wasn't either psychic *or* running the fortune-teller's scam. Maybe he and my client had talked about me, and he'd picked up this tidbit from *her*. For some reason, the thought gave me a serious chill.

"Would you like to come back sometime when you are not 'working'?" Jordan asked.

"Uh, maybe," I found myself saying. Postulating a shadowy relationship between Morgan and the good doctor would take me much too far afield. I cleared my throat. "But right now I am working," I said. "We were talking about Eric Vessey?"

"Yes, I think that you would be interested," he said wistfully. Then his expression changed, as if he were returning to the here and now. "Well then, Vessey," he went on. "A man obsessed. But I doubt very much that that's what killed him. Or perhaps I should put it a bit differently. Among his many obsessions, the one most closely held is unlikely to have caused his death. But of the others, who can say?"

"Is he the type who would have gotten careless about his air?" I asked.

"Unquestionably. A man of great *hubris*."

"So you think it was an accident."

"I don't think anything. The physical body inevitably passes away. Under what conditions is, in this case, a matter of importance to you. It is the resolution of your mystery. But for me it resolves nothing, so why, then, should I speculate? Now you, it is your employment. You will do your job. You will do it, I would say, as best you can. Yet however Mr. Vessey died, it will not ultimately affect what you take away from here."

The statement made me a little uneasy. "What do you mean?" I asked.

"There is more to you than meets the eye, Detective Swift."

With that he began to walk down the gravel path, away from me. Over his shoulder he said, "Are you sure you don't want to see the ornamental pears?"

"Next time," I said.

"Until next time," he said.

He clasped his hands behind him as he walked. I found myself having difficulty focusing on him as his figure receded. It was that white-on-white business, I told myself. His hair, his clothes. It all ran together, blurring his parts into a featureless blob, like a ghost.

I went in the other direction, toward the parking area. The day remained warm and still. The air was delicately touched with the scent of pine.

My car was in sight when I heard someone call my name. I turned. At first I didn't see anyone. Then the small figure emerged from among the trees. It was the boy who'd been in the Institute building, the one who had stayed home from school.

Everyone, it seemed, knew my name. Daffy old men, strange children.

The boy came up to me. "I know you," he said with a sly smile. "You're a private detective."

He looked funny with that little cowlick. I didn't think they allowed them on people any more.

"Guilty," I said. "How'd you guess?"

"You were on TV. Like Magnum."

Yeah, I'd even been interviewed on TV once.

"Kid, you've got a good memory," I said. "And just for the record, there are some fairly important differences between me and Magnum, namely about six thousand miles, half a year's worth of extra summer, and maybe forty million women. So who are you?"

"Danny Jordan."

"You a private eye, too?"

He grinned. "I want to be."

"Well, I'd say you're off to a good start if you can remember me from the TV. You're Grover Jordan's . . . ?"

"He's my grandpa," he said. "Well, not exactly my grandpa. His sister was my grandma. That's sort of like the same thing, isn't it?"

"Sort of. What are you doing here, Danny?"

"I live here. Grandpa Grover takes care of me."

"How come? Where are your parents?"

He shuffled his feet in the gravel, staring at the furrows he created. "I don't have a dad," he said. "My mom left me with Grandpa Grover. She comes back, and then she goes away again."

"Well, I'm sure she misses you," I said. I didn't really know what to say.

"Nah. She's old. I mean, older than you. But not as old as Grandpa. She doesn't want to fool with a kid." He'd been looking away, but now he looked back at me. His face brightened. "Anyway," he said, "what are *you* doing here, Mr. Swift?"

"You can call me Swift. I'm working on something."

"A case?"

"Yeah, sort of."

"Neat. What's it about?"

"You read detective stories, Danny?" I asked.

He nodded vigorously.

"Then you know I can't reveal what I'm doing. That's between me and my client. If I betrayed a client, then no one would hire me anymore."

He looked crushed.

"But," I went on, "that's not to say that I couldn't use a little help in the matter."

I looked at him conspiratorially. He brightened once again.

"You mean . . ." he said.

"I mean that it would be good to have someone on the inside here. Someone who's smart and, well, who *notices* things."

"That's me, Swift! I notice *everything*."

I put my hand on his shoulder and gave him a critical appraisal. "You sure you're up to it?" I said.

"You bet. What is it, a murder case? Drugs? What?"

"Can't say. But I tell you what. You keep your eyes open, you see anything unusual, anything out of the ordinary, you let me know the next time I'm out here. Okay?"

"Right. When'll that be?"

"I don't know. But I have the feeling it won't be long. This looks like a very . . . *peculiar* case."

He lowered his voice. "Anyone in particular you want the low-down on?" he asked.

"Not right now. Just general stuff. If something develops, we may have to get into specifics later on. And of course," I added, "no one must know that you're my ally."

He looked offended. "Don't be a twit," he said.

"Good. I am counting on you, Danny."

I turned to go.

"See you later," he said. "Partner."

Then he hurried back toward the main house, ready to do some serious detecting work.

CHAPTER
5

When I thought about it, it was a pretty off-the-wall job. I was being paid to chase a dream. Now, Lord knows, I'd chased some dreams in my life. But I'd never been paid for it before.

The spring day was balmy. I rolled down the window in my orange VW as far as it would go, about three-quarters of the way, and enjoyed the fresh air. I turned on the radio, pretending that it still worked. Amazingly, there were The Grateful Dead—playing *Ripple*, one of my favorite songs. I kept time by slapping the steering wheel and sang along. I'm not known as much of a singer, but then, though I do love his guitar work, I don't think Jerry Garcia is much of one either. I feel like I do a passable imitation.

I dawdled along U.S. 29, heading north, back toward Charlottesville. There was no hurry. The highway sliced through the foothills of the Blue Ridge, some of the loveliest land on the planet. Traffic was light, except for the steady flow of eighteen-wheelers on their way to D.C. and New York. They rumbled past Clementine on the downgrades, leaving her shaking like a limberjack in the slipstream.

When I left the Institute, I didn't really know what my next stop was going to be. Along the way, I decided.

Patrick had recently gotten himself a real office. He was Patricia Ryan's kid brother, and had taken up computer programming when a midnight encounter with a drunk driver had ruled out professions requiring full use of the legs. A couple of years later he was one of the top three microcomputer experts in the city. Not exactly a slow learner.

He'd founded Shenandoah Consultants, Inc., and for a while had run the business out of his sister's house. But now he was too successful for that. He had an office. He was ten years younger than me and had something I'd never been able to afford.

The office was located in a frame duplex that he shared with an insurance agent, on the west side of town. A hanging wooden sign announced his tenancy. It featured the name of his company against a background of a mountain sunrise. Or sunset, depending on your point of view.

When I walked into Patrick's domain, he had a keyboard in his lap and was working the keys for all they were worth. I didn't think humans could type that fast. I *knew* they couldn't type that fast and make something coherent happen on the screen.

Patrick was surrounded by the tools of his trade, all carefully situated within arm's length of a seated person. There were disk drives, monitors, printers, oscilloscopes, boxes of floppies, circuit boards, and all manner of electronic I-don't-know-whats. I'm still not truly prepared for the computer age, a fact that Patrick never lets me forget.

He turned his wheelchair toward me and a big Irish grin appeared on his freckled face. He has the same auburn hair and green eyes as his sister.

"Hey, Loren Swift," he said. "You know your ASCII from your elbow yet?"

Among his other accomplishments, Patrick Ryan is a smart-ass kid. A smart-ass kid who has three times my brain and makes ten times as much money. I'd probably hate him, or at least exhibit some ugly envy symptoms in his presence. Except, for one thing, that I'm in love with his sister. And except, for another, that he saved my life not once but twice one memorable evening. Minor considerations like that.

"As a matter of fact, I do," I said. Patrick had actually

taught me a few things. "Ass-key is a computer language." I patted my butt. "And that's my elbow."

He laughed. "Good job, Swift," he said. He motioned to a vacant terminal. "Want to sit down and blast some code?"

I sat down. "As a matter of fact," I said, "that's exactly what I want to do. But not in the same way you mean it."

I produced my little spiral notebook and got out the page containing the gibberish I'd found among Eric Vessey's gas mileage records:

O NW Quad

lO N

DuE Edge

85 D

X X

I gave the page to Patrick.

"What do you make of that?" I asked.

"Ah," he said, "that kind of code." I nodded. "And Charlottesville's most famous private detective is humbled before it? Like an IBM expense-account exec before an Egyptian hieroglyph?"

"Just the facts, kid," I said. "You can skip the travelog."

He studied the notebook page for a while, then said, "Well, it's not actually code, of course. It's shorthand."

"Uh huh."

"Not much chance of figuring out what it means unless we already know kind of what it means. If you know what I mean."

"Take a guess," I said. "You're supposed to be the boy genius."

"I don't know, it looks like directions to me. Is this a buried treasure case?"

"It isn't an anything case yet. Tell me what you think the directions say."

"Well." He furrowed his brow like he was really thinking, though I knew this kind of thing was kid stuff to him. "If we assume that the first line tells us where to begin, then 'NW

Quad' probably means the northwest quadrant. Of whatever it is. And the zero is a reference point to start from. But zero what? It could mean anything. That's going to be a problem for you. If our first assumption is correct, the rest will be useless to you until you know what the zero stands for."

"Okay," I said. "So the second line would mean 'ten paces north.'"

He shrugged. "Paces or feet or miles. Who knows? Then I'd say you turn due east and continue along the edge of something until you get to some point that's not specified. Whatever you're after is buried eighty-five feet down. That's pretty deep."

"The guy who wrote this was a diver. It could just mean eighty-five feet of water."

Patrick's face lit up. "The stiff in the quarry," he said. "The one you and Patricia found."

"Yeah, the stiff in the quarry."

"Far out. How'd *he* hire you? You getting into voices from . . . *beyond the grave*?" He had a voice like John Newland when he wanted to.

"Don't be cute." I found myself becoming a little uneasy at any mention of psychic phenomena. "My client is very much alive," I went on quickly. "But there appear to be some, uh, incongruities about the way the gentleman died."

"Ooh, I like that word, 'incongruities.' You pick that up at U.Va.? I thought you were only there for a semester?"

I sighed. "What about the two X's?" I said.

He shrugged again. "X marks the spot? Double X's mark two spots? A warning of some kind? Poison here. Beats the hell out of me."

"Try this. Suppose it's directions to some place in the quarry itself, where something's hidden. That'd explain why he was diving. And remember, Patricia told you that the first thing she spotted was a come-along. So presumably whatever he expected to find was too heavy to move by hand."

"Okay, Swift," he said. "But how big's the quarry?"

"Pretty big," I admitted.

"So you're still not much better off than you were before you found that stuff in the notebook. You already guessed that he must have been doing *something* down there. That's good, Sherlock. That and a few weeks underwater might get you an answer. Of course, *now* you've got what you think are directions of some kind. But you don't know *when* he wrote them down, you don't know *what* they refer to, and you can't *follow* them. You're still in for a hell of a lot of bottom time."

"I know," I said.

"Sorry."

"It's not your fault. In case I hadn't told you, that's what the detecting business is all about. Cutting your bottom time. We learn to do the best we can."

"I'll take a computer any day," he said. "It only thinks in binary. On or off, yes or no, plus or minus. And it never goes diving at night."

I laughed. "Yeah, I suppose it's simpler when you don't have to deal with people. But I'm too old for job therapy, you know that."

"Also too stubborn. And probably too dumb."

He returned the code and I put it back in my notebook and got up. "Hey, I'll see you later, kid," I said. "Thanks for the expertise. Always a big help."

"Anytime. Good luck."

"Sure. And don't bet all your chips in one place," I said as I left.

My talk with Patrick hadn't really netted me any new information. Even if Vessey's cryptic shorthand did relate directly to his death, which was by no means certain, I still had no idea where it was pointing me, nor what I should expect to find when I got there. Until that became more clear, it'd be futile to put in a lot of time on decoding.

My next stop seemed obvious. I drove to Underwater Charlottesville, the local dive shop. I had made the acquaintance of the proprietor, Jonathan Searle, during my certification course. I'd rented the necessary equipment from him. Mask and fins and snorkel and B.C. and the ever-popular wetsuit.

Searle was a soft-spoken guy about my own age. He had seemed nice. There wasn't enough demand in Charlottesville for a five-day-a-week operation, so he ran the store on a part-time basis. He had some kind of teaching job where he got off in the middle of the afternoon. After that, he'd open the dive shop for a few hours.

The shop was located in a rundown section of town.

Dingy cinderblock buildings, warehouses, industrial supply operations. The kind of area every town needs, to accommodate those who can't afford the rents elsewhere.

Underwater Charlottesville was a small, one-room affair, housed in one of the cinderblock buildings. Behind the single front window hung a straw man dressed in a wetsuit. Beneath him was an arrangement of rocks and fake seaweed. A few tropical fish were painted on the glass. Above the door was a wooden sign with the shop's name painted in dark blue, against a background of light blue water filled with tiny white bubbles.

I went inside. There was one long glass display case. It was filled with regulators, diving knives, compasses, gauge consoles, and other tools of the trade. There were several tubular aluminum floor racks, such as would hold sport jackets in a men's clothing department. They were hung with Lycra bodysuits, insulated vests, shorty wetsuits and Farmer Johns. Different brands of B.C.'s were hanging on wall hooks. Behind the display case was some cheap metal shelving that held books and spearguns, masks and mask defoggers, plastic squeeze bottles of insect repellant for those Caribbean killer mosquitoes, and a special solution to combat "diver's ear."

In addition to all this hardware, there were more people than there ought to have been. The shop was jammed with college-age kids. They were milling around, inspecting equipment, trying on wetsuits, jostling and stumbling over each other in the limited space. If someone had yelled "Fire!" there would have been a mess of death.

I looked at the kids, with their neatly styled hair and their designer jeans and their Reeboks and their orange U.Va. sweatshirts, and I wondered how I could possibly have gotten so old so fast. What in God's name, I wondered, would I be like if I were that age and in college today?

Useless speculation. I pushed my way through the mob, not really caring whose feet I was stepping on, until I reached the far end of the store. Jonathan Searle was there, busily writing up receipts in an attempt to impose some order on the chaos.

A perky blonde coed, apparently thinking I was trying to butt in ahead of her, begged my pardon. Very politely, of course; the ideal of the ever-gracious Southern lady is far from dead. She even called me "Sir," a form of address I find particularly loathsome. I gave her the wordless tough-guy look that I've borrowed from Sylvester Stallone, and she cringed and backed away like the President's former buddies once the scandals hit the front page.

Some guy, maybe her boyfriend, started to say something. I gave him more of the same, trying my best to seem like a murderous psychotic who's just about to drift across the yellow line. It's a difficult act for me, but I'm reasonably good at it. At least with teenagers. Whatever the guy was going to say, he thought better of it. The two of them began to inspect wetsuits in the latest designer colors: lime green, pink, lavender, all the shades that look especially ludicrous on the human body.

For a moment I felt just a little guilty. Then the feeling passed.

Ronald Reagan, I thought. He wasn't right about much of anything else, but he was right about this: We are becoming a nation of wimps. We've grown afraid of standing up for ourselves, we tolerate the most contemptuous kind of behavior from our elected officials, we file suit when any little thing goes wrong in our lives, we feel national pride only when the military is out defending our honor against some Third World backwater that couldn't possibly put up decent resistance.

I finally got Searle's attention. He was a slender man, with long wavy brown hair, boyish features, and the kind of puppy-dog brown eyes that are sometimes called "soulful."

"Hey, Swift," he said. He spread his hands in a gesture of helplessness. "The University group is getting ready for its checkout dives. It's a bit more of a madhouse than that course you took was. Just hope I've got enough rental equipment to go around."

"I need to talk to you, Jon," I said.

"You ready to buy your own gear?"

"Nah. It's business, I'm afraid. I'm working on a case and I need to tap your expertise."

"Sure, no problem. But I'm kinda tied up, as you can see. Why don't you come by the house later tonight. You know where I live?"

I shook my head and he gave me his address.

"Any time after seven-thirty," he said. "I'll be there."

"Thanks," I said, and I shoved my way back out of the store. No one gave me any hassle.

There was a convenience store a block from the dive shop. It had a pay phone out front. I fished around in my pockets and managed to come up with a quarter, which I used to call Morgan Vessey. She was at home and told me to come on over.

Morgan Vessey lived in a condo near the center of old Charlottesville. It was a semi-detached house on the edge of a cluster of eight such buildings. The house had plastic siding done in a dull gray, to give the look of well-weathered wood. Its roof, by contrast, featured a pair of modern skylights and a solar panel to help heat the unit's water.

These condos were on the pricey side, I knew. The art and collectibles market must be bullish. Either that or the little psychic dynamo had a supplementary source of income. In a sense it was odd to be working for someone about whom I knew next to nothing. But if I screened the people who bought my time as much as I'd like to, I'd wind up with maybe two cases a year and I'd soon be reduced to having to work for a living.

Morgan Vessey answered my knock looking as petite and blonde and mousy as she had the last time. She had on a severe gray business suit and a pair of plain gold hoop earrings. She was dressed for success, as we have come to define these things, or else she had attained it.

"Come in, Swift," she said, and I did.

I found myself in a spacious entrance hall, open all the way up to the skylight. There was a set of stairs to my right, the kind that seems suspended in the air.

There was track lighting along every wall, for the purpose of illuminating the paintings. They were everywhere. There were a number of different styles represented—different artists, I assumed—but they were all what I'd term "modern." That is, none of them pictured anything that I could recognize. I didn't care much for them, though some of the more brightly colored ones did remind me a little of my old concert posters. I wondered if maybe this was what those same folks were doing, twenty years down the road.

"See anything you like?" Vessey asked me.

"Not really," I said.

She nodded. "I didn't think so. But then, your taste is a bit . . . stuck in the past, isn't it?"

I shrugged. "Art isn't my field," I said.

She fixed her eyes on mine, and it happened again, the thing that had happened in my apartment the previous morning. My head kind of twitched. At the same time, though I wasn't at all physically attracted to the woman, I could feel my body heat beginning to rise.

"You like doing this?" I said.

"Doing what?" she asked. All innocence, like Tuesday Weld in the movie *Pretty Poison*.

"Nothing," I said.

She continued to look at me as though she was trying to get inside. "You're a strange one," she said. "Have you ever been psychically evaluated?"

"No."

"You should. I'd be interested to see what the results were. I think they might surprise you."

"No, thanks. I'm not much for that sort of thing."

"Ah yes," she said sweetly. "The skepticism of your trade. Tell me, how did that come about? Is the cynic attracted to the work, or is it the work that makes the person?"

"I'm not a cynic," I said. "I just don't believe in the supernatural."

"And yet you've had some paranormal experiences. Like I said, you are a strange person."

I had no idea where she was heading with this, but I was pretty sure I didn't want to make the trip.

"You were going to give me the key to your brother's house," I said.

She gave me the intense look for a moment longer, then said, "Yes. Come on into my office."

I followed her through the nearest door on the left. It was a small room, the kind of office you'd expect to find in someone's home. A desk, a couple of chairs, filing cabinets. On top of the desk was an IBM PC. Its printer was in one corner of the room. In another corner was a stack of paintings leaning against each other. They were unframed, with their fronts turned away so that I couldn't see them. Probably just as well.

Vessey took the chair behind the desk and indicated that I should sit down too. I did.

"Anything to report?" she asked.

"Not a whole lot," I said. "I visited the Nelson County sheriff. He didn't tell me anything I didn't already know. He's inclined to believe it was an accident, and I'm still inclined to agree with him."

"No, it wasn't," she said firmly.

"Suit yourself. Then I examined the area around the quarry, just to see if maybe the sheriff's boys had missed anything of importance. They hadn't. Then I checked in at the Institute. That got me exactly nowhere, though I did meet Grover Jordan. He told me about the little chat you had with him."

I said it casually, but I was carefully watching her reaction. All I saw was puzzlement.

"What chat?" she asked.

"The one where you told him you'd hired me."

"I'm sorry, Swift. I don't know *what* you're talking about."

She was an expert actress, or else she really didn't.

"He knew about my dreams," I said. "I assumed you told him."

She laughed. "No," she said. "Not me. Dr. Jordan's just amazingly perceptive. He can tell things about people. The more contact you have with him, the more impressed you'll be."

Her answer seemed sincere enough. I didn't know whether the old guy could read minds or what, but there wasn't any sense in pursuing it further.

I shrugged. "Okay," I said, "back to business. Tonight I'm going to meet with the local divemaster, which I don't have much hope for either. Actually, the only unusual thing I found all day that might be relevant was this."

I opened my notebook, took out the page containing Eric Vessey's code, and passed it to her.

"That look like your brother's writing?"

She nodded. "What is it?" she asked. Her response appeared genuine. I was pretty sure she didn't know what she was looking at.

"Some kind of directions, looks like. I found it in a notebook that was in Eric's glove compartment. He had his gas mileage in there, and this thing."

She handed it back. "It makes no sense to me," she said.

"Me either. But if it is directions to something, then it might well have to do with why your brother was diving in the quarry that night. Especially since it was in the car."

"I see."

I slipped the code back in my notebook and put it away. "On the other hand, it isn't much," I said. "One of those items to put on the back burner until I'm a little more sure what I'm looking for. Which brings me to why I'm here."

"My brother's house," she said.

I nodded. She opened one of the desk drawers, took out a set of keys, and gave them to me. There was a small white tag attached to the key ring, with the house's address on it.

"And you'll need this," she said, handing over a magnetic card key. "To deactivate the alarm system."

"Your brother had a burglar alarm?"

"Yes. Very good quality, too. Typical of Eric."

I looked at the key and couldn't help but laugh.

"Something's funny?" she said.

"Private joke," I said. "I did some work for this company."

"They don't make quality stuff?"

"No, quite the contrary. It's just . . . never mind. It's a very long story and it's not important."

Not important to her, that is. It was very important to me. Eric Vessey's alarm system had been manufactured by Fail-Safe Detection Systems, the very people who were responsible for my newly acquired wealth. She accepted my dismissal of the subject with a nod.

"Okay," I said, "has anyone been in there since Eric died?"

"I don't believe so, not unless they were real professionals. It's sealed until the will's been probated, and I've made sure the alarm's on at all times. I'm the executor, of course, so I suppose it's all right if we make an . . . exception in your case."

She was advising me not to let anyone catch me in there.

"I'll make my visit as brief as possible," I said. "But I want to do a thorough search."

"Naturally."

"I'll return the keys tomorrow, and I'll let you know if I find anything."

I got up to go.

"Swift," she said.

"Yeah."

She stared at me for a long moment, as if making up her mind about something.

"I don't know," she said finally. "I've just got this feeling. I think you ought to be careful, that's all."

I couldn't read anything in her face.

"I'm always careful," I said.

CHAPTER
6

Ihad a yen for a thick deli sandwich, so I drove over to the Corner. This is an area near the university that caters specifically to the needs of the student population. During my own fleeting undergrad days, I'd been a frequent visitor to the Corner, and it wasn't because of the food. I'd had a fake I.D. and very little idea of better ways in which to spend my time.

As I settled into a window seat at the deli, I thought that, well, at least I didn't get carded anymore.

From where I sat, I could see across the street to Grounds, as the University of Virginia's campus is known. There was a low stone wall, defining boundaries. Inside, the flower of civilization, Mr. Jefferson's stately academic village. Outside, a chaotic scramble as the rest of us fought to keep our individual gigs running.

Beyond the wall, a wide expanse of open lawn was pastel green in the fading light of the early spring day.

Uphill of me, I could just see the tail end of Brooks Hall. It was my favorite building on the campus. Ugly like you wouldn't believe, but that wasn't why it was my favorite. I liked it because it didn't belong there. Literally. It had been designed for Harvard, but there had been a mixup and some laudanum-crazed ninteenth-century architect's assistant had shipped the plans down here instead. Thing was, Virginia had been expecting some plans, too. The builder, what did he know from style? So he went ahead and built the thing.

The result was Brooks Hall. It sits there still, squat and graceless, completely inconsistent with the Jeffersonian elegance of the rest of the campus. You gotta love it.

I munched my sandwich and chips, and drank my Stroh's. Patricia had been trying to get me to curb my drinking. She was probably right, if I wanted to live longer and all that. But you had to drink beer with a deli dinner. They went together like politicians and deceit.

There were several tables set up on the lawn across from me, on either side of the walkway the students used to get from Grounds to the Corner. There were petitions and leaflets and large, hand-lettered signs. I watched as the kids manning the tables collared other kids to try to sell their particular point of view. The two sides of the walkway offered two opposing solutions to the problem. The problem was AIDS.

One table represented the Southern Campus Christian Crusade, the other the Gay Student Union. I didn't have to hear what was being said, or read any of the literature, in order to know what kind of argument was going on.

And argument it was. When not trying to persaude the uncommitted, the two groups were hurling insults at each other. There was a lot of heat, but then it was an emotional issue. It had the entire country in a sex-fearing sweat.

A burly city cop hovered near the tables, looking like he was itching to bust a few heads should things get even a little out of hand. There wasn't much doubt which heads he'd go for first. Charlottesville, even though it has for some reason attracted a rather substantial gay population, is still first and foremost a conservative Southern town.

Though I'm not sure that "conservative" is a word that means a whole lot anymore. My idea of conservative is those parts of the Constitution that begin "Congress shall pass no law" and go on to spell out all the ways in which our numbnut leaders are not allowed to screw around with our lives. I take it that not too many people agree with me. So I tend to avoid talking politics or social issues. In the end we'll get more or less what we deserve.

I finished my dinner, such as it was. It was still too early to head for the next stop on my agenda, so I bought a copy of the *Daily Press* and ordered another Stroh's.

The paper's lead story, no surprise, was about AIDS. There was no escaping it. This particular story concerned some Richmond cops who had been called in to break up a fight. One of the participants was irate at police interference in what he considered his own business. He also had AIDS. During the ensuing scuffle, the man had spit at one of the arresting officers. Now the cops were charging him with attempted murder.

Well, who the hell knew? I wouldn't have wanted to be on the jury charged with untangling that mess.

I turned to the sports page.

Another Stroh's later, I'd finished the paper. I'd forced myself to read everything in order to pass the time. There was nothing new in the news.

I took a walk to the far side of Grounds and back, to shake the effects of the beers and sitting on my butt for more than two hours. Then I drove to Jonathan Searle's house. I got there a little before eight.

The house was in the Belmont section of Charlottesville, not far from where I live. Belmont's one of the less fashionable addresses in town. People like Jonathan Searle, with decent but not great jobs, own houses there. People like me, with less than minimum wage jobs, rent apartments there. It's not a seedy area. The houses are kept up and there's even a fair measure of community spirit. If I had a choice, I'd still live there, rather than in one of the intellectuals' ghettos near the university or the monotonous middle-class sprawl north of the city.

Searle's was a modest frame house set halfway up one of Belmont's hills. It was maybe forty years old. The small lawn was well tended and the siding didn't need paint. There was a mailbox in the shape of a scuba tank.

When I rang the doorbell it played the first five notes of *I Can't Get No Satisfaction*. A man after my own heart.

Searle answered the door. He was wearing jeans and a T-shirt silkscreened with the *Underwater Charlottesville* logo. He greeted me with a smile and let me in.

The door opened into a tiny entryway. There was a flight of stairs on the left. Upstairs would be two bedrooms and a bathroom. The living room was on the right, with the kitchen/dining area beyond. There'd be a full basement under us. I guessed that it would store a lot of equipment related to the scuba business.

"Come on in," Searle said. "We were just having something hot to drink."

I followed him into the kitchen. It was small but functional. There was a table set up against one wall, with a chair at either end and one tucked under the middle. A boy sat on the chair at the far end. He had a steaming mug of what looked like hot chocolate in front of him.

The boy was about fourteen. He had short brown hair and a complexion as smooth and unblemished as a baby's. His eyes were also brown. They were extraordinarily large and moist. They looked capable of expressing all of the world's sorrow. Otherwise, his face was completely impassive.

"Benjy, this is Mr. Swift," Searle said. "Swift, Benjy."

"Hi, Benjy," I said.

I held out my hand but the boy didn't take it. He looked at me without saying anything. The face was still blank, but there was something like confusion in the eyes.

"Sit down, Swift," Searle said as though Benjy and I had had a normal introduction. "What can I get you? Water's still hot. Coffee, tea, hot chocolate with whipped cream?"

I hadn't had a hot chocolate with whipped cream in about twenty years so I went for it. I sat in the middle chair. Benjy was still looking at me. For some reason I felt incapable of looking back. I stared down at the tablecloth while Searle fixed my cocoa.

"There we go," he said, setting a heavy china mug in front of me. He took the chair at the other end of the table.

I took a sip and glanced over at Benjy. His eyes were brimming with tears. As I watched they spilled over and began running down his face. I looked at Jonathan. He appeared unconcerned with what was happening.

Benjy got up and came over to me. He put his arms around me and pressed his cheek against mine. He hugged me close. It was unlike anything I'd ever experienced. I was flustered at first, but the boy radiated warmth and it spread to me. I hugged him back.

After a long moment, he moved away from me a little. He was grinning broadly through his tears. He looked at Jonathan and nodded his head vigorously.

Searle said. "Mr. Swift and I would like to talk now, Benjy," he said. "Okay?"

Benjy nodded again. He gathered up his hot chocolate and left the kitchen. I could hear him clumping up the stairs. A door closed above us and the house was quiet.

"Benjy can be a little disconcerting," Searle said. "But he's a good kid. And he likes you."

"He seems nice," I said carefully. "What, ah, was that all about?"

Searle rested his forearms on the table and leaned forward. He paused for a while before answering. He looked at me as if weighing considerations.

"Benjy's very sensitive," he said finally. "He discerned something sad about you, right off. There's been some terrible sadness or tragedy in your life. He wanted to show you that he feels it too, whatever it is. That he'll help share it. And then he let me know that you've overcome it to a great extent, that you're basically a good person."

"Oh," I said. "I, uh, don't quite know what to say."

"Did you feel like he was drawing something out of you?"

The question hit me like a stone. "Yeah, actually I did," I said. "It was the strangest feeling. How do you know about that?"

Searle shrugged. "It's something that he does," he said. "I can't explain it, but people always feel a lot better after he's done it. As far as his assessment of people goes, well, he doesn't make mistakes."

"Always a first time. I'm really a number one bastard. I park in *No Parking* zones and put a fake clergyman's ID in my windshield, for example."

He laughed. "Like I said, he's never wrong."

I sipped my chocolate, licked a trace of cream from my upper lip.

"Who is he?" I said. "If you don't mind my asking. Your son?"

"Does look a bit like me, doesn't he?" he said. "But no. He's my nephew."

"He lives here?"

There was another pause. Jonathan had a cup of tea in

front of him. He turned it around and around on the table-cloth. Then he took a drink and set the cup firmly back down.

He looked me in the eye. "Do you believe in evil, Swift?" he said.

"Yes, I do," I said without hesitation.

A nightmare scene flashed through my mind, a terrifying scene from my life in which a very large man had caved in the back of Patricia's skull with no more emotion than if he'd been swatting a fly. Yeah, I believe in evil.

"Yes," he said. "Does it have to do with the sorrow that Benjy felt from you?"

There was another scene. A blond teenager lying in a pool of her own blood, victim of an act of mindless, malignant violence. I had tried to save her life and I'd failed.

"I guess it does," I said, a little hoarsely.

"I think that you understand," he said.

He took a deep breath and let it out slowly.

"My brother was an evil man," he went on, "and I don't use the term lightly. Benjy is the result of his evildoing. The boy was locked in a room from the time he was a baby. My brother visited him only to abuse him."

I felt ill. "For God's sake," I said, "why?"

"Yes, for God's sake. At least that's what my brother said. God spoke to him directly and told him what to do. Benjy's mother had died in childbirth. Somehow, 'God' had decided that that was Benjy's fault and that he should be punished for it. My brother was merely carrying out God's will."

"What happened to him?"

"He's in a hospital down in southwestern Virginia. He's virtually catatonic. I think he must have been torn apart by what he was doing, and eventually his body and mind just shut down."

"I'm sorry," I said.

"I was too. But then, now Benjy lives with me and he's brought a lot into my life. You've seen how sensitive he is. They think it was compensation. He wasn't allowed to develop in normal ways and this brought out his other gifts."

"Can he talk?"

"A little. By the time someone figured out what was going on, he was way past the age when speech should have developed. It's hard to go back when that happens. But he does have some verbal ability. He never talks in front of strangers, though. He's perfectly happy communicating in other ways."

"You must have an extraordinary relationship," I said.

"Yes, we do. Benjy's life is more important to me than my own. And believe me, I never thought I'd say that about another person. In my younger days, I was your classic selfish American male. I used people and threw them away. Benjy's forced me to grow up, and I'm glad. Do you have anyone whose life is more important to you than your own?"

"I don't know. I like to think so."

"It's a wonderful thing, and a huge responsibility. Especially with someone like Benjy, who can't care for himself. But I don't mind. I'd do anything for him. He's someone who brings only positive energy into this world. He's that extraordinary. He needs me for some things, but how badly we all need him for others."

I realized that I felt very comfortable, sitting there talking with Jonathan. The fact that he'd shared all this with me had something to do with it. But it was also that I seldom ran into guys my own age whom I enjoyed shooting the breeze with. One factor is Charlottesville's population, a big slice of which is always under twenty-five; nothing personal, but students now seem very young to me. Another is that those folks who are my peers tend to be the kind of upwardly mobile yuppie types that have me reaching for a second drink before I've finished my first. And then there's my line of work, which constantly throws me in with people I would otherwise shun. The end result is that I don't have many friends and I don't meet many people who are likely to become friends.

Being with Searle was a small pleasure.

"Thanks for telling me," I said.

"No reason not to," he said. "Nothing there that I'm ashamed of. How about you? You have any kids?"

"Me? No."

"Never wanted any?"

"I don't know," I said, and I didn't. I was very accustomed to being a loner. "It's never been an issue. My ex-wife didn't want any kids, period. Patricia and I, we haven't talked about it yet. And there wasn't anyone in between that I would have considered."

"I was probably a lot like you. Then Benjy came along. Since then I haven't found anyone who wants the kind of instant family I've got. It's a major change, caring for another human. But you get an awful lot back. You should try it some time."

Patricia came to mind, our conversation about whether to send a child to school with another kid who had AIDS.

I cleared my throat. "Well, ah, maybe I will. Anyway, in the meantime, I did come here on business. If we might . . ."

He chuckled. "Sure," he said. "What would you like to know?"

I thought about it, then decided what the hell. He'd been open with me, I'd be open with him.

"You know," I said, "that Patricia and I are the ones who found Eric Vessey's body in the quarry." He nodded. "Now I have a client who thinks that Eric Vessey's drowning might not have been an accident. I'd like to get your opinion on the thing. And anything else you might know about it."

"Okay. But I gotta say I think you're on a wild goose chase. Where do you want to begin?"

"Well, the equipment seems the logical place. He rented it from you."

"Right."

"And it was in good shape?"

"Hey, *all* my rental equipment's in good shape." He laughed. "Well, maybe not everything. There's those gloves with the holes in them. And that B.C. with the punctured bladder. . . . But yeah, Vessey's stuff was fine. The really important things, like the regulators and the pressure gauges, I check them out every time they come back, before I rent them out again."

"Did you recheck the equipment after he drowned?" I asked.

"Uh huh. The Nelson County sheriff held it for a week. Then they brought in an impartial third party, an equipment expert from a big dive shop in Richmond. I tested everything out at my place, under his supervision, and he certified the results. Vessey's regulator and his gauges were working perfectly. There's not much chance it was anything but a routine accidental drowning. That's what I believe it was."

" 'Not much' chance?"

"Right."

"What do you mean?"

"C'mon, Swift," he said. "Somebody *could have* done Vessey. Of course. Almost any accidental death can be faked."

"This one could have been?"

"Sure."

"How?"

He thought about it. "Well," he said, "there's a number of ways. All of them, I think, are going to involve another diver. First," he ticked off number one with his finger, "there could have been somebody else in the quarry with Vessey. He had a lot of lights with him, so he would have been easy to find. The other person could have sneaked up on him and jerked the air hose out of his mouth."

"Okay," I said, "but if that happened, it seems likely to me that there would have been some sign of a struggle. Vessey was a big guy. He would have fought."

"If he'd just sucked in a lungful of water, he might not have fought very hard. But I agree, killing someone that way is not easy to do. Everything has to go just right. Still, it is a possibility."

"Okay, what else?"

He ticked off another finger. "Again, it would have to be another diver. He would have had to have access to Vessey's equipment. And he would have had to have a pretty good idea of when Vessey was planning to dive.

"The most logical thing would be an equipment switch. For example, substitute a faulty pressure gauge, so that when the tank was empty the gauge would still read five hundred pounds or something. Then hope that Vessey wouldn't be able to deal with an unexpected out-of-air situation, which is a pretty big question mark."

"The other person would have had to be on the scene when Vessey went down," I said.

"Right. He'd have to wait until Vessey's bubbles stopped coming to the surface. That'd be a pretty good indication that Vessey had drowned. Then he could dive down and replace the faulty gauge with the good one that I originally rented out.

"There's a problem with this, though. Where'd he get

faulty equipment? I'm the only supplier in town, and he didn't get it from me. I haven't had any theft and all my rental stuff's accounted for."

"All you're really saying is that he was a good planner."

"I suppose. But there aren't but so many sources. Unless he was very, very careful, you could trace it. And there's another thing. Nobody sells faulty equipment, not knowingly. So your hypothetical person had to have the know-how to be *able* to modify a pressure gauge."

"Anyone in town have that kind of expertise?"

"Sure, me." He laughed. "But I didn't do it, boss. Honest."

"Anyone else?"

"I don't know," he said. "Probably Steve Furniss, your instructor. But I don't see Steve as the bad guy type. And some others, perhaps a sizeable number. There's a lot of divers in this town. Who knows how many have picked up the technical stuff somewhere?"

"Can you give me a list of the most likelies?"

"Yeah, I guess."

I tore a page out of my notebook and gave it to him. He thought for a while, slowly compiled a list of about a dozen names. None of them was familiar to me, outside of Furniss, his assistant, and one guy I knew was another instructor.

"Thanks," I said.

"Swift," he said, "look. I know these guys. They're all long-time divers. I really think you're wasting your time."

"Probably. Just like Eric Vessey probably accidentally drowned. But it's the way you do the job, Jonathan. You try this, you try that, you see if something shows up that connects with something else. It's not so much that I suspect your friends of being involved with Vessey's death. But suppose our second person *approached* one of them about equipment sources or to get some unusual modifications done. You see what I mean?"

"Oh. Yeah, I see what you mean."

"Nobody approached you, did they?"

"Nope."

"Okay," I said. "Now . . . let's see, what other possibilities do we have?"

"Not many," he said. "There is a remote chance that the other person wasn't a diver. That would mean that if there was an equipment switch, it was done while the equipment was in the sheriff's office."

"Pretty farfetched."

"I agree. And we still have the problem of where the doctored equipment came from."

I paused to drink some of my hot chocolate. It was no longer hot. Cold hot chocolate is never going to catch on.

"That it?" I asked as I put down the mug.

"That's about it."

"Okay, let me think about these things, see if I can come up with anything else. In the meantime . . . I don't know, what was *your* take on Eric Vessey?"

He shrugged. "Didn't much know him," he said. "Seemed like an intense man, but he didn't talk a lot. He was a decent diver, far as I could tell. Never bounced a check. If you're asking do I know why someone would want to kill him, I can't help you."

I thought some more, and it came to me.

"One other thing," I said. "You must keep a rental log, right?"

"Of course."

"I'd like to see it."

"No problem," he said. "In fact it's here. The shop was such a zoo today I didn't have time to enter all the information from the tickets, so I brought it home with me. I'll get it."

He left the kitchen and came back a few moments later. He set a large leather-bound book in front of me.

"This year's," he said. "Complete up to this afternoon."

"That ought to do it," I said.

"Good. Can I get you some more hot chocolate?"

"Make it coffee this time. I've still got things to do tonight."

He made the coffee and I studied the log. It was very carefully set up. After each entry (person's name, address, home phone, work phone, degree of certification) there were columns for: the dates of rental, itemization of equipment, notation that the equipment had been checked before rental and after return, variances in equipment condition, before and after tank pressures, amount paid in advance, balance due, assessments for equipment damage, balance paid, and a flag for delinquent accounts. There was also a space for comments like, "Don't ever rent to this person again!" and "Interested in acquiring a dive buddy." The space beside one woman's name carried the notation, "Single—yes." I smiled.

I worked my way from the first of January to the present. On more than one occasion, I said out loud, "Well I'll be damned." When I'd finished, I'd noted a handful of names, including the following: Morgan Vessey, Paula Slate, and Drake Vessey. I asked Searle who in the hell Drake Vessey was.

He looked at me with puzzlement. "Eric's brother," he said. "You didn't know about Drake?"

"No, I didn't."

"But you knew he had a sister."

"Morgan. Yeah, I knew about her. This is a real diving family we got here."

"Uh huh. Eric started it," he said. "A few years back. I got the impression that he'd always been the one who was out front, from the time they were kids. Morgan took it up next. She's his twin, you know, so. . . ." He shrugged as if that explained why they'd do many of the same things in life. "Drake, he was last. He's the least active of the three. More bookish. The most intelligent one too, I'd guess. I think it was more that he wanted to prove that he *could* do it, than that he really wanted to."

"You know Dr. Slate?" I asked.

"Paula? Sure. They've run a lot of tests on Benjy over the years, out at the Institute. Because of his psychic abilities. I met her then."

"So she's new to diving?"

"Relatively. I think she got certified about a year ago. She's a very curious person, and when we started using their quarry for training it got her curiosity up. That's when she took the course."

"How'd that come about, using the quarry at the Institute?"

"It was my doing," he said. "I discovered the quarry when I used to go out there with Benjy. I knew immediately that it'd be perfect for practice dives, so I asked Dr. Jordan if we could use it. He was resistant to the idea for a long time, pictured a bunch of people coming out and trashing the place. And there was always the possibility that somebody would . . . drown. With the legal hassles of that, should it happen.

"But I was finally able to convince him that we were responsible types. So far, the arrangement's worked out real well for the local diving community. We've never had an accident in any of the classes, and the divers always carry out their garbage. Now I don't know what'll happen. Dr. Jordan has closed the quarry for the time being. I don't want to sound cold-blooded about a man's death, Swift, but it was a freak accident that never would've happened if he hadn't broken every rule in the book. I hope it doesn't put the quarry off-limits to everyone else. You know what I mean."

"Sure," I said, "I know what you mean. People die and the rest of us keep on trying to make it a little smoother for those who haven't."

"Something like that."

Though time had passed easily, it had been hard on my rear end. There's something about a kitchen that's conducive to conversation despite its obvious drawbacks in the comfort department. I've never quite understood it.

"I think that's enough for one night," I said. "I'm gonna get going. Thanks for the help, and the speculation."

"Any time," he said. "Of course I do hope your client is wrong. And I believe he or she is. No offense."

"At this point, I'm inclined to agree with you, even if I'd dearly love to know what Vessey was doing in the quarry that night. And no offense taken. I didn't know Eric Vessey, so it's just a job like any other. I get paid either way."

He smiled. "You do cultivate that cynic stuff, don't you?" he said.

I patted my chest. "Heart of gold underneath. I'll call you if I think of anything else."

"Or stop by. Benjy and I are here most nights. He does like you."

"Tell him I like him too."

I left Searle's. It was now time to see how the late Eric Vessey had lived.

CHAPTER
7

Eric Vessey's house was in a fashionable area north of Meadow Creek, just over the Albemarle County line. It was a long, low brick structure, with a garage at one end. The garage door was closed, which was probably just as well. I snugged my VW to the curb, a little down the road, and walked back.

There was a door at the far end of the house from the garage, with three steps leading up to it. Next to it was a little amber bulb, glowing its warning that the alarm system was in operation. It gave off just enough light that I could see the *Fail-Safe* logo. I smiled to myself.

Below the light was a slot. I inserted the magnetic card key into it and the light went out. One of the other keys fit the door lock. I opened the door and let myself in.

I groped with my right hand, found a wall switch and flipped it. What the hell. Somebody could call the cops on me, sure. But if there were things to be found out about the late Mr. Vessey, this was the place to start looking for them. And the looking would go a lot easier if I didn't try to do it by flashlight. I could worry about complications when they happened. I'd talked my way out of worse spots.

I found myself in a spacious hall that extended for some distance in front of me. The switch I'd flipped had turned on a series of ceiling lights. So, though it wasn't apparent from the front, the house was actually L-shaped. It was very quiet inside, and the air was stale. I stood still for a few moments, to see if anything came to me through the old occasionally reliable sixth sense. Not much did. It felt like an empty house. It also felt like it had been empty for some time, but then that's what I would have expected.

Out of habit, I moved slowly, quietly. It wouldn't make the slightest difference, of course. If I clomped down the hall in jackboots, the neighbors weren't going to hear me, and if there was someone else in the house I was going to be discovered. But habits are habits. You stick with them for that one time in a thousand when they save your life.

There were four rooms on my left, three with their doors open. I could see what they were by the hall lights. The first was a large kitchen with a cozy breakfast nook. The second was what I guess you would call a "game room," dark wood paneling and leather chairs. Its focus was a regulation-size pool table. It looked to be slate and undoubtedly was. Third came a bedroom with the appearance of being for guests.

The door to the fourth was closed. I opened it cautiously. It was a big bedroom, most likely Vessey's. Definitely one of the rooms to be searched after I got the layout of the house down. I left the door open.

Opposite the four rooms was a wall with lots of glass. It looked out over an interior courtyard featuring a large rectangular swimming pool. Beyond the pool I could see another wing of the house in the nightglow. So the place wasn't L-shaped either. It was U-shaped. Rather a substantial house for a single man who had few friends and never entertained. I suppose it's predictable that if you have more money than you can use you spend it on stuff you don't need.

I went back down the hall and turned into the section of Vessey's house that was visible from the road. The prickly sensation of being an intruder was beginning to leave me, and I moved more casually now.

First stop was a large formal dining room. There was a

table set for eight. It looked like it had been set for the same eight since the time when *aids* was just a word that meant you were helping someone. On the walls was a lot of art, presumably from the Morgan Vessey collection.

The dining room gave way to a monstrous living room that took up all the rest of the space in this part of the house. The light from the far hall was dim now, but I could make out the important stuff. There was a sofa big enough for the Red Sox's starting lineup and a very expensive home entertainment center. There was a wet bar. More art hung on the walls. There were sliding glass doors leading to the pool area.

I crossed the living room and found a hall that was the mirror image of the other one. A wall switch turned on an identical series of ceiling lights. There was the same glass looking out over the pool, this time on my left. On my right were another four rooms. The door to the second was closed, the rest of them open.

The first room was an entertainment center of another kind. I guess you'd have to call it a bathroom, but it was half the size of my apartment. It had a Jacuzzi and a sauna and a couple of home Nautilus machines.

I opened the door to the second room. Bingo. Vessey's office.

Quickly, I checked the remaining two rooms. Both were guest bedrooms for the decedent's nonexistent guests. I returned to the office, closed the door behind me, and hit the light switch.

What came on was an antique brass lamp on Vessey's desk. It gave plenty enough light to see by. I saw a large desk with an executive's chair behind it and two other chairs for visitors. The latter were more modest than the big man's chair, but they were still expensive places to park your butt. There were two heavy four-drawer steel filing cabinets, the kind that have steel bars that pop out when you unlock them. Both were locked.

And there was a fancy computer setup. An Apple MacIntosh with a hard disk, color monitor, and laser printer. There were wooden boxes with rollback plastic tops, filled with floppy disks. Notebooks and user manuals. Boxes of continuous printer paper. It looked like everything one would need to go into the desktop publishing business. Each element had its own niche in the computer furniture that seemed to have been custom designed for this particular system.

A desk, eight hanging files, and racks of floppies. Any of which could contain relevant information. It was intimidating. A long night without sleep was strongly suggested. But then, I just might get lucky. I set to work.

I searched the desk first. There was a drawer with credit card bills and receipts, another with tax forms, another with office supplies. And so on. Nothing much, except in the center drawer. There, I found a small book on coins. It seemed a little odd, so I set it on the desktop. I'd take it with me when I left.

When I'd finished with the desk, I eyed the file cabinets. They looked like they'd resist anything less than oxyacetylene. I didn't have a blowtorch. I checked the key ring Morgan Vessey had given me. None of the keys was the right size. There had been a few keys in one of the desk drawers. I checked them. None of them fit either.

I thought some more. Would Eric Vessey hide the keys in question? If he did, would he hide them well? I found that I didn't have the slightest idea. So I checked out all the obvious places.

There was nothing taped to the underside of any of the desk drawers. Nothing behind either of the two paintings hanging on opposite walls. Half the front wall was a floor-to-ceiling bookcase stuffed with books. There might be a hollow one among them, but I sure didn't want to go hunting for it.

I picked up a paperweight that was sitting on the desk. It was a cast brass human skull, mounted on a wooden pedestal. The pedestal had a little plaque on its front that was engraved with Eric Vessey's name and, underneath that, the year *1954*, a dash and a blank space. Well, whatever got you off. I suppose it served to remind him of his mortality until fate—or one of his fellow humans—tacked a real meaning onto the word.

I fooled around with the skull, a little uneasily, and found that it was screw-mounted. When you unscrewed it you discovered a little hollow place. In the hollow were two small keys. One for each of the filing cabinets.

Vessey had saved me a lot of trouble by arranging his files according to date. I unlocked one of the cabinets and pulled out the top drawer, the one marked with the current year. It rolled open as smoothly as if it were skating on ice and it made almost no sound. A quality piece of office equipment.

The drawer was crammed with hanging files, each of them tabbed by subject. I leafed slowly through. And there it was, a folder marked "Jordan." Just like that. The detecting business should always be so easy.

I carried the file over to the desk, holding it as if it were breakable. Inside there was a manila folder. It was thick but not bulging. I settled myself into the executive's chair, noting that it had controls for heat and vibra-massage and stereo music input from some remote source, to be played through the speakers up around ear level. I didn't use any of the accessories. The anticipation already had me good and wired. I opened the manila folder.

The first item was a puzzler. It was a Xerox copy of an article that had appeared in the local paper in the summer of 1940. Someone named Charles "Boots" Henry had been stabbed to death at his country estate outside of Charlottesville. The police had no suspects but were assuming that Henry had been killed by a burglar who had been surprised in the act of burgling. There was no hard evidence, except that some valuables were obviously missing. There were no solid leads. The cops were not optimistic.

Henry himself was pictured as something of a recluse. He was obviously a person of some considerable wealth, but had no visible income. It was rumored that he'd amassed his wealth in the bootlegging business, back in the Twenties. At that time he'd been tagged with the "Boots" nickname and it'd stuck. The tone of the article suggested that Mr. Henry was not someone who was apt to be widely mourned.

I turned the page over. There was nothing on the back. The second item was a short article from the same paper several days later. The police were looking for a neighbor of Boots Henry, a man named Greg Jarvis. Jarvis had apparently disappeared around the time of the murder and the cops were requesting anyone with knowledge of his whereabouts to come forward.

Nothing on the back of the second page. The third item was a Xerox of a lined page from some kind of notebook. Vessey had written at the top, "Henry diary, Book 9, p. 157."

And then the light went out.

Automatically, I felt around until I found the brass lamp and I turned its switch a couple of times. Nothing happened. There were no windows in the office, so I was in pitch darkness. I sighed and leaned back in the chair. Hell of a time for a power outage.

About a minute passed. Then I began to get the creepy crawlies. The house was still dead silent, but it no longer felt like I was alone.

I called a picture of the office into my head and held it there until I was confident that I could move around without maiming myself. I got up. The leather chair creaked like the deathbed voice of a very old person. I put my hand reassuringly on its arm as if it were in fact alive.

Carefully, I moved around the desk, stepping slightly to the side to avoid the wastebasket I knew was just about there. The heavy carpet absorbed any sound of footsteps. I made my way to the wall and inched along it until I came to the door. My hand rested on the knob. I moved again, keeping touch with the knob, so that the door would now open away from me. A simple precaution to keep my face from being pulverized if someone were really out there and chose this moment to come on in.

Staying to the side, I opened the door a crack and stepped backward, to see if I could see anything. There wasn't much, but I was able to make out the ghostly form of a part of the swimming pool and a tiny pinpoint of light in the distance. Assuming the pinpoint to be a streetlight, and the pool to be still illuminated by the cityglow, then the power outage was not general.

I turned and flattened my back against the bookcase that made up this section of the wall. I thought about the situation. If the house had lost power for some reason that I'd laugh about later, then okay. But what if parties unknown had thrown the master circuit breaker? That could only mean that the perpetrator knew I was in here (or knew that somebody was in here) and would rather keep me in the dark. Why? I couldn't think of a reason that made me feel at all comfortable.

What to do. I could try to sneak out. Or I could stay where I was and see what happened. Or I could exit the room making a lot of noise and hope to scare him off. I wasn't carrying, of course. I have a couple of handguns and I'm allowed to conceal them on my person, but I rarely do. Too much chance they might be used against me. And as yet I'd had no warning that this particular case might be hazardous to my health.

I decided to stay where I was for a while. I waited and nothing happened. I began to get more and more nervous, and still nothing happened. The lights didn't come back on, there were no suspicious sounds from anywhere in the house. Yet there was the sensation of another presence, close to hand.

Finally I couldn't take it anymore. I felt the same way I had when my brother locked me in a closet for three hours when I was eight years old.

There was, I recalled, a door in the opposite wall that let onto the pool area. It was catty-corner from the office and not far away. It was undoubtedly locked, but I thought I remembered a locking button in the knob. If I was right, I could be through the door in a couple of seconds. It wasn't a great idea, but it seemed like a better bet than going slowly dinky dao in the dark.

Then I thought about the Jordan folder. And I thought: suppose it's not an ordinary burglar but, by a bizarre coincidence, someone who's after the same thing I'm after, even though I don't have a clue what it is that I'm after. The thought came and went. I regretted not having the folder in my hand at that moment but them's was the breaks. I wasn't about to turn my back on the door and go groping for it.

I took a deep breath and stuck my hand in the crack I'd made between the door and the jamb. I shoved. The door swung open without much sound. Vessey kept his house up. Used to keep his house up.

When I moved, it wasn't at top speed but I didn't exactly dawdle. I went through the office door, turned in the direction of the door to the pool. And stopped like I'd hit the centerfield wall. The light in my eyes felt like the flashguns of all the *paparazzi* of the world, all going off at once. I raised my hand instinctively.

There was a brief low chuckling sound, then the light was out of my face and I caught a fleeting glimpse of a hefty figure before a fist was driven into my belly. The guy's blow was powerful and well-placed. The wind went out of me in an instant.

I stumbled backward, clutching at the doorframe of the office. A strong hand grabbed my shirtfront, straightened me up without much effort. Another hand clubbed the side of my jaw. I staggered, took another couple of steps back into the office, lost my balance, and. . . .

. . . And that was it. No dramatic explosion in my head. No stars and whirling planets. Nothing until I blinked my eyes with almost no notion of where I was. I focused on the thick gold carpet. Pieces of lint and tiny fuzz balls. I was lying on my left side, slumped against something very solid. Where? What had I been doing before . . . ?

Slowly, it came to me. I was in the late Eric Vessey's office. The solid object at my back was his desk.

The light was on in the office. Of course, you idiot, I thought to myself. How else would you have been able to see the fuzz balls? And what was the *significance* of that? The significance was . . . that the light hadn't been on when I . . . lost consciousness.

I'd been unconscious. Okay.

I moved, very tentatively, and my body told me right away where all the pains were. The middle of my gut, my jaw, the base of my skull. The sequence of events was clear. Someone had trapped me in the darkened house. He'd punched me in the gut, then in the jaw. I'd stumbled backward into the office and. . . . The rest was lost. But I must have fallen and hit my head on the desk. That'd put me out for the count.

I sat up, my back still to the desk. My head hurt a lot. I started to retch and bent forward, but nothing came up. The room tilted a little, first one way, then the other. I closed my eyes. After the queasiness had passed, I opened them again.

With what seemed a superhuman effort, I brought back what I'd been doing in that office in the first place. It came slowly, but it came. When I was satisfied with my state of recall, I looked at my watch. I'd been out for something like half an hour. Then I got to my feet, using the edge of the desk to steady myself. I took as careful a look around as I could.

The office was not as I remembered it. I had left the Jordan file on the desk and now it was gone, along with the coin book. Other drawers of the filing cabinets stood open. The desk had been gone through. Some of the boxes of floppy disks had obviously been rifled as well. I had no doubt that whoever had hit me had been looking for the same thing I was, whatever it might be. And I had no doubt that if it had been there, he now had it. Which meant there was probably no point to further searching.

As hurriedly as I could in my condition, I set the office straight. Closed the drawers, locked the filing cabinets. Then I got the hell out of Vessey's house. I wasn't cute about it, either. If the intruder was still there, he could have another shot at me. I wouldn't be able to do anything about it. If he wasn't, he might have called the cops or any damn thing.

The house was empty. I switched off the lights and beat my retreat. I set the outside door to lock automatically. Then I dug in my pocket for the magnetic card to reactivate the alarm. It was gone, as were the rest of the housekeys. I tried to remember if I'd left them on the desk in the office. I couldn't. But so what? If I had, they were inside and I was locked out. It made no difference. I headed for my car.

As I walked to the street, I had a moment of thoroughly irrational doubt that my VW would be where I'd left it. But it was. I got in and drove directly to Patricia's.

Patricia was less than thrilled to see me in the middle of the night. She still had a real job, got up in the morning and went to work the same time real people do. Then she *saw* me. There would have been a nice bruise on my cheek, some dried blood in my hair.

She checked me over. "You all right?" she asked.

"Yeah, I suppose," I said. "I don't think I got concussed. My jaw's not broken. My brain's only a little more scrambled than it normally is."

"Hospital?"

"Uh uh. That's where people go to die."

"Very funny."

Unthinkingly, I shook my head. Very foolish. I had to close my eyes until the nausea eased.

"It wasn't a joke," I said. "You got some Irish?" I insisted that she keep a bottle of Jameson's on hand, though she never touched the stuff herself.

"Of course. You want some Tylenol #3 too?"

I wasn't sure how that'd go down on my dented stomach, but I said yes anyway. Anything was better than trying to endure the hellfire in my head.

I settled gingerly onto a chair at her kitchen table and she brought me the emergency medical kit. I took four Tylenols with codeine. A lot, but then they had a lot to do. I chased the pills with three stiff shots of the world's best Irish whiskey. I figured that ought to be enough in the way of downers to at least let me sleep off some of the pain.

Patricia washed and degermed the wound at the base of my skull. She told me it didn't look all that bad. I told her that made me feel a hundred percent better. She asked if I wanted her to kiss it and make it all right. I said that there were other parts of me where kissing might be more effective. I suggested what some of those parts might be.

Her green eyes sparkled and she slipped me her lascivious smile. She had the finest lascivious smile I'd ever known. The auburn hair and seemingly innocent freckle face only served to set it off the more.

"Later," she said. "Right now I want to know what happened to you."

"I thought you had to work in the morning," I said.

She just gave me a look. It was a look I'd long ago learned not to argue with. So I cranked up the instant-replay machine and ran the tape for her:

The Nelson County sheriff's office. The quarry. The Jordan Institute. Her brother. Underwater Charlottesville. Morgan Vessey. Jonathan Searle and Benjy. And last, but far from least, the little duet at the home of the late Eric Vessey.

When I'd finished, I realized I'd had an eventful if not exactly fun-filled day. It was also good for me to have gone over it with her. I could tell she was conscious of that too, by the way she coaxed the story out of me. Telling it helped fix the events in a brain that was apt to resemble oatmeal in the morning.

"So," she said, "you didn't get a look at whoever conked you."

"No," I said. "Just half a second's peek. He was a big guy is all I know."

"Or she."

"She?"

"There are large women," she said patiently. "Like this Dr. Slate, for example. How can you be sure of sex when you'd just been nearly blinded and saw a vague outline at best?"

"It was a guy," I grumbled.

"Okay, okay. *No* woman could knock *you* out. And you think *his* being there has something to do with this case."

"Of course. Why else would he take the Jordan file?"

She shrugged. "Because he realized you'd been looking at it in the middle of the night and thought it might be valuable?"

"Possible," I said. "But if he was an ordinary burglar he left behind some pretty fancy hi-fi equipment and a computer and the art and I don't know whatall other valuable stuff. And he grabbed a coin book that he could probably pick up at the library."

"Yeah, I guess I tend to agree with you. And if you're right there are certain conclusions to be drawn."

"Such as?" Though I knew exactly what they were. But she wanted to get her detective's license.

"Such as: There is, or was, something among Vessey's possessions that was valuable enough that our intruder was willing to assault you in order to get it before you did. Such as: If someone's not hesitant to beat you up when you get in his way, then maybe he's not hesitant to kill, either. Such as: Morgan Vessey and her ESP may be right."

"All true enough. But if the damn thing's so valuable, why'd he wait until tonight to go after it?"

"I don't know," she admitted. She thought for a minute. "Okay, here's an idea. He's not a professional burglar, so he doesn't know how to get through an alarm system. Tonight he was driving by, saw the inside lights on and the alarm light off, and made his move."

She looked pleased with herself. As well she should have. It was a pretty good idea.

"Or else he was following me all along," I said.

"Wouldn't you have known that?"

"Nope. I don't automatically check for a tail. Not unless I have some reason to believe there might be one."

"So there you have it," she said.

"This is have did," I said.

"Huh?"

I tried to remember what I'd just said, but I couldn't. The codeine was beginning to mix with the alcohol and the results were going to be unpredictable. I shook my head gently. It didn't feel nearly as bad as it used to.

"I think it's time for bed," she said.

"Munh hunh."

She led me to bed and slid in next to me. The mattress felt as though it were oozing up around my body. The blacksmith inside my head was hammering his iron somewhere out of sight.

I felt Patricia's hand on me, fondling me gently.

"Just relax," she whispered, barely stifling a small giggle. "This won't hurt a bit."

Relax was actually the one thing that I probably couldn't do more of. I drifted away, somewhere far beyond the possibility of mere physical arousal. Then again, she was very good at this. . . .

A half hour later I finally did go to sleep. My next-to-last thought was that I was probably never going to wake up. My last thought was that I didn't care. I'd been loved like the only man on earth who was worth it, and all my aches and worries had floated away with the tide. It was a wonderful time to check out.

The dream came sometime near dawn. Bad ones always happen near dawn. The hour of greatest vulnerability, I've been told. The hour when you meet those hairy, shambling creatures with rotten stumps for teeth, the ones that try to gnaw through the twine that keeps you wrapped.

I was underwater, diving at some unimaginably great depth. The water pressure was intense. My mask was jammed into my flesh, contorting my features into an ugly grimace. My eardrums felt near to bursting. Only maximum suction brought any air down through my hose. I was gasping, struggling to feed sufficient oxygen to my starving brain.

The water itself was murky and had the consistency of a thick syrup. I pulled hard, trying desperately to raise myself to the surface, but the resistance I encountered canceled out my efforts. Large, shadowy shapes bumped against me in the gloom. I couldn't tell what they were, or which direction they were coming from. Whenever one of them would touch me, adrenaline would jolt my system, my heart would pound, the demand would go out for more air, more air, and there wasn't any.

Despite my frantic efforts, I was sinking. The pressure crumpled my mask against my face like a used Kleenex. I could no longer see. Somehow, I began to sob. My body

shook with convulsions more massive than any it had ever
known. I gulped at the air hose and my mouth filled with
water.

I threw my head back and suddenly there was a moment
of suspended time. The water cleared. I could see again, all
the way to the surface, far above me, far out of reach. My last
air bubbles trickled upward like tiny crystal spheres. The
sunlight was playing on the faraway surface, turning it into a
vast, dazzling mirror.

In the center of the mirror there appeared a face, a gigantic
face, framed by a cat's cradle of swirling white hair. It was the
face of Grover Jordan. He was smiling down at me, the
picture of God as a gentle, genial grandfather. Then the face
blurred, changed. It became someone else, someone familiar
yet not quite identifiable, someone who caused my body to
shake with primal terror.

I screamed soundlessly. When my lungs pumped again,
there was only water. The unrelenting pressure forced my
chest wall outward, until it was about to explode—

And Patricia had her arms around me, stroking me,
comforting me. I was sitting upright in bed.

"It's just a nightmare," she was saying. "Just a nightmare.
It's okay now."

I was still gasping. My hair was damp and sweat was
running down my face. I could taste the salt.

"Loren," Patricia said softly, "what was it?"

The familiar features of Patricia's bedroom came slowly
into focus. Her words penetrated a consciousness that was
suspended somewhere between realms. My pulse rate
began to slacken.

I caught my breath. "I drowned," I said. "I—I think I
know what it was like to be Eric Vessey in that last moment."
I raised my knees and rested my forearms and chin on them.
"It was very convincing."

"Uh, this kind of gives me the creeps," Patricia said.

"Well, it's only a dream, isn't it? Only a nightmare."

"I don't know. Is it? There are some very strange things
about this Vessey business. I'm not exactly comfortable with
what it's doing to you."

I thought about it, tried to see things from her point of
view. She could often read me before I knew what was
happening myself. But the more I looked inside, the closer I

came to the edge of a vast emptiness. Paradoxically, this emptiness seemed to be firing images into my head. When I was awake, I could keep the scattergun cinema under control. But when I dreamed. . . .

Yeah, maybe I should just drop the case. Maybe there was nothing more sinister about Vessey's death than that he'd had the misfortune to end up sucking for air where there wasn't any. Maybe all I was going to do was unearth more of the peculiarities of his life, and so what if some of them were criminal? And then I'd end up spending even more time with people who were twisting my mind violently around on an axis that was unsteady enough on the best of days. Not to mention that my poking into Vessey's affairs meant a possible threat to my physical being as well.

Just quit. Uh huh. And when was the last time *that* happened?

"I know what you mean. But it's not hard to understand," I said with a very large lack of understanding. "I've been hanging around some peculiar people. It's bound to rub off a little. We're all suggestible to some extent. Even me. Besides, somebody just put a dent in my brain, remember? And then the codeine on top of that. Which reminds me. . . ."

Now that the dream shakes had subsided, I was again aware of the violent pounding inside my head. I got out of bed and tottered off to the bathroom for some more Tylenol #3. The floor wasn't pitching and rolling under my feet all that much.

I looked in the bathroom mirror for signs of intelligent life, and didn't see many. What I saw was a stranger staring back at me. For just an instant I felt that the stranger was telling me, in the same way the dream had tried to, that Eric Vessey had in fact been murdered. Then the feeling passed. I shook my head at my suggestibility and returned to bed.

"I'll be all right," I told Patricia. "I'll be fine in the morning."

But it was already morning, as I became increasingly aware. Patricia fell quickly back asleep. I couldn't make it. After fifteen minutes or so I gave up and got quietly out of bed. I went to the kitchen and made some coffee. The caffeine would mix with the painkiller and help ease the pressure in my head.

I got out my notebook, an unlined pad and a pencil, and I

set them in front of me on the kitchen table. Then I sat there, sipping my coffee, allowing my thoughts free play, doodling on the pad as the ideas came and went.

The case had broadened out quite a bit. The job I'd originally been hired to do—find out whether Eric Vessey had been murdered—was still my job, of course. But I hadn't really believed in Morgan Vessey's dream. I thought I could poke around, discover that there was nothing to be dis- covered, and pick up my paycheck. Now I'd had my head bongoed and dreamed a little weirdness of my own. It was time to take the prospect of murder seriously.

There were two threads to follow. The first one was the one I'd been pulling on so far. Why might he have been killed? The working assumption was that it was connected with the reason he was diving in the Institute quarry at all, and I felt certain that assumption would hold.

The second thread was: Who might have wanted to kill him?

Eventually, of course, the two threads would tie together. If in fact murder had been done. But for now it was possible, and more efficient, to keep them separate.

With regard to the first question, I'd made some progress. I knew that Vessey was looking for something in the quarry, and I knew that it was valuable. Maybe it was coins; he'd had that coin book in his desk. I might even have directions to whatever it was, though I couldn't decipher them just yet.

And then I knew that he'd kept a fairly hefty file marked "Jordan." I couldn't be positive, but this strongly suggested that Vessey was interested in something to do with the Jordan Institute, or Dr. Jordan himself, or both, rather than simply with the quarry.

In addition, before the lights went out I'd seen the first three items in the file. Two of them were newspaper articles concerned with the murder of a suspected bootlegger close to fifty years earlier. How he fit in I couldn't imagine. He must, though, because I'd seen, just for an instant, a page from one of his diaries. There was probably some vital information on that page. But then the intruder had arrived, with immaculate timing. All I could remember was the diary's book and page number.

Book . . . Page . . . And then I realized that they were

gone. I concentrated, but to no avail. My friend had knocked the two numbers clean out of my head. I swore.

Well, at least I knew that there was something somewhere in Boots Henry's diaries. I made a note to find out more about the very late bootlegger. I knew just the man for the job.

My second question was still surrounded with haze. Eric Vessey might have been diving for an unimaginable pile of goodies and yet not been murdered. If he had been, though, it wasn't too early to take a closer look at those people known to have been involved with him. I made a list: Grover Jordan, Paula Slate, Drake Vessey. Then I added Morgan Vessey. Why she'd murder her brother and then hire me to find her out was a puzzler, but I couldn't discount the possibility.

As I stared at my list, another thought surfaced. An important one. If I was beginning to think in terms of suspects, I'd have to begin watching what I said to whom.

Next to the first column I made another one and labeled it "Friends and Lovers." The only thing I put there was a question mark. And next to that column I started one called "Fringe People." Here I wrote "Steve Furniss," "Jonathan Searle," "Other Divers?" and "Business Cronies?"

For the time being, I decided not to place speculative motivations against any of the people's names.

CHAPTER
8

One of the first things I had planned for the day was to call Drake Vessey, but he saved me the trouble by calling me.

After my session at the kitchen table I'd gone back to bed and, despite the coffee, had racked out for several hours. When I woke up, Patricia had long since gone to work.

I ate a light, very tentative breakfast, found that it stayed down okay, and drank some more cofee. My jaw was swollen, but my belly was unmarked except by the growing evidence of too much beer. My headache had receded to a tolerable background noise, so I could stay clear of the hard drugs and make do with plain aspirin. I even whistled a little, though it wasn't a happy song.

After breakfast I called the answering service I've been using while I wait for monthly office rents to drop into double digits. The lady at the service gave me my one message in a voice filled with promises that would never be kept. She's never seemed concerned about my not keeping mine.

She told me that a Drake Vessey had telephoned and left a number to call back. I called.

Vessey had a deep, authoritative voice. He used it to say that he wanted to see me. I wanted to see him too, but I didn't say so. I pretended that I had no idea who he was and suggested that he meet me at my apartment. Around noon, if that was convenient. It was.

When I'd finished talking with Vessey, I called my friend Jonesy, who worked for the *Charlottesville Daily Press*. Every year in late March we get together in front of his big color TV, to flog our favorite basketball teams through the NCAA Tournament. I supply the Moosehead, his current favorite. In return for the beer and the pleasure of my company and the first crack at whatever juicy stories I stumble over, he lets me tap his encyclopedic knowledge of the area whenever I need to.

"Swift," he said, "my main creditor. How you doin'?"

"I don't know, Jonesy," I said suspiciously. "Am I somehow in your debt?"

"C'mon, don't be a stiff."

"I'm not. I had a rough night."

He laughed.

"If you think it's funny," I said, "you should see the Technicolor skin."

He laughed even harder. He finds it amusing that I'd choose a trade where I have to take the occasional lump.

"Okay," he said, "you're *not* putting me on, are you? The Tournament, remember?"

"I missed it."

"I figured you would, when you realized what a stupid bet you'd made. Carolina never could win the big ones. And it must've killed 'em to have to finally give Tark the Shark his national championship. But UNLV takes the Tourney, they gotta be number one. 'Course me, I got nothing against the guy. He doesn't do anything the other coaches don't do. The rest of them just get around it by designing curriculums even *you* could finish."

"Let's not get into that now," I said.

It was a running disagreement we had. Tarkanian had often been accused of recruiting kids who didn't have a chance in hell of graduating. And maybe he did. Jonesy believed that everyone else did too, only they hid it better.

The problem, he said, was that there simply weren't enough "student athletes" to go around. And his solution was to make college basketball a play-for-pay proposition. End the hypocrisy once and for all.

Somehow, that just didn't sit right with me. I might not have accomplished much in my single semester at U. Va., but I didn't think that we should turn our college athletes into professionals before they got out of school.

Okay, he'd remind me, but if they enforce academic standards, then we're going to have to settle for a lower level of play. I'd tell him that was fine with me. One of the major appeals of college ball, to me, has always been the contagious enthusiasm with which it's played. That more than makes up for any deficiencies in execution. If I simply wanted to see consummate skill, I could always watch the pros.

"All righty," he said. "But you still owe me twenty-five bucks. Don't tell me your rough night canceled your memory."

"Yeah, I remember now. Next time. You know I'm good."

"Sure, Marlowe. So you didn't call to talk sports."

"You're such a perceptive reporter," I said.

"Oxymoron. Except in my case, of course. What you need?"

"Guy named Boots Henry. Bootlegger who lived out in the county someplace. Died in 1940. You ever heard of him?"

"Nope."

"See what you can find."

"That it?" he asked.

I thought about it, then added, "And anything you've got on the Jordan Institute."

"That I *have* heard of. You in a rush?"

"Tomorrow's fine."

"Gee, thanks Swift. I'll give you five-to-one you can't remember the all-Tournament team either. What do you say?"

"Jones, today I'll be lucky if I can remember my *own* name."

"That bad, huh?"

"That bad."

"Okay. Later."

I had sufficient time to go home, take a very leisurely, very hot shower, shave, and generally make myself look a little less like a person who'd been involved in some unintentional close-range carpet inspection.

Drake Vessey arrived right when he said he would. He was about four inches taller than my five-ten and he had maybe forty pounds on my one-seventy. Dark eyes, dark hair. The Vesseys apparently came in all sizes and colorings.

He had the deep voice I'd noted over the phone, but other than that was almost devoid of presence. His haircut was conservative, his basic blue suit nondescript, his face as free of stubble as a child's. He wore glasses with nerdy plastic frames.

When I first saw him, I almost laughed out loud. He bore an uncanny resemblance to Christopher Reeve as Clark Kent.

I stifled the laugh by asking him if he worked for IBM.

"Why no," he said. "Why do you ask?"

"I don't know. You look like an IBM executive."

"Thank you," he said.

He declined my offer of a drink, it being too early in the day. Coffee he accepted. He took his with cream and sugar. I took mine with Irish whiskey. In my case, the time of day did not apply.

We settled ourselves in my living room and I asked him what was on his mind.

"Well, you probably recognize my name," he said. "It was my brother whom you . . . found in the quarry."

"I'm sorry," I said, though he seemed to me the sort of guy who'd usually be doing the apologizing.

"Thank you. He was the only brother I had. I have a sister Morgan, too. Eric and Morgan and Drake. Our father was fascinated by men of the sea. You probably guessed that." He smiled faintly. Actually, it hadn't even occurred to me, but I nodded. "Well," he went on, "I hope you won't think it's . . . crass, my coming to you like this when Eric's . . . The truth is, I'd like to hire you, Mr. Swift."

"Just Swift is fine. What for?"

He shifted nervously in his chair. "I don't know exactly how to put it. I'm not used to dealing—"

"—with people in my profession. I know. Put it as simply as you can, Drake."

"I'm sorry," he said. Yup, I was right about the apologies.

"You must hear that a lot. But I'm afraid it isn't simple. You see, I get these feelings sometimes, I don't know if you'd call them premonitions or what. But they're usually right. I have a feeling about my brother's death, that there are things about it that haven't come out. And . . . and I feel like I'm in danger of some kind. What I'd like is for you to, to help me investigate what happened to Eric and . . . well, protect me, if I need it. You do do that sort of thing, don't you?"

Jesus, I thought. Here we go again.

"Ah, yes I do, Drake," I said. "But I've got to tell you something right now. I have a client at the moment. Normally, that might not prevent me from taking your case too. But in this instance I'm afraid that there is the possibility of a conflict of interest. So I'm going to have to turn you down."

"May I ask who your client is?"

"You may, but I'm not allowed to tell you."

He gave me a close scrutiny, as if *I* were the one who wanted to hire *him*. Then he visibly relaxed. His mouth widened into a good-natured grin and I saw his teeth for the first time. He had perfect teeth.

"What did I say funny?" I asked.

"It's my sister, of course," he said.

"What's your sister?"

"Your client, dum-dum. Your client is my sister, Morgan Vessey. It has to be."

"I can't divulge the names of any of my clients. Et cetera, et cetera."

"Okay," he said, "I'll play. I bet she hired you to prove that Eric's death wasn't an accident, didn't she?" He nodded the answer to his own question. "What I bet she didn't tell you is *why* she wants you to prove that. Interested?"

Of course, but I didn't say anything. I knew he'd go on, and he did.

"Sure you are," he said. "In fact, you're interested in anything at all about my late brother."

He raised his eyebrow. His whole demeanor had changed completely, just like that. Now we were co-conspirators in some little scheme that only we knew about.

"I might be," I said as noncommittally as I could.

"It's Eric's will," he said. "Eric was a real paranoid, always worried that someone was going to kill him for his money. So he put in this clause whereby if he died in some mysterious way Morgan was authorized to investigate what happened to him. Expenses to come out of his estate. Then, if Morgan comes up with his murderer where the cops couldn't, she gets a whole pile of money that otherwise goes someplace else." He paused, then added, "You're surprised."

That I was. I suppose it showed.

"That's the strangest thing I've ever heard," I said.

"Yes, isn't it? But then, it's just like Eric. He liked to cause friction between Morgan and me."

"I don't understand."

"Didn't she suggest to you that I killed my brother?"

"No comment," I said.

"Well, if she didn't, she will. Remember I told you that."

We sat in silence for a minute. I certainly didn't know what to say and he seemed to have talked himself out. His manner was changing, too. He fidgeted more. The confidant was turning back into the Milquetoast.

"Swift," he said finally, "please. I do have these feelings. If you won't let me hire you, at least let me be in touch with you. He was my brother." He gestured at something that wasn't in the room. "We might not have been the best of friends, but he was still my brother. And . . . I'm afraid."

His dark eyes were moist. Though he was a bigger man, he made me feel protective. I couldn't help it. There was just this aura of helplessness about him. Even when he'd been my co-conspirator he'd been more like a kid than an adult.

"Okay," I said.

"Thank you," he said shyly, and then with more animation, "I can help you. I knew Eric better than anyone. He was my brother."

I made a decision. I decided to let Drake Vessey tell me whatever he wanted to about Eric, himself, Morgan. He seemed eager. And there was no necessity for me to admit that his sister was my client. Even as I made the decision, I questioned it. It might be much better to just cut the guy loose. He could seriously complicate things. But then, I might get to the heart of the matter more quickly if I had his help. I opted for expediency over caution.

"What do you do for a living, Drake?" I asked.

"I'm a historian," he said. "Well, not exactly a historian. I don't teach or write history books or anything. I do historical research."

"You work for yourself?"

"Uh huh. People hire me. Like if someone was writing a history of such and such a family in Albemarle County, they'd hire me to help do the research."

"Really? You know a lot about Albemarle County?"

"Um, yeah, I guess so."

"Don't be modest," I said. "You ever hear of a character named Boots Henry?"

He looked at me blankly.

"Suspected of being a bootlegger. Murdered in 1940."

"No," he said. "But I could look it up for you."

"Forget it," I said. "Somebody already is."

He was turning his head, looking around the room as if for the first time. His movements were segmented and jerky. My *Quicksilver Messenger Service at the Avalon Ballroom, Summer of '67* seemed particularly to fascinate him.

"They're concert posters," I said, "mostly from San Francisco. Nowadays they're called poster art and you get charged a lot of money for them, if they're in good condition."

"San Francisco," he said, wrinkling his nose. "Lot of homos out there. AIDS."

It'd been years since I heard anyone use the term "homo." It sounded odd, especially since Drake didn't seem to be the hard-core bigot type. It seemed more like there might be things that were just offensive to him, in an ingenuous kind of way. And yet, there was a peculiar undertone to what he'd said, something I couldn't quite put my finger on.

"There are a lot of homosexuals in Charlottesville," I said. "And three or four AIDS victims. One of them's only a kid."

"I know," he said, shaking his head with what appeared to be genuine sadness. "A terrible thing, terrible." He looked down at the floor.

"What are you working on now, Drake?"

"Oh." He perked up. "You mean professionally?"

"Uh huh."

"Well, nothing really. I'm between jobs. I just finished a private family history. And then I'm going to be helping a woman who's doing a historical novel. Civil War period. But that's not until later in the month."

"How is the research business? If you don't mind my asking. Do you make a living at it?"

"Oh, I enjoy it," he said. "I mean, I'm not wealthy, not like Eric. He sort of inherited the family real estate business. I didn't have much talent for that. But Daddy left us all some money, so I guess I'm doing okay."

"And how long have you been diving?"

If the question surprised him, he didn't show it. "Not long," he said. "About a year and a half."

"You take it up because Eric did it?"

I watched closely, to see if he'd betray any signs of resentment of his brother. He didn't. Instead, he began to cry. It wasn't a sobbing kind of cry, but he was fighting it. He swallowed hard a couple of times and a few tears ran down his face. He wiped them away.

"I'm sorry," he said a little hoarsely. "Sometimes it just hits me."

"I understand," I said.

"I'm not sure you do. Do you have any brothers?"

"One. And a sister too, like yourself."

"Younger or older?"

"My brother? He's a year older."

He nodded. "Eric was two years older than me," he said. "He was always my hero. Did you idolize your brother?"

I chuckled. "Hardly."

"We fought a lot, like brothers do. Even after we grew up. But he was what I would like to be like, if I wasn't who I am, if I was strong and good-looking like he was."

"And that's why you took up diving?"

"I guess so. He made it sound like so much fun, and it is. But I never would have thought to do it on my own. I would have been afraid. He convinced me that there wasn't really anything to be afraid of."

"You done it much since you got certified?"

He looked at me suspiciously. "What do you mean?" he said.

"Nothing," I said. "I was just wondering if you kept up with it or if the enthusiasm wore off."

He must have believed me, because he looked a little guilty when he said, "I haven't dived in quite a while. Eric didn't invite me when he went to the Caribbean. He liked to have dates and I'm not very good on dates."

I cleared my throat. "Drake," I said, "can I ask you a personal question?"

"I don't know. What?"

"If Eric was your hero, how could your sister suggest to anyone that you wanted him dead?"

"She's greedy," he said emphatically. "She always wanted him all to herself. It's unnatural, if you ask me." He paused. "I mean, she doesn't like me. Besides, she'd like to get her hands on the money and she doesn't care how."

"But why would anyone believe her?"

"She can make you believe things. She has powers."

He said it the way he might have said she had a birthmark on her right shoulder. The strange thing was that I kind of agreed with him.

He was nodding to himself. "Is this helping you?" he asked.

"Yes," I said. "You're helping me very much."

"I want to help you. I want to know what happened to my brother. He was a very good diver, you see. Do you know why he was diving in that quarry?"

"I'm sorry, no. I only found him. I don't know very much about him at all."

He smiled. "I might know," he said.

"You might?"

"But I'm not going to tell you right now." He got up abruptly. "I have to go. I'd like to talk to you again sometime."

I got up and shook his hand. "Sure," I said. "Anytime. Anything you feel like talking to me about is fine. Okay?"

"I want to help you," he said, and he left.

CHAPTER
9

After Drake Vessey had gone, I couldn't help but wonder who'd done his wiring. It looked like they'd cut some corners. And I wondered if old Eric had been as strange as his sibs. If he was, the circumstances surrounding his death might be as convoluted as a disarmament negotiation.

In any case, Morgan Vessey owed me some explanations. She's the one I called first. She was available and agreed to see me in half an hour.

Then I called Ridley Campbell. Rid's the chief of police (formerly sheriff) of Albermarle County. He and I have a relationship that can turn pleasant or sour at a moment's notice. I've crossed him in the past, but I've also done him some large favors. Since my investigation was clearly bumping into criminal activities—if nothing else, I had been assaulted—it was time to take the professionals into my confidence. Next time I ran into my assailant I wanted someone Campbell's size around.

Must have been a slow day. Ridley said that unless there

was an emergency he could meet with me later in the afternoon.

My last call was to the Jordan Institute. I wanted to talk with Dr. Slate again. She agreed.

It was one of those days when everyone's free and willing to chat. Perhaps I'd come through it intact.

I'd worked up a pretty good head of steam by the time Morgan Vessey opened the door to her townhouse.

"Swift," she said, "how are you?"

"Pissed."

"Your face . . ."

"Yeah, I tried to hit somebody with it, but he didn't go down. Look, we can talk about it later. Right now—"

I tried to shoulder my way roughly past her. She caught my eye and I felt that little electric jolt again. It was enough to stop me in my tracks.

"Swift," she said calmly, "is it me you're angry with?"

My tongue was all twisted up and I couldn't get anything out. I just stood there.

"I see," she said. "Come into my office."

She turned and led the way. It was as if she'd slipped the leash off. I followed, now more angry with myself for being a wimp than I was with her.

The office looked the same as it had the day before, except that there were two easels set up next to her desk. Each was displaying a painting. The subjects were, I think, a man and a woman. A couple, perhaps. It was a little hard to tell if they were supposed to be people, because they'd been painted as if they were some twisted hybrid of human and machine.

Vessey saw me looking at the paintings.

"What do you think?" she asked.

I shook my head. "They look like Transformers," I said. I was sort of vaguely aware that Transformers were the most popular kids' toys of the year. And that's what these creatures looked like, a shape that was about to change into something entirely different. And unexpected. And possibly evil.

"Very good," she said. "That's the artist's intent, of course. She's making a statement about the extent to which we have come to resemble our toys."

"Terrific."

"Do you think so?" She sat behind the desk and I took one of the chairs. "I'm trying to decide how much I like them. Well, actually I'm trying to decide whether the buying public will like them. I think they have the potential to be very big. But it's always a guess, isn't it?"

"The art world, or the rest of life?"

She smiled. "What is it that you're angry about?" she asked.

"Let's start with your brother."

"Eric?"

"Uh uh. The living, breathing one."

"Drake," she said. "What about him?"

"I wasn't aware that he existed before he turned up on my doorstep this morning. I don't like that."

"Why not?"

Damn her. I didn't know why I didn't like it. I just didn't.

"He would seem to be relevant to this investigation," was the best I could come up with.

"Maybe so," she said. "But I certainly didn't fail to mention Drake because I was keeping something from you, Swift."

"Morgan, if you're looking into somebody's life one of the logical starting points is his family."

"Drake and Eric didn't have much to do with each other."

"Are you saying they didn't get along?"

"Not very well, no."

"And how do *you* and he get along?" I asked.

"I don't see him much, either."

"Real close family."

She got a bit of a nasty look on her face. "Don't judge us, Swift," she said.

"Why didn't you tell me you were a diver?" I said quickly.

For once I think I caught her off-guard. But she dealt with it simply by pausing.

"How did you find that out?" she asked.

"I'm a detective. Surprise."

"So I dive. What difference does that make?"

"Come on," I said impatiently. "Your brother was a diver. He died in a diving accident. If it wasn't an accident, chances are pretty good that it was another diver who killed him. You're another diver."

"You think *I* murdered Eric!?"

"I don't think anything at this—"

"You're insane. Why in God's name would I hire you to find Eric's killer if I killed him?"

"Money," I said.

That shut her up. She leaned back in her chair and stared hard at me. I tried to read her. She was more cautious now, curious, maybe just a little apprehensive. I think she was also looking at me with increased respect. And I felt she was assessing the possible courses this conversation might take. The wheels turned, the decision was made.

"What do you mean?" she said finally.

"I know about the will," I said.

I'd weighed what I was going to say, too. There was an advantage in not letting her know that I knew about the will. But only if I intended to play a very devious game myself. I'd concluded it wasn't worth it. Better to be straight with her and hope that she'd return the favor.

"I see," she said.

"You might have told me up front," I said.

"And what good would that have done?"

"At least I would have known what your motivations were."

"Don't patronize me, Swift!" She seemed genuinely angry. "I told you that I wanted justice for Eric and that's exactly what I want. I don't give a damn about the money."

"I understand that it's a considerable sum."

She didn't say anything. She continued to look at me like I was unworthy of the gift of life.

"Okay," I said. "You want to try looking at it from my point of view? There's a clause in the will awarding you a substantial amount of money if you can prove that your brother was murdered. Now people do a lot of things for money, strange and violent things. They scheme and they lie and they take the lives of their fellow humans, even including members of their own family.

"Assuming you knew about the will, let's say that you decided to kill Eric in such a way that the blame would fall on someone else and you'd be free to collect the reward. But it didn't work. The cops ruled his death an accident. The cash was slowly slip-sliding away. So you decided to hire me, in a last-ditch attempt to keep your chances alive. How's that sound?"

Amazingly, she still hadn't warmed up.

"It sounds like maybe you're not the right person for this job," she said.

"Morgan," I said, "you can fire me if you want. It's your right. But I just wanted you to realize the implications of being selective in what you tell me. I assume I made my point?"

I felt as if we'd locked horns on more than one level. The room was almost claustrophobic with the tension between us. She was working hard to regain control of me and the thing was, I wasn't sure she couldn't do it.

So I cheated a little. I got up. I turned my back to her. I walked over to the paintings and examined them with considerably more interest than they deserved. In my mind I tried to transform the figures into the human beings who might or might not have served as models.

For the first minute I figured she'd be having a fit. Then, I figured, she'd be deciding whether she was going to fire me. Then she'd be ready to lay her decision on me. I gave her another long minute after that, just to let her know that I didn't really care what happened.

By the time I turned back, she was smiling again.

"Swift," she said, "I must admit that there is something about your style."

I put a pleasant look of expectation on my face and waited.

"I didn't kill my brother," she said.

I sat back down.

"I take it this means I'm still employed," I said.

She sighed. "Truce," she said, "okay? I want you to finish the job. I didn't kill my brother and I want to know who did."

"Do you think it was Drake?"

"*I* don't know. But I wouldn't be surprised. Eric was the classic overachiever. Drake was the classic sibling in the shadows."

"He doesn't seem like a killer to me."

"How much time did you spend with him?"

"I don't know, maybe half an hour. He struck me as a Milquetoast."

"Swift," she said seriously, "Drake's a complex man. I wouldn't underestimate him. You know that Eric was in a fight shortly before he died?"

"The sheriff told me about that."

"Well, I think it was Drake he was fighting with."

"Based on what?"

She shrugged. "Another feeling. And I can't imagine who else it might have been."

"Let's back up here a minute," I said. "You say Drake and Eric rarely saw each other, and yet you think they got into a fight. You don't even mention Drake to me at first, yet you feel like he might have killed his brother. I'm not sure I understand what's going on."

"I wish I did," she said slowly, "but I don't either. Please try to remember that these are my *brothers* we're talking about, Swift. I've already lost one. My twin. The other may have had something to do with it and in a way, I want to know that. But in another way, I don't. I'm afraid, because if he did, it means that I'll lose him, too. Do you see? I want it all to somehow work out, and it can't."

"Yeah," I said, "I guess I see. But if I'm going to do the job, I won't be able to alter the facts. And you need to tell me everything that you know or suspect."

"I realize that. The other thing was, I kind of wanted you to walk into this cold. I didn't want to say a lot about Drake and prejudice you before you met him. It's sort of the same thing with the will, too."

"Okay. Your concerns are noted. From now on, though, honesty is the only policy. Deal?"

"Yes, it's a deal," she said shyly, except that I doubted she was ever shy about anything.

"How long has it been since you last dived?" I asked quickly.

"I don't know, quite a while. I rented some equipment recently, but I returned it without using it."

If she was jerking me around, she was awfully good at it. She'd answered without hesitation. Of course, she knew I'd gone to see Searle. From that, she might have deduced that I'd find out about her equipment rental. And she might have decided beforehand to admit it if asked, in order to look like she was being completely candid with me. If all of that were true, she was extraordinarily clever and practiced at the art of deception. Which she might well be.

"Why'd you rent it?"

"You're *still* trying to make me into a suspect, aren't you?"

"No," I said, "I'm trying to turn you into a non-suspect."

"Here I am," she muttered, "paying someone to investigate *me*." She sighed. "All right," she continued, "I rented it because the scuba club was going to make a dive on the U-boat off the North Carolina coast," she said. "It sounded exciting and I thought I'd join them. Then Eric drowned and it just . . . didn't sound like fun anymore. So I turned the equipment back in, unused."

She'd given me something that could be corroborated by a third party. Good. I didn't like asking her questions that sounded like a criminal interrogation. I'd had to, and now I could stop.

I could check out her story with Jonathan Searle. He was vice-president of the scuba club and he'd know if she had really signed up for the North Carolina trip. He'd also know if the equipment had been used. If she was telling the truth on all counts, it wouldn't mean she absolutely hadn't been involved in her brother's death, but it'd improve her credibility with me, as well as make her involvement less likely.

That and the fact that it couldn't have been her in Eric Vessey's house with me the previous night.

Speaking of which, "You're probably wondering what happened to my face," I said.

"You're prying into my affairs," she said. "Not vice versa."

"Well put. But actually it has to do with the business at hand."

"Oh?"

"Uh huh. I went to Eric's house last night, after dark. After I'd got the layout of the place, I settled myself in his office. Figured that was the logical spot for him to have kept his secrets. I searched his desk and some filing cabinets. I'd just found a couple of interesting items when the lights went out."

She looked at me quizzically. "You mean, literally? Or figuratively?"

"Both, as it turns out. Literally, first. Someone turned the electricity off. There are no windows in the office, and I'd closed the door, so I was quite in the dark."

"How do you know 'someone' did it?"

"When I opened the door I could see some stray lights outside. It wasn't a general power outage. Besides, I met the gentleman."

"Well, who was it, for God's sake?"

"I'm afraid we weren't properly introduced," I said. "There was a flashlight beam in my eyes for a few seconds. Then there was a low chuckle. And then he put *my* lights out. His punch would suggest a decently strong fellow."

"I'm sorry, Swift," she said, and her concern sounded legitimate. "I didn't expect that this job would put you in any . . . physical danger."

I waved my hand, brushing off physical danger like I was one of those real tough guy private dicks.

"Hazards of the trade, my dear," I said. "My gut's a little sore from where he hit me, and my jaw's a little sore from where he hit me, and my head's a little sore from where I hit myself. But no real harm to the first two and my brain's no more mushy than it ever was. The question of interest to us, however, is: Who was the fella and what did he want in there?"

"Should I have an idea?" she asked.

I shrugged. "I don't know. Do you?"

"I don't think so. You?"

"Not about who he was. But I do have an inkling what he was after. The same thing I was. Did your brother collect coins?"

"I— Uh— What are you talking about, Swift?"

"Coins," I said. "Was Eric a collector?"

"No . . . I don't understand."

"I found a book on coins in his desk. You know, one of those books that tells you values and stuff like that."

"I have no idea why he'd have that. There's probably a dozen reasons."

"Probably. And then," I said, "we come to what I wanted and didn't get." I paused briefly, wondering if it was right to tell her, then told her. "I didn't take his file on the Jordan Institute. They of course own the quarry where he drowned."

"What was in the file?"

"Good question. I opened it and then the lights went out." I'd told her enough for the time being.

"Meaning that . . ."

"Yup. Meaning that when I woke up it was gone. The coin book too."

She shook her head. "Damn," she said. "Why would he

have a file on the Jordan Institute? I mean, if they were trying to sell it and he was handling the sale, he'd have a file. Sure. But then why would whoever knocked you out want to steal it?"

"I've asked myself the same. I think we have to assume that there was information in the file that would shed light on your brother's death, or at least on the circumstances surrounding it, like why he was diving in the quarry in the first place. Also it seems likely that that information would be damaging to someone. It's impossible to believe that it was an ordinary burglar. He left the stereo and the TV and all that."

"Did he take anything else?" she asked.

"I don't know. I hadn't really gone through the files that thoroughly. The Jordan name caught my eye right away. Would you know if something was missing?"

"No. I never looked in my brother's files."

"So he might well have taken something I hadn't yet seen."

"This is weird," she said.

"Yeah, but most things are weird before you know how they work."

"And what did you expect, Morgan?" she asked herself. "You *knew* it wasn't an accident. Now you know for sure."

"I'm sorry," I said, "but it doesn't confirm that he was murdered. It only means that he had something worth stealing, something more valuable than a TV. That might be equally true if he were still alive."

"You've got to admit that you're suspicious, Swift."

"I admit it."

"And I won't be devastated if you don't want the job any more."

"Ah, I'll stick it out for a while."

"Then consider your salary raised to three hundred a day. Hazardous-duty pay."

"Offer accepted."

"Okay," she said. "What next?"

"Let me run down a few ideas I have. At some point I may want you to come with me while we go through the house, but I doubt that our friend will have left anything useful."

"I agree. Can I help in any other way?"

"Well, if you have any contact with Eric's friends or business associates, you can ask around, try to find out what he may have been working on the last couple weeks of his life."

"I'll do what I can, but I don't think it's much."

"Oh yeah," I said. "One other thing. I don't have the keys to your brother's house anymore. I think I might have left them on the desk in Eric's office, but I'm not sure. The intruder may have gotten them."

She nodded. "I'll take care of it," she said.

I got up. "Good. I'll be in touch," I said.

"Swift, I'm sorry. About . . . about everything."

"Just try to keep from messing with my head," I said.

CHAPTER
10

Ridley Campbell had an unpretentious office in the county office building. He looked out of his element sitting behind a desk, and he was.

Campbell was a throwback to the days when cops preferred to be out on the streets, talking to people and making their presence felt, rather than putting in chair time with their computer printouts spread in front of them. He was an imposing man, with a strong resemblance to Jack Lambert, the former Steeler linebacker, in both looks and build. He was probably as tough as his twin, and as easily intimidated.

Unfortunately for the criminal element, he also had a pretty fair mind.

I wasn't sure the same was true of the people walking up and down in front of the county office building. It was an anti-AIDS (meaning anti-gay) demonstration. The movement was picking up some steam. There were a couple dozen picketers out there.

Mostly what they wanted was a ban on gay schoolteachers. They had signs saying things like: "Our Children Are Your Future" and "Dirty Hands Off Our Kids." Another carried a big blowup of one of the last photos of Rock Hudson. Hudson's wasted face had a bold red circle drawn around it, with a red stripe across its center. Yet another sign said: "Cancel AIDS to Schools."

I was accosted by a leafleter. I hate being accosted by leafleters, no matter what they're leafing. I have this thing about being able to walk the streets in peace.

It was a middle-aged man with the last of his hair combed from the back of his head up over his bald pate and sprayed in place. I had to flick my elbow to get his hand off my arm.

"Lack of interest," I said. It didn't faze him.

"Brother," he said, trying to foist a flyer off on me, "won't you help us? Make sure your children aren't exposed to AIDS."

I kept my hands at my sides and I kept walking up the stone steps.

"I don't have any children," I said.

A woman broke ranks to say, "Well, *we* do," as if childlessness was a criminal act.

"If you're not with us, you're on the side of the plague," she added.

"Look you two," I said without breaking stride, "you've got a right to be here. You've got a right to demonstrate and you've got a right to believe whatever you want. But I've got a right to be left alone. So if you don't stop bothering me I'm going to cram the end of that sign up your butt whether it's got AIDS on it or not."

The man's face got grim but he stopped following me. The woman shrank away as if I did indeed have the dread disease.

"Faggot!" someone cried after me.

I went inside. Normally, I hate office buildings, but this one, at this moment, felt just fine. Even the packaged air seemed cleaner than the stuff I'd just been breathing. I hiked up to the office of the chief of police.

The man himself looked like something out of an ad for ugly pills, but his smile was not unfriendly.

"Swift," he said, "what can we do you out of?"

"Courtesy call, Rid," I said.

"Trouble, to put a word to it."

"I certainly hope not, Chief, but I have a client—"

"Skip the stuff I already know, will you?"

I smiled. "Okay," I said, "last night I was assaulted."

"Yeah," he said, "I noticed the beauty mark on your cheek. In my jurisdiction?"

"I believe so." I gave him Eric Vessey's address.

He nodded. "My bailiwick. You're here to file a complaint, you don't need me."

"That ain't exactly it. That was just sort of to get your attention."

He sighed. "Swift," he said, "how come every time I see you you got something on your mind more twisted up than two teams grabbing for a loose fumble?"

"I'm a complex man, Rid. I attract complex problems."

"Yeah, and I'm the goddamn Duke of Earl. What do you want?"

"Courtesy, like I said. I give it to you, you give it to me."

"So give."

There's always the question of how much to tell official law. In this case I didn't see a good reason to be evasive, so I decided to tell most of it.

"I'm looking into the death of Eric Vessey," I said.

"Who's he?" Campbell said.

"Guy that drowned in a quarry down in Nelson County. Couple of weeks ago."

"Oh yeah, I heard something. What about it?"

"My client suggests the possibility of foul play."

"What's this got to do with me?"

"I realize he *died* in Nelson, but he *lived* in Albemarle. That's your county."

"I know my damn county, Swift," he said. "But it's still Nelson's ballgame. If they suspect something, they can ask for my help and I'll be glad to give it to them. They ain't asked."

"I'm not surprised. The death's been ruled accidental."

"Then what are you doing fooling with it?"

"C'mon, Rid. You know Floyd Davis?"

He chuckled. "Sure," he said. "I know Floyd."

"Then you know the acting sheriff is just putting in time until they get a more permanent replacement for Faber Jakes. If a death looks accidental, then that's what he's gonna say and not make any kind of fuss about it."

"And you think different."

"I don't know what I think, Rid. My client thinks different.

And I agree with my client that there are some strange things about this accidental drowning."

"Such as?"

Without revealing anything about Morgan Vessey, I filled him in on the case's peculiarities, my conjectures, and such evidence as I had. He nodded from time to time. He was as good a listener as any experienced cop. I took him up to the events at Vessey's house. That would be just a little tricky.

He was sitting back in his chair, his hands folded across his belly. When I paused, he said, "Now is when we get to the part about you being beat up?"

I grinned. "That's right," I said. "It was at the address I gave you earlier, which happens to be Eric Vessey's house."

His look got serious. "Swift," he said, "I am not gonna countenance no burglary on your part."

"Still like those fifty-cent words, eh, Chief?" Campbell liked to flex his vocabulary from time to time, see if you were paying attention.

He was not amused.

"Sorry," I said. "Little humor there. Actually, I didn't break into the house, of course. You know me better than that. I got permission to enter the premises from the executor of Vessey's will, who is also the next of kin. It's all legal."

"I can check," he grumbled.

"Fine."

I made a big production of searching my wallet for Morgan Vessey's card and gave him her name and number as if I barely knew her and had talked to her only in her official capacity.

"Then what happened?" he asked.

"Somebody switched off power to the house and jumped me in the dark. I never got a look at him. When I woke up he was gone."

"He take anything that you could see?"

"I'm not sure," I lied. "But he was no ordinary burglar. He passed over a bunch of fancy electronics. I think it's safe to assume that whatever he was looking for is more valuable than that stuff."

Campbell was silent for a while. He chewed on the inside of his lip while he thought over what I'd told him.

"I'm gonna be put out with you if there's more to this than you've told me," he said finally.

"That's it, Ridley," I said.

"Okay. I might as well tell you, in terms of the law all we got's a leaky hose here. But . . . I admit that the damn thing does sound, I don't know, peculiar."

"I'd like to continue with my investigation."

"I can't stop you there."

"What I mean, Rid, is that I'd like to continue it with your knowledge. And your protection, if I need it. Whoever beat me up was big. He could've killed me if he'd hit me in the wrong place."

"Sure," he said. "You keep me informed. If there's something criminal going on, I'll get behind you."

"Thanks. And maybe you could do me one small favor?"

"I shoulda known. What?"

"Just whatever the word on Vessey might have been. Any suggestion he was into illegal activity. Whatever you happen to hear."

"I'll ask around," he said tersely. It went against his grain to do favors. He belonged to that endangered species, the honest cop. But he owed me several large, and he knew it, so he helped me out if it wasn't an inconvenience. For my part, I never asked him to compromise the rules of his job and I slipped him information if it didn't compromise my own. Not exactly a marriage made in heaven, but a working relationship that had been known to serve us both in time of need.

"I appreciate it," I said. "And don't worry, anything I find out that you need to know, you got it yesterday."

"See it happens thataway. Now get on out of here, I got work to attend to."

"You have a nice day too, Chief."

I left Campbell's office and went immediately to the nearest pay phone. I called Morgan Vessey, explained to her what had happened and why I'd had to use her name, and told her what to say to Albemarle's chief of police if he called. She thanked me for my concern and said that she would have figured it out anyway.

Afterward I tried a quick lunch, to see if it would stay down. It did. I wasn't great, but I was better.

Then I drove to the Jordan Institute. It was another beautiful spring day, with the temperature pushing eighty, so I took the back roads down into Nelson County. Roads that followed the path of least resistance through the mountains, roads that were trails before the invention of dynamite, and suggestions of trails before that. The woods all around were just beginning to leaf out. Redbuds and dogwoods were flowering everywhere.

Five miles outside of Charlottesville, you'd never know there was a town of any size nearby. A lot of people still live in houses a hundred years old, or older, and a lot of them live by a personal code that is generally considered extinct.

There's a long and heavy history of violence to these hills. The violence of one race against another, of parents against their children, of husbands against wives, of brothers and sisters against their own. It's a violence that's never far from the surface, even today. You can see it any Saturday night you care to go drinking in the wrong place; you can see it at the cockfights they hold every weekend back up in the dank hollows; you can see it in the haunted, bruised faces of the women and kids waiting in hospital emergency rooms—as the poor always wait—for someone in white to stitch up their lives.

If you're smart, you steer clear of it all. Because it doesn't matter how much malice there is among those who've been at each other's throats for generations. That's nothing, compared to what they feel for someone from the outside who comes butting in. If you don't belong, you're the real enemy.

Dark thoughts for an afternoon full of light. Patricia says I'm way too much on the gloomy side, that I miss the beauty of the landscape and see only the blood that has soaked the earth in this corner of the planet. She may be right, though I try hard to preserve the side of me that likes to laugh and dance and make love in peculiar places. I tell her I'm just the end result of the irresolvable conflict between my father, Byron Swift, the dour product of centuries of English inbreeding, and my mother, Justine Carbuccia, first-generation Italian-American.

A perfect combination for a detective, I say. The British flair for deduction, the Italian leaps of imagination. I can solve cases either way.

I turned into the drive that led to the Jordan Institute. My mind felt neither particularly imaginative nor rational. It felt as if it had been stressed by a solid blow to the skull, which it had.

I met Paula Slate in her office and was again impressed with the imposing nature of her presence. For a fleeting moment, I wondered what kind of punch this woman could throw. Then I reminded myself not to do any wild theorizing in advance of the facts.

"I'm glad you phoned, Mr. Swift," she said. "If you had not, I believe I would have eventually called you."

I was settled in my leather chair. The good doctor had thoughtfully provided a most welcome cup of coffee. It didn't hurt that they made quality coffee at the Institute.

"What about?" I said pleasantly.

"What did you want to see *me* about?"

"I didn't know you were a diver."

"I have a very large curiosity about human experience, Mr. Swift. Always have had. Diving provides some rather unique modes of perception. Since the instructors were using our quarry, I thought I might see for myself what it was all about."

"Done any recently?"

She leaned back and smiled. It was that condescending smile again and it irritated hell out of me. I was successful in keeping my annoyance hidden. For the time being.

"No, I haven't," she said. "But I think we're connecting up with what I wanted to talk about."

"How so?"

"You found out somehow that I'm a certified diver and now you want to know if I ever did any diving with Eric. Correct?"

"Among other things."

"The answer is no, I didn't," she said. "But we talked about doing some together. In fact, we were planning a trip to North Carolina shortly before he . . . before he died." The slight catch in her normally even, precise delivery was a window through which I saw for just a moment the human being inside. Someone capable of caring and of being hurt, like the rest of us.

"I'd even rented the equipment," she continued.

"So you knew Eric Vessey a little better than you let on," I said.

That was evident, and she nodded. I recalled the first time

we'd talked, when I'd asked her if she'd known Vessey well. The pause and the little smile that indicated she might have, before she proceeded to deny it. I'd wondered if their relationship was more than just psychic. It was.

"I'm sorry," I said.

"It's all right," she said with a conviction that rang only about ninety-eight percent true. "Through my work here, I've learned to see death in a different way than most people. It doesn't have that same sense of finality for me. Though I do miss him, of course."

"Would you mind telling me how close you were to him?"

"We were lovers."

She said it in a very matter-of-fact way, as if she revealed their relationship to anyone the subject interested.

"I see," I said, which is the one thing you always say when you don't. "May I ask why you told me yesterday that you didn't know him socially?"

She thought about it, then said, "I don't know, really. I guess part of it is that I felt the instinctive urge to protect someone with whom we'd worked here. We don't enjoy the kind of protected privilege psychiatrists have with their patients, although I believe we should. In addition, I suppose I felt that my relationship with Eric was none of your business."

"And what made you change your mind? That's what it feels like you've done."

"A change of mind, yes. I simply thought about why I hadn't wanted to talk to you, and what harm it would do if I did. I realized that there was nothing about Eric's and my relationship to be ashamed of, and that nothing we discussed could do his memory any disservice.

"In addition, I pondered the reason why you had come around asking questions. I considered the possibility that there might be more to Eric's death than there seemed. If that were indeed the case, I would certainly want the facts to come out. Since the sheriff is obviously uninterested, you would appear to be the one most likely to make that happen.

"And finally, Eric and I had ceased our involvement over six months ago. There seems little point in being close-mouthed about it at this point."

It was a very reasonable explanation. But then, she was such a reasonable woman.

In the course of things she'd also explained her recent rental of diving equipment, before I'd made any mention of it. Like Morgan Vessey, though, she was highly intelligent and might have guessed that I'd find out about it. She too might be trying to derail any suspicions I had about her motivation.

"Okay," I said. "Let's talk about Eric Vessey then."

She nodded her willingness. "What would you like to know?"

"One thing you told me yesterday was that you had no knowledge of any of Vessey's business dealings and no idea if he had any enemies. Was that true?"

"Yes. You have to understand the nature of our relationship, Mr. Swift. I was a good bit older than he, of course. I don't think there was ever any question that our . . . involvement was going to lead anywhere, if you know what I mean."

"You didn't intend marriage," I suggested.

"Nor living together, or anything of the sort. There was just a very large attraction between us. It began during the psychic sessions, which can become highly charged, and it spilled over into our lives. It was an electric thing. Other than that attraction, we didn't have much in common, and we didn't pretend to. Because we so obviously had no future together, there was little incentive for me to become familiar with the details of his existence, such as what he did for a living, who else he was dating, people who loved and hated him, if any, and so on. It was quite sufficient for us to merely do the things we did together and let it go at that."

"So you have no reason to suspect that his death might have been anything but the accident that it looks like?"

"No, I don't. If I were you, though, I'd get to know his sister. Morgan Vessey."

"Why?"

"It's difficult to put into words. They had a very odd relationship. There were twins, for one thing. But it went beyond that."

"Odd in what way?"

"I don't know. Sometimes when I would see them together, the things they would say, the way they would look at each other, it was—" she shrugged "—*strange*. Like they weren't quite two separate entities."

"I'm not sure I follow you," I said.

"You have to understand, Mr. Swift, that I'm continually involved with things that most people would call supernatural, if they'd deign to discuss them at all. But to me they're as natural as any other aspect of the universe. I study them, I look for what lies behind them. One of the results of this is that, while I'm not psychically gifted myself, I am very *attuned* to the physical and psychic vibrations of others, which are merely different facets of the same reality. The vibrations between Morgan and Eric were quite unlike any I'd ever observed before. So much so that they eluded all my attempts at classification. The only thing I can say is that they were a *very* interesting pair of siblings."

"I have talked with her," I said. "Not at any great length. But she did this thing to me. She looked me in the eye and it made my head twitch. Damned if I know how she did it."

"Yes, I know what you mean. It isn't a trick. She is a very talented person in this area, as was her brother. She is able to project a small part of herself into the mind of another person. That's what you felt, a fragment of her psychic energy. I'm not sure she has full control over what she does. She would never admit to any of it being conscious. I didn't believe *that*, but as to extent, who knows?"

"What about the other sibling?" I asked.

"Ah, you've discovered Drake, have you?"

"It seemed like I should."

"He's another strange one," she said.

"Anyone in this family who isn't?"

She chuckled. "Actually," she said, "they all swear that their parents were the most normal people imaginable. Hard to believe, but I didn't know mom and dad. Anyway, Drake is kind of a recluse, I take it. I only met him once, very briefly. I've no idea if he shares any of the talents of his sibs. From what I heard of him, I take it that he prefers the company of books to people."

"All right," I said, though I didn't have a clue in hell what was all right about any of this. "Now Dr. Slate, is there anything that you remember Eric having said, anything at all, that would have indicated what he was doing diving in the quarry?"

She thought about it, shaking her head all the while.

"No, nothing," she said.

"Is there anything you've ever heard about the quarry that would suggest there's something valuable down there?"

"Valuable? I scarcely think so. If it were valuable, I don't think they'd have abandoned it."

"There has to be, though, don't you think? Do you see Eric diving out there alone at night for fun?"

"I suppose if you put it that way, no, I don't."

"Think about it," I said. "Maybe something will come to you. Some chance remark that didn't seem to mean a lot at the time." I got up. "If you do think of anything, please give me a call, will you?" I gave her my phone number.

"May I help you in any other way?" she asked.

"Possibly. It might come down to my having to dive in the quarry myself. I don't know when, but I'd like your permission to go in there."

"Of course. Perhaps, when the time comes, if you need a buddy, I could dive with you."

"That's a possibility, too. I'll think about it. And there's one other thing," I added. "I wonder if I might talk with Dr. Jordan for a few minutes?"

"I believe that can be arranged," she said. "He's out in the garden. I'll take you there."

CHAPTER
11

The area behind the Institute's main building was, in a word, breathtaking. I stopped and stared.

Marble steps led down to a a large, circular grassy area, with teak benches and a fountain at its center. The fountain had been cast in the shape of the Greek god Pan, dancing up on one leg while he played his pipes. Water jetted from the ends of the pipes and cascaded down over the body of the man/goat.

The circle was ringed with apple and pear trees, all of which were in full bloom. It was a spot almost too peaceful to truly exist.

"It's something," Paula Slate said, "isn't it?"

"Yeah," I replied. "It sure is."

"All Grover's work. He's been here a long time, starting with just the bare bones. Little by little he made the place over to his own vision. It's our good fortune that his sense of aesthetics is a match for his intellect."

I followed her down the steps. We crossed the grassy circle and walked down a green corridor of lawn that lay beyond it. There were low ornamental hedges on either side of the corridor. Behind them, grape arbors.

At the end of the corridor was the vegetable garden area. There were four rectangles under cultivation. Each rectangle contained half a dozen raised beds, with sawdust walkways between them. The beds were each about fifty feet long and five wide. The early, frost-resistant crops were in. Peas, broccoli, cauliflower. The lettuce would be germinating but hadn't poked through yet.

Dr. Jordan was kneeling by one of the beds, carefully mulching broccoli. We came up behind him. I noticed that each broccoli plant had a little white plastic sleeve around its base.

"They keep the cutworms away, Mr. Swift," he said without turning around. I'd seen no sign that he'd been aware of our approach. "They run up against the plastic and they don't know what to do. Very effective."

He got up and faced us, brushed the dirt from his hands. He was dressed in his peasant white again. The washed-out blue eyes had that twinkle to them. He gave me one of his little Oriental bows.

"I'm pleased to see you again," he said.

"Impressive," I said.

He looked around him, at the order that had been imposed on the land.

"A lot of hard work," he said. "Not much else. Foolish, in its own way. The illusion of control. But not without its rewards."

"Actually, I didn't mean the gardens. I mean the way you deduced I was here."

"I didn't deduce it, Mr. Swift. You have a rather strong presence. I'm able to perceive when you arrive. It's the same as when you walk into a house and you immediately know if there's anyone else there."

He gave me a cryptic look. I suddenly wondered if he somehow knew what had happened at Vessey's the previous night.

"And how did you know I was looking at your cutworm defense?" I asked to hide the uneasiness I felt.

He laughed. "A guess! But not entirely a shot in the dark. Your eyes would follow the line of my arm and your attention would be drawn to the broccoli plant and then to the strange plastic horse collar around it."

"You oughtta been a detective," I said.

He laughed again. "But I am," he said. "Come, let me show you around. I'll see you later, Dr. Slate."

"In my office?" Slate said.

"Fine."

She left. Grover Jordan guided me through the garden, showing me what was planted where and describing how the whole thing would look after the real growth started.

In between stops on the tour, we talked.

"What brings you back so soon, Mr. Swift?" he asked me. "Did you decide to have yourself evaluated?"

"No. The case has taken some strange turns since yesterday. I'm beginning to believe that Vessey's death may be suspicious after all."

"You've been in a fight, for example."

I touched the side of my jaw and wished I hadn't.

"Not quite a fight," I said, and I told him what had happened to me at Vessey's house the previous night.

"Interesting," he said when I'd finished, "how the activities of the living are superimposed on those of the dead."

I looked at him a little blankly, then said, "You mean how whatever happened to Eric is determining what happens to me?"

"Certainly. Or take me for instance. Take this garden. This piece of land has been occupied continuously for hundreds of years. The things that are growing here do so from soil enriched by the decomposed flesh of those who previously worked it, not all of whom were as extravagant as my immediate predecessor. That—" he pointed to a substantial granite crypt at the far end of the garden "—entombs his worldly remains. One Charles Henry, somewhat less than affectionately known as 'Boots,' now encased in stone. *He* has not yet returned to earth, but when I finally eat the broccoli, I will in fact be dining on those who came before him."

"Huh? Boots Henry?" I said. I suppose I said it rather stupidly, because he glanced over at me.

"Yes. He owned this place before I did. Well, not precisely before. I bought it from his heirs. It sat here unused for a number of years after he died. Why, do you know of him?"

Perhaps I should have guessed. I certainly had enough information. Perhaps the blow to my head had temporarily scrambled the deductive process.

In any case, I could now assume that the primary reason Vessey had been diving in the quarry had to do with the late Boots Henry, and not with the Institute. Otherwise, there was no reason for him to have a file containing those newspaper clippings and the page from Henry's diary.

But Henry had been dead for almost fifty years. Why the sudden interest? What had he left behind that was worth making a risky night dive? Could whatever it was have been a motive for murder?

"No," I said a little too quickly. "Who was he?"

"You do know him," he said.

It was senseless to try to put anything over on this old man. I wouldn't bother any more.

"His name came up," I admitted. "In the course of the investigation."

"I see. How was that?"

Well, what the hell. There were an awful lot of people in this world who might have beaten me up. But when they came marching in, the frail elderly gentleman in front of me was definitely not going to be in that number.

"Before the burglar put my lights out," I said, "I got a look at one of Eric Vessey's files. It was marked 'Jordan.' I thought it might be about you, or about the Institute. Instead, when I opened it I found a bunch of stuff about this Boots Henry, whom I'd never heard of. That's when he cut the power."

"What kind of things, about Henry?" he asked.

"Some newspaper clippings. His death, the search for his killer. And a page from a diary of his. Unfortunately, I had barely identified what it was before the room went dark. I didn't see what he'd written about on that particular page. When I came to, the whole file was gone."

"Let's sit, shall we?" he said.

He'd known exactly when to suggest it.

"Thanks," I said. "I don't think my equilibrium's quite back to normal yet."

We'd made a circuit of the garden and walked back along the green corridor. We sat on one of the teak benches in the grassy circle. There was no one else in sight.

Spring was literally busting out all over. The sky was blue, the air warm and heavy with the scent of fruit tree blossoms. Honey bees were going crazy. The fountain was bubbling merrily. From where I sat, I could look right into the grinning face of the Pan figure. I didn't feel as merry as all that, but I grinned back anyway. Eric Vessey sucking water at eighty feet seemed like something that had happened in another lifetime.

"What do you think of life, Mr. Swift?" he asked. "Do you think that it is eternal?"

His words had an eerie connection to what had just been on my mind, but I was beginning to get used to that.

"I don't know," I said. "I guess I usually believe that we get our one shot and that's it."

"You are a believer in entropy, then."

I'd seen the word once or twice in my readings, and had looked it up.

"That's the theory that the universe is getting colder, right? That it will eventually sort of go out."

"More or less," he said. "Newton's Second Law of Thermodynamics. The nonavailability of energy in a closed thermodynamic system. To put it simply, the energy that is currently available is all there is. As it is consumed, it cannot be replaced. Therefore, since energy is what keeps everything in motion, once it's gone the universe must inevitably become inert. Without motion, without heat, life is impossible, of course."

"A depressing thought," I said.

"Yes, it is. I found it so, too. That's why I built the Institute."

"You're gonna try and heat the universe back up?"

He laughed. "In a sense," he said. "Though it's not *me* who is going to do the heating. We're all in a box, you see. Here at the Institute we're not looking to set fire to the box. What we're looking for is a way *out* of the box.

"Let me explain. If the Second Law is correct, and we have no reason to believe that it isn't, then its conclusions follow as the night the day. The Law cannot be defied, it cannot even be modified. A hopeless situation, one would think.

"The only possible catch is that it applies to a *closed* thermodynamic system. Suppose, then, that our universe is not truly closed, that it is something more than the stuff that appears to make it up."

"I can't," I said.

"That's all right. You don't have to imagine it literally. All you have to do is accept that it's possible. If it is, then the law of entropy may not apply and we may have a way out of the box.

"Many years ago, I read a science fiction novel called *The Triumph of Time*. In it, a space traveler finds himself in the emptiest, most remote corner of the universe, and there he hears a tiny pinging sound. It turns out to be the sound of hydrogen atoms springing into being from nothing, or from somewhere beyond the universe. Our traveler has found the point of creation. If such a point existed, then instead of seeing our universe as inexorably running down, we could see it as steady state.

"I was very affected by that book. It pointed the way out of the box. From the way it was written, I felt it entirely possible that the author had had some direct perception of what he was writing about. He couldn't have gone there physically, of course. I assumed that he had been there psychically.

"And so the Institute. We do many types of psychic research here. But the most important thing we do is train people in psychic projection, so that they may then seek the point of creation."

To tell the truth, it sounded like a bunch of voodoo mumbo jumbo to me. But then, I suppose that's how Einstein would've come across if he'd taken me aside for a little relativity lesson.

"Found it yet?" I asked.

"We like to think so. Of course, it's not the kind of thing one can be positive about."

"And what does this all have to do with Boots Henry or Eric Vessey?"

"Mr. Vessey was a seeker," he said. "Mostly after material things, it's true, but he had that other side to him. You are a seeker, as well. It comes out in your obsession with mysteries. I offer you the greatest mystery of them all. We would be happy to have you join us in our quest."

"Uh, let me take a rain check on that," I said. "What do you know about Boots Henry?"

"Not a great deal."

"What is there about him that would have attracted the interest of a seeker after material things, someone like Eric Vessey?"

"I don't know. But perhaps we can guess. Mr. Henry was a bootlegger, you realize. Or so they said."

I nodded.

"Then it's possible," he went on, "that he had amassed a personal fortune of some size. It's rumored that he had. Or so said the realtor who sold me this place. He also told me that, while Mr. Henry did leave a good bit of money behind, it was only supposed to be a fraction of what he had hidden away somewhere. We must remember, of course, that the man was trying to sell me some land. Hints of buried treasure wouldn't hurt his cause."

"Light bulb," I said. "Vessey somehow gets ahold of the old bootlegger's diary and finds that Henry had hidden the bulk of his ill-gotten gains in the quarry. That gets Eric's interest up. He sneaks out to the quarry at night and goes diving, looking for the stuff.

"But if that's true, if Henry wrote down where he'd buried the money, then whoever inherited his papers should have found it. Who'd he leave everything to?"

"There was no will, so his sister got it all. She was his only living relative. And I'm afraid she was past caring by the time he died. She could take care of herself, but that's about it. It's why this place went to ruin for so long. She wouldn't do anything to keep it up, but she refused to sell it until my realtor came along. To be honest, I think he tricked her somehow. But I didn't care, I really wanted the place and she obviously didn't. It was perfect for the Institute."

"What happened to her?" I asked.

"She died a couple of years after I moved in here."

"And you never went hunting for the Easter egg?"

He shrugged. "I have, as I'm sure I've made clear, far more important things to do. I wrote it off as one of those stories you use to entertain guests."

We sat in silence for a while. Jordan was one of those rare people who seem comfortable in someone else's presence whether there's conversation going on or not. I sorted through the thoughts in my head, trying to line them up in a way that they'd form the kind of questions I knew needed to be asked.

"I guess I still don't see how Eric Vessey fitted in," I said finally.

"You'd first have to know his twin sister," he said. "A remarkable woman, Morgan Vessey. They had both inherited money, as much as they needed for a reasonable life.

Eric Vessey's response was to try to keep doubling and redoubling his stake. I've never understood this fascination with money for its own sake, but whatever it is he had it. Perhaps he was just a born gambler.

"His sister, on the other hand, is much more conservative. She used her inheritance to start a small business, dealing in art and collectibles. She's done fairly well, though she's not wealthy. More important to her, she's doing something that involves her sense of aesthetics as well as her talent for commerce. I think she might have been an artist herself, but she doesn't have quite that level of skill. And the kind of person she is, if she couldn't be very, very good she wouldn't want to do it at all."

"You met her first," I said.

"Yes, she read about the Institute and she came out to see me. She'd known about her psychic abilities for a long time and she wanted to explore them further."

"Paula told me she froze up in the lab, though."

Jordan laughed. "She would," he said. "Dr. Slate and I have somewhat . . . different objectives."

I looked at him questioningly.

"Don't be surprised, Mr. Swift," he went on. "There is room in the world for diversity, you know. What I described to you earlier was my personal vision. Other people here are allowed to pursue their own goals. I am primarily interested in what you might call the 'big picture.' Dr. Slate, for example, is more directed toward exploring the use of psychic energy in everyday life."

"I'd like to come back to her later, if I might," I said. He nodded. "So you did work with Morgan."

"And still do. Miss Vessey shares my interests. While she does not do very well in the kind of experiments Dr. Slate favors, she has become an integral part of the quest for knowledge that is most important to me."

"I've met her. She's managed to transfer some of her abilities to everyday life, from my experience."

"I don't doubt it. It's only under the very controlled laboratory conditions, with very specific objectives, that she fails. I think it's the stress of the demand to perform."

"Yeah," I said, "well, out there in the real world she can really bend your head around. I've had women who could do that to me before, but not in quite this way."

"You tend to have been ruled by your libido?"

Now that was an area I definitely didn't want to get into with a guy in his seventies.

"Aren't we all?" I said to cover my embarrassment, and then added quickly, "So then what happened? Morgan brought her brother out here?"

He smiled to acknowledge my change of subject and said, "Yes. I don't think he was that interested, but they had the kind of tight relationship that twins often do. He indulged her if something was important to her."

"Did you work with Eric?"

"Some. But he wasn't inspired by my particular quest."

"Paula had more luck, I take it."

"Yes. He and Dr. Slate worked together very well."

"They were lovers, she told me. She didn't seem at all reluctant to admit it."

"I knew that they were," he said.

"You had no problem with that, your staff becoming involved with a, what did she call him, an 'associate'?"

"Not at all. It wasn't disruptive to the Institute; she's a mature adult. I don't judge what people do with their personal lives. And as far as it went professionally, she had some very good results with him."

"Do you think he wanted to see if he could use his psychic abilities to make money?"

Jordan laughed. "I wouldn't doubt it," he said. "But he must have thought he'd learned all that he could. He stopped coming out about six months ago. Until he started diving, that is."

"And what about Dr. Slate?" I asked.

Shifting gears never fazed him. I wondered what did faze him. Maybe coming face to face with the point of creation.

"An excellent operations manager," he said. "She's really built up the workshop program. We're almost a profit-making organization now."

He spoke of her as if typing up a job evaluation. I felt strongly that there was no real warmth between the two of them. I'd felt the same way when I'd seen them personally interact. But it was impossible to think of the old man as actually *disliking* anybody.

"A first-class mind, too," he added. "She's done a lot of important research in the field."

"Actually," I said, "what I meant was, what about her and Vessey?"

He looked at me as if, for the first time, he didn't understand what I was saying.

"Dr. Jordan," I said, "Paula Slate and Eric Vessey were lovers. The possibility exists that he might have shared with her what he was doing."

"I rather doubt that."

"Still, it's a possibility. She's a diver, too. Maybe he asked her to help him find whatever's in the quarry."

"You think that she might be involved. . . ."

"I don't think anything at this point. With these people, I don't even trust my own mind. But the man's dead. All I'm doing is investigating those folks he was associated with, to see if any of them might profit by his death."

"Of course, Mr. Swift," he said. "Well, here is my opinion: Dr. Slate is perhaps not the most comradely person one would ever meet, but I know her rather well and I feel that she is quite incapable of murder."

"Given that any of us is capable of it under the proper conditions?"

"Given that."

"Thank you," I said. "I value your opinion."

He nodded toward me. We'd covered a lot of ground. I thought back over what had been said, wondering if there was anything else he could tell me. I couldn't think of anything.

As if reading my mind once again, he said, "Are you out of questions, Detective Swift?"

"I guess I am, for now."

"I have tried to be candid with you."

"Yeah, I realize that. I appreciate it."

"In return," he said, "perhaps there is something you would do for me."

"As long as it's legal."

He smiled. "Quite," he said. "I'd like to work with you for a short time."

"You mean psychically?"

"Yes. Would you consider it?"

"You realize that I just had my head caved in last night."

"I realize that. Not to be insensitive about it, I think that could even be beneficial. Stress can be a catalyst for high levels of achievement, in many things."

"Well, what the hell," I said. "It doesn't hurt, does it? I'd rather not deal with any more pain right now."

"It's painless, I assure you. And it won't take much of your time. I'm just . . . curious, you see."

"Sure, why not. Let's do it."

I got up. The time I'd spent out in the garden and here by the fountain had revitalized me. I felt almost like a whole person again.

"Wonderful," he said.

He led me back up the marble steps and into the main building. We climbed to the second story and went down a long hall with a polished hardwood floor. A series of doors marked with numbers led off the hall. None of them was open. Several of the doors had small sets of lights set into the wall next to them. One red, one green. Either might be on, but not both.

At the end of the hall was door number twelve. Next to it the little green light was on. Jordan opened the door and we went inside.

The room was small and windowless. There was a partition about six feet high that stretched from one wall nearly to the other. It divided the room roughly two-thirds to one-third. In the larger section was a stretch-out kind of couch. The walls were painted a muted blue and the corners had somehow been rounded off so that they were indistinct in the soft, indirect lighting. The carpet blended with the wall so that there was little sense of where one began and the other left off. It was a room, I imagined, that resembled the inside of an egg. I couldn't see behind the partition.

Jordan closed the door and said, "Basic accommodations. One of our early units. But it will suffice for our purposes." He gestured to the couch. "You may lie there if you like. I think you will find it extremely comfortable. Loosen your clothes if that helps you relax."

I walked over and lay down. He was right about the couch. I adjusted my position until I felt I could fall right asleep. A moment later he came over. Next to the couch was a wall hook, with a pair of headphones hanging from it. He lifted them off.

"I'm afraid you'll have to wear these," he said. "But again, I believe you won't find them uncomfortable."

He fitted them to my head. They were very light. I hardly noticed them once they were in place.

"Now," he said, "I'm going to go behind the partition. I can speak to you through the headphones. I'm also going to play you some music. What I'd like you to do is relax, concentrate on the music, and try to blank your mind of everything else. At some point you will hear a single high-pitched tone. It will last for about five seconds. When it stops, please say the first thing that comes into your mind. You don't have to speak loudly, I'll be able to pick up anything that you say. Afterward, the music will start again. The high-pitched tone will happen three times. Each time just say whatever comes into your head. After that the session's over and we can talk about it. Simple enough?"

"High-pitched tone, speak my mind," I said. "I think I can handle that."

He smiled. "Good," he said, and he went behind the partition.

Shortly after that, the lighting went down even further. The room became a fuzzy, undefined space. The effect was soothing. At the same time, sounds started coming through the headphones. I relaxed, folded my hands on my stomach and closed my eyes. I'd always liked listening to music through headphones. Nothing quite like it for blotting out the rest of reality.

Only thing was, it wasn't exactly music that was filling my head. Well, it might have been music of a sort. But the Rolling Stones it wasn't. I don't know quite what to compare it to, except maybe two orchestras playing different things at the same time, and neither of them playing anything that even vaguely resembles a melody.

It probably sounds unpleasant, but it wasn't. I relaxed some more. I didn't have to blank my mind, as Jordan had suggested. The music, or whatever it was, did that for me. Pretty soon I wasn't thinking at all.

Just when I might have dropped off to sleep, the sound porridge was replaced by the single high-pitched tone I'd been told to be alert for. It shrilled for a short time and then there was silence. The silence seemed overwhelming, in comparison to what had gone before.

I knew that I was now expected to come up with something. For a moment there was nothing. I was still not thinking. *What am I supposed to say?* flashed through my mind. And then there was an image.

"An ugly man with a beard," I said out loud and I

chuckled, also out loud. It was a wacko image out of nowhere.

As soon as I spoke, the "music" started up again. The same pattern was repeated.

The high-pitched tone came again, then the silence, and this time I said, "Hickory dickory dock!" I thought that was pretty funny, too.

But the third time was the funniest of all. "A penis!" I said and I cracked up laughing. It wasn't even *my* penis. But this was obviously some kind of Freudian game and I'd just passed with flying colors. I took the headphones off.

"Hey Doc," I called, "is that it? That was fun."

Jordan spoke from behind the partition. "That's it," he said pleasantly. "Very nice. You can join me here if you like."

The lights came up as I walked back to where Jordan was.

There wasn't much there. He was seated before a small console, in which were set some dials, cassette decks, VU meters and the like. He had a pair of headphones, which he'd draped around his neck. Next to the console was a small table. There were several objects on it.

"How'd I do?" I said with a grin. "Am I the next Morgan—"

Then I looked closely at the items on the table.

"Now wait a minute," I said, "you're not going to tell me . . ."

Jordan was smiling with genuine amusement. The Paul Newman eyes were sparkling.

"What I like to do," he said, "as a first test, is a simple send and receive. I'm a very good psychic transmitter, so if the subject is at all good at receiving we should get something. The tones you heard through the headphones may have sounded random. They are anything but. They have been refined over a long period of time and are exceptional at inducing a psychically receptive state. But then, you know that."

I didn't say anything. Couldn't.

"You don't want to admit it," he continued. "I sense that that is part of your nature. But I'm afraid you're going to have to, Mr. Swift. Here is the evidence. I held one of these objects in my hand at the time of each high-pitched tone and concentrated on sending an image of it. The results are obvious. You are an excellent subject."

I stared some more, still quite speechless. A trick. People can do amazing tricks. Bend car keys, predict next week's newspaper headlines. All a matter of sleight of hand. Somehow . . . But how? Magicians rely on misdirection of attention. They usually need a cooperative assistant, and I knew *I* wasn't in on this. He couldn't possibly have known.

"Surely," he said, "you don't believe that I keep a few thousand common objects in this room and that I quickly sorted through them whenever you spoke." He laughed at the idea.

I shook my head dumbly.

"Of course I didn't. Here is item number one. A Lincoln penny. Your ugly man with the beard, obviously. And then my watch." He chuckled as he put it back on his wrist. "Hickory dickory dock, indeed. That was very good. And last but by no means least, the penis." He gestured toward a small ceramic ashtray in the shape of a mushroom. "Pretty close, I'd say."

I finally found my tongue. "This is very strange," I said.

"Not really." He got up and put his hand on my shoulder. "It's quite simple, once you understand the principles. The only reason people don't do this sort of thing all the time is that they've closed themselves off to the possibility."

"Look, Dr. Jordan, I had a rough night last night and I'm not at all sure what's going on here today. I think I better be getting on home."

"Do consider becoming a regular visitor. You have a lot of potential."

"Yeah, well, we'll see. This is kind of outside of my experience. Let me sleep on it a couple of times."

He smiled that smile. When he did, he was a hard man to resist. He could sell me snake oil or any damn thing. Maybe he *was* trying to sell me snake oil.

"Look," I said, "I've got to get going, okay?"

He nodded and I beat it out of there. I didn't stop to look behind door number three or any of the rest of them. I was tired and my headache was coming back. It was late in the day. All I wanted was a cold beer or two and a good night's sleep. The case could go on hold until the following morning.

I almost made it to my car.

CHAPTER
12

I was crunching across the gravel of the parking lot when the kid stepped out of the pines.

"Hi, Swift," he said.

Danny Jordan, the boy detective. I really didn't want to play with him but there he was. I didn't have the heart to just walk on past, so I stopped.

"Danny," I said.

He looked pleased that I'd remembered his name from one day to the next. Kids are easy.

"You're back again," he said.

"Yeah, some developments in that case I'm working on. I needed to talk to some people."

"This have to do with that guy Vessey?"

"Why do you think that?"

"Elementary," he said.

"Come on, Sherlock."

"I been listening, like you told me to do. Besides, him drowning's the only exciting thing that's happened around here in ages. That's got to be it."

"Well, as a matter of fact I am looking into Eric Vessey's death, Danny. You know anything about it?"

"Sure. He was a creep. I didn't like him."

"Anything else?"

"You bet. Him and Dr. Slate were having an *affair*." He said it in the overly self-assured way of someone who isn't quite certain what an affair is.

"How'd you know that?"

"Ah, you can tell. The way they'd sneak off together after their sessions. Once I walked in on them in her office and they were kissing and stuff. I heard them talking about it, too. I heard her say, 'This isn't a *relationship*, Eric, this is a *physical attraction.*'"

He did a pretty fair imitation of the way Paula Slate talked and I laughed. He was pleased once again.

"You're a good detective," I said. "When did all this go on?"

"Last year mostly. In the summer. Then I didn't see him for a long time, not since before Halloween. I guess they weren't having their *affair* anymore."

"Maybe they were just having it some other place."

He shook his head. "I don't think so. Dr. Slate hardly ever leaves here, you know. She doesn't take vacations or anything. Mostly all she does is work."

"Well, that's interesting," I said, "but I don't—"

"Wanna know what else?"

"What else?"

"They had terrible fights, too."

"Did you see them fight?"

"Uh huh."

"Did they hit each other?"

"Once I was, well," he hemmed and hawed a little, "I guess you'd say spying on them, over in her apartment. They were arguing about something and he slapped her. And she slapped him right back! Boy was *he* surprised! He walked right out of that apartment. I had to hide in the bushes quick or he woulda seen me."

"Do you know what they were arguing about?"

"I don't know." He frowned, trying to remember. "Something about she said he was using her for something and he said he wasn't. Something like that."

"When was this, Danny?"

"A while ago."

"Last summer?"

"No, no," he said impatiently. "He came back, that's what I'm saying. I didn't see him for a long time and then I started seeing him again."

"And Dr. Slate was seeing him, too?"

"Uh huh. That's when they had their fights. That's when I saw them fighting in her apartment."

"*When* is when you saw them fighting?"

"A while ago," he said again. "That one time it was, it was that day when it was real warm and then a few days later it snowed. That's when it was."

The last week of February. We'd had a day when the temperature went up to seventy. Then a cold front had moved in and and three days later we picked up four inches of snow. A month before Eric Vessey died.

"And after that he began showing up around here again," I said.

He nodded.

"Was that the only fight you saw?"

He grinned. "Bet you'd like to know," he said.

"C'mon, Danny."

"Will you let me shoot your gun sometime?"

"Sure. I'll take you to the gun club range. We can shoot all afternoon. I promise."

"Really promise?"

"You got it, kid."

"They had a fight down at the quarry," he said.

"At the *quarry*?"

"Yup. That Vessey guy, he was diving there more than once. I seen him. Always at night. When he drowned, that wasn't the only time he was in there."

Now he really had my attention. The kid was bright and he was observant and he was a world-class snoop. Maybe he'd seen something important. I looked around the parking lot. It was still empty, but I'd begun to feel apprehensive. What if Danny *had* seen something and what if it incriminated Paula Slate and what if she happened to see us talking together and later realized that he'd been the one to feed me the information and what if . . . ?

"How'd you like to go for a drive?" I asked him.

"What for?"

"You ever been in a detective's car before?"

"Uh uh."

"Well, there you have it. Besides, it'll give us a chance to talk in private." I said it as if privacy were very important to our partnership.

"Well, okay," he said.

"Good. We won't go far."

We walked over to my VW and got in. I took a last look around. No sign of anyone.

"Her name's Clementine," I said, patting the steering wheel affectionately. "She ain't much to look at, but she gets me where I want to go. Usually."

"I don't know anyone who has a car like this," he said.

"They're kind of a rarity these days. Believe it or not, fifteen years ago almost everyone owned at least one of these."

"Is it worth a lot of money?"

I laughed. "In a way," I said. "I could sell it for about the same as it cost when it was new. But what then? I'd have to walk everywhere."

It occurred to me that a good place to talk might be the quarry, so I drove there. I parked Clementine so that I'd see anyone following us before they saw me and I could tell the kid to scrunch down in the seat if need be.

I cut the engine and turned so that Danny and I were facing each other. I rested my arm on the back of his bucket seat. Just us two detectives getting together to talk shop. His little cowlick was backlighted and looked like an exclamation point atop his head.

"Okay," I said, "what were you doing down at the quarry when you saw Vessey there?"

"Hey, I know this place pretty good, Swift," he said with an air of self-importance. "I like to walk around at night. It's fun. I pretend I'm lost and then find my way back. One night I saw lights down by the quarry, so I sneaked down to see what was going on. It was him, and he was diving. I checked it out after that and he was back there every night, doing it again. Except two nights it was raining and I didn't go out."

"How many nights all together?"

"Oh, three or four, I guess."

"The same week?"

"That same week. Before he drowned."

"And all this was after that first fight you saw."

"Oh yeah, way after."

"Okay," I said, "let's see if I've got this straight. Eric Vessey and Dr. Slate had an affair last summer that ended sometime before Halloween. After that, he didn't come around the Institute anymore. Then in February he showed up again and you saw him having a fight with Dr. Slate in which they yelled and hit each other. Did you see him in the weeks after that, before he started diving?"

He nodded. "He was out to see her a few times."

"But you didn't see any more fights."

"Not those times."

"How did the two of them seem to be getting along?"

"I dunno. How can I tell that?"

"You can't," I said. "A lot of the time, none of us can. Anyway, a month or so after the fight in her apartment you saw Eric Vessey diving in the quarry. For a week he did it almost every night. Then one night he drowned and that's it."

"Right."

"Who else knew about what was going on at the quarry? That Vessey was diving there."

"Nobody. I didn't tell nobody."

"Why not?" I said.

"It was neat," he said. "Just me knowing. I thought I'd spy on him until I found out what he was doing. Then I'd *really* have a story to tell. That wasn't wrong, was it?"

"No, of course it wasn't wrong. Tell me, did you ever see Dr. Slate down at the quarry with him?"

"Nope. Just that one time, when they had the fight."

"Did you ever see anyone else with him?"

"Nope."

"Now, exactly when did you see them have the fight down there? Do you remember that?"

"Sure, I remember that real well. It was the night before you found him."

I was getting excited and had to caution myself to keep the lid on. This stuff might mean something and it might not.

I said, "You're sure?"

"'Course I'm sure," he said like it was a real jackass question. "That was a big day. The sheriff and everything."

"Did you tell someone from the sheriff's office about this?"

"Nah. They didn't want to talk to me. They hardly even talked to Dr. Slate or Grandpa Grover. I mean, why should they? He just drowned, didn't he?"

"As far as we know, he just drowned accidentally. But there are some things about what he was doing out there that I have to look into. Now this is important, Danny. Tell me exactly what happened that night."

"Well, I was playing out back of the big house," he said carefully. "It was night time, but not real late night. I was over behind those hedges?" He looked at me and I nodded that I knew what he was talking about. "And Dr. Slate came out of the house and she walked off toward the woods, like she knew exactly where she wanted to go. The way she was headed, it looked like she was going to the quarry. So I followed her. I mean, I didn't follow right behind her. She was heading for the main path, so I went a different way and I waited to see if she'd show up. And she did."

He paused to catch his breath, then went on. "I hid in the woods and watched. That guy Vessey was unloading his diving gear from his car. He hid the car in the woods so you couldn't see it driving in, but I could kind of see from where I was.

"Dr. Slate must have heard him moving his stuff around, because she walked right back in there. And I heard her say something like, 'I told you I didn't want to do it this way.'

"And he said, 'What are you doing here?'

"And she said, 'I saw your headlights, you can see them from the second floor, and I *knew* it was you. I should have known all along you'd try to do it at night.'

"And he said, 'Yeah, well I'm doing it this way and you're not going to stop me.'

"And she said, 'Damn you, have you found anything yet?'

"And he said, 'I'm not sure I'd tell you if I have.'

"That made her really mad. I never seen her so mad. She yelled and screamed and swore at him for a while, but whatever she said he just talked back at her like he didn't care.

"Finally she called him some more names and said that she wasn't going to help him anymore and that she wasn't going to have anything to do with him anymore and that he'd get it over her dead body and she turned and stomped back off into the woods before he could say anything.

"What were they fighting about, Swift? Do you know?"

I didn't know what I knew. This was a hell of a story. It sounded like something that might easily have happened, but I had to remember the source. Though he seemed extremely perceptive and had terrific recall, he was still a young kid. Any part of what he'd told me could be exaggerated or just slightly skewed, especially if he didn't like Vessey, or Paula Slate, or both of them.

"I'm not sure," I said. "But it might be important to find out. You have a remarkable memory, Danny."

"Thanks," he said, looking very pleased. "It helps in school. If I can remember stuff, I don't have to work as hard."

"You're a detective at heart, son. And a better partner than I deserve. Now what happened after Dr. Slate went storming back into the woods?"

"Well I didn't know what to do. It was kind of exciting, all this stuff going on and I'd already seen that guy diving in the quarry so I followed Dr. Slate. I wondered what she was going to do next.

"Which was that she went back to her apartment. I, maybe I spied on her a little. I could hear her stomping around in there. Then in a little while she came out and I just got behind a bush in time so she didn't see me. She was carrying a little bag and I followed her to the parking lot. She got in her car and drove away.

"So I hurried back around the big house. I figured if Dr. Slate was gone I might see what was happening at the quarry, and I ran smack into Grandpa Grover. He wanted to know where I was going in such a hurry and I didn't really want to tell him, so I told him I was playing a game and that the Mafia was chasing me. He said it was too late for me to be out and that I should go to bed now."

He paused to catch his breath and I asked, "Did you?"

"Yeah," he said apologetically. "Grandpa Grover's good to me and I try to do what he wants."

"That's fine. I believe that he's a good man. I don't think he'll ask anything of you that isn't what's best for you."

"Uh huh. But anyway," he said with more enthusiasm, "I couldn't sleep, of course. So I waited until it was *real* late and then I snuck out again. I didn't want to disobey Grandpa Grover but, you know . . ."

"Sure, I know."

"I went back to the quarry. I was pretty scared, but I figured I could hide good and no one would see me. And there wasn't anyone there. It was *very* spooky."

"Was Vessey's car still there?"

"I don't know. I took the main path, so I couldn't see back in there quite as good and I didn't do much looking around. There was something about it, it was *too* quiet. It really gave me the creeps. I stayed about a minute and then I got back to my room as fast as I could." He shrugged as if he'd made some tactical error. "Did I do all right?"

"You did great," I said and, all things considered, he had. "What about the next morning? Did you go down to the quarry at all?"

"Not until the sheriff and them came. I knew there was gonna be diving class, so . . ."

"Okay. Now Danny, have you told anyone else *anything* about all this?"

"Uh uh. Well, just Grandpa Grover."

"And what did he say?"

"He said he was proud of me for having told him. But that Mr. Vessey had drowned and so it didn't matter what him and Dr. Slate had been fighting about and it didn't matter why he was diving in the quarry. He was dead. Grandpa said he didn't think Dr. Slate would want to be reminded of any of it and that the best thing for me to do would be to just put the whole thing out of my head if I could."

"I think he was right," I said. "And now I'*m* proud of you for having told me. But no one else must know. No one. Until I solve the case I'm working on, with your help. Do you understand?"

"Sure," he said confidently. "We're partners. Nobody could get it out of me."

"Good. Now we better split up."

"You want me to get out of here?"

"I think it's best. It's important that no one know you've been talking to me. If I drive you back, there's a chance we'll be seen together. You can go through the woods, no problem, right?"

He nodded.

"Just make like you've been out playing. And anytime I

come out here in the future, pretend like you don't know me. If I need to contact you, I'll find a way. Okay?"

"You bet. You can trust me, Swift."

"I know. Same deal as before, too. Keep your eyes and ears open for anything strange."

He nodded again.

"All right," I said, "get your butt moving, partner."

He winked at me and got out. He looked around, then hightailed it for the woods.

I watched him go, the little figure darting nimbly here and there among the rocks, and I was filled with a terrible sadness. In my business I tend to see only the underbelly of human behavior. I see greed and cruelty and violence and entirely too much death. Over the years I've developed defense mechanisms to cope with this steady assault on the part of me that still believes in compassion, love, humanity, those things that seem to have flown from the lives of the people I get involved with.

For the most part, my defenses work. I stay detached. I use my sense of humor a lot. I keep my hopes low and don't fret about it when even my minimum expectations aren't met.

But there are times when it all breaks down. A lot of those times are when children are involved, because they are almost never to blame. I can handle the things we do to each other; I can't handle what we do to our children.

As Danny disappeared among the trees, I spoke to whatever gods might be running the show down here.

Please don't let the kid get hurt, I said.

CHAPTER
13

On my way home, I tried to sort through everything I'd learned. It wasn't easy, considering my physical condition and the little tango Grover Jordan had done on my head. But a vague outline was becoming visible.

It looked like it had all begun a year or so earlier, when Morgan Vessey got involved with the Institute. She had done some psychic testing there and had eventually persuaded her twin brother to try it too. Eric wasn't all that keen on the subject, but he did it as a favor to her.

While working his psychic muscles at the Institute, Eric had met Paula Slate and they'd become involved in muscle work of a more physical nature. They'd gone at it for as long as the attraction held, apparently for the previous summer and partway into fall. Then one or the other of them had had enough and called it off. Eric dropped his psychic workouts at the same time.

About six months later Eric had discovered that, coincidentally, there was something of great value hidden in the quarry on the Institute grounds. Or he came to believe that there was. Chances were that this something—it might be rare coins—had been hidden by one Boots Henry, a rumrunner from the 1920's and the former owner of the Institute property.

Vessey had been a greedy bastard. Everyone I'd talked to had concurred on this point and, having been inside his house, I was inclined to believe. Everything I'd seen indicated that the man liked to travel first class.

In any case, Vessey had decided that the next thing he wanted was Boots Henry's legacy, whatever it might be. In an effort to get it, he'd apparently rekindled his relationship with Paula Slate. They'd fought over his tactics, with her accusing him of trying to "use" her.

Here things got a little fuzzy. Perhaps he was unsuccessful in the attempt to enlist Slate's cooperation. Or perhaps he just decided to cut her out. Whatever, about a month later he'd started diving in the quarry by himself. At night. Presumably without telling anyone. Certainly without telling Slate, who was furious when she found out.

And then he'd drowned. The night that it happened, Vessey and Slate had fought at the quarry. Slate had stalked off and gone back to her apartment. A little while later, she'd emerged carrying a small bag. She'd gotten in her car and driven off. Where she'd gone, and for how long, was unknown.

But it was possible that she'd driven back to the quarry. It was possible that the heavy diving gear she'd rented (tank, backpack, wetsuit, and weightbelt) was in the trunk of her car. It was possible that she'd gone inside for the light items—face mask and regulator and fins—and stuffed them in a small bag. It was possible that she knew Vessey would ignore her outburst and dive anyway. It was possible that she went in there after him and pulled his plug.

All that, though, was a large sackful of conjecture. And it had one gaping hole in the middle of it.

Jonathan Searle, my authority on the subject, had said that if someone were to successfully fake a diving accident it would require careful planning, especially if the perpetrator didn't have a lot of equipment expertise.

So . . . if Dr. Slate *had* in fact murdered Eric Vessey, it would have to have been a premeditated act. Yet Danny's description of the fight at the quarry suggested instead a woman who was angry at discovering something she hadn't expected.

She wasn't off the hook, of course. I might be missing an important piece of the puzzle, or Danny might have misremembered some vital part of the scene.

Then again, Vessey might have drowned accidentally after all.

But here was something else: Why had the good Dr. Slate rented the diving equipment? Because she'd been going to North Carolina, on a dive trip with Eric Vessey, she'd said. Would they have been planning a trip together if they'd been getting along as poorly as it seemed they were?

Unfortunately, the person who held the answers to some very key questions was Paula Slate, and I couldn't go at her directly. Not without exposing my source, and if there was one thing I was intent upon, it was protecting Danny as best I could. How to handle Slate would require some thought.

What was now certain was that Eric Vessey's death, accidental or no, was not a simple matter. What he'd been doing in the quarry was possibly illegal, and it involved other people. There was something solid to give Morgan Vessey for her money.

Or should I?

I thought about Morgan, and how best to deal with her. She was employing me, and paying me damn well. She deserved to know whatever I found out. On the other hand, there was the possibility she was just using me. The whole business of the hidden valuables in the quarry might be irrelevant to her brother's death. She could have seized on his pursuit of them as the perfect opportunity to do away with him, pin the crime on someone else, and walk away with her enlarged share of his estate.

Farfetched? A little. But how about this? I'd heard that she and Eric were extremely close, the way only twins can be. People who are extremely close can also have extremely violent fallings out. She may have wanted him dead for other reasons entirely, and only found out about the peculiar provisions of his will later on.

What to say to Morgan, therefore, would also require some thought.

Then there was Drake Vessey. He could well have been a pivotal figure in the drama. He was a historian. Perhaps in his researches he had come across some reference to Boots Henry's treasure. Perhaps he'd shared his discovery with his brother. After that, who knows what might have happened? Yeah, he was in there too.

Grover Jordan? There was absolutely no evidence that he was involved in this thing in any way. Except . . . Except that he knew what Danny had seen, had told Danny to forget about it, and had then failed to report Danny's observations to the sheriff's office. I was sure of that, because the fight between Vessey and Slate on the night of his death was something even Floyd Davis would have investigated.

And there was another small matter yet to be cleared up. Namely, who had punched me out the previous night at Vessey's house, and why? And who had stolen the file I'd been looking at? I assumed that the two were the same unknown person but, of course, they might not be.

So where did all of this leave me?

A whole lot further along than I'd been when I awakened in Patricia's bed in the morning. But with many dark corners and blurred shapes still to contend with.

First I needed answers to a few simple questions. I pushed Clementine (insofar as she *can* be pushed) up U.S. 29, a good, four-lane divided highway. No back roads on the return trip. If I hurried, I could make it to town before Underwater Charlottesville closed.

I did, just barely. Searle was locking the place up but he seemed happy to see me and let me in.

"Swift," he said, "you gonna become a regular around here?"

"Maybe," I said. "But I'm afraid this is strictly business again. There're some things I need to know."

"Sure."

He motioned and I followed him through the hodgepodge of equipment to the counter at the back of the store. He set me up with some very welcome end-of-the-day coffee.

"Same case?" he asked.

"Yeah. There've been some developments. Accident is still the going theory, but I'm a little more inclined to think it might not have been."

He held up his hand. "I won't ask," he said. "What can I do for you?"

"Thanks. I need to know if the dive club sponsored a trip to North Carolina around the time Vessey died."

"Yep. The old U-boat dive. Weekend before last. Steve and the guys scheduled it that way. He likes to take off for a serious dive after futzing around with beginners for ten weeks. No offense."

"You got the sign-up list?"

"I do."

"Ah, can I take a peek?"

He hesitated. "These are my friends, Swift," he said. "It's not like it's some secret list or anything. But . . ."

"I understand," I said. "But I'm just double-checking something. I'm not trying to incriminate anyone on the list. Believe me. I don't even really *have* to see it. All this is going to do is save me a little time."

"Okay."

He got the dive club folder out of his filing cabinet, extracted the sign-up list, and handed it to me. Sure enough, there was Morgan Vessey's name. And there was a pencil line drawn through it.

She'd been telling the truth. It didn't mean she told the truth in all things, but it was a point in her favor.

"Find what you wanted?" Searle asked.

"Yeah. Thanks a lot, Jon," I said. "I appreciate it." I handed him back the list. "One other small favor," I added.

"Shoot."

"I'd like to see the rental log again. Is it here?"

"It's here. I got it pretty well straightened out after you left last night. Those classes are a big headache, but they're the meat and potatoes."

He got the log for me. What I wanted to know I should have noted the previous night. In less than a minute, I had my answers and I gave the log back to Jonathan.

"That didn't take long, either," he said.

"Nope, just routine double-checking. Let me ask you one other thing. When Drake Vessey rented his equipment, did he tell you what he wanted it for?"

"Let me think . . . Yeah, he did. In fact I asked him. He hadn't been in here since his certification, which was a while back. When they go that long, I like to know what they're up to. Don't like to see folks getting into something they can't handle. You don't use your skills, you forget them.

"Anyway, he told me that he realized he was rusty and he wanted to do a little quarry diving to bring the skills back up. He said his brother, who dived a lot more, was going to be his buddy and help him. That was about the extent of it, as I recall."

"Makes sense," I said. "Well, thanks for your help, Jon."

"Sure. See you whenever."

On the drive back to my apartment, I integrated what I'd just learned into my understanding of the facts so far.

The one critical thing I'd previously overlooked was: What kind of equipment had people been renting?

This was important because what you rent depends on what you intend to do. If you plan to dive locally, then you need the entire kit, including B.C., wetsuit, tank, weights, etc. And Underwater Charlottesville is the only place to get this stuff.

However, if you're going someplace else, someplace where diving is a common activity, then you *don't* need it all. You might want to rent your wetsuit and your regulator and some other items here in town, because it might be cheaper to do so than to rent them in a resort area like the North Carolina shore. Those things are relatively compact and travel well. But you definitely wouldn't get heavy stuff like a tank or a weightbelt and haul it around on a trip of several hundred miles. No reason to. You'd rent *that* kind of gear when you got where you were going.

I'd thought of this distinction as I was returning from Nelson County and I'd kept it in mind when I studied Searle's rental log.

Eric Vessey's name had appeared five times. The first time, some two weeks before his death, he'd rented everything, of course. He was going as far as the quarry and that was it. On his subsequent visits to the shop, all he'd done was refill his tank.

Morgan Vessey had rented her equipment a few days before her brother died and returned it a few days after. The list was short. She'd checked out a mask, snorkel, fins, and regulator. This was entirely consistent with what she'd told me, that she was going on the North Carolina trip. Everything else she needed could have been easily had down at the shore. She said that she had returned it unused, and she probably had. There was nothing she could have done locally with just these few items.

Once again, as best I could determine, Morgan had told the truth. The points in her favor were beginning to add up.

Next was Drake Vessey. He'd been in the day after his sister and had rented the whole kit. That made sense, since he'd told Searle that he was planning to quarry dive in the area. He'd also said he planned to dive with Eric. *That* sounded highly unlikely. Eric was at that time already well into whatever he was doing out at the Institute.

In any case, I had no way of knowing how much, if any, diving Drake had done since he rented the equipment, because he hadn't returned it yet. On my mental chart, I put a very large question mark beside his name.

Finally, there was Dr. Paula Slate.

She had rented her gear two days after Vessey and she'd checked out the full set. This meant that she'd probably lied to me.

I had originally thought that Eric and Paula might have reconciled between the time of the first argument that Danny overheard and the second one at the quarry. Enough so that they could contemplate taking a dive trip together. But if that had been the case, her checklist would have looked more like Morgan's. Logic dictated that she had never intended going to North Carolina.

Now I had to consider the possibility that at rental time she intended diving *with* him in the quarry, that they were still partners in the search for whatever it was, and that they had the more serious falling out later on.

Or she might have decided to have a look in the quarry on her own. This was unlikely, since she hadn't been back for an air refill, but possible.

It could also be that she'd rented the equipment for some other reason, as yet obscure.

In any case, she hadn't returned the stuff yet. So there was no way to tell if she'd used it.

However I looked at it, the whole thing was still a solid knot. I had some ideas about where to start unraveling it, but there weren't any that couldn't wait until the following day. I was tired and sore and in need of about ten hours of quality sleep. There was no reason I shouldn't have what I needed.

Except. . . .

My intentions were good. I drove straight back to my apartment. I called Patricia and told her that I wouldn't be of any value, no matter how hard she tried. She made some lewd suggestions anyway. We both laughed. Then she asked me, more seriously, if I was doing okay. I told her I was tired and sore, but that nothing was broken that wouldn't mend itself. I said I'd see her in about twenty-four hours and we agreed that that was fine and we hung up feeling good about each other.

I had some cold cereal with milk and my stomach accepted it without complaint.

I had fluffed my pillows and gotten out a paperback mystery by Janwillem van de Wetering, a Dutchman whose police procedurals are the strangest ones around, and among the best. I was ready to read until my eyes would no longer let me.

Then the phone rang.

I considered ignoring it. I let it go half a dozen rings. Still the caller persisted, and I knew I was going to give in. I'm just not the sort who doesn't answer a phone. Whatever that says. I sighed and got out of bed.

"Swift," he said, "it's Drake Vessey. I wanted to see how the investigation is going."

"The investigation's going fine, Drake," I said. "But I'm a little beat. I've had a long day, I didn't get much sleep last night. Can this keep until morning?"

"Oh don't hang up, Swift. I won't keep you. But it's important to have someone to talk to, don't you think?"

His manner had changed character once again. The voice was kind of singsong, like it was disconnected from the sense of the words it was saying. This guy was a bit of a loon. Maybe more than a bit. I was beginning to have an uneasy feeling about Drake Vessey.

"I've got plenty of people to talk to," I said. "It's what I do for a living. But right now I'd rather sleep."

"You see my sister today?"

"I'm not at liberty to discuss my investi—"

"She tell you I killed my brother?"

I wanted to hang up. I should have hung up, probably. But I didn't hang up. Like it or not, Drake was a part of this case and he might conceivably have something to say to me.

"Did you?" I said.

He laughed. It was a shrill, unpleasant sound. But then his voice got very sober, very serious. It was the deep, reassuring voice I'd first heard over the phone.

"I didn't kill Eric," he said. "You've got to believe me, Swift. Please. If anyone tries to convince you that I did, you must not believe them. I did not kill my brother."

His sincerity was almost palpable, and impossible to resist. Even for me. And I'm used to people lying, exaggerating, running every imaginable con. By this time, I'm immune to it all. But Drake was so convincing that I was ready to believe anything he said. His voice had that kind of power. Everyone in this family, it seemed, had powers of one kind or another.

I had to forcefully remind myself that only a moment earlier I'd been certain he was whistling Looney Tunes. That was too much for my aching head. I started to lose my balance and I had to sit down.

"Drake," I said, "I don't know what to say. To my knowledge no one has accused you of anything."

"I want to help you," he said.

"You already told me that. If I need your help, I won't hesitate to ask for it."

"No, I *really* want to help you. Do you know why Eric was diving in the quarry?"

"Not exactly, but I've got a pretty good idea."

"I might be able to help you there. What have you found out so far?"

"I'm sorry. Nothing I can discuss."

"That's too bad," he said. "I think we should go diving out there, me and you. Put what we know together. I think we could find it."

"Find what?" I asked.

"What Eric was looking for."

"Which is?"

"Oh no." The little boy voice. "You're trying to *triiick* me now. Keep it all for yourself. We need to share. Uh huh, huh *huh*." Then a sudden shift back to serious. "Let's meet tomorrow and discuss our mutual interests."

Okay, he might know something. But my gut feeling was that he didn't and that he was trying to find out what *I* knew and that meeting with him would be a waste of time. There were other avenues to pursue, ones that would probably be more fruitful.

"Tomorrow looks pretty busy, Drake," I said. "I've got a lot of things I want to run down. How about if I call you Thursday morning? We can set it up then."

There was a pause. When he spoke again, there was something like genuine disappointment in his voice.

"I'm sorry. This is a mistake," he said. "I was hoping to be able to see you."

"I'll see you," I said apologetically, "don't worry. Just give me time to get some work done."

"This is your work."

"I know. And I appreciate your help. Thursday morning, then. 'Bye."

"Good-bye, Swift."

I hung up. I returned to bed, opened my book, and rejoined the quirky detectives Grijpstra and de Gier on the streets of Amsterdam. A couple of quick chapters and then to sleep, I thought.

Not ten minutes after I'd finished with Drake Vessey, there was a knock at the door. I couldn't believe it. I fumed and swore under my breath and told myself not to get up. The knock came again, louder. Whoever was out there could see through the glass pane, could see the light leaking under my bedroom door.

Then came the voice. "Open up, Loren! I know you're in there!"

The voice was muffled by the two doors and the intervening distance. It was hard, insistent, somewhat familiar but not enough that I could identify its owner. He was evidently not going to leave quietly. It didn't matter. I'm even less capable of ignoring a live visitor than I am a ringing phone.

"All right!" I yelled. "I'm coming! Keep it down!"

I pulled on some pants, stumbled out into the living room, turned on lights, unlocked the wretched door.

And I stared.

My first thought was the same as always, how very much he looks like me. Just barely older, a hair taller, a tad heavier. A little more stubble on the face than I'd let accumulate. Minor things.

I sighed.

"Hello, Ashley," I said.

He grinned. "Invite me in?" he said. "Or you gonna leave your only brother standing on the outside while your life spins slowly away from you?"

I held the door for him.

"Thanks, little bro'," he said as he entered the apartment. "The hell you doing in bed at this hour anyway?"

"I was in a fight last night, Ash," I said. "I need some sleep."

He turned, made a show of inspecting my face.

"Well, I'll be damned," he said with another big grin. "And at your age. You still doing that, going out to bars and getting in fights?"

"It wasn't a bar fight. And it was you used to do that, not me."

He looked at me for a long moment, then said, "Ah Loren, it's good to see you."

And he hugged me. I didn't respond at first, but then I hugged him back a little. It was very difficult, showing affection for my brother. We had a checkered past.

"Hey," he said, "I got something for you."

He had on a grimy khaki jacket. From its pocket he pulled a small bottle of Scotch whisky. It was a pretty good brand, probably better than he could really afford.

"You're still a juicer, ain'cha?" he said.

"Been known," I said.

He stripped off his jacket, threw it on my couch. He dropped his knapsack on my floor. Then he went into my kitchen and returned with two juice glasses. He set them down on my eating table and pulled out a chair for himself.

"Come on," he said, "let's have a drink together."

"Ash, I wasn't actually *in* a fight last night. I got beat up. I don't feel that terrific."

He poured each glass half full. "All the more reason. Cut the pain. Help you sleep." He raised his glass. "Loosen up, kid," he advised me and he took a healthy swallow.

I knew that if I joined him, the one drink would turn into several. After that, the probability was that we'd either end up in a heated argument or slobbering over our family tie, swearing as to how much we cared for one another. Neither prospect was very attractive. Nevertheless, down I sat. After all those miserable years, he still had the older brother's hold on me.

"This is great, isn't it?" he said after I'd had a test taste of Scotch. It went down like liquid peace.

"Yeah, great," I said.

"So . . . You're still out there chasing down the mundane mysteries of life?"

I shrugged. "It's a job. And you're still out there trying to turn them into truths."

"Right," he said, laughing. He spread his arms. "The poet and the gumshoe. What a thing to do to poor Dad. If it hadn't been for Delia, how much sooner the stroke would have come."

He was probably right. My poor father's New England insurance executive's heart could never have rested easy once he saw how his sons were turning out. My younger sister Cordelia had, however, actually broken precedent and finished college. Better yet, she'd gone right from college into corporate finance. She now made more in a year than I am likely to in ten. That might have been some consolation at the end for the old man. But when it came to parents and their children, you never knew.

"It's mother's fault," I said. "Those Italians. Too much passion, not enough responsibility."

In actuality, though, Ash and Delia represented the extremes in temperament. I was somewhere between my sister the achiever, and my brother the irresponsible but irrepressible artist. In my younger days, I'd been more a lover of good times and no regrets, like Ashley, but I'd grown away from that. A lot of the change had had to do with my work. Someone in my line inevitably sees where so many of the good-time people end up.

"And praise God for that!" Ashley said, raising his glass. "Days of heaven and nights of Cabiria. Let the bloody British suffocate in their own righteous sputum!"

"How's Mother doing?" I asked.

"Good, last I saw her. Let's see, maybe six months ago. She's got all those cousins and nieces and whatnot, half the North End's related to her, so she hasn't been hurting for company since she moved back to the city. A bad life it isn't. Wine and cheese and pasta and gossip and Dad's investments."

"I'm glad. I don't get up to Boston much. The money's usually in short supply."

I felt a little guilty saying it. I hadn't seen my mother in nearly two years. Not even after I'd lucked into my current fat bank account. The truth was that I was now a Southerner and I hated it up north. I had no friends up there anymore. Patricia Ryan was here, and she was the most important person in my life.

And then there was Mother herself. Since she'd begun associating exclusively with the Italians of her childhood, she had sloughed off a great deal of the person she'd had to create in order to stay married to Dad. I could see now that much of what I'd thought was her, as I was growing up, was only a mask. I still loved her and cared what happened to her. But lately, she'd become more and more of a stranger.

When I went back, I wound up drinking too much and having a lousy time. Mother understood. Given the chance, she'd light into me for being such a miserable son, in order to maintain her good Italian self-respect. But she understood.

"Speaking of which," I said, "how's the poetry business? You look alive."

I knew what the answer was. It was always the same. He called himself an *itinerant* poet. He went from here to there, he gave readings, he participated in workshops, he spoke anyplace an audience would gather. He got published and his books sold in the hundreds. When he got hungry, he did carpentry, at which he was first-rate. I suspected that Ashley was just a born wanderer, with the "poet" label tacked on to give him at least a crumb of respectability. He had no home anywhere, no continuing relationship with a woman, no children ("that I know of, little brother"), few possessions beyond what he carried with him. He was working without a net. I envied him and I pitied him, depending on whether I was seeing him as the last of the troubadours, or as Cain.

"Not bad," he said. "Just gave a reading up in D.C. Close to a hundred people. Hey, I made enough money to buy some Scotch. Then I thought, while I was in the neighborhood, you know . . . Look, this bottle's getting pretty low, what say we go out somewhere. This is a college town, ain't it? Ought to be some lively places to be found. Good friends, *scintillating* conversation, dahling."

It was my chance to bow out before we drank ourselves to the point where something I didn't want was bound to happen.

"Ash," I said, "I really can't. I feel awful. I'm in the middle of a job that's going to take a lot of my time tomorrow. I need some sleep. Why don't you go ahead without me." I gave him the name of a bar and told him how to get there. "That's a good spot for you. Lot of MFA candidates drink there. In fifteen minutes you should own the place."

He'd love it, and they'd love him. They were mostly pretentious literary kids who were less worried about their writing than they were about where next year's grant money was coming from. He'd be an instant hit, the *gen-yew-ine* article, as close as any of them would ever get to the traditional lifestyle of the destitute artist.

"Tomorrow night," I said, "I'll take you out for a nice authentic Italian dinner." We both laughed. "And maybe we'll make some rounds afterward, if I feel better."

"Well, okay," he said. After a pause he added, all innocence, "Hell of a pretty night. Virginia sweet magnolia. And it's not *that* long a walk, is it?"

I sighed, dug out my car keys.

"Same orange Volkswagen," I said.

"Get outta here."

"Nope. She's still running."

"I *love* it! An antique! The last gasp of rationality in our mechanical contrivances. *Sieg Heil!*"

"Just try to bring it back in one piece, will you, Ash? I'm shooting for an early start in the morning and I need that damn relic to get me around. And remember they're tough on drunk drivers in this state."

"Hey, you know me."

I did. I knew there was no way of telling where my car was going to end up. But I also knew that Ash could drive better after a few drinks than anyone I'd ever met. And I knew that if he got *too* drunk he'd crash out in the back seat rather than stay on the road.

He put on an old sweater with patches at the elbows and mussed his long wavy hair some. He rubbed the stubble on his cheeks as if testing it for texture.

"I look the part now?" he asked.

"Yeah, you look the part. If you don't want to be a poet you can play a fisherman down on his luck. That'll go over nearly as well."

He said seriously, "Sorry I came at a bad time." I nodded.

"But tomorrow's bound to be another day," he added more brightly. "It cannot be else. I want to hear all about your case. I *love* a good mystery."

"Tomorrow, Ash," I said.

And he was gone.

That was the way it often was. The Ashley Swift disappearing act. He had to move, to keep moving. If you couldn't keep up with him, if you couldn't stand the pace of the all-night bull sessions and the drinking and the spouting of spontaneous poetry and the endless pursuit of the closest accessible woman, then you got left behind. Even if you were a brother who hadn't been seen in so long you wondered if you counted.

And yet he was the one who was there when Dad struggled against the stroke, and didn't make it. He was the one who always went back to check on Justine. Mother.

There were still a couple of fingers of Scotch in my glass. I swirled the amber liquid around, brooded into it, drank it slowly and with the sweet bitter awareness of passing time.

Ashley and I, separated by just under a year, had grown up as almost contemporaries. The key word is *almost*. I've come to think that being so close in age is worse than being a little further apart. His year's head start meant that he hit all of the milestones a half-step ahead of me. First to go to school, first to make puberty, first to have a girlfriend, and so on. Yet he knew I was always right behind him. Maybe it made him insecure, I don't know. All I do know is that he rode me mercilessly, about everything, everything that he did before I did.

Growing up with Ash was not fun.

One of the least fun things was that he made a play for every girl I was ever interested in. He had that extra year on me and was always more outgoing than I was. We looked a lot alike. It's no surprise that he took most of those girls away from me. I don't think he truly wanted them, any of them. It was all in the challenge, and to be able to get me once again.

I hated him for that. It made my teenage years even more lonely than they invariably are. It is something that perhaps cannot be forgiven. I have tried, and not been able to.

When Ash got out of high school, he tried college. It was no more the place for him than it was for me. He stuck it out for a year, before deciding that a poet could only be destroyed by school. He dropped out and hit the road with a pencil and paper and a knapsack. He never left that road.

I didn't drop out, I got kicked out. And when I did, I got drafted. I went to Vietnam. Ashley had told his draft board he was a homosexual and they'd given him a deferment. He could be very convincing. At the time of my army physical, he'd hurried home to counsel me to do the same as he'd done. I listened to him, but I couldn't do it.

I'd seen a war, and Ashley hadn't.

After Nam I lived in Boston, got married, used some of Dad's contacts to become an insurance investigator, got divorced. I saw Ash fairly often, since he came back regularly to visit the family, have a guaranteed place to sack out for a few days, and get enough to eat.

When my divorce was final, I'd moved to Virginia. I rarely saw my brother, only when he was "in the vicinity" and dropped by. The times I'd been back to Boston, except when Dad died, he wasn't there. We didn't keep in touch.

There were times when I missed Ashley. But I think that what I was really missing was the brother I never had. The one who treated me with kindness and respect. The one who walked point for me and told me what the future was going to be like. The one who left my girlfriends alone.

Patricia. The last time Ash was in town, I hadn't known her. I wondered if I was going to introduce them.

That was too much for my weary head, which was throbbing away as it was. I chased the Scotch with a stiff shot of good Irish, put some aspirin on top of that, and went to bed. I didn't bother with the novel. It wasn't five minutes before I was gone.

Oddly, the last person I thought of was not my brother. Nor was it Patricia. The image I passed out on was the enigmatic Clark Kent face of Drake Vessey.

CHAPTER
14

The phone woke me.

True to form, I got out of bed, trudged to the living room and picked it up.

"Yeah," I said.

"Swift, you sound like hell," Jonesy said.

Actually, I didn't feel all that bad. I hadn't gotten my ten hours of sleep, at least I didn't think I had, but I seemed to have had enough. Jonesy had his crisp morning newspaperman's voice on.

"I'm all right," I said. "What in God's name time is it?"

"Eight. Don't you ever get up the same time as working people?"

"I pay my dues. What've you got for me?"

"I got one Charles 'Boots' Henry, born 1895 to an old Virginia family. Claimed, in fact, to be a direct descendant of Patrick Henry. Maybe, maybe not. Lived in Richmond during the Twenties and early Thirties. Rumor has it that he kept our capital city in the booze during Prohibition. Retired in 1933 and bought a spread in Nelson County. Great big house, just for him. Became something of a recluse, considered eccentric by the good folk of the day. Died in 1940, by violence."

"I know that part," I said.

"Bit of a stink to it. They didn't discover the body for about a month."

Jonesy's journalistic sense of humor. "Very funny," I said. "And after he was murdered, the estate went to seed, right?"

"So it would appear. His beneficiary was his sister. All he had. Unfortunately, Ellen Henry was on the daffy side. She spent the money he'd left in his various accounts, twenty thousand or so, but she didn't want to live in his house. As you say, it fell into disrepair."

"Did they find any money in the house?"

"Not much. They surmised that the burglar got away with whatever came to hand."

"And they never caught the guy?"

"No. There were apparently suspicions about a fella who lived down the road, name of Jarvis. Mainly, I think, because he vanished right about the same time. But his name never shows up again. I suppose the cops eventually just lost interest in the case. Henry was a cheap crook nobody missed. So why bother?"

"Sounds reasonable," I said. "Now, what about the rest of Henry's belongings? Where'd they go?"

"Whatever had cash value, sister Ellen sold off. Until there was just the shell of the house left. His books and personal papers and stuff got donated to U. Va. Supposedly some of it was historically important. The Patrick Henry connection and whatnot. I imagine it's all still there in the library someplace."

"Okay," I said as if that information didn't interest me at all. "How long did the estate sit there unoccupied?"

"Ten years."

"Then Grover Jordan bought it and set up the Institute."

"You've been doing your homework too, I see."

"Teacher's pet," I said. "How'd Jordan manage to talk Sis out of it?"

"Good realtor, good with the sweet talk. Plus by 1950 our Miss Henry was getting slam-dunked somewhere over the far rim. The guy probably waved the paper in front of her and told her if she signed it she'd become the Queen of Denmark."

"I've met this guy. Once or twice. So what do we know about the good Dr. Jordan?"

"Not a lot," Jonesy said. "Originally from California. Psychology degree from Cal. Came here with enough of a stake to get the Institute started. The house and grounds were in pretty bad shape when he bought them. From what I understand, he restored them singlehandedly."

"I've seen the result. It's impressive. How's the Institute's reputation?"

"Tops. For what they do."

His jaded tone of voice indicated that he had little use for the field of psychic research.

"A disbeliever, eh?" I said.

I could see him shrugging his bony shoulders as he said, "If it helps people get through the night, I got nothing against it."

"Dr. Jordan tested me, Jones. I'm very talented."

"C'mon, Swift, don't start that stuff with me."

"I'll tell you about it sometime."

"Later. Much later."

"Okay," I said. "You got anything else I need to know?"

"You want the setup at the Institute?"

"Sure."

"Nonprofit corporation," he said. "Purpose: research into the workings of the human mind. Three-person Board of Directors."

"Jones, you are a miracle man."

"Grover Jordan, big *P*, little *h*, big *D*, Chairman of the Board."

"Surprise."

"The other directors' names are Paula Slate, also with a *P* and an *h* and a *D*, and Jonathan Searle, no following initials."

Now that was interesting. It was something to talk about with Jon and the evasive Dr. Slate.

"Thanks, pal," I said.

"That's it," Jonesy said. "What's in it for me?"

Jonesy always expected a big story out of me every time I pumped him for information. He'd gotten a couple, too. One of them—involving a cocaine processing plant in central Virginia—he was supposedly turning into a book for which he supposedly had a publisher lined up. It was going to make us both wealthy, he said. I was ready to believe it when I got the first check.

"A case of Moosehead," I said, "for now. But stay tuned."

"Ah-right, I know better than try and beat it out of you. But you owe me two cases. I had to do some real digging for this stuff."

"Fine. Plus the twenty-five bucks. And you'll get the story, too, if there is one. Don't worry."

"Meher Baba."

"Huh?"

"Meher Baba. One of them *guru* types. Went around saying, 'Don't worry. Be happy.' Like it was the world's easiest thing. I wish."

"It'll happen for you. Later, Jones."

Since my talk with Grover Jordan, there wasn't much in what Jonesy had told me that I didn't already know. But what there was, was quality stuff. Jonesy had done quite a job. That was typical. He'd pursue something like a shark with blood up its nose.

The most important piece of news, of course, was the location of Henry's papers.

It made the following scenario seem highly probable: Drake Vessey had come across the papers while researching something in the University library. In them, he'd found a reference indicating that Henry had hidden something of great value on the grounds of what was now the Jordan Institute, probably in the quarry. The reference was undoubtedly on the page of Henry's diary that I'd almost seen in Vessey's office before the lights went out.

Drake had then told his brother about his discovery. After that, some combination of Drake, Eric, Morgan, and Paula Slate had become involved in the search for the loot. That search had ultimately cost Eric Vessey his life, with perhaps an assist from one of the other players.

The other new thing I'd learned about was the corporate setup at the Institute. I could barely see why there'd be a Board of Directors. And I certainly couldn't imagine why Jonathan Searle or Paula Slate would be on it. Little details. Unimportant details? I didn't know. It seemed like they should be and yet, there was a nagging creature in my brain that said these were things I should find out more about.

In any case, they would have it wait. The direction of my

day's activities had now been determined for me. The first thing to do, obviously, was to go to the University library and find Boots Henry's diaries. Once I located that elusive page, I would know at last what Eric Vessey had been doing in the quarry.

I had a full breakfast and I enjoyed it. The last reminders of the night at Vessey's house were rapidly fading.

As I was finishing up, Drake Vessey called again.

I debated whether or not to run some part or all of my scenario by him. I decided against it. The old occasionally reliable sixth sense was cautioning me to treat this guy as if there were a bunch of extra jokers in his deck. Besides, it would be better to save it for when we were face to face. I wanted to see his reactions.

Drake continued to try and interest me in diving the quarry with him. By that point he was one of the last people on earth I'd care to dive with, but I didn't say so. I put him off gently, said I still had that very busy day in front of me.

He hinted that he had answers to some of my questions. And that other answers lay hidden in the quarry. Which I already knew. He aroused my curiosity, but not enough. I just didn't want to deal with him until I had the story more solidly filled in.

I told him I was still planning on contacting him the following morning and rang off.

Next I questioned whether I needed to speak with Morgan Vessey, in light of what I'd learned at the Institute. I decided that I didn't. After I'd uncovered Henry's secret, then I'd call her.

There was nothing else that needed doing. I was ready for my trip to the University library.

Only trouble was, I didn't have a car.

When I'd gotten up, I'd tossed a coin. There was a fifty-fifty chance Ashley would be asleep on the couch. Tails, I lost.

I was standing in the middle of the living room, hands on hips, wondering if I'd have to walk all the way across town to the University Grounds, when in the door walked my brother.

"Ash," I said, "this is getting weird."

"Huh?" he said. He didn't look but about half-awake.

"Do you believe in ESP?"

He smiled. "Loren," he said, "mind is the stuff of the universe. The very *stuff*. I been trying to tell you that for years. About *time* you listened."

He dropped the VW's keys into my hand.

"She's a good car," he said. "Pulls a little to the right, though."

"I know that, for Chrissake. I'm trying to be serious with you. Some very strange things are happening to me. This case, everybody I meet is involved with ESP or I don't know what kind of psychic weirdness. I think it's screwing up my head."

"Probably screwing it *on* right."

"Thanks, you're a big help."

"Loren, it's been a bit of a night. There was this grad student who just *had* to read me her poetry. Terrible crap, of course. But if you let 'em read you their poetry, they'll do *any*thing for you. Except let you sleep, which I will do now so that I can talk to you later about the structure of the universe. Dinner, yah?"

I nodded. "I'll plan to be back here at five. Call you if I get hung up."

"I oughtta be up by then."

I hesitated, then said, "Go ahead and use my bed."

"Planned to," he said, and he tottered off in that direction.

I wondered why I'd hesitated, then decided it wasn't worth thinking about. Morgan Vessey was doling out the bucks and it was time to make it worth her while.

Clementine seemed okay. I gave her a quick visual inspection. No new dents, no broken glass. She drove fine, too, except that she pulled to the right a little. Which she had ever since a homicidal teenager had run me off the road two years earlier.

I parked on the street. Just in case I was in there longer than the two-hour limit, I propped my clergyman's credentials behind the windshield. I didn't know if they did any good, but I never got parking tickets.

Then I walked up the University Avenue hill and into the library. It was a familiar place. Not that I'd used it much during my student days. But since then I'd become a consumer of books. I think that, more than anything, it had to do with not being *forced* to turn those pages.

In all my visits, though, I'd never been looking for the

kind of thing I was currently after. I went over to the check-out desk. There was a young girl sitting behind it. She was very pretty, but then she turned her eyes on me. Empty. Bored with life at twenty. She was the perfect end result of an overly affluent society, entirely ready for nothing more demanding than a few dozen years' worth of deciding when the BMW needed to be tuned next.

She didn't know *what* I was after and didn't care. She referred me to someone else, an older guy who I suppose had a degree in library science. Library *science*, for God's sake.

The scientist was more helpful. He informed me that the historical collections weren't housed in the main library building. Then he directed me to an annex in another part of Grounds. It wasn't that far, so I walked it.

Not as warm as it had been, it was nevertheless a fine spring day. Hundreds of students passed me by. Clean students. Students with spotless clothes and glowing complexions and the general air of well-tended money. I looked at them and I tried to generate some hope.

The Byrd Annex was a smallish two-story building. It was—what else?—Jeffersonian brick. The front door was wood, painted white. It had a huge brass handle. I pushed down the thumb-latch and walked right in.

There was a small, carpeted entrance foyer. There was some dark wood paneling. And there was one desk. Behind the desk was a boy with short hair, pasty skin, and thick-lensed glasses. He had his feet up and was reading a book on fluid dynamics. His own fluids didn't look all that dynamic.

He set his book down and said, "Yes, sir. Can I help you?"

I gave him one of my lawyer cards, but forgot to mention that I wasn't one of the partners listed on it nor connected with that particular firm in any way.

"I'm working on a case," I said, which was certainly true. "I need to see some papers that I believe you have here."

"Well," he said, "I have to warn you that this can be a tough place to find things sometimes. But let's give it a try. Whose papers?"

"Charles Henry *aka* Boots. Resident of Nelson County. His papers would have been donated during the 1940's."

"Doesn't ring a bell," he said after a moment's thought. "Hold on."

He went to a card file that stood against the far wall, rummaged around, then came back to me.

"Bad news," he said.

"They're not here?"

He shrugged. "Oh, they're probably here, all right. But the only thing the file says is 'north basement.'

"Let me explain. The University, you see, gets hundreds of donations a year. A lot of paper. Way more than the staff can possibly catalogue and microfiche and then file properly. Now if it's something important, say the lost diaries of Thomas Jefferson, obviously it'd get immediate attention. We'd probably put something like that on display. But some of the other stuff, well, it can get neglected. Unless it's a special interest of one of the professors, it can get lost in here."

"The north basement," I said.

"Right. We've got four basement rooms under this building. Anything that hasn't yet been catalogued goes in there. The rooms *are* divided up by quarters of the alphabet. That's some help. The north basement is G through L. So the Henry papers ought to be in there. Want to go take a look?"

"Please."

"Right this way."

We went through a door into a narrow stairwell and down two flights. The floor and walls down there were concrete. Everything was painted ugly institutional green. The fluids nerd opened a heavy metal door and turned on some overhead flourescent lights.

"Voilà," he said, motioning me inside.

The air in the room was pleasantly cool and dry, but that was the only indication that important things might be stored down there.

It was a gigantic room. It was filled with floor-to-ceiling steel racks. Rows and rows of them. The racks were fitted with heavy steel shelves. The shelves were filled with cartons. Each row of racks was associated with a monorail that was bolted to the ceiling. Movable ladders could be shuttled up and down the rails, giving access to the upper shelves.

A warehouse of the dead and gone.

"And this is just G through L," I said.

"Uh huh."

"Any rhyme or reason to it?"

"Kinda sorta," he said, making it likely he was a native Virginian. "The more recent stuff is to the front here. And the alphabet tends to run from north to south." He indicated the compass points for me. "Unless of course someone took the stuff out and put it back a different place."

"Gee, thanks. At least there's only one set of papers to a carton, right?"

"Usually."

"I surrender," I said, raising my hands. "Doesn't *anybody* have an idea where specific papers might be?"

"Actually, Bill does. He's been around a long time. He doesn't know everything, but . . ." He shrugged and glanced at his watch. It had a black plastic case and a built-in calculator. It probably also went *beep-beep* every hour. I hated watches like that. "He should be here at one," he added as if his watch had somehow confirmed Bill's time of arrival.

"In the meantime . . ."

"In the meantime, I've got to man the desk upstairs. You're welcome to look all you like. I'd start about three-quarters of the way in, for the Forties. If you do find it, let me know. We've got some nice reading rooms you can use."

I sighed. "Okay," I said. "But would you please send Bill to see me as soon as he gets here?"

"Sure," he said, and he left me alone down there.

It looked like a long, incredibly tedious job, unless I got very lucky. But it was something I had to do. It didn't help that one of the reasons I'd made such a poor college student was that I loathed research work. Bored me out of my tree.

There was nothing else but to begin. I gritted my teeth and waded in. I took the nerd's advice and started about three-quarters of the way back.

It was a mess. Most of the cartons were labeled. But some weren't. And some, I discovered, were mislabeled. I had to check the contents of each one. They were crammed four and five deep on the shelves. Eight shelves between floor and ceiling. How many feet of rack per row I didn't even want to guess.

The alphabetization was haphazard. Most of them were *G* through *L* though. Most. And the dates did tend to cluster. This might have been a help if I knew the exact year the papers were donated. Unfortunately, I wasn't even positive of the decade. Was it while Henry's sister was still alive, or after she died?

I slogged on. I'm sure there were some very interesting stories in there, but I didn't stop to read any of them.

At ten minutes past one, Bill showed up. By that time I'd done a lot of eliminating, but no locating.

Bill was a tall, skinny guy with wire-rimmed glasses and a carefully tended salt-and-pepper mustache. He was about forty. When he stood he clasped one of his hands with the other and let both dangle in front of him. I suppose it was his way of appearing relaxed and friendly.

"I understand you're after the Henry papers," Bill said.

"Yeah," I said wearily. "This place is a nightmare."

"Well, we're understaffed, of course. And there's a lot of things donated that no one will *ever* want to see. It's why we have these basement rooms.

"In any case, you're in luck. I happen to know just where the Henry papers are."

I started to look some daggers his way but caught myself. It wasn't his fault. I should be grateful he was working today.

"Excellent," I said.

"Yes, it's quite an odd coincidence," he said. "Normally, an obscure person like that, we wouldn't have two requests in ten years. But someone else was here looking at the same collection, let me see, it couldn't have been more than a few months back."

I described Drake Vessey for him.

"Yes," Bill said, "that sounds like him. He was doing research for a book on the Virginia Henrys. Commissioned by a family in Richmond, I believe it was. We went through the subject index and this was one of the items we came up with. Is he a colleague of yours?"

"No, not really. But I know him. He's the only other man in town I can think of who might be interested in this."

"Well, I hope you don't end up duplicating one another's efforts."

"Oh, don't worry about that."

"In any case, I put the Henry papers away myself. Right over here."

He led me two rows deeper and down to the middle. He slid the ladder over and climbed up to the seventh shelf, pushed some cartons aside and rooted around in there.

"Yes," he said, "here we are. I'll hand them to you."

Boots Henry had left the world four large cartons full of paper. When I had them all, Bill climbed down and brushed his hands off before clasping them in front of him.

"Of course, they've never been properly catalogued," he said. "Actually not catalogued at all. There's no telling what you'll find in there." He chuckled. "But it there's any money, you've got to give it to the University."

Money? I thought. Maybe. Though I don't think he hid it in here.

"I'll remember that," I said.

"Here," he said, "let me give you a hand."

Together we hauled the cartons out to the elevator. We rode up to the second floor, where there was a nice reading room with lots of windows and big, wide tables to spread your research out on. A few scholarly types were hard at work. None of them paid me the slightest attention.

"Good luck," Bill said. "I'll be downstairs if you need me. When you're done, just crate it all back up if you would. We'll take care of putting the cartons away." He grinned. "Got to make sure they go in their proper place."

"Okay, thanks," I said.

I sifted through the boxes. Whoever had donated the papers had included everything imaginable. From tax records to bills for improvements on the house to letters from creditors to copies of Henry's birth certificate. I didn't bother with any of the small stuff. I wanted the diaries.

They were in box number three. All ten of them, each a couple of hundred pages thick. Each page was covered with script. I groaned. The long hours stretched out in front of me.

I sat down, made myself as comfortable as I could on the hard chair, and opened the first diary.

Fortunately, Henry's script was pretty legible. I was able to skim along, hitting the high points.

Under other circumstances, I suppose it would have made fascinating reading. Henry hadn't left anything out. There were long flashback passages about his childhood in turn-of-the-century Richmond. Descriptions of some early scams—he was apparently always a con artist. There was a detailed account of how he got into the bootlegging business and how it all worked. There were bloodcurdling tales of violence and brushes with death. His sexual escapades were covered in great detail. And so on.

By 1930, at the age of thirty-five, he was a wealthy man. He never needed to work another day. And the end of Prohibition was in sight. Henry had made his enemies. It was time to get out.

He came to the Charlottesville area, found the property in Nelson County and bought it for next to nothing. In those days it was considered very far out of town. He retired to the property in 1933.

In the late Twenties, he made the decision that undoubtedly was to lead to the death of Eric Vessey sixty years later. He began to turn all of his money into gold.

Henry, like many before him, had a deep distrust of paper. He realized that no matter what happened to a nation's currency, the demand for gold would remain high. He liked gold coins, gave much space in his diaries to how they looked to his eye, how they felt in his hand. He was especially fond of the St.-Gaudens twenty-dollar gold pieces. He obviously appreciated them for their aesthetics as well as the stability of their monetary value. Henry was perhaps no common thug.

He bought gold and bought more gold. A part of the diaries was devoted to a catalogue of how much and when and where and amount paid. He kept good records, and told no one what he was doing.

Coincidentally, he moved to Nelson County the same year that President Roosevelt halted the minting of U.S. gold coins forever. Henry hadn't anticipated this by too much, but when it happened his entry for that day couldn't conceal his happiness. The worth of his holding, already substantial, was about to start multiplying.

By my rough figuring, at the time of Roosevelt's action Boots Henry held about 12,500 coins, with a face value of a quarter of a million dollars. A great deal of money at a time when a four-course roast beef dinner could be had for sixty cents. Enough, probably, for even a paranoid to feel comfortable with his nest egg. And my estimate was based solely on the purchases that he had actually recorded. There might, of course, have been others.

No matter what, it was a hell of a lot of gold.

After he got out of the illicit liquor business, his diaries' subject matter began to change. The early entries had been pretty straightforward accounts of the events of his life. In the later ones, he turned increasingly introspective.

It was apparent that having provided for his material wants was no longer enough. He sought answers to the larger questions. He got involved with theosophy and spiritualism.

At the same time, he began to worry that someone was going to try to steal his gold. And so, known only to his diary, he personally constructed a vault beneath his house, a single room with concrete walls a foot thick. He collected all of his gold coins together, from hiding places in the house and on the grounds, from bank safe deposit boxes (with banks failing at a record clip, he no longer considered them very "safe"), and placed them in the vault.

And where was the entrance to this vault? That was the question. Assuming that the collection had remained pretty much intact, the answer to that question was worth a large number of dollars.

On this subject, old Boots was very coy indeed. About all he would say was that it was where "no one will ever stumble upon it accidentally," and that if it was undisturbed for any period of time it would seal itself away from the world forever.

That was apparently exactly what had happened.

I got up and stretched, took a walk around the room, drank some water, looked out the windows at the boys and girls of spring. But I couldn't stay away from the diaries for long. The answer was in there somewhere. It had to be.

I continued to read and on page 157 of the ninth volume I found what I was looking for. Even looking right at it, I couldn't remember having seen it before. But it was the page Eric Vessey had Xeroxed. That was certain.

The entry said:

"I am now convinced that we visit this earth not once, but many times. And we are guided to our destinies in ways that we cannot fathom with the limited knowledge of one life cycle. It is evident, as well, that I am preparing for my own return. In my next life, if I do not achieve it in this one, I am destined for greatness.

But who can say into what circumstances I will be born? All that may be done is to make provision, should those circumstances prove a hindrance to my progress.

Today I have taken steps to provide for my future self. I have written down instructions for finding the entrance to the vault. I am fully confident that, should I need these resources, I will in my next life be inevitably directed to find what I am writing here, and from this the rest will follow.

I speak to the person I will become. Locate the estate formerly owned by Charles Henry, fronting on Least Pasture Road, in the County of Nelson, south of the town of Charlottesville, Virginia. On said estate, locate an abandoned soapstone quarry. Divide the quarry into fourths by lines running due east and west, north and south. Immediately adjacent to the northwest quadrant, locate an iron post in the ground. From the post, proceed ten paces north, turn due east and walk to the edge of the quarry. Drive a stake into the ground and attach eighty-five feet of weighted rope. Drop the rope over the side, so that it hangs plumb. Descend into the quarry. At the end of the rope, locate a large stone with two X's cut into it. Remove this stone and those around it to reveal a cavity in the rock.

Within this cavity I have placed a box. It has been proofed against the weather to the maximum. The instructions inside it are completely sealed in wax. They reveal the procedures necessary to the reopening of the vault. This is a major undertaking, since the vault will have self-sealed, and the procedures should be followed with care.

Know that if you are reading this, you have been directed to do so from the next life, for you are me. Take care with the contents of our vault, and let us find together the greatness which is our destiny."

Boots, I thought, you are an interesting character in your way, but I sincerely hope that I am not you.

Of course, with all the weird things that had been happening, anything was possible.

I now had most of the pieces to the puzzle. Boots Henry had left the gold for his reincarnated self and placed directions to it in a quarry that was dry at the time but now contained a hundred feet of water.

Suddenly, I thought of Eric Vessey's shorthand directions, the ones I'd found in his gas mileage log the first day I was on the case. No wonder Patrick and I had gotten nowhere with them. What we'd taken for a zero—the directions' starting point—was actually a simple representation of an iron post. I smiled to myself.

In any event, Vessey's state of mind was very clear. The gold was far and away sufficient motivation for several risky night dives. As it was for murder. But had murder actually been done? And if so, by whom? I was still a good ways from being able to answer either of these questions.

Though I had what I'd come for, I continued to read. Couldn't stop myself. There wasn't that much left. The balance of volume nine, and the tenth, which wasn't completely filled. I went through them very quickly. It was almost as if I were expecting it all to be a novel, with some kind of tricky ending.

There wasn't one. There was a spaced-out chronicle of Henry's evolving spiritual beliefs. And considerable ink given to one Sally Jarvis, a neighbor lady who shared his interest in the beyond and with whom he apparently had a decided physical relationship as well. No doubt she was related to the Jarvis for whom the police were looking after Henry's murder, as related in the newspaper article I'd seen in Vessey's house. This fellow was also a likely candidate for "Brother J.," a character who showed up here and there in those last two diaries.

Volume ten ended abruptly. How could it not? I told myself. The man didn't know he was going to be stabbed to death.

I'd discovered nothing of importance after the bit about the quarry. I leaned back in my chair and allowed my brain to sort through what I'd read. It was a wild and woolly tale, all right. And how much effect it had had on so many of us, so many years down the road.

I didn't sit around for long. There was something I wanted to do. It was late in the day, but there should still be time. Hurriedly, I repacked the Henry cartons. Then I went back downstairs and told Bill I'd finished.

"Find what you were looking for?" he asked politely.

"No, not really," I said. "I may have to come back another time."

"I'm sorry. But you're always welcome, of course. Now you know where the papers are."

"Thanks. Do you have a phone book?"

He nodded and produced one from within the desk. He looked discreetly away while I used it.

I opened the Yellow Pages to the listings for "Coin Dealers." The first one in the column was called "Buddy's Coin and Stamp." It was over near the center of town, not far. It'd do.

Once again I thanked Mr. Bill. I left the library and drove over to Buddy's. It was half an hour before closing when I got there.

Buddy was a young guy. He was short and overweight, with a genial unshaven face and the kind of smile that probably doesn't wash off.

I introduced myself and said, "I'm afraid all I want is a little information."

"Gee, could you come back after the rush?" he said.

The shop was empty.

I chuckled for him. "I'm interested in the St.-Gaudens twenty-dollar gold piece," I said.

"Yeah, aren't we all?"

"Like to know how much one is worth."

"Well, that depends," he said. Outwardly, his expression hadn't changed, but there was some sort of shrewd calculation going on behind his eyes.

"On what?"

"Lots of things. The year, the mint, the condition. You name it. Some of them are incredibly rare."

"These would be in good condition."

"Which?"

"Good?" I said again.

"No," he said, "that's not what I meant. I meant, *which* would be in good condition?"

"The ones I might be interested in."

"Do you have some St.-Gaudenses to sell, Mr. Swift?"

"Not exactly, no."

"You have access to some?"

"Maybe."

"You know," he said, "this is very interesting. I had a guy in here a couple of months ago asking the same questions." He described Eric Vessey. "You wouldn't be working with him, would you?"

"No." I'd picked the first coin shop in the book, and so had Vessey.

"Okay, Mr. Swift. Don't tell me anything. I don't want to know anyway. If you have some St.-Gaudenses, I will be most happy to broker their sale for you. No questions asked.

I have more contacts than anyone in town and I will do the best possible job for you. How's that?"

"Great," I said. "So how much are they worth?"

"Well, what'd you mean by 'good' condition? Did you mean 'uncirculated'? That's the term we use for something brand new, never used as coin. Then there's 'extremely fine' and 'very fine' and on down to stuff that isn't worth much more than the gold itself. And there are different degrees of each of these categories, too. Appraising coins can be a rather complex business."

"I'd say they would be uncirculated, or close to it," I said. The diaries had indicated that, whenever possible, Henry had bought his coins fresh from the press.

Buddy dug out a well-thumbed copy of a coin catalogue. He turned pages while giving me a little spiel.

"The St.-Gaudens double eagles," he said. "Commissioned by Teddy Roosevelt. Generally considered to be the most attractive U.S. coin design ever. T.R. called it the first coinage worthy of this country. Minted between 1907 and 1933 in lots as big as four million and as small as ten thousand. You're probably not interested in all this."

"No, I find it very interesting," I said without much enthusiasm.

"Sure you do. And here we are, the bottom line," he said. He ran his finger down one of the columns on the page. "The only thing the man really wants to know. Now you understand that this is pretty theoretical, since I don't know what we're talking about. But let's assume a coin in 'extremely fine' condition. Let's assume an average year. Book value is six hundred twenty-five dollars. If you've got something from a year with one of the smaller runs, say a 1926D, bump it up to twelve hundred. If you've got a 1907 high-relief, we're talking five thousand. And if you've got *anything* from the early Thirties, the bidding starts at ten K."

I swallowed kind of hard. "That's per coin," I said.

"Of course per coin. What do you think, these babies are like Lincoln-head pennies?"

"No, I mean, I guess I don't know what I thought. Well . . . thanks. I think that gives me a pretty good idea. Maybe one other question? If you don't mind. You know the history of these things, right?"

He looked insulted.

"Of course," I said quickly. "So if there'd been a major

discovery, a large number of these coins, you'd know about it."

"What do you mean by 'a large number'?"

"Oh, five thousand, something like that," I said, deliberately underplaying it.

"That'd be an incredible find," he said. "Whoever found those would be an instant millionaire. And several times over at that." I could almost see him begin to salivate.

"Anybody in this area ever offered a lot like that for sale, say in the last thirty-five years or so?"

"You know, my friend, I wish I knew what was going on around here. That's exactly the same question that other guy asked. But what the hell, I'll tell you exactly what I told him: Are you kidding? There've hardly been any lots like that available *anywhere*, let alone Charlottesville. And I doubt there ever will be again, either.

"You see, the going assumption in the business is that the St.-Gaudens coins we know about are all that are left. We assume that the rest of them got melted down somewhere along the line, for one reason or another. If a lot like you're talking about has somehow stayed hidden all these years, a large number of people are going to be very surprised. Before they run for their checkbooks, that is."

I shook his hand. "Okay," I said. "That'll about do it. Appreciate your time."

He held my hand a moment longer than necessary. "Let me just say one thing, Mr. Swift," he said. "If you've been going through your grandma's attic and you found something interesting, I suggest you bring it on down here as soon as possible. I might could make you a wealthy man." He handed me a card. "Or call me. Anytime, day or night."

"Thanks, Buddy," I said. "I'll remember that."

I left Buddy's thinking that I knew Eric Vessey even better now. Henry's gold coin collection was still out there, sealed in a vault on the Jordan Institute property, waiting for some lucky fool to cash it in.

How much cash? Well, assume that Henry's coins were in nice condition but he'd bought only the most common ones. In that case, the Institute was sitting on a *minimum* of nearly eight million bucks. And the key to locating it lay in eighty-five feet of water.

For that kind of money, well, I might just go after that little box in the quarry myself.

CHAPTER
15

I walked from the coin shop to the downtown pedestrian mall and put in a call to my employer. She was with a client but told me to come by in forty-five minutes. Then I called my brother. Surprisingly, he was at the apartment. I told him I was going to be late and if he got hungry to go ahead and fix some dinner for himself. Whatever he could find.

To pass the time, I bought a copy of the daily paper and took it to one of the little wooden benches that dot the mall. I sat next to a cast-iron sculpture of a woman's silhouette. The woman was big and she was toting an equally large shopping bag.

The paper's lead story had to do with AIDS once again. The private school had announced that morning that they had decided to expel the young boy with the disease. Some unhappy people had immediately gone to the county office building, to see if they could get someone in power on their side. There, they'd run into the same group of protestors I'd encountered the previous day, the ones who wanted all AIDS victims quarantined if not jailed. Angry words were exchanged, then blows. The cops were called in. Arrests were made.

It was a depressingly familiar story. I quit reading it halfway through and turned to the sports section. Baseball season was underway and there was hope in every manager's heart. The Red Sox were talking about finally getting the Series monkey off their back. Steinbrenner was guaranteeing a championship for the Big Apple. Tommy Lasorda was scarfing bowls of pasta and dealing out toothy smiles. The Mariners were aiming to finish as high as third in their division.

The little rituals of spring. Silliness, I suppose. Trivial. Unworthy of an adult's attention. Well, maybe so. But I see the sports pages as the only place in the paper where I'll find any optimism. They provide a nice contrast.

I took it easy, read all the boxscores, then at the appointed time I walked to Morgan Vessey's condo, which was only a few blocks away.

She was wearing a pale yellow silk dress that effectively draped her body and made enticing sounds when she moved. Different type of client, different outfit, I guessed. We went into her office, where the computer's printer was clacking away. She pushed a button on the printer, putting it on hold. A tiny green light began blinking.

"You look better," she said after we'd settled ourselves. "No more violence."

She sat across from me, her eyes fixed on mine. The image that came to me was *rodent of prey*. I had to stifle a laugh.

"Only at the county office building," I said to cover myself.

"Terrible. That poor boy."

"I agree."

"Sometimes I wonder how we could have gone so wrong. People must have lost touch with their inner beings. I don't know . . ." She spread her hands against the hopelessness of trying to find your inner being, once lost. "But no more violence directed against you."

"No. I do have something for you, though. I have the key word. And that word is: Gold."

"Gold what?"

"Coins, actually. What your brother was hoping to find when he made those dives in the quarry."

I then took her through the whole story, step by step, as best I understood it at that moment. I did some condensing, for instance with the details of Boots Henry's life. And I omitted some things that I didn't think she ought to know yet, like the affair between Eric and Paula Slate, and their subsequent spats. If she didn't already know about it, there was the risk that she'd go after Slate before all the evidence was in.

When I was finished, all she said was, "I should have known."

"Known what?"

"That Eric would get himself involved in something like this." She banged her fist on the desktop. "Damn him!" she said. "He didn't need the money. He'd done the best of any of us. Why, Swift?" Tears had welled in her eyes, but she didn't let them out. They hovered there, as if poised to make a graceful swan dive off her lower lids.

She'd asked the eight-million-dollar question. Why did someone who had so much money already, become obsessed with acquiring more and more? I didn't know why, though I'd wondered from time to time. It was a common enough pattern. I suppose the only way I'd ever find out was if I first became wealthy myself. In other words, I'd never find out.

"I don't know," I said with a shrug. "It's just one hell of a lot of money."

There was a silence, during which I imagine she integrated the new information and got herself back on track.

"Well, now what?" she said finally.

"I either keep working or I don't," I said. "In all fairness, I have to say that there's still no evidence to suggest that it wasn't an accidental drowning. Although we do now have a clear motive for murder."

"I know what I know. I want you to keep working."

"All right. Well, the first thing we have to face is that it had to be Drake who started the ball rolling. He was poking around in these moldy old papers and found the references to the gold. I'm assuming that he took the information to Eric."

"That would make sense," she said with assurance. "Drake wouldn't have known what to do next. He probably asked Eric for a little of his real estate expertise. Find out where the Henry property was and who owned it now. That would have been simple for Eric, but it wouldn't have satisfied him to do the favor without knowing why. He would have leaned on Drake until he got the whole story from him. I can just see Drake, hemming and hawing and shuffling his feet, and finally blurting it all out."

"I agree. Because we know it was Eric, and not Drake, who went to Buddy's coin shop to find out exactly how much the gold was worth and whether anyone had discovered it yet."

"And once he found out, he'd immediately start thinking of ways to minimize Drake's share."

I cleared my throat. "You realize what you're saying," I said.

"Yes. It's motive, isn't it? If Eric was maneuvering to cut his brother out."

"A strong motive. But you've always believed Drake was involved, haven't you?"

She nodded. But she didn't seem too happy about it.

"Anything you haven't told me?" I asked.

"No, nothing. I have these feelings, that's all. They're usually right."

"I have feelings, too. I call it the old occasionally reliable sixth sense. You think that's ESP?"

"Probably. I'd have to hear the details. What does it have to do with all this?"

"Well, Drake called me last night. He told me he didn't kill his brother."

"So?"

"So I believed him."

"Swift," she said with annoyance, "I thought you understood that he's not as much of a wimp as he seems to be."

"I know that. But there was something in the way he said it. You have your intuitions and I have mine. I know he was involved now, but . . ."

"I'm warning you, Swift. Be careful of Drake. You underestimate him and you could get hurt again."

"You think he's the one who beat me up?"

"I don't know," she said, "but it seems likely. Especially after what you've told me today. It would be just Drake's style. He'd want to get everything about the gold out of Eric's files. But he's so ineffectual about some things. He wouldn't know what to do about the burglar alarm; he'd be terrified of breaking in and getting caught, especially if he's guilty of something else. He'd stew about it. Then, for lack of anything better to do, he'd cruise by the house every night, hoping I'd forget to turn the alarm on one time.

"On Monday night, he would've seen that there was somebody inside. So he stops. He sneaks up to the window and sees it's you, a stranger. He probably figures you're a burglar, since no one's supposed to be fooling around in there until the will is probated. It's a perfect situation, from his point of view. He knows the house and can get around in the dark much better than you can. So he kills the lights, goes in, knocks you out, steals what he wants, and leaves you holding the bag if anybody else shows up.

"The other thing is, you can be sure he checked your wallet while you were out, to see who he'd bopped in case he ever ran into you again. That means he saw your license. When he did, I'll bet that he immediately assumed you were working for me. So he knows who you are and he knows what you're doing and that's why he's calling you up. I'd take that into account, if I were you."

Yeah, it could've happened that way, I thought. And he could have decided to dog me for the next few days, to try and find out what my investigation had turned up so far. And if he thought I was getting too close to the gold, what then?

She cocked an eyebrow at me and shot a question mark into my head.

"It makes sense," I admitted. "I can't think of anyone else who would have wanted that particular file so much."

Actually, I could. Paula Slate. But I didn't want to discuss that possibility with Morgan Vessey.

"He's a strong man, Swift," she said. "I'm sure he's the one who bruised Eric all up. Plus he's tricky. Very elusive. His personality can change drastically from one minute to the next." That I knew. "You may think you can read people, but Drake's someone you're never going to get a handle on."

"All right," I said. "Advice noted."

"It's your bones."

An offhand remark, I suppose, but it iced me right to the core. No need for her to put any psychic energy behind it.

"It is," I said. "Maybe you'd better tell me where your brother lives. Just in case."

She gave me directions to a place out in Albemarle County, north of Charlottesville. Told me it was a small old farmhouse on about ten acres of ground. I wrote the information in my notebook.

"Now, we still have a major problem," I said. "The box in the quarry only contains a note telling where the gold is and how to go about getting at it. It isn't the gold itself. From the diary, it would appear that reopening the vault is not going to be an easy matter. You see what I mean? A person couldn't just walk onto the property and walk away with the gold. Retrieving the box would only be the first step."

"Eric would have figured something out," she said. "Knowing him, he was probably already working a deal with the owner of the place. Knowing him, he was also probably rigging the deal so that he'd come out with the gold and the other guy'd get nothing."

"He never hinted to you what he was up to?"

"No."

"Okay. Well, I guess my next move is to go back and talk to the people at the Institute, see if I can find out if Eric approached them. Now is there anything else you've heard that might be relevant? Something your brother let slip, or something I said today that rang a bell? Anything at all?"

She thought about it, then shook her head slowly. "No," she said, "I don't think so."

I told her I'd be in touch the following evening and walked back to my car. Hurried back, actually. It was late again, but once again there was a chance I could make it to Underwater Charlottesville before closing. This visit, it was equipment I was after. Scuba gear. After the revelations of the day, my curiosity had grabbed ahold of me for fair. I wanted to see for myself what was down in that quarry.

As I drove, I tried to think who I might buddy up with for the dive. Drake Vessey had suggested it, but I certainly didn't trust him. I didn't trust Paula Slate, either. Patricia I didn't want sucked into this thing, besides which she'd hassle me for even considering it so soon after being bopped on the head. Someone like Searle or Steve Furniss or one of his assistants was a possibility, but all those guys worked normal jobs and if I wanted one of them I'd have to wait for the weekend at best. The more likely options were: dive alone—which went against my training and was what had cost Eric Vessey his life—or dive with Morgan. Both of those left me feeling uneasy.

The uneasiness changed to frustration when I arrived at

Underwater Charlottesville. The shop was dark. I sat in my car in front of the concrete building with its colorful sign and cursed. I was itching to dive.

I decided to drive over to Searle's house and see if he was home. He was.

"Well, hi stranger," he said when he opened the door.

"Hi, Jon," I said. "I tried to catch you at the shop, but . . ."

"I had to close up early today. Come on in."

We stepped into the little entryway. Benjy had come out to see who it was. When he saw it was me, he smiled, at first. I said hello to him. He approached me and laid his hand gently against my cheek.

Then, slowly, his smile changed to a strange, fearful expression. His eyes grew wide. He opened his mouth and a noise like the howling northwest wind came out. It was a frightening sound. Involuntarily, I took a step backward. I had goosebumps all over.

Searle went and comforted him and he began to calm down.

I recovered enough to say, "What is it, Benjy?"

He didn't say anything, just looked from Jonathan to me and back again. They were apparently communicating nonverbally, because Searle nodded.

"Okay, Benjy," he said. "I'll tell him. Now could you please wait in the kitchen. We'll just be a few minutes."

Benjy gave me a final distressed look and left. Searle turned to me. He seemed concerned.

"What's going on?" I said, a little shakily.

He wet his lips with his tongue and cleared his throat.

"That's only the third time he's ever done that, that I know of," he said. "It's a warning. The last time was . . . was right before the accident."

"Huh? What accident?"

"Four years ago. Another car skidded in the rain and slammed into mine. I got banged up pretty bad. I was in the hospital for a while. Benjy tried to warn me."

"What are you saying, Jon? That he can see the *future*?"

He shook his head slightly, as if to clear it.

"I don't know what it is," he said. "Benjy can pick up things the rest of us can't. You saw some of that the last time you were here. I've come to think of it as a human ability that's somehow been lost over time, like the ability to track an animal by its scent, which we also once had. Except that, occasionally, it shows up again, in certain special individuals like Benjy." He shrugged.

"I don't know what to say," I said.

"I understand. Just take it for what it's worth. Benjy is letting you know ahead of time that you're in danger. Perhaps from that case you're working on. If I were you, I'd trust him. Be a little more cautious than you usually are. Since he was able to warn you, it's unlikely you'll come to any serious harm. Like me. The accident was bad, but I came through it fine."

Great. Just what I needed. My sense of how the world is put together had already taken some nasty jolts. Now this. And the thing of it was, I was prepared to accept what he was saying. When Benjy had made that noise, I had somehow *felt* for a moment what he was feeling. I had known, intuitively, that whatever he was trying to tell me, I should listen to it.

"Thanks," I said. "I guess."

He smiled. "I know this must all be hard for you," he said. "But hang in there. So . . . what brings you by?"

"Oh yeah. That. Well, like I said, I tried to catch you at the shop. What I need is to rent some equipment. I think I know why Eric Vessey was diving in the quarry and I want to go down and have a look for myself. Unfortunately, the shop was closed and I was wondering if maybe, if it's not too inconvenient, ah . . ."

"If we could go down and get it this evening?"

"Uh huh. I'm sorry to ask you like this, but I'd really like it before tomorrow afternoon. If it's a bad time just tell me."

"No, I think we can take care of you. I can put dinner on hold. Let me tell Benjy."

I waited in the entryway while he went into the kitchen. A few minutes later he returned and said we could go.

"It's okay to leave him?" I asked.

"Oh, sure. Benjy can take care of himself, within limits. We won't be that long."

We took my car. On the way, I decided I might as well ask him a few questions.

"Case has taken some strange turns," I said.

"Oh?"

"How'd you happen to end up on the Board of Directors at the Institute?"

"You discovered that, did you? Well, I suppose I should have expected that you would. We don't tend to talk about it, but not because it's some state secret. Dr. Jordan just likes to do things in a private way. I don't mind talking to you, but I'd prefer it if you didn't repeat anything I say."

"You have my word," I said.

Searle paused, then said, "It started when I first took Benjy out there for psychic testing. Grover and I got along right away. Over time, he talked about his goals with me, and I became interested in them. When he decided to restructure the Institute a couple of years ago, he asked me to become part of it."

"What was the restructuring?" I asked.

"Up to that time, he'd been owner and sole director of the Institute. As he got older, he became concerned about what would happen when he died. He was also concerned with the prospect of becoming senile."

I laughed. "He seems pretty sharp to me."

"He is," Jonathan said. "But Grover is also, despite the direction of his research, a very practical man. He knew that senility was always a possibility, no matter how alert he might be right now. And, of course, one can always die at any moment. What he wanted to be sure of was that the Institute's efforts would be carried on, and in much the same way.

"So, he came up with the reorganization. A three-person Board of Directors, each with an equal vote on matters affecting the Institute. Two out of three votes would decide an issue, though so far we've always been unanimous.

"The idea was that this would guard against his losing his judgment. If he did, and it was obvious to us, we could override any bad decisions that he tried to make. And if he should die, we have the power to appoint someone new to the Board and to keep the Institute running.

"He was very clear about the makeup of the Board, too. He wanted one person from outside the Institute, to supply the perspective of someone uninvolved with its day-to-day operation. That turned out to be me. And then he wanted someone from within. Dr. Slate was the logical choice there. She knows the Institute better than anyone besides Grover, and she has the skills necessary to make a smooth transition if he were no longer there.

"Does that answer your questions?"

"I guess so," I said. "Sounds logical. Let's see, one other thing. Have either of the Vesseys been in today, or Paula Slate? It could be important."

"Nope," he said. "Very slow day."

We had arrived at Underwater Charlottesville. Searle opened the shop for me and then sat by patiently while I fitted myself for wetsuit and hood and gloves and booties. Then I selected a face mask and flippers. The all-important B.C. Tank and backpack and weightbelt. I even rented a diving light and one of those knives you strap to your leg.

The full kit. I wasn't going anywhere but Nelson County.

When I'd finished we loaded the gear into Clementine and I drove Jon home. I apologized again for bothering him and we agreed to get together socially sometime, after I'd wrapped up the case.

Then he said, "Swift, you're not going to do anything stupid, are you?"

"Like what?"

"Like diving alone."

"No," I said. "Of course not."

"See that you get yourself a good buddy," he said.

"Sure."

I left him standing on the sidewalk, looking as if he'd decided he'd done the wrong thing.

It was after seven when I finally got back to my apartment. And wonder of wonders, Ashley had made dinner. He'd hoofed it down to the neighborhood market, picked up the proper materials, and put together some manicotti. From scratch, just like Justine made it. It was still baking when I arrived.

Ash was like that. One day he'd have you assaulting the wall with your head, the next he was busting his butt for you, singing a merry melody, and you couldn't resist him.

He had a bottle of valpolicella, too, for which I was exceedingly grateful. Even though it probably meant he'd discovered I had a charge account at the grocery store.

We sat at the table and drank some wine while we waited for the manicotti to start bubbling.

"So what were you talking about this morning, little bro'?" he asked.

"I don't remember," I said. "What *was* I talking about?"

"You asked me about ESP."

"Oh yeah, that. I think I might be getting a little goony, Ash. And it's worse now than it was then."

"Hey, runs in the family. No problem. You just have to bear in mind, when you to that last left turn, keep going straight." He spread his hands. "I'm still here, aren't I?"

"Thanks, you're a major help."

He put his hand on my shoulder and I jerked away reflexively.

"You *are* wired," he said. "If you want to talk about it, talk about it."

So I did. I told him the complete story of the Vessey case. It was good to be able to bounce it off someone and not have to carefully edit what I was saying, as I did with each of the principals. I could have talked to Patricia, of course, but she wasn't there, and Ashley was.

The conversation continued into dinner. Manicotti with a rich marinara sauce, a spinach-and-tomato salad with red wine vinegar and olive oil dressing, and hot garlic bread so spicy it scoured out the sinuses. The whole was a fair imitation of Justine's cookery. I dug in as though I hadn't eaten in two days, which wasn't that far from the truth. My stomach took it all in stride.

I finished the story about the time we were mopping our plates with the garlic bread. Telling it like that, the whole thing, made me realize just how complex it was, and how strange, and how many questions there were that still needed answering.

"The thing is," I said to Ashley, "I don't *know* if Eric Vessey was murdered, I only have a *feeling* that he was. I'll probably never be able to prove it."

"Well," he said. "If you want my opinion, I think this business has been good for you. The universe is full of weirdness, Lor. You've never wanted to admit that, because it interferes with your logical mind. You're like Dad that way."

"Now wait a minute—"

He held up his hand. "No offense," he said. "I don't mean it pejoratively. There's nothing wrong with logic. It pays your rent, right? But it just doesn't cover everything."

"This case, for instance."

"Exactly. You're being exposed to people who can show you the far side of things."

"Well, what do *you* think?"

He grinned. "I think we should go for the eight mil."

I couldn't help smiling too. "It is tempting," I said.

"But you won't. Not old Mr. Straight Arrow."

"C'mon, Ash, don't start that crap. You have your life and I have mine. I like mine and I don't begrudge you yours."

"It's not really his money, you look at it that way."

"It's not mine, either."

"So you're gonna come out of this as poor as you went in."

"We'll see. I think when I show Dr. Jordan where it is, he'll probably want to give me some kind of reward. With all that money, I'd say he's apt to be generous."

"Ah, it's all neither here nor there anyway. Take my word for it, the most important thing that's gonna come out of this is how your head is rearranged. That's worth more than all the Saint goddamn Gaudenses."

I was feeling oddly content. Dinner was sitting well, we'd finished the bottle of wine. Being with my brother was not the strain that it might have been.

Then, suddenly, I began to lose my equilibrium. My fingertips no longer sensed anything solid. There appeared to be a thick plate of glass between me and the rest of the world. I felt as though I might slide down through the chair, and the floor, and the earth, until I ended up in some vast empty space devoid of light.

I stared at Ash, with what kind of expression I have no idea.

"Jesus Christ!" he said. "What *is* it?"

What it was was that his face no longer belonged to Ashley Swift. It was a glob of liquid flesh, forming and reforming itself. It became the face of Morgan Vessey. Then it dissolved and became Drake Vessey. Then it dissolved again and I was looking at the gray death mask of Eric Vessey.

"What the *hell* is going on?" Ashley said.

He got up and came around to my end of the table. He must have got his arm under mine and hoisted me out of the chair, but I couldn't be sure because I couldn't feel anything. All I knew was that I was being propelled toward the couch. Then I fell into it.

"You need a drink, boy," he said.

I thought that was very funny and I laughed a lot.

He went and rummaged around in the kitchen and I heard him call and ask didn't I have any liquor left in the house. I laughed some more. He came back in the living room and announced that he was going out for some.

"Give me the car keys," he said.

I didn't know where my keys were. I didn't know *what* my keys were. So I didn't do anything.

"Jesus," he said.

He stuck his hand in my pocket and got my keys out. He looked around, grabbed a jacket of mine that was draped over the chair at my desk. He started for the door, then he stopped.

"You stay right there," he said to me. "You're gonna be all right, ain't you?"

I grinned at him.

"Stay put," he said again, and he hurried out the door.

I stared across the room, at the swirling Dayglo colors of one of my posters. It advertised a concert by Big Brother and the Holding Company. At its center I could see the colors shaping the face of Janis Joplin, that smile of hers. Her warmth filled me up. She opened her mouth and I could hear that incredible voice. It sent out waves of sound that wrapped me up, lifted me from the couch, carried me to the source. There was the voice and there was a liberating darkness. . . .

The pounding awakened me. It sounded like it was inside my head. I moved, felt the fabric of the couch with my hands. I was lying down, my body bent to accommodate itself to the limited space available. The pounding continued, and I heard a voice shouting. There was someone at the door.

"Swift!" the voice said. "You in there?!"

I pushed myself up. I felt a little lightheaded, but otherwise quite normal. How had I happened to fall asleep? I wondered. The wine. Must have been the wine. It occurred to me to look at my watch. It was after midnight. Quite a little nap.

The man stopped knocking. He opened the door and walked into my apartment. It was a cop, a detective, one of the few city boys with whom I'm on reasonable terms.

I must have looked a little strange, because he asked me if I was okay.

"Sure," I said. "I'm fine, Craven. What's up?"

"You better come with me, Swift," he said.

I sighed. "What's the charge this time?"

"That ain't how it is. Come on. I'll explain along the way."

"I don't like this."

"I don't like my wife's dog. Let's get moving."

We left my apartment and got in his vanilla Ford. I really don't like getting in cop cars. It invariably means that something ugly is going to happen. But he did put me in the front seat with him. The door could be opened from the inside.

"What's going on, Craven?" I said.

He took a healthy breath and blew it noisily out his nose.

"There's a guy in the hospital," he said. "Somebody shot him getting into your car."

My mouth went dry. "Ashley," I managed to say.

"That his name? He didn't have I.D. on him."

"What's he look like?"

"Little like you. Not quite as neat. One of your neighbors called it in. Said it *was* you. You know the guy?"

"He's my . . . he's my brother."

"Shit," Craven said. "I'm sorry, Swift."

I didn't want to ask, but I did. "How is he?"

"On the table. But they think he'll be okay."

I realized I'd been holding my breath for quite a while. I let it out. There was a long pause, during which I stared out the windshield at streets that suddenly seemed unfamiliar.

Then Craven said, "I did the paperwork at the hospital. Then I drove over to interview the neighbor, a Mr. Pipkin. Older guy, lives catty-corner to you?"

He looked over at me and I nodded that I knew who he was talking about.

"Pipkin said he was looking out a window and he saw you getting into your car. Then there was a gunshot. You fell in the street and somebody was running the other way. It was too dark to tell anything about the shooter. Then there was a car starting up and taking off, but it was somewhere he couldn't see it. He rang up 911 immediately and fifteen minutes later we had your . . . brother in the hospital. Ten minutes after that they went in after the slug.

"When I finished up with Pipkin, I decided to check out your place, see if there was anyone there. First thing I seen was your light on, so I knocked a bit, then I decided to hell with regulations and I stuck my head in there."

"Thanks for doing that," I said.

"No problem," he said, and he shook his head. "Witnesses. How we ever get a straight story I'll never know. What about your brother? Anybody around might want to kill him?"

There probably were, any number of people. But not in Charlottesville. On the other hand, several people came to mind who might want to kill *me*.

"No one," I said. "Everybody likes Ashley."

"Always the good ones, ain't it? Well, here we are."

He let me off at the hospital emergency entrance. Before I got out of the unmarked car, he put a hand on my arm.

"Look, Swift, I don't want to bug you tonight. Go see about your brother. But we need to talk. This is a serious matter here. I'll be back a little later, okay?"

"Okay."

I went into the emergency room and presented myself at the desk. Ashley had been John Doe'd in and was still in surgery. I filled out the admittance forms for him. There was the awkward moment when they asked if he had insurance. Knowing Ash, I was sure he didn't. They asked who was going to guarantee his bills. I said that I would.

For one crass moment I couldn't help but think that there went the first money I'd had in the bank in my entire adult life.

Then I mentally slapped my own face. What a stupid, selfish thought. Ashley might have been a pain and a bully, and he might have stolen all my girlfriends, but I'd landed him in the operating room with a bullet in him. It didn't balance.

Ash, I thought, *there have been times when I hated your guts. But I didn't ever want this, I swear it. Just pull out of it. When you do, I'm going to come clean with you, get it all out front. Things are going to be different with us. And I will find out who did this to you and I will punish him.*

I sat in the impersonal fluorescent glare of the waiting room. There were stacks of back issues of *Woman's Day* and *Family Circle*, even a few *Sports Illustrated*, but I didn't look at them.

Who? I thought. *Drake Vessey? Paula Slate? Morgan Vessey? Or someone else altogether, someone from a previous case.* I tried to think of anyone who was in the slammer due to my efforts and who might now be getting out on parole and who would be sufficiently pissed to take a shot at me. I drew a blank.

It wasn't long before they paged me. I checked my watch

and made it about four hours since they would've brought Ashley in.

The doctor's name was Abelard. He was a tall, gray-haired fellow who looked remarkably fresh considering the time of day and the long hours he'd just spent in surgery.

"I understand he's your brother," Dr. Abelard said.

"Yes," I said. "How is he?"

"He's a lucky man. To put it simply, the bullet entered his back and hit a rib, where it broke in two. One piece went straight on and exited his chest. The other went upward, hit another rib and eventually lodged just below his shoulder. The first fragment punctured a lung, but that's the most significant damage. Neither of them hit the spinal cord, heart, major blood vessels, or other organs. The bones shattered, of course, and there was a good deal of internal bleeding. But all things considered, he's in excellent shape. Lucky, as I said. We're talking a matter of half an inch here, a quarter-inch there."

"Can I see him?"

"Well, he's in Intensive Care right now. You can go down there if you really want to, but there's not much to see. He won't be awake until morning."

"I want to see him," I said.

"Of course."

Dr. Abelard led me to the Intensive Care Unit. It was a large room with space partitioned off by curtains. The spaces were small. Ashley's contained only his bed, a machine for monitoring vital signs, a rolling table with odds and ends on it, and the metal contraption they hang I-V bags from.

Ash didn't look good. In his drugged sleep, his features seemed sunk into his face. His eyes appeared bruised and his skin had an unhealthy pallor, though that might have been due in part to the lighting. Oxygen from a wall unit was supplied through two flexible tubes with curved ends that fit into his nostrils. He had an I-V needle in one arm. The fluid from two different plastic bags was mixed and dripped into his vein. Antibiotics, Dr. Abelard said, and glucose. If he did happen to come awake, a painkiller could be added.

The monitor showed a strong, steady heartbeat. *Ashley*, I thought, *you don't look great, but you're alive.*

I didn't want to touch him where he'd just had surgery, so I rested my hand on his knee for a moment. *Hang in there, big bro'*, I thought.

"All right," I said to Dr. Abelard.

Abelard took me back to the emergency waiting room. Craven was there. The detective sat me down in a quiet corner and asked his questions.

I'd thought a little bit about what I was going to say. There were two main options: tell him everything or tell him nothing. There wasn't much in between, because once I started to talk he wouldn't be satisfied until he had the whole story.

The tell-everything option had its advantages. It'd get the cops involved, though it'd be a jurisdictional nightmare. Drake Vessey lived in Albemarle County, as had his brother, but Eric had died in Nelson, and Ashley had been shot within the Charlottesville city limits. The state police would probably have to be called in to sort things out.

Whatever, there would be cops and they would be investigating the Vesseys. This would take the heat off me, at least for a while. If Ashley's assailant (presumably the same person who beat me up) were among the principals in the case, he or she would likely go to ground. The cops might even solve the thing. In that event, I'd still get paid and the streets would be relatively safe for me and my brother again.

On the other hand. . . .

I had no evidence to link anyone in the Vessey case to the attack on Ashley. It was possible the cops would stir up a lot of people to no end. That'd make it tougher for me to continue with the case. Even if one of the Vessey principals *did* shoot Ash, it could be a disadvantage to have the cops run that person to ground. He or she might become all the more difficult, and hazardous, to flush out.

Then there was my personal involvement in the case. Someone had beaten me up. Someone had tried to kill me and in the process come close to wasting my brother. I wanted the satisfaction of dealing with that person up close enough to smell his sweat.

The private investigator's First Commandment rang in my ears: *Thou shalt not become personally involved in thy cases.* And I did try to follow it, Lord knows I tried.

But I decided I would do what had to be done, on my own. I told Dectective Craven nothing.

CHAPTER
16

Ridley Campbell, however, was another story.

Early next morning I was headed up the steps of the county office building, bound for his office. There were no demonstrators or counter-demonstrators out trying to enlist me in their crusade. Good.

I'd had a small amount of sleep after Craven drove me back to my apartment. When I woke up, I immediately called the hospital. Ashley was resting comfortably. No complications.

Then I called Drake Vessey. I told him that my brother, who was visiting me, had been suddenly hospitalized. I'd have to be spending time with him. Also, I had some urgent business to attend to out at the Institute. Consequently, I would have to put off our meeting until the following day.

Drake was very gracious over the phone. If any of what I said surprised him, it didn't show. He agreed readily to the postponement and hung up with best wishes for my brother's speedy recovery.

Though it had been the most civilized conversation

imaginable, it left me with an uneasiness that went straight to my bones. I wondered if this was really the right thing to do. Because if Vessey was in fact the person behind all the violence, then I was deliberately lighting his fuse.

I shook off my doubts, called Morgan Vessey, and arranged to meet her later in the morning.

Then I called Patricia at work. I explained what had happened to Ashley.

"Good God," she said. "Is he all right?"

"Expected to recover fully," I said. "I'll be checking in on him from time to time throughout the day. But I wonder if you could do the same, maybe on your lunch break. Just go ahead and introduce yourself if he's conscious."

"Of course I will. But where will you be?"

"I'm, ah, still working on the Vessey thing."

"Loren," she began, and the disapproval in her voice was heavy.

"It's okay," I said quickly. "I've almost got it wrapped up."

"Damn it, Loren! Does what happened to your brother have to do with this case?"

It was a question I knew I'd have to face, and I'd dreaded it. One of the things I hate most is having to lie to Patricia. She doesn't appreciate it either. But if I told her truthfully what I intended to do, she'd do everything she could to prevent me. She can't stand it when I do stupid things. She might even go straight to the cops.

So I lied.

"We don't think so. We think it was a guy I helped send to prison five years ago."

"Who's *we*?" she asked suspiciously.

"Me and the city cops. They've got a good lead already. They found a witness."

There was a lengthy pause. I could almost hear her drumming her fingers on the desktop.

"All right," she said finally. "But will you *please* be careful. First you get beat up and then your brother gets shot. So maybe there's no connection, but I still don't like the way this case is going."

"Don't worry," I said. "I'm not going to take any unnecessary risks." Miraculously, I got the words out without choking on them.

"Okay, I'll bring Ashley some flowers or something."

"I love you," I said, and I got off the line before I tripped over my deceit.

After a quick bowl of cereal, I decided to check my guns. The Walther locked in my desk drawer, the Police Positive taped to the wall behind my couch. I was feeling more than a little paranoid. Someone was trying to kill me. I didn't feel like I wanted to start *carrying* a gun yet; that's always a last resort with me. Still, I needed to know that they were there and ready for use if it came to that.

The Police Positive was right where it ought to be.

When I went to check the Walther, though, I noticed something. My middle desk drawer was open a little. Out of a detective's habit, I never leave it that way.

The hair raised up on my arms. Someone had been in my desk. It could have happened when I was passed out, when I was at the hospital, when I was asleep, anytime. It could have been anyone. They could have stolen something, or left something—like a bomb.

A bomb? *Come on*, I told myself.

Still, I stared at that damn drawer for about two minutes before I finally started inching it open.

There was nothing missing. And there was nothing that hadn't been there before, except a single sheet of paper, with something written on it in longhand. It was a poem.

> *the rain fall*
> *soddens bleak Byron's grave,*
> *Justine*
> *in mud in black becoming*
> *a clacking, a withered crone*
>
> *and Delly,*
> *sweet Delly in corridors,*
> *now*
> *lost*
> *in dollared time*
>
> *and you and I,*
> *the rain the same,*
> *our own graved feet*
> *together dance*

I read the poem and I read it again. I gazed for a long time at the sheet of paper, then it blurred and my mind was flashing scenes from the past.

Ashley, I thought, *damn you, Ashley, you never do play fair, do you?*

I put the poem carefully away. I checked the other drawer and found the Walther in its appointed place.

Then I gathered together the things I'd need later in the day. Face mask, snorkel, fins. Regulator. Rope and compass. The rest of the equipment was still in my car. I double-checked everything and packed it all in a red nylon carry-on bag.

And now I was in the office of the Albemarle County chief of police.

He was sitting behind his desk, looking as though he ought to be chiseled into Mount Rushmore instead.

"I heard about the shooting," he said. "He related to you?"

"My brother."

"Sorry. Didn't know you had one."

"He hasn't been much of one, until now. I want the guy who did it, Rid."

"Can't blame you," he said. "Who do you like?"

I fed him the details of the Vessey case, the parts I'd learned since the last time we'd talked. I told him everything I thought was relevant.

When I'd finished, he said, "You tell this to the city cops?"

"No."

"You're hanging your ass out again. This is an attempted murder, Swift."

"I realize that," I said. "But I've got nothing that adds up to squat. Whoever tried to kill Ashley, thinking it was me, may or may not be involved in the Vessey business. So I'm not withholding any real evidence. The biggest tie-in is the attack on me Monday night, and that's your jurisdiction and I'm telling you."

"Why?"

"I want your help. The way things are going, I ought to be able to break the case in a couple of days, at the most. When I do, I'd just as soon have you there."

Campbell chewed on it for a while. Inside that ugly head was, I knew, a first-rate mind. Ridley was also an honest cop.

And he had an unusually healthy perspective when it came to his job. He was hard-line on crimes of violence. Very hard-line. He knew that a lot of the bad guys were so bad they should never be allowed on the streets, and he did his best to keep them locked away. But when it came to those who weren't harming others, the people who bet the football pools or grew a little pot for their own consumption, he ignored them.

He and I agreed about many aspects of our legal system. We both thought that about half the laws on the books should be tossed in the trash and the other half truly and fairly enforced. We both thought the perpetrators of victimless crimes should be immediately set free and replaced by those habitual criminals who were out walking because of some ridiculous technicality. And then, if there were any spaces left in the prisons, we both felt they could be filled with a random sampling of lawyers and politicians, and society would be much the better for it.

"I don't like this, Swift," he said finally. "I think I better talk to some of these people myself."

"Give me a couple of days, Rid," I said.

"I don't know."

"One day. Come on, just one day."

"You know what you're saying here? You're using yourself as bait, is what you're doing."

"Hopefully not."

"Yeah, but maybe so, too. If your theory's right, somebody out there killed one guy, beat you up, then almost killed a innocent bystander in your place. I'd say they're dangerous."

"That's why I want to flush him out now. Or her."

"I still don't like it."

"We'll be in touch the whole way," I said. "Look, I've already got Drake Vessey on alert. Today I'm going back to the Institute, ask a few more questions, put some burrs under people's butts down there. Then I'm going home and sit tight. You can put a car outside my apartment, or a man inside if you want. If nobody shows up by morning, I'll keep my date with Drake, and you can go along with me. How's that?"

"You're putting me in a real bind, Swift."

"I'll cover for you. If it goes into the crapper, I'll say I never gave you all the facts. You can trust me. Goddamn it, I *want* whoever it is, Rid, and this is the best way. You know it is."

"Maybe."

"Deal?"

He shook his granite head. "No deals," he said. "You do what you have to do, and I'll do what I think's best. You just make damn sure there's *nothing* I don't know about."

"Thanks, Rid," I said.

I felt confident as I left the building that Ridley had given me my one day. And I knew if I got into trouble he'd be there.

For a moment, I wished I'd told him the whole truth. But if I'd said I was planning to dive the quarry myself, I know he wouldn't have gone for it. It would have queered the whole deal. Better to have a lapse of memory and face the consequences later.

Sorry, Rid, it just slipped my mind. Been having a hard time of it, you know. Hit on the head, and then all these weird psychic things happening to me. You understand.

It didn't sound that great. If things worked out the way I hoped, though, I wouldn't have to make excuses.

In any case, I was definitely still going to make that dive. If at all possible, I wanted that little box in my hands before I started confronting people. The odds were long, I knew—Eric Vessey had dived four times and failed to find it—but I had to take a shot. The box would give me tremendous leverage.

My next stop was the hospital. Ashley had been moved from the Intensive Care Unit and now had a private room. He was awake when I got there.

"This your doing?" he asked me.

"Yeah," I said. "Might as well be."

"Jesus, what'd I ever do to you, little bro'?"

"Nothing to deserve this."

"You know who did it?"

"Not for sure. But it shouldn't take me long. I'm gonna nail him for you."

"Well, don't get carried away, Loren. I'm fine. Be out of here in no time."

"You do that. We've got a lot to talk about."

He smiled weakly. I took his hand and held it for a minute. Then I left.

From the hospital I went to Morgan Vessey's snappy townhouse. I told her what had happened.

"Oh my God, that's terrible," she said.

She seemed genuinely horrified. I was becoming more and more convinced that she was innocent of anything except perhaps coveting the reward specified in her brother's will.

"Yes, it is," I said.

"And it's all my fault. What do we do now?" she pleaded.

She was distraught. Her self-assurance had been punctured, limitations placed on her psychic power. She had not foreseen that it might turn out this way.

"You think it was Drake?" I asked.

"I don't know what to think. Why don't you just drop the whole thing. I'll . . . I'll pay you. A bonus, something. I just don't want any more killing."

"I don't either, Morgan. But like it or not I'm in the middle of it now. Drake, or whoever it is, is not going to believe I quit. I've got to see it through, until that person is safely behind steel. I have no choice."

"I see. All right, what can I do for you?"

"I'm close," I said. "I can feel it. Can you be available to me for a day or two? I may need you."

"Of course. I wasn't planning on leaving the area anyway. If I have to go out for any length of time, I'll leave a message on my answering machine telling you where I can be reached."

"Thanks."

"Where do you go from here?"

"I'm going back down to the Institute," I said. I smiled. "See if I can find me some gold."

"But . . . Well, isn't that dangerous? What if whoever else is after it finds out what you're up to?"

"That's the general idea."

"Wait a minute. I don't think I like this."

"You're not the only one. But I'm a big boy, Morgan. And it was my brother. I've made the decision. Just stay close to home if you possibly can."

She wasn't the type to enjoy being put in this position, but she swallowed it fairly gracefully.

"All right," she said.

I left her and headed for the Jordan Institute. I'd notified two of the principals about what I was doing. It was time to make sure the rest of them got the word.

It was another cool day, sunny and pleasant. I didn't hurry; I wanted to see if I was being followed.

Traffic was heavy in town, so it was hard to tell. I headed out Ridge Street, went west one exit on Interstate 64, then turned onto U.S. 29 South. Here traffic was lighter. I ran the old VW up to 70, which is about her limit, held her there for a few minutes, then dropped back to 55. If I had a tail, he wasn't making any effort to pace me.

But then, if Drake Vessey wanted to follow me, he wouldn't have to do it too closely. He already knew where I was going. And ditto for his sister.

As I drove, I thought about what had happened to me the night before. Or tried to think about it. It was just so far outside any previous experience. But then, so was much of what had gone down since Morgan Vessey walked into my life.

The only thing I could compare it to was being drugged. Even there, I didn't have much basis for comparison. I'd smoked marijuana a few times. It had been a little like that, but far more intense. My disorientation had been total. I wondered if it was similar to what happened when you took LSD.

I hadn't *been* drugged, though, I was sure of that. Unless you counted the wine, and I've drunk a lot of wine and never gone completely out of my mind. The truth was, every time I ran through the sequence of events, all I came up with were questions.

Had it been some sort of temporary nervous breakdown, brought on by the bump on the head and the stress of my brother's unexpected visit?

Had it been a waking dream, like the D.T.'s?

Or was it a bizarre ESP episode? Was it possible that one of the psychic people I'd recently fallen in with was capable of projecting images into my brain and badly loosening my hold on reality? A week earlier I would have laughed at such a notion. Now I wasn't so sure. There were my strange dreams, Benjy, Grover Jordan's experiment, Morgan's little trick. All leading up to the collapse that had sent Ashley out to meet a bullet.

What about that? If someone was putting thoughts into

my head, had he or she really intended it to be me rushing from the house?

I shivered. I didn't even want to consider something like that. All I wanted was to wrap up the case and start hanging out among the normals again.

I stopped the car after I left the main highway, and again when I turned onto the road that led to the Jordan Institute, checking for a tail. No one familiar passed me either time.

When I reached the Institute, the parking lot was again uncrowded. I went in the main building and down to the offices. Dr. Slate was in and not terribly delighted to see me again so soon.

So I didn't bother with the social niceties. "When'd Eric Vessey tell you about the gold?" I said. It seemed a reasonable shot to take.

There was a lengthy silence. Within a few seconds it was obvious to me that I'd been right, that she knew. But she was cool. She wasn't going to answer in haste. When she finally spoke, she betrayed little emotion.

"How did you find out?" she asked.

I shrugged. "I guessed," I said. "But it wasn't hard. Once I discovered what it was that Vessey was after, it stood to reason that he would have enlisted the aid of someone on the inside, someone on the Board, if possible."

She winced at that. She'd accused him of using her at least once, and the memory was probably still painful.

"You admitted to having had an affair with him," I continued. "That made you by far the most likely candidate."

"I see. And how did you find out about the gold?"

"A long story. To make it short, I did some investigating."

"I see," she said again. I felt that I could peer right into her brain, could watch her turn the various alternatives over and over, searching for the one that would benefit her the most. Or do her the least harm.

And then she surprised the hell out of me. She started to cry.

All the fancy college degrees, all the psychological training, all the sensitivity to psychic vibrations, all the self-control and the manipulativeness and the assured business-person façade and the condescending manner, everything went right out the window. She was a human being who was hurt, and she was crying. It suddenly seemed highly unlikely that she could have murdered anyone. I cautioned myself that she could be both hurt and a killer.

It wasn't a flat out, heavy sobbing kind of cry. That would have been too out of character. She just sat there in her fine leather chair and closed her eyes and let the tears run down her cheeks until there weren't any more. Then she wiped her face and blew her nose.

"I'm sorry," she said. Her composure was coming back fast.

"No," I said, "*I'm* sorry. I go around stirring up the past and I inevitably step on some toes. I try not to cause people grief, but. . . ."

"I understand."

"If it's not insensitive of me to ask, would you like to talk about it?"

"I suppose it doesn't matter any more." She was back in control now, but the person inside was still showing through far more than it had. "Where do you want me to begin?"

"Wherever seems appropriate," I said.

"I was in love with Eric. I guess I always was, from the very beginning. You had to know him. He was a selfish, greedy sonofabitch, completely unprincipled. But there was something about him. He was magnetic, in his way. Morgan has much the same kind of power, as you've probably noticed. Whatever Eric wanted, he got. And if he was taking it from you, you gave it gladly. I found him irresistible.

"When we first got together, I lied to myself. I told myself that it was just a fling. There was the difference in age, and the fact that I didn't really *like* him very much. I wasn't going to get involved." She smiled without humor. "But of course love always defeats your best intentions."

"Yeah, I know," I said. I thought of my ex-wife, Marilyn. I had loved her, still did, though we were totally unsuited to one another.

"Well, it was very nice while it lasted," she went on. "We had last summer. After that Eric lost interest, not just in me but the Institute as well. We drifted apart. I gave myself to my work, and I healed.

"Then, suddenly, he was back. Told me he'd missed me and wanted to spend time together again. I didn't really believe him, but you know how it is, I *wanted* to believe, so I humored him. It didn't take long to find out what he was after."

"The gold."

She nodded. "I was insulted at first. He was using me, just like he used everyone else in his life. If we hadn't been such lovers . . . well, that's stupid, isn't it? The thing is, I'm not proud of it, but he could be very persuasive. Almost before I knew what was happening, he had *me* interested in the gold, too. I never would have been, if it weren't for our physical relationship, but once I was involved in that, do you see? It all became part of the whole."

I wasn't sure that I saw but I said I did. "What'd he want to do?" I asked.

"He wanted to buy the place. That was the only way to be sure of getting the gold. He knew it wasn't going to be anywhere he could just pick it up and carry it off. So he pulled me into his plot, using our relationship as the enticement. Grover will never sell this place as long as he's in his right mind. Eric knew that. The only way to get him would be through someone close to him. Me. I'm a member of the Board of Directors. Grover trusts me. He knows how much I've done for the Institute. He respects my professional judgment.

"The way Eric saw it was, he had some very good cards. He knew there was this gold hidden somewhere on the property. Worth millions of dollars. And only he knew how to find it. He figured that together we'd convince Grover to sell, in return for a share of the money. Knowing Eric, the gold was probably a lot more valuable than he told us."

"What'd he say?"

"Four million."

"It's worth at least twice that."

"I'm not surprised," she said wearily. "I should have known Eric was out to cheat us all. Otherwise, why would he insist on clear title to the land? He was probably juggling three different ways to screw us above and beyond a simple misrepresentation like that.

"Anyway, he proposed that we split the four million among us. It sounded like a great deal of money. You have no idea how much it would mean to my research to have access to a sum such as that. Right now, I have to keep a careful watch on the budget. We get some grant money, and the courses bring in some more, but we still operate at a loss. All that keeps us going is Grover's trust fund, and that's been slowly depleted over the years. There will be a day when we'll go broke. And it could be soon. Eric's plan seemed to offer economic relief for a long time to come."

"What did he say was in it for Dr. Jordan?"

"He proposed leasing the Institute back to us for some nominal yearly fee. That way everyone would make out. Eric would enrich himself, while we would still have a place to work and the money to do whatever we wanted. You can see how persuasive his argument was."

I could. I could also see how he was trying to maneuver them into a spot where his superior financial and real estate expertise could be used to do them out of everything. I wondered if that had ever occurred to the practical Dr. Slate, or if she'd been too dazzled by the prospect of her 1.3 mil.

"Dr. Jordan didn't go for the idea, I take it," I said.

"Right. He built this place with his own hands. No promises of mere money could ever entice him to sell it. I told Eric that we were probably wasting our time, and we were. But he had to try. We did. Grover said no and refused to discuss it any further."

"How did you feel about that?"

"Disappointed, of course. But there was nothing I could do. I didn't know where the gold was. I hadn't even known there was any. And I certainly didn't know how Eric had found out about it. He kept all of those details to himself. He was very good at that sort of game.

"The other thing was that I respected Grover's decision. The Institute is really his, despite the way we have the Board set up. He should be allowed to do with it what he wants, so long as he sticks to the principles upon which he founded it. That was exactly what he was doing in this case. I resigned myself to going along with his wishes."

"But Eric didn't."

"No, of course not," she said. "He was determined to get his hands on that gold, whatever it took. I told him to just let it go, but he wouldn't listen. We fought about it."

"When did you find out that there was something important in the quarry?"

"Not until just before he began diving," she said bitterly.

"And you were going to dive with him? That's why you rented the equipment?"

She chuckled humorlessly. "No," she said, "what I told you about the equipment was true. Ironic, isn't it? We were in one of our smoother periods and he actually convinced me we were going to take a pleasure diving trip together. To North Carolina. I don't suppose he ever really meant it."

"But you rented the full outfit," I said. "Including a tank and weights. You wouldn't have needed the heavy stuff unless you planned to dive around here."

"We *were* going to dive around here. Eric suggested we do a quarry dive before we went to the ocean. As a warm-up. He thought I might be a little out of practice. And it'd give us a chance to get familiar with each other as diving buddies."

Simple. Logical. Maybe I'd been looking for something sinister where there wasn't anything at all.

"All this was after Dr. Jordan had rejected your offer?" I said.

"Yes. Eric didn't mention anything more about it for a while. He said he was going to work some other angles. I don't know if he ever did, but the subject was dropped for so long I assumed that he'd given up.

"Then, the week before he died, he told me the key to finding the gold was in the quarry and that he was going to dive for it. He asked me to join him. I said no, I didn't want to betray Grover. He said he was going after the gold with or without me. We fought. I told him to stay out of the quarry, that I'd see what I could do to get Grover to change his mind.

"He started diving anyway. After dark. I never knew about it until I saw the lights down there one night. Somehow, I knew immediately what was going on. I stormed down there and found him suiting up. I was furious. We had a terrible fight. He said he wouldn't need me once he had whatever it is that's down there. I told him that this wasn't right. I told him that I would stop him one way or the other. Then I left. I was still in a rage."

"What night was this?" I asked.

"The night he . . . died." She paused. A look of horror spread across her face. "Oh my God," she said, "you don't think. . . . Yes, you do."

"I don't think anything. I'm just trying to find out what happened."

I was breathing a little easier. This had all come out quite naturally. It felt like Danny was safe now.

"I couldn't have. I loved him," she said, as if killing a lover was something without precedent.

"What did you do after you stormed off?" I asked.

"I came back to my apartment. I had no idea what I was going to do. I'm not used to having a lot of conflicting emotions at the same time. I didn't want him in that quarry, and yet in another way I did. It was difficult for me. My first impulse was totally irrational. I wanted to get away, to spend the night somewhere else. I even threw a few things into an overnight bag, got into my car and started to drive.

"I drove out to Route 29. Then I turned around. I was very confused, but I was calming down. I decided to go back to the quarry and confront Eric again.

"But there was this car in front of me. It had passed me while I was pulled over on the shoulder, then I'd lost it. I . . . I saw it again. At least I think it was the same car, the taillights looked the same. There's that last rise you come over on our road, where you can see for nearly a mile. When I came up there, I could see all the way down to the road to the quarry, far in the distance. And that car was turning into that road."

"*What?*"

"Someone was going in there, and it wasn't Eric."

"What did you *do?*"

"I didn't know what to do. I couldn't imagine why Eric would be meeting anyone at the quarry at night. And when it came down to it, I really didn't want to know why. It looked like he was up to another of his schemes. I was disgusted. And a little afraid, too. More than a little. He'd said he was going to do it with me or without me. I didn't know what that meant. I guess I didn't have the courage to go down there and confront him and whoever was with him. So I went back to my apartment. And the next day I found out that he'd . . . drowned."

"You didn't tell the sheriff about this?"

She shook her head. "It seemed clear that he'd accidentally drowned," she said. "But that's not the real reason. I was scared. What if whoever he'd been with *had* killed him and found out that I'd seen his car? What might happen then? And another thing. If I told what I'd seen, there would have been more of an investigation. They would have found out I'd been with Eric that night. They might have found out we'd been quarreling. *I* would wind up as a suspect. I didn't want that. And nothing I could have done would bring Eric back. We understand here that he's just exchanged one reality for another. It seemed best for all concerned to let the whole thing lie. Do you understand?"

"Yes," I said, though I didn't. I have a different view of possible homicides.

"I guess it's all going to happen anyway, isn't it? My worst fears. Your investigation has done that. Gotten people wondering about Eric's death."

"It's difficult to hide a murder, Paula," I said. "And I don't think it's right. I appreciate your telling me all this, but we still don't know if it's murder we're dealing with. I'd like to find out. I think you can help me. What kind of car was the other person driving?"

"Well, when it passed me, I remember seeing *4WD* on the back. It was a station wagon. A foreign one, I think. That's about all I can tell you. I wasn't expecting to have to remember it."

"That may be enough. All right, will you do me one large favor?"

"If I can."

"You can. Just don't mention this conversation to *anyone* for the time being. I think I know who it was out there with Eric that night."

"You *do?*" She seemed genuinely astonished.

"Maybe," I said. "But there are some questions yet to answer. Will you keep quiet?"

"Of course."

"I need a little time. Also your permission to dive in the quarry this afternoon."

"You're . . ."

"I'm going to try to find what Eric was after. If I do, I'll be able to answer my questions a lot faster."

She looked confused.

"Don't worry about it," I said.

I got up and left, thinking that if she'd killed her lover she was a damn good actress.

But whatever she was, it was time to make that dive.

CHAPTER
——17——

$\mathbf{A}$s I pulled out of the Institute's parking lot, I thought I saw, just for an instant, a face in the pines. By the time it had registered and I'd turned to look again, it was gone. I couldn't be sure what I'd seen. The way my sense of reality had been twisted around the past few days, it might have been real or it might have been a hallucination or it might have been some sort of psychic projection.

I shook my head to clear it and continued down the drive. It wouldn't be good to go diving in anything less than a lucid state. I was still new at the game and I needed to concentrate on all the dos and don'ts.

I thought about Boots Henry and his gold and his forays into the spirit world. When he was hiding that box in the quarry, didn't he realize that someday it would be under water? He must have. Perhaps his spirits had directed him to make it as difficult to find as possible.

Then again, perhaps he'd never really hidden anything down there at all. Perhaps the diary entry was just another trick, or a fragment of an even more obscure code.

For a moment, my feet felt very cold. Here I was, planning to scuba dive, something I wasn't at all comfortable with yet. On top of that, I was going solo, which even the experts seldom do. On top of that, I was looking for something that might or might not be there. And on top of all that, if the box *was* there my chances of finding it were discouragingly small; Vessey, a much better diver than I, hadn't managed it.

It was crazy.

Why did I feel compelled to do it?

The answer was that I didn't know. Outside of the obvious. Which was that possession of the box would allow me to resolve this case in a hurry and maybe flush out a murderer. But somehow that wasn't enough. It didn't fully explain my motives. What did? I gave a mental shrug. I was being urged on by something buried, some part of me that I couldn't bring to consciousness. It pushed and pulled and wouldn't let me stop to reconsider.

I thought again of my dream, and the strange incident the previous evening.

Descending into that quarry, I realized, was going to be a deep dive into something more than just water.

The area around the quarry was deserted. It was a pleasant day, sunny, with the temperature around sixty. Water temperature would be at least five degrees less. Not great, but in the wetsuit I'd barely be aware of the cold.

I stood at the edge of the quarry and looked down. Its surface rippled just slightly in the modest breeze. The water was nearly opaque. I could see a couple of feet below the surface, but only out at the edges. For a moment I spaced out and felt as though I were looking into a black hole, looking at the black emptiness between the stars. The hole began to rotate. Before the sensation was able to overpower me, I turned my back on the quarry, returned to my car.

Very carefully, I assembled my gear. I checked to make sure everything was there, and then I checked again. I cracked the valve on the air tank. Air came blasting out. For some reason, that noise in the stillness took the edge off. What I was doing no longer seemed quite so insane.

Next I took my compass and rope from the red nylon bag and followed Boots Henry's directions. I located the iron post in the northwest quadrant of the property. From there it was ten paces north. How big a pace? I knew that Henry had stood about five-eight. I did my best to adjust my pace to what I thought his might have been. After pacing off ten, I turned east and walked to the quarry's edge. I drove a garden stake into the ground. To it I tied my rope. The rope had knots at seventy-five, eighty, eighty-five, ninety, ninety-five, and one hundred feet, and a short length of chain attached, to weight it down. I threw it over the side.

Then I hauled my gear to a big log that rested near the rim of the quarry. There was a circle of stones next to it, with the charred remains of a fire within. People had picnicked here.

People had died here.

I put the thought out of my mind and began the laborious process of suiting up. First I stripped down to my underwear. The Farmer John, the full wetsuit, went on over that. My skin seemed excessively dry and trying to pull rubber over it was like trying to extricate your fingers from one of those Chinese finger traps. I grunted and groaned and eventually I managed it.

The booties were easier. I'd brought some thin polypropylene socks and I slipped the booties on over them. They snugged beneath the Farmer John at the ankle, sealing up my feet. Just above the right bootie, I strapped the diving knife to my calf.

The hood went on next and tucked under the wetsuit collar. Then I assembled my backpack. This one, like the one I'd worn on my check-out dive, was integral with the buoyancy compensator, the B.C. The air tank fit inside similar heavy circular nylon bands with nonskid rubber on one side. These were attached to the hard plastic backpack frame, as was the B.C. jacket, a blue and yellow nylon bag enclosing an inflatable bladder.

I clamped the tank tight with the nylon bands and tried to move it. It wouldn't budge. I screwed the first stage of the regulator to the air tank's valve. Facing the pressure gauge away from me (that way, if it was defective and exploded under pressure it wouldn't spray glass in my face), I opened the valve. The seal was good; no air was leaking around the valve seat. The gauge didn't blow up. It showed an honest 3,000 psi.

Three thousand pounds per square inch, as opposed to the normal atmospheric pressure at sea level of fourteen point seven. This is what makes diving possible, the ability to fill an aluminum 80—the type of tank I was using—to 3,000 psi. What it means is that eighty cubic feet of air are crammed into a metal cylinder that will ride easily on your back.

An enormous pressure. So great that you always handle a tank with extreme care. There have been terrible accidents. Before the first stage of the regulator is clamped to the tank, all that's holding the pressurized air in is a single valve. Drop the tank and that valve's seal can break. When that happens the action of the escaping air propels the tank forward in reaction, turning it into a runaway missile. A twelve-inch concrete block wall will barely slow it down.

Yet you strap all that contained fury to your back and you forget about it.

Three thousand psi was enough to last a good diver close to an hour. I wasn't going to push it beyond about half that.

I checked to make sure that things weren't backwards, that the regulator hose would be coming over my right shoulder. It was. I attached the power inflator hose, which would allow me to transfer air directly from the tank to the B.C. I put the regulator in my mouth and tried a few breaths. The air flowed smoothly. It was cold and tasted like cotton.

The backpack was ready. I set it on the log behind me, slipped my arms through the straps, and cinched it tight. I leaned forward, testing it for weight and balance. It weighed about as much as my car, but the balance was good. I strapped the weightbelt around my waist. More pounds. I was a very ungainly creature, but all that would change when I hit the water.

I picked up the rest of my gear and got shakily to my feet. My body felt like someone else's. Someone who'd made way too many trips to the pastry table. I plodded over to where I'd tied the rope to the stake and sat on the edge of the quarry.

The final three items. First, fins. You don't want to put your fins on until you're ready to dive. Walk around in them and you're liable to fall on your face with the full weight of your gear on top of you. I rinsed my fins, slipped my bootied feet into them, and pulled the straps tight around my heels.

Second, mask. I spit into mine, rinsed it out and put it on. I ran its edge carefully under the hood, for a positive water seal.

And, finally, gloves. These have to be dead last because, once they're on, your fingers have the dexterity of a two-by-four. I made sure the gloves' cuffs were tight against the wetsuit at my wrist.

The Mr. Spaceman outfit was complete. I ran my left hand through the lanyard that held my dive light and fastened the little clasp that would make sure the lanyard didn't slip off. The light dangled from my wrist.

I picked up my prybar, the single piece of rock-moving equipment I had with me. Unlike Eric Vessey, I didn't own a come-along. But I wouldn't have brought one anyway. I didn't want to get involved in any major excavations down there. If Vessey had already done the grunt work for me, fine.

The prybar went into one of the loops on my B.C. jacket. It was secured in place with a Velcro tab.

One last time, I mentally ran through my equipment list. Everything accounted for. I thought of Patricia and me, readying ourselves for our certification dive, only two and a half weeks earlier. I'd been nervous then.

No point in doing any more thinking. My mask was beginning to fog up and I was sweating inside the suit. I inserted the regulator between my teeth, bit down on it, and took a few breaths. Working fine. I let air into my B.C., using the power inflator. Then I bent forward and tumbled into the quarry.

There was a slight initial shock from the cold. But soon I was as cozy as I'd be in my bathtub, at least in terms of temperature. I bobbed on the surface, buoyed up by my partially inflated B.C. There was still a little fog, so I cracked my mask a tiny bit and let some water in, swirled it around until the fog cleared, and dumped it.

The diving console, an oblong hunk of rubber, hung by my left side. I brought it up to my face. It contained the air pressure gauge, the depth gauge, and a compass. There was also a small digital stopwatch set into its face. I pushed the button that started the stopwatch going. The last thing I wanted was to overstay my welcome at eighty-five feet and wind up with the bends.

The U.S. Navy dive tables said that I could safely stay at that depth for about thirty-five minutes. I planned to make it twenty-five instead. Thirty if I got onto something. That'd give me ample time to get back to the surface at sixty feet per minute, the recommended maximum rate of ascent.

I let the console fall back to my side, touched it once to make sure I knew where it was. Then I detached the plastic gizmo—the one used to manually inflate or deflate the B.C.—from its Velcro strip. I held it above my head with my left hand. With my right I pinched my nose. I pressed the deflate button and the air went out of my B.C. I sank.

Water pressure increases by one atmosphere each thirty-three feet. This means that pressure doubles in the first thirty-three but doesn't double again until you get to ninety-nine. Relative to air pressure at ground level, there is a proportionately greater increase the closer you are to the surface. One result is that you have to equalize pressure on your eardrums much more frequently near the top of your descent than you do lower down. Conversely, you have to be more careful near the top of your ascent. Novices have died disregarding this. If you take a full breath of pressurized air at ten feet, heading up, and hold it in, the amount the air will expand is sufficient to explode your lungs.

I equalized constantly as I descended, forcing air into my pinched nostrils until my ears popped.

Beneath the surface, the quarry felt colder, although it wasn't significantly. It was dark, despite the bright sunny day. There was a good bit of silt suspended in the water and visibility was on the poor side. Using my fins, I turned myself slowly around, in an attempt to reduce the sense of claustrophobia brought on by the dark and the tunnel vision created by the mask.

At ten feet I stopped. I let a little air back into the B.C., so that my buoyancy was just slightly negative. With minimum effort I was able to hang there for a moment, letting myself relax. There was the sensation of weightlessness, of being able to fly, that I'd found so exhilarating the first time I'd dived.

When I felt comfortable, I swam over to the quarry wall and located my rope. I took it in my right hand and moved it until it fell more or less plumb. Then, following the rope, I descended again.

There were ledges in the wall, about every ten feet, so that there was a tapering effect. No telling whether Boots Henry had meant eight-five feet measured straight up and down or on the slant. Compounding the problem were the effects of weathering. Near the top of the quarry, the walls were fairly sheer. The deeper you went, the more places there where chunks of rock had broken off and fallen downward.

At sixty feet I turned on my dive light. Its narrow beam was highly visible in the murk, like a shaft of sunlight in a dusty room.

I continued to descend. There were more and more rock slides. I began to realize that the dive had been a pretty stupid idea. I'd had a crazy notion—perhaps brought on in part by Jordan's saying that I had psychic gifts—that I could just drop down here and somehow be guided by my instincts to the exact spot. It wasn't going to happen. The box was probably buried under tons of rock, the X's might well have long since weathered away. Hopeless.

I almost gave it up, and then I hit my first knot. Seventy-five feet. Well, I'd come this far. I shined the light here and there to examine my immediate surroundings.

A lot of stone, layered with a fine silt that billowed up in clouds when I swam too close. I dropped down another five feet, to the next knot. Now there was some evidence of Vessey's efforts. Places where rocks had been obviously moved. Freshly chipped spots where he'd picked and pried.

I went down to eight-five and looked at the stopwatch. Ten minutes gone. Fifteen to twenty minutes of work time available. I detached the prybar from its loop and held it in my right hand.

A few feet lower, at about eighty-eight, and off to the left, there were a couple of places Vessey had been concentrating on. Slides that had piled up on the ledge at ninety. He'd moved a ton of rock, it looked like, but then he'd had the come-along. I swam over to the first site. My breathing was slow and deep and regular, for the most efficient use of oxygen.

There was a huge boulder. All around it, Vessey had been excavating. It looked like a reasonable thing to do. If the boulder could be dislodged, a large area behind it would be opened up. I played the light around the boulder's perimeter.

Suddenly, there was movement. My body jerked and my heart pounded. I would have jumped backward if I'd been standing. A huge staring eye flashed past mine. I swung the prybar, but the resistance of the water turned it into a slow-motion move. I sucked frantically at the regulator.

It was a bass, a good-sized one. He'd been hovering, motionless, beneath the boulder and I hadn't seen him. He was probably prepared to tough it out until I put the light on him. Then he wiggled his tail a few times and he was past me and lost in the gloom.

My breathing and heartbeat slowed again. But I realized just how out of my element I was. Fish lived down here. They could breathe.

I returned my attention to the boulder. It seemed as though, if I was able to dislodge some of the surrounding rocks, it might tip and go bounding to the bottom of the quarry. That looked like it had been Vessey's plan. Worth a try, anyway.

The trick would be to loosen the rocks restraining the boulder and be in a position so that when it came loose, it didn't crush me underneath it. Things might weigh less underwater, but this monster didn't weigh enough less to make much difference.

My plan was to start from near the middle and work outward. I maneuvered myself so that I could reach in with the prybar. Then I got very nervous. The boulder loomed above me like the fist of God. There was no telling when it might pop free. I made a strategic withdrawal.

I examined the situation again. There were some fair-sized rocks at the edges of the boulder. I could work them without getting in the way, which seemed like a more prudent tactic. I inserted the prybar behind the first of them and levered it. It resisted and I pulled harder, then harder still. I was beginning to think I wouldn't be able to budge it when it shot out with considerable force. Enough to have stunned me had I been in the way. As it was, it bounced harmlessly down the slope of the rock slide.

Meanwhile, the boulder creaked and shifted in my direction. I shrank back instinctively. Any sound underwater seems ominous. This one was particularly so.

It was evident that the boulder was poised rather precariously on its supports. I swam to the other side by going up over the top. No need to take chances.

I located another rock that looked critical to the balance. I jammed the prybar behind it. This one was lodged even more tightly than the last. I braced my feet and pulled on the lever for all I was worth. It gave an inch, another inch, then it too shot straight out.

The sudden release of tension threw me backward. My tank slammed against stone and my outbreath popped the regulator from my mouth. I flailed in a panic as I took in water, searching for the regulator. Then I remembered my training. What to do in this situation. They'd pounded it into us. I bent forward and to the side, moved my right arm back in a sweeping motion. I hooked onto the hose, ran my hand along it until I found the regulator and guided it back into my mouth. The cold, dry air tasted like the essence of life. I coughed a couple of times through the mouthpiece and I was okay.

The boulder was teetering. There were grating sounds of rock on rock. I backed away. Some small stones clattered down the slope. And then it came free. Slowly, as if rising up and stretching its arms and legs. There was a point of perfect suspension before it finally toppled and went crunching toward the quarry bottom. The noise rattled in my ears.

I was looking at a virgin section of wall. There was a U-shaped space in the rockslide where the boulder had been resting. I swam in for a closer look, being careful not to nudge any of the remaining stones. I could easily upset the new equilibrium and end up with my leg pinned under more weight than I could move.

Visibility was very poor. I had to examine the area from a distance of a couple of feet. I was so close that I almost didn't see what I was looking for.

Henry had only been concealing a box with one crummy piece of paper inside. So I'd supposed I was looking for a little rock with some small X's cut into it. It was actually a rectangular slab stood on end, and the X's were three feet high. I'd only been able to see them because I spotted the point where the two lines crossed to form each letter.

I finned backward until I could take in the whole thing. For a moment, I hung there. As I played the light over the rectangular slab, I felt a chill, and it wasn't from the water. I'd done it. It was a near impossibility, but I'd done it.

The slab was large, but not especially thick. I estimated that I could easily dislodge it with the prybar. I glanced at the stopwatch. At the outside, I had a fifteen-minute cushion. Best not to waste any more time. I swam back toward the slab.

I never made it.

Visibility in the silty water was poor, but it wouldn't have made any difference if I'd been swimming in the gin-like clarity of one of Florida's springs. When you dive, there are blind spots you can't do anything about. One of them is directly above you. That's where he must have been hovering. I had no way of knowing for how long.

I was about six feet from the rock when he made his move. A simple, effective way of quickly disabling a diver. He reached down from above and ripped off my mask.

The sudden change blinded me. In the tiniest fraction of an instant, the thought flashed through my mind that I'd made a terrible mistake. I'd offered myself up as bait. Now a very big fish was about to take it. And he had all the advantages.

Instinctively, I went on the attack. I twisted my body away from where I thought he'd be and brought my right arm around. There he was, to my blinded eyes just a meaningless black blob. I struck out with the prybar, aiming as best I could for the head.

But he could see. He saw the bar coming, slowed by the water. It was a simple matter for him to grab it. He snatched it from my hand like he'd sneezed and was taking a Kleenex. With his other hand he tore the regulator out of my mouth. I felt a slight tug and then there was a pop and the water was filled with an explosion of bubbles.

I knew immediately what had happened. He was very strong and he'd yanked the regulator's second stage—and my mouthpiece—out of its hose. My air supply was cut off.

The rest was acted out purely from instinct. I'd learned the techniques in my certification course, but no course in the world could have prepared me for this. My conscious mind shut down and the naked will to survive kicked in.

I'd just breathed in when I lost the regulator. That undoubtedly saved my life. It gave me one precious breath to work with. I windmilled my arm, got the regulator hose in the crook of my elbow, and directed the stream of bubbles toward my assailant. What with the water's normal cloudiness, the extra silt we'd stirred up, and the bubbles, visibility dropped to zero.

I began to let my breath out. At that depth, my buoyancy dropped quickly past equilibrium and I sank. He could come after me, following my trail of bubbles. If so, I was dead. I hit the slope of the quarry wall, bounced and rolled deeper into the pit.

My body turned so that my back was up. When it did, I detached the accordion-pleated B.C. inflator hose from its Velcro strip and clutched it in my hand.

I settled to rest in the rocks, face down. This was the critical moment, when I'd find out if he was coming or not. I waited until I couldn't wait any more. The remainder of my final breath was dribbling out the side of my mouth. My eardrums were close to bursting.

He didn't come.

And since he couldn't see down here, as long as the bubbles continued to rise there was no reason he wouldn't assume that I'd gulped water and quickly drowned.

I might be able to breathe from the bare, bubbling hose. But I might not. I didn't know if the unregulated pressure would be so high it would blow my lungs apart. Besides, if I bit down on the hose, my assailant might notice that the bubbles were now rising in a pattern and figure out what had happened. I had to try something else.

So I slipped the mouthpiece on the B.C. inflator hose between my lips. I was about to try something I'd read about but never practiced. It was my only chance. I pushed the button that opened the valve. With the last of my air I blew in, to clear out the water. Then I inhaled, not knowing what I'd get a lungful of.

It was air. Wonderful sweet air from the B.C. The technique worked. I was going to live, at least for the next few moments.

Once I knew that, the first thing I did was pinch my nose and relieve the horrible pressure in my ears. That in itself was almost like being reborn. Then I stopped running on instinct and forced myself to think.

The air was running out of my tank at an alarming rate, and I'd already used up close to half of it. I squeezed the damaged hose, slowing the rate of loss as much as I thought I could without attracting the attention of whoever was above me. But wasted air continued to bubble away. I didn't have a lot of time.

On the other hand, if I tried to ascend too soon I'd run into my attacker once again, down here or after I reached the surface. Either way, he'd have no difficulty finishing me off. I had to stay under as long as I possibly could.

I maneuvered the light and the console so that they were right next to my face and I could read the gauges and stopwatch without my mask. My safety cushion was down to five minutes. Worse yet, I was at ninty-seven feet, deeper than I'd expected to go. There was the bends to worry about.

Yet there was nothing to do but wait. I lay there and waited, helpless, fighting panic every second. Resisting the urge to rise was the most difficult thing I've ever done.

I used the power inflator to let air into the B.C. and then I sucked it out. The tank pressure dropped steadily. By the time it fell into the red, meaning less than 500 psi left, I had to take my chances and act. I turned myself over, gathered together a collection of heavy rocks, as best I could in my half-blinded condition, and stuffed them into the pockets of the B.C. jacket. Then I inflated the B.C. until I was afraid the bladder would burst, hoping the weight of the rocks would counterbalance the excess air enough that I wouldn't bob to the surface like a cork. That would be certain death.

The B.C. filled but I stayed put.

The air stream from the tank slowed, then came to a virtual stop. All that was left was what was in the B.C. If I rationed it, it'd last for a while. But if the other guy was still down here, I was dead. I stuck the stopwatch in front of my face again. The news was bad. I was over five minutes into borrowed time already. I had to go up or the bends was a certainty.

I didn't even have a free hand for my remaining weapon, the dive knife—not that it would have done me much good blinded. But I needed one hand to work the inflator hose, my air supply. With the other, I began to jettison rocks. I started to ascend.

I soon passed the point where I'd discovered the slab. I aimed the light over there. It was difficult to tell without my mask, but it looked like there was a hole where the slab had been. Frankly, I really didn't give a damn.

My assailant was gone, too. Which was a relief, but the rest was still a very tricky business. The air expanded as I rose. That gave me more air, but it also made me more buoyant. I'd cast off a rock, pick up too much speed and have to hold myself back with my flippers. I didn't dare slow my progress by dumping any air.

Eighty feet. Sixty. Forty. Twenty. The closer I got to the

surface, the more the water lightened. I was going to make it. I concentrated hard over the last twenty feet, making sure never to hold my breath.

A safe ascent from close to a hundred feet would have taken a little under two minutes. Because of my struggles with buoyancy, over five had passed when I broke the surface, slurped a lungful of normal, everyday air, and cut loose a cry of happiness. The sky was a brilliant, astonishing blue, the first spring leaves a soft green that glowed and pulsed with life.

It had been twenty-five minutes since I was attacked. My companion might still be around, stowing the last of his gear. If he was, now would be the perfect time to put a bullet in my head and end this nonsense once and for all. But somehow, it didn't matter any more. I floated briefly, offering my body as a target.

There was no bullet.

I swam slowly to the edge of the quarry and pulled myself out. It was a strain. I was exhausted and the heavy equipment felt like an elephant on my back.

When I finally managed to get myself up onto the rim, I scanned the clearing for the first time. Except for my car, it was empty. There was only the gentle breeze and the raucous cawing of a single crow perched at the crown of an oak.

An ill omen, crows. So I grinned and raised my thumb to him. My adversary must have left the scene only moments before.

I knew I had to get out of my wetsuit. In the water, it was protection. Out here, it was robbing my body of heat. Already I'd begun to shiver.

In my weakened condition, it was a laborious task, but I did it. I stripped off everything, including my T-shirt and briefs.

The long ascent would work in my favor but still, I'd been under ten minutes longer than the U.S. Navy tables deemed safe.

Naked and spent, I lay in the sun, waiting for the first symptoms of the bends.

CHAPTER
—18—

Whenever you dive, there is a buildup of nitrogen in the blood and tissues. This is a natural process, the result of the body being able to dissolve more of the gas under increased pressure. After a safe dive, it is slowly released and expelled through the lungs, allowing the nitrogen level to once again normalize for ground level.

Problems arise when the diver either stays down too long at too great a depth or ascends too fast. Under these conditions, the nitrogen can come out of solution too quickly. Bubbles can form and expand. The effect is similar to shaking a soft drink can, then opening it. The shaking builds up pressure inside the can; opening it suddenly decreases the pressure. Carbon dioxide bubbles come rapidly out of solution and the soda sprays everywhere.

Imagine that happening inside your body and you've got a good mental picture of the bends.

The bends is an unpredictable beast. Variables include water temperature; the degree to which the dive was unsafe; the physical condition of the diver; the presence in the bloodstream of contaminants such as drugs and alcohol; and blind, stupid luck. One diver may get bent even though the Navy tables—which are based on a statistical average—said he should have been safe. Another can violate the tables all to hell and walk away unharmed. You never know.

In a very mild case, the nitrogen bubbles are small and the diver may notice almost nothing. In a severe case, blood vessels rupture and tissues are torn apart. Unless the person so afflicted is near a special decompression chamber, death is inevitable.

The first place the bends is normally felt is in the joints. Usually, symptoms are apparent at once, though there may possibly be a slight lag.

I'd been lying by the quarry for a while, had soaked up a good deal of solar energy. Amazingly, I was still alive, my body hadn't twisted itself into an impossible knot. I felt strong enough to get to my feet.

My left knee hurt, but I could walk on it. I'd been slightly bent, I was sure, and I could only hope that the knee was the extent of it. If this was the worst that happened, I'd gotten off easier than I deserved.

I hoofed it over to my car and got into some clothes. I didn't bother with the equipment. Then, working the clutch a little shakily, I drove back to the Institute. One name repeated itself over and over in my head. Drake Vessey, Drake Vessey.

I barged into Dr. Slate's office without knocking. She was bent over some papers on her desk. She didn't look wet. I no longer really suspected her, but I had to be positive.

"Where have you been for the past hour?" I demanded.

"Mr. Swift, what—"

I leaned my knuckles on the edge of her desk. "Just tell me," I said icily, spacing each word out.

"How dare you—"

"*Where!?*"

That got through to her. She said, "Oh, for goodness sake, I've been right here. I—"

"Can you prove it?"

She got to her feet. "Now see here," she said. She was angry, but a little concerned too, since she couldn't be sure exactly what I was up to. I continued to give her my coldest stare.

"Grover knows I was here," she said evenly.

"Take me to him."

She hesitated.

"*Now!*"

Without another word, she led me out back. Jordan was seated on one of the benches near the fountain. Paula Slate and I stood before him.

"Grover," she said, "would you kindly attest to my whereabouts during the past hour."

He ignored her. Instead, he said to me, "Mr. Swift, sit down. I've been expecting you. It's all coming to an end, isn't it?"

I didn't know what to say. Paula and I just stared at him.

He chuckled. "Could you leave us alone, Dr. Slate?" he said. "Mr. Swift and I have much to talk about."

"Hold on a minute," I said. "Somebody just tried to kill me."

Paula gaped at me. She had no idea what was going on. She was innocent.

"Kill . . ." she said.

"In the quarry," I said. "Someone tried to drown me."

Jordan, however, wasn't fazed. He waved his hand and said, "I'm not surprised. But I assure you it was not Dr. Slate. She's been here the whole time."

I took a deep breath and let it out. I turned to Paula Slate.

"I'm sorry," I said. "But I had to be sure. A half hour ago I was as close to dead as you can get and make it back."

She looked stunned. She nodded and didn't say anything.

"Now, if we might, Dr. Slate . . ." Jordan said.

She nodded again, turned and walked back into the house. Jordan patted a spot on the bench next to him. I sat down. For a moment, he just looked at me. Looked into my eyes, looked deep into my soul, it felt like.

The kindly old face. The white hair and beard. The silly sombrero. It was the image from my dream, my protector. I suddenly wondered if he'd known all the time that I was down there, fighting for my life. How could he? And yet, why not? He'd been able to project pictures into my head.

Two thoughts collided violently in my mind. *He* was the one, he'd somehow killed Vessey, he was behind everything. *No!* Impossible! A frail old man, a kindly man. No, he'd *saved* me. He'd not only known I was down there, he'd been with me and he'd guided me, made sure I'd done all the right things.

No. . . . Impossible. . . .

My head was spinning. I held on to the back of the bench for support.

"I'm happy to see that you're still alive," he said, and he was. My doubts vanished. "I suppose this is all kind of a shock to your belief system."

My power of speech was returning. "Yeah, you might say that," I said.

He smiled and shook his head gently. "Money," he said. "Such a foolish pursuit."

"You know about the money?"

"Yes, I know."

"Is there anything you don't know?"

He smiled again. "A great deal," he said. "There is at least as much that I don't know as you *do* know."

"I don't understand. What's that supposed to mean?"

"Me, for example. You know who I am."

"Huh?"

He didn't say anything more, just looked into me with that look. Who *he* was? It made no sense, yet. . . . A strange feeling came over me, like I was slipping once again into a different state of consciousness. It was the same feeling I'd had when I was looking down at the quarry and it seemed to turn into a black hole. And then the goosebumps raised up along my arms. I *did* know. I didn't know how I knew, but that was a question I was no longer asking.

"Jarvis," I said softly.

He nodded. "Very good," he said. "You see, I was right about you."

I was tongue-tied. "But—" I said. "Wh— I don't—" And then, finally, "Why'd you kill him?"

"Yes," he said, "that's where it begins, isn't it? Do you believe in justifiable homicide, Mr. Swift?"

"No."

"An unequivocal answer. I like that. I'm not sure I believe in it anymore, either. But I was a much younger man then. At the time, it seemed the only appropriate response."

I might as well have been nailed to my seat. The Vessey case, my own close brush with death, the bends, all of it drifted to the back of my mind.

"What happened?" I asked.

For once, his eyes ceased their relentless boring into mine. They turned inward.

"Boots Henry was my friend," Jordan said. "I knew about his past, of course, but by the time I met him he had changed. Or so I thought. He was deeply involved with spiritualism, which was really the forerunner of modern psychic research. Crude. Much of it hoax. But it kindled an interest in things beyond the reach of our physical senses.

"I was thirty years old. I'd done nothing with my life so far and had no idea what I was going to do with the rest of it. Then I met Boots Henry and an entire new dimension was opened up for me.

"It was my sister, Sara, who first became involved with him. She'd always been a very spiritual person. Very quiet, introverted, but kind and gentle. A rare person. She was highly attracted to what he was doing. She drew me into it. The three of us became extraordinarily close."

Not as close as you believed, I thought. Sara had a big role in the diaries. "Brother J." didn't.

He paused. I don't think he was any longer aware that I was there on the bench with him. His expression changed. For the first time, I could see that he felt anger and pain, just like anyone else. I didn't dare speak for fear of breaking the spell.

"Unfortunately," he said with an unconcealed bitterness that reached back nearly fifty years, "he was highly attracted to her as well. In the physical sense. Despite all the dabbling in the spiritual realm, he continued to be ruled by his baser desires. He hoarded his gold and seduced his women. At heart, he was the common criminal he'd always been.

"Poor Sara never knew what happened to her. She was that trusting, and she had no experience of men. She got pregnant.

"Once she did, Henry discarded her like so much rubbish. He closed the doors of this place, to both of us. The bond that we'd felt vanished as if it had never been.

"Sara had a nervous collapse, but there was nothing we could do. We had no money. I helped her through the pregnancy as best I could. It was a horror. By the time she gave birth, she had wasted away to almost nothing. She . . . she lived only a few more days. They couldn't save her. I couldn't, as much as I loved her. No one could. She wanted to die. Watching it happen was the most unbearable experience of my life.

"I named the baby Sara, after her mother. I brought her home as soon as I could. I cared for her through those difficult first weeks, planning carefully what I was going to do. As soon as I felt she could travel, I went after Boots Henry. What do you think about justifiable homicide now?"

I cleared my throat. "I don't know," I said honestly.

"Nor do I. But, as I'm sure you know by now, Henry paid for my sister's life with his own. I searched the house, this house, taking whatever money and valuables I could quickly lay my hands on. All told, it came to close to ten thousand, which was a substantial amount in those days.

"The same night, I got little Sara and left for California. We never looked back. California was wide open then. The country was headed for war. People were flooding in from everywhere. I became Grover Jordan, another immigrant hick with a motherless child. No one asked any questions.

"The difference was that I had a stake. I decided to go to college. That's where I spent World War II. Since I was Sara's sole support, I didn't have to fight. I went to school, worked nights in a munitions plant, stretched the money I'd taken from Boots Henry.

"And I discovered that my interest in the nonmaterial world stayed with me. I majored in psychology. After I had my B.A., I just wanted to keep on going. I got my master's, and then my doctorate.

"By then, the war was over, and millions of men were suddenly back home. College got very popular, because of the G.I. Bill. There was a tremendous demand for teachers. I got a job without any trouble. When I wasn't teaching, I was doing some very elementary research in the field of ESP, which was brand new at that time. I was happy, I suppose. We were happy. I might have gone on like that for a long while, except. . . ."

He paused. A faraway look came over him. The pause went on for so long that I finally said, "Except?"

"Except that I was in an automobile accident," he said slowly. "I was out for three days. When I came to, I was a different person. I'd had one of those near-death experiences you read about. In fact, I'd traveled to what I now consider the interface between life and death. I remember clearly being poised on the brink, that it could have gone either way.

"And at that point, Boots Henry appeared to me."

I was flabbergasted, and I must have looked it, because he smiled and said, "It was quite a shock to me, too. I would more likely have expected my sister, or almost anyone else. But I saw his face as clearly as I see yours now. And he spoke to me.

"He told me I was forgiven for what I'd done. He said he'd been the one who was wrong, but that it was part of a larger plan that he could see only after he died. He said that I must return to the world of the living, because there was much I had yet to do. And he was going to help me. That was to be his last act in our little drama.

"He told me I was to return to Virginia and found the Institute. That this place was its natural home. That I could purchase it for a pittance, he'd see to that. That I would do important things here.

"When I regained consciousness, that's exactly what I did. I'd grown a beard and aged ten years, so there was little chance anyone would remember me. I'd had few enough friends to begin with, and no family left alive. So I gathered up Sara and we came home."

I'd heard stranger tales, but not many. There was another lengthy pause, which I eventually ended.

"End of story?" I said.

He came back from wherever he had gone in his mind. He grinned. "Not exactly," he said.

He got up and motioned me to follow him. We headed down toward the garden area.

"Little Sara was ten when we moved here. But she grew up, of course. I don't know if it was genetics, or her childhood, or what, but she was a wild one. I couldn't control her. She ran away when she was in her late teens, went back to California. I'd get letters occasionally.

"Apparently, she thought she was barren, and with her lifestyle she must have been close to it. She was well into her thirties before she ever got pregnant. At that point she rediscovered her uncle. She wasn't going to be much of a mother and she knew it. So she brought her son here and left him with me."

"Danny," I said.

He nodded. "He's a good kid. I've never minded. Though it's kind of odd when you think about it. I raised Boots Henry's daughter, and now I'm raising his grandson."

It was more than odd. But there was a kind of justice to it. Grover Jordan, the kindly old man in the white sombrero, was, after all, a murderer.

"I like him, too," I said.

"Oh? You've had a chance to talk to him?"

"Yeah. He's been playing hooky this week, I think. He told me he wants to be a detective."

Jordan smiled. "He has that kind of mind," he said. "Restless. Like mine. Or yours."

We crossed the garden and stood in front of Boots Henry's crypt. There was a heavy wrought-iron gate across its front. Jordan pulled it open and gestured for me to go inside. I hesitated.

"There's no danger from the dead," he said.

"All the same," I said, "after what happened to me this afternoon. . . . Is there some reason for this?"

"Yes."

I didn't like it, but I went into the crypt. It was dank and gloomy in there, if that's not flogging the obvious. In the center of the thing was a heavy granite sarcophagus, resting on a stone slab. There were carved stone figures at its head and feet. Guardian spirits or demons, I didn't know. Jordan walked over and rested his arm on the coffin. This was turning into a Grade *B* horror movie. I hung back near the entrance, ready to run for it if something jumped out at me.

"Boots Henry," he said with a gesture at the stone box.

"Uh huh."

He smiled. "Don't worry," he said, "I'm not going to show you his bones. But there is one thing remaining, isn't there?"

"Uh, I don't know." I'm not sure I'd truly understood the meaning of the word *befuddled* before that moment.

"The gold, of course," he said.

"The . . . gold . . . ?"

"Don't fail me now, Mr. Swift."

He grasped the head of the carving nearest him and twisted it. Nothing happened immediately. But then he put both hands on the sarcophagus and pushed it. It pivoted on some invisible hinges and I was looking at a black hole. It went through the slab and into the ground.

"Henry told me one other thing when he appeared to me," Jordan said. "He told me where the gold was."

"I— I don't believe this," I stammered.

"You should. After all you've been through. But if you don't want to, there's an alternative explanation. Perhaps Henry had dropped some hint about the gold, back when we were supposedly friends, and I'd forgotten about it. Perhaps my accident jarred that memory loose. My imagination could have done all the rest. Does that square a little better with your rational detective's mind?"

"I don't know," I said.

I stood there, staring at the hole like it was the gateway to madness.

"Well," he said, "don't you want to see the gold?"

I wasn't at all sure that that *was* what was down in the hole. Even if it was, I wasn't sure that I wanted to go down there to see it. But I went anyway. The loose ends of the case were tying themselves up and the gold was central to everything. I had to personally verify its existence.

I walked slowly over to the hole. Jordan reached down and came up with two flashlights. He handed me one. He'd obviously prepared for this moment.

"A nice touch, don't you think?" he said. "Building his crypt above his hoard."

I wasn't in a light mood and I told him so. He shrugged and invited me to follow him into the ground, which I did. We went down a short ladder and found ourselves in a tiny room with a stone foundation. I had to stoop over a little. There was a small door at one end of the room, but beyond it only dirt. Jordan played his light over the scene.

"Henry's design," he said. "The timbers rotted and the passageway sealed up. It's the only way into the vault. I excavated it myself when I first moved here. And then I filled it back in."

"The vault's . . . empty?" I said, not quite able to believe.

"Disappointed?" he asked.

I didn't know what to say.

He motioned with his light and we went back outside. On our way up to the house, he told me the rest of the story.

"Once I got into the vault I immediately moved the gold, of course," he said. "Into safe deposit boxes. Then I contacted a broker in New York. Over the years, little by little, I've sold it off."

"A little at a time," I said. "That's why the sales never attracted any attention. That's why Vessey thought the coins were still here."

"I needed the money. First to renovate this place. Then to set up the Institute. Then for operating expenses for the past thirty years. I told people I had a trust fund and no one questioned it. In addition, I've been able to provide modest support for some other organizations doing research similar to mine."

"Jesus," I said, shaking my head. "It's all been for nothing."

"Greed," he said. "Everyone believes what they need to believe."

"How much is left?"

"Not much. My feeling has always been that money is the great corrupter. That's why I've never told anyone about the gold. Too much chance of attracting people here who were interested only in it. People like Eric Vessey, constantly scheming to get their hands on it.

"By the same token, I've also felt that if I passed over leaving a great deal of money behind, there was a good chance it would be squandered. Better to leave the Jordan Institute itself as my legacy, with someone in charge who would work hard to keep it running on a self-sustaining basis. That's why Dr. Slate is here. She's intelligent, an excellent organizer, and dedicated to the work. If anyone can preserve the Institute, she can."

"So what happened?" I said, more to myself than to him. "Vessey, working through Paula Slate, comes to you and offers to buy the place, thinking you don't know about the gold and he's going to make a killing. He says you can lease the Institute back for peanuts and keep a couple of million dollars. You can't imagine how he knows about the gold, but to his chagrin you turn him down flat. End of discussion. I suppose you don't know yet how he found out."

He shrugged. "Your turn to enlighten me," he said.

"He found out the same way I did. Henry wrote all about the gold in his diaries. They're in the U.Va. library, for anyone to read. Drake Vessey came across them while he was doing some research and told his brother. Eric took the information Drake had given him and tried to work a scheme so that he'd end up with most of the gold himself.

"That sounds like Eric," Jordan said. "And where does the quarry come in?"

"Right, you don't know about that. Well, you thought your refusal would be the end of it. But it wasn't. Eric had to have that gold.

"So he decided to come at the problem from another angle. He kept up his pressure on Dr. Slate. At the same time, he tried to find out where the coins were actually buried. It seems your friend Henry believed that he was going to return to this life, but was worried that he might not remember certain important details when he did. To help his future self, he wrote out directions to the gold and hid them in a box in the quarry, which wasn't yet full of water.

"Then, he recorded directions to the box in his diary. Those directions let Eric know approximately where to dive. He decided that the box would be a good bargaining card, so he went after it on his own." I shook my head. "That useless box."

"And he found it?"

"No," I said. "He drowned before he did. *I* found it. Today."

He shook his head sadly. "And someone tried to kill you for it."

"Uh huh. I've got a pretty good idea who."

"It must be Eric's brother. Did he kill Eric too?"

"I don't have a lot of hard evidence, but it sure looks that way. He'd been involved since the beginning. Eric had a big fight with somebody just before he died, and Morgan's pretty sure it was Drake.

"At the least, he's almost certainly the one who attacked me in Eric's house three nights ago. *And* he's almost certainly the one who tried to kill *my* brother."

He looked at me with shock.

"Oh yeah," I said, "there's that as well. Somebody shot my brother last night, thinking it was me. Drake Vessey, I'm pretty sure.

"Plus he *had* to be the one in the quarry today. Only three people knew I was coming out here. Paula's time is accounted for and Morgan's too small.

"That leaves Drake. He must have followed me yesterday,

after he knew for sure that I was on the trail of the gold. Assume that he saw me pick up the dive shop owner and drive down to the shop. It's dark along that street, so he could have parked and watched for a while. I don't know his car, wouldn't have spotted it. He would have seen us load the equipment into my VW. That meant I was ready to dive for the box myself, which meant that I was too close for comfort. So he hung around my house, hoping I'd come out and he could take a shot at me. But my brother took the bullet instead.

"Today he would have learned of his mistake, and then I made things easy for him. I told him where I was going. So he didn't have to follow me that closely. As long as he was patient, all he had to do was hide his gear in the woods near the quarry and then wait for me to show up.

"The rest we know. Now the only problem I have is proving it. Fortunately, I know the chief of police in Albemarle County. He's a good man. Tough, smart. I think together we can make a case."

We'd stopped by the fountain.

"Mr. Swift," Jordan said, "I don't quite know what to say. I'm sorry for all this. I should have suspected what Eric might do. How much we might have avoided if I'd just told him he was wasting his time. It was foolish not to."

I held up my hand. "No apology necessary," I said. "You haven't done anything."

"Yes, I have. I killed a man. Are you going to turn me in, Mr. Swift?"

"For something you did in 1940? I don't think there's much point. And if what you say is true, you've fulfilled Boots Henry's destiny for him."

He made a slight bow in my direction. "I was certainly right about you," he said. "When . . . this is all over, perhaps you'd like to become involved with us here at the Institute."

"Ah, well, we'll see. But there is something you could do for me in the meantime. Use your psychic power to direct us to some hard evidence against Drake Vessey. The gun he used on my brother, or something like that."

"Hmmm," he said.

And then Paula Slate came hurrying out of the house.

"Grover," she said. "Swift." She was breathless. There was no animosity toward me in her voice.

"What is it?" Jordan asked.

She looked from him to me and back again, then said, "Danny. He's gone."

I felt something cold and terrible in the pit of my stomach.

"What do you mean?" I said.

The words came fast and furious. "He's been home sick this week," she said. "Though he's always in and out. I indulge him a little that way. But he never goes far. The house and the grounds. I can always find him.

"When you came back from the quarry in the state you were in, I realized that I hadn't seen him in a while and I got a little worried so I went looking for him. I can't find him anywhere."

"Did you look down by the quarry?" I asked.

She nodded vigorously. "Everywhere," she said. "All his favorite places. He's not here." She was on the verge of hysteria.

Take charge.

"Do you think—" Jordan began.

"Take me to a phone," I said sharply.

Nobody moved, so I grabbed Slate's arm and shoved her toward the house. That got her going. I hurried up the marble steps after her.

Assume the worst. Assume that Danny had seen me arrive or, more likely, been out playing near the quarry when I pulled in there. Or, more likely yet, chanced on the scene at the quarry after I'd gone in and perhaps after Drake had gone after me. He'd recognize my car, so assume he'd hung around to see what was going on. Drake would come out of the water without me. Danny might not know immediately that something was wrong. He might ask Drake what was happening. Drake, thinking I was dead, would see the kid as a very inconvenient witness. And then. . . .

I refused to think about *and then*.

I followed Paula Slate into her office. She stood next to the phone, wringing her hands, confused and terrified at the same time. Jordan was right behind us, his placid exterior shattered. I felt sorry for them, but it wouldn't do any good to spell out my fears. And there was no time. I dialled

Campbell's office. *Be there, Ridley,* I said to myself. *Come on, be there.*

He was.

"Rid," I said, "it's Swift. I can't explain. Please, trust me. Is that pet judge of yours, whatshisname, is he there today?"

"Yeah, I think so."

I felt a slight relief.

"Get him to sign a no-knock for Drake Vessey's house." I told him where it was. "Suspicion of kidnapping."

Slate gasped. Jordan stared at me.

"What the hell is this, Swift!?" Campbell said. "We never talked about no kid—"

"Vessey's the one we want," I cut in. "The one who shot my brother, too. The gun should be there."

"Good*damn* it! I can't just—"

"*Ridley!*" I shouted. "He's the *one!* It's an eleven-year-old kid, for Christ's sake! Get the goddamn warrant!"

There must have been more than a little hysteria in my own voice, because he immediately said, "All right. You got it."

"How soon?"

"I don't know. Fast as I can make it up and find the judge."

"Hurry, Rid. I'm down in Nelson. I'll meet you at Vessey's as quick as I can get there."

I hung up. Slate and Jordan were staring at me like I'd emerged from the mind of Steven Spielberg.

"You two stay put—" I started to say. Then I said, "Never mind, come on with me. Let's *go!*"

They moved it. The fastest available car was Slate's Toyota, so we took that. I drove, pushing the car as much as I dared, hoping this wouldn't be the day I came under a radar gun.

Along the way the old images kept flickering on and off. A blond teenager lying in a pool of blood. Patricia with her head caved in. A bright young detective raped and beaten within an inch of her life. *No more violence,* I prayed. *Please, no more violence. Not Danny, please, not a little kid.*

The hardest part was threading our way through the traffic around Charlottesville to get north of town, where Drake Vessey lived. There were endless lights and city police cars to contend with. I drove my hardest, but it was still over forty-five minutes before we got there.

It was a small, one-story white frame house, set back from the road on about two cleared acres, with woods all around. Ridley and his men were already there.

The boy was with Ridley, in the chief's cruiser. When he recognized the Toyota, he came flying out. He jumped into Grover Jordan's arms and squeezed the old man for all he was worth. Slate got in from behind and the three of them stood there, hugging and crying.

I went over to Campbell.

"Mind telling me what this is all about?" he said politely.

"Later," I said. "What happened here?"

"When we arrived," he said, "somebody came out the side. I guess your man Vessey. He jumped in a four-wheel-drive Subaru and drove straight into the woods. I didn't have the right car for pursuit, so he's gone. But he won't get far. Once we found the kid, I put out a pick-up call, local and state."

"Subaru *wagon?*" I asked.

"Uh huh."

The 4WD Japanese wagon Paula Slate had seen the night Eric Vessey died. Hard evidence.

"You need to get him," I said. "He killed his brother."

"You can back it?"

"I can back it. He's the one who shot Ashley too."

Campbell immediately got on the radio and passed along the new information about Drake Vessey, along with my detailed description. Consider suspect armed and dangerous. Approach with caution. Kidnapping for sure, suspicion of attempted murder and homicide.

"Where was the kid?" I asked.

"Locked in the root cellar. He's fine."

"What'd he tell you?"

"The guy was diving in a quarry on the kid's grandfather's property. The same quarry where that guy drowned?" I nodded and he made a small grunting sound. "Kid discovered him there. He was very confused because he saw *your* car and was expecting you. Then this stranger came up out of the water, holding a little box. Kid asked him what was going on and the guy eventually snatched him and brought him here. The rest you know."

"Why didn't Danny run away from Vessey?"

Campbell shrugged. "Said he was the nicest guy. Looked

like Clark Kent. Vessey told him he was your friend and the two of you had been diving looking for the box and that you'd be coming up shortly, after you got through digging out something else. Kid helped him get his equipment off and everything. Then they went and fetched his car, which was parked in the woods somewhere. Vessey got his gear loaded up and pulled a gun. Kid was scared. I don't blame him."

"Thanks, Rid," I said. "Thanks for trusting me."

Danny had finished the family reunion. He came over to me and hugged me around the waist. I patted the top of his head, tried to smooth down the little cowlick, but it popped right back up again.

The boy had helped Vessey get his equipment off, thereby cutting the time needed to do it and enabling Vessey to leave the scene that much sooner. There was a good chance he'd inadvertently saved my life, while almost losing his own.

"I didn't know what happened to you, Swift," he said. "I was afraid."

"Hey, I'm doing fine," I said. "You're just too good a detective, son."

"I'm not sure that's what I want to be anymore."

I laughed. "Well, think it over, Danny. You're plenty brave enough, I'll tell you that."

There wasn't much else to do. Paula Slate and the two Jordans took her car and went home. Ridley notified the Nelson sheriff to have someone guard the Institute until Vessey was captured. Meanwhile, his men searched the house, but didn't come up with a gun or the worthless box.

Campbell drove me to town. On the way, I told him everything. We went to his office and prepared a statement and I signed it. He even had a couple of his men drive down to the Institute and retrieve my car for me. Such service.

"You know, I don't much like the way this one went down, Swift," he said when we were finished. "You damn near got yourself killed, and who knows what would've happened to the kid if you *had* wound up at the bottom of that quarry for good."

"Well," I said, "I don't feel great about what happened to Danny. But he is okay. And we wouldn't have Vessey if I hadn't flushed him out."

"We don't *have* him yet."

"You know what I mean."

"Yeah, I know what you mean. But you know what *I* mean too. This was a grandstand stunt, Swift. Maybe it worked. This time. I don't want there should be a *next* time, is what I'm saying to you. You got it?"

"Sure, Rid," I said. "I got it. Now can I go? I've had kind of a rough day."

"All right, go ahead," he said.

I walked to the door. Limped a little. My knee was still stiff. When my hand was on the knob, I turned back.

"Ridley," I said. "Get that bastard off the street, will you? It gives me the creeps, him out there."

CHAPTER
——19——

The phone woke me up.

After leaving Campbell's office, I'd checked in with Ashley at the hospital. He was hanging tough. His room was now brightened by several vases full of flowers, bless Patricia's little Irish heart.

Next I screwed up my courage and drove to Patricia's house.

I finally had to tell her the whole story, of course. I knew she'd be furious. And she was. She stormed around like a maniac for about two minutes. Then her anger ebbed. She does have a temper, but she's basically too level-headed to let it control her for long.

She soon accepted that, despite my stupidity and having had to lie to her, things hadn't turned out all that badly. The case was solved, Danny was safe, Drake Vessey would soon be apprehended, and I'd come out of it with little more than a sore knee and a disinclination to do any diving for a very long time.

She also realized that I was in need of some loving care, and she gave it generously. Afterward, I drove home.

Now normally, after a day like I'd had, you couldn't have pulled me away from Patricia with a come-along. But I was spooked. The case wasn't quite closed yet. There was still a crazy man out there who might believe that I was dead. Or, after the raid on his house, he might not.

The last time there'd been a loony out gunning for me, Patricia had gotten in the way and she'd been seriously hurt. I didn't want to chance that happening again. So, until such time as they got Drake Vessey put away, I'd spend the nights in my own bed, alone. I went to sleep with my right hand cradling the .38 Police Positive under my pillow.

I didn't sleep for long.

When the phone rang, I knew who it was. The old occasionally reliable sixth sense was working overtime. Or maybe it was my newly documented "psychic sensitivity." Whatever, I knew.

And as soon as I answered, then *he* knew *I* was alive. He didn't say anything, just chuckled. It was the same chuckle I'd heard in Eric Vessey's darkened house three nights— could it have been only three?—earlier. I was sure it was. It raised the hair on my arms.

He chuckled once, then hung up.

I probably should have called the cops immediately. But then I thought, if I surround myself with cops, he'll just continue to lie low until I relax again. Or he might find out about Patricia, and go after her. And I had no idea where he was. He might be three hundred miles away by now, just letting me know he was still on the loose.

So I didn't call the cops. I made myself the target once again. I couldn't go back to sleep, of course. I sat in my kitchen, the Police Positive in my lap, and I waited.

An hour passed and nothing happened. Then, suddenly, I thought of Grover Jordan and a feeling took violent hold of me. I felt compelled to leave the apartment. To go out and find Drake Vessey.

I fought against it. This was insane. To go out would be to expose myself. And where was I going? I wasn't sure. And how could I know I was going to find him? I just knew. And why should I go alone? Because if I brought help, it wouldn't work.

It was a wild goose chase. No, it wasn't. I was going to end up dead. No.

The feeling pulled and pulled at me and I was powerless to resist. In a daze, I got up, shoved the revolver behind my belt, and walked out of the house.

It was a clear, cool moonless night and I didn't have a jacket on. I shivered. But I didn't go back to get something heavier to wear. I couldn't. The compulsion to keep moving was too powerful. I had a strong sense of time running out. That if I didn't act now, there would be terrible consequences.

I started my car. Only then did I know where I was going. Except that I guess I'd known from the moment he chuckled. That was his way of telling me where he was. If he wasn't really there, I'd feel like a fool running around in the middle of the night. And if he was. . . .

I drove to Morgan Vessey's condo. It took her a long time to answer the door. She was not pleased to see me.

"What the *hell*?" she said. She tried to drill me with her eyes, but this night I was immune. "Do you know what time it is, Swift?"

I looked at my watch. "It's two-thirty in the morning," I said.

"What are you *doing* here?"

"I'm sorry," I said. "You haven't heard from your brother, have you?"

"What are you *talking* about? Of course I haven't heard from my brother. Did you get me up at—"

"Morgan, Drake is wanted by the police. He tried to kill me today, among other things."

She just gaped at me.

"I think he killed Eric, too. But I need to check something out. I know it's late, but I have to find out tonight. I need the keys to Eric's house."

"What . . . what's there?"

Her hand was resting in the hollow of her throat. She looked frightened. It hadn't even occurred to me that she might be in danger, but she might. So strong was my sixth sense, though, that I was completely confident we'd have Vessey before she ever came to harm.

"Evidence," I lied. "Possibly important. Did you ever find the keys I lost on Monday night?"

She shook her head.

"Change the locks?"

"No, not yet."

"Okay, you have another set of keys, don't you?"

"Yes."

"Get them."

I was in control of the psychic energy tonight. She went and did as I'd asked, without the slightest hesitation. She dropped the keys into my hand, along with a magnetic card for the alarm system.

"Now," I said, "go back inside and lock the door. *Stay put.* Don't open the door for anyone but me. If you hear from Drake, call the police immediately. I should be back before long and we'll talk about what to do next. Clear?"

She nodded. I could see her struggling with the conflicting emotions.

"Do it now," I said.

She closed the door and I heard the sound of a deadbolt being thrown.

Eric Vessey's house was unlocked and dark. The burglar alarm light was off. I thought again about calling Ridley Campbell. But once again the sense was overwhelming that if I did, I'd lose Drake. I'd never thought much about fate, but that was the word that came to mind. It was my fate to meet him back here, alone, the way it had happened the first time.

Strangely, there was no fear. I'd left most of that back in the cold and gloom of the quarry. This time, the outcome was destined to be different. I went into the house with confidence, the gun loose and ready in my hand. I burst through the door, flicked the wall switch, stepped quickly to my left, crouched.

Nothing happened. No one was there, no lights came on. There was no sound of electricity at work. The power's been cut, I thought. Okay. Just like before. The challenge had been made. He was here somewhere, as the chuckle had been meant to tell me. And he'd expected me to come in the door prepared. He hadn't been waiting right there, where I might get him before he got me. He was someplace else.

I thought about getting out of there, immediately calling the cops. But I didn't do it.

Instead, I reached out with my foot and eased the door

shut. Then I stood still, listening for some telltale sound of another human being. The house was silent.

From memory, I put together a mental picture of the layout. U-shape. Four rooms down the hall ahead of me. Kitchen, game room, two bedrooms. The formal dining room and huge living room to my right, with the swimming pool out back. In the other wing of the U, the Jacuzzi bathroom, the office, and two more bedrooms.

I didn't move for ten minutes. Slowly, my eyes adjusted to the dark. And it was very dark. I remembered that there had been drapes that could be pulled across all the glass that looked out over the pool area. The house had heavy shades for every window.

He must have pulled everything. Setting the stage for a last little game. Thinking that, having been here longer and knowing the house better, he'd be less blind than I. Well, if that's the way he wanted it, it was fine with me. The way I figured, he'd actually handed me the advantage. In Nam, you trained yourself to use your night vision and use it efficiently, and you learned to move very, very quietly.

My confidence hadn't waned a bit. I felt as though I could put myself right into Drake's mind. He'd be waiting. Patience was what he was good at. He'd waited outside my apartment for hours, on the off chance that he'd get a shot at me. He'd waited by the quarry for who knew how long, with only the expectation that yesterday would be the day I'd go diving.

So now that's what he'd be doing again. He'd sit tight until I came to him, then he'd do whatever he intended to do. I had to assume that his plans involved the gun that hadn't yet turned up, the one he'd used on my brother.

I didn't know if I'd be able to outwait him. Maybe. I've become pretty good at it through the years. You have to, or detective work will drive you nuts. But in this case it didn't seem like the best plan. If I didn't go to him, he might give it up at dawn and slip away and then I'd have to do this all again another day, or another night. I decided to go to him.

First, to prepare. I took the chance that he wasn't going to come at me right away. He could. He knew where I was. But I needed to strip down if I was going to seize the initiative. I had to risk a little noise. As quickly as possible I took off my shirt, pants and shoes.

Nothing happened. Now I was ready. I was going to be very hard to hear.

With the .38 clutched in my hand, I got on my belly and slithered silently down the carpeted hall. I crawled into the kitchen. He wouldn't be in there, I was sure of it. He wasn't a kitchen person. I was so sure of myself that I stood up and groped my way carefully to the long butcherblock counter. There had been a couple of wooden carousels containing kitchen implements. I slipped the gun behind the elastic at the back of my briefs and moved my hand, inch by inch, until I found them. I picked them off the counter. I'd managed the whole thing without making a sound.

Crouching, I stepped quickly to the door. I breathed deeply, then I threw one of the carousels into the air, back behind me. At the same time, I took off down the hall, toward the far end. The carousel crashed to the kitchen floor, scattering utensils everywhere. I dumped implements from the other carousel as I ran, keeping them to the side of the hall away from the windows, but he wouldn't know that.

I dropped to all fours when I reached the far bedroom door. There were now a lot of things for him to step on if he came this way and, except in the kitchen, I knew more or less where they were. If he'd fooled me and was actually lurking about the kitchen somewhere, he was trapped. He wouldn't be able to move without my hearing him.

There was no response to my racket. I hadn't expected there to be, but I paused for five minutes anyway. It'd work on his nerves, if nothing else.

I considered again where he might be. The office was a good bet. He was attracted to places like that, and there was a certain poetic justice to us having it out there. He'd expect me to try it. On the other hand, there wasn't a lot of room to maneuver and the room was windowless. That'd be a problem if he wanted to try blinding me by suddenly letting some outside light in.

The living room was most likely, I concluded. There was a lot of space. Plenty of furniture. And if I was going for the office, I had to pass through it.

I retrieved the gun from the bottom of my briefs, where it had fallen, and went silently back up the hall, being careful to avoid the junk strewn along the way. Every six feet or so I stopped and turned sideways, my back to the windows, a precaution against his deciding to spray a few random bullets in my direction.

There were no bullets. I dropped prone when I reached the door to the dining room. For a few minutes, I listened. I projected the sixth sense. No sounds, no feel of anyone in the room. I crawled through the doorway and propped my back against the nearest wall. The revolver was balanced on my knee, aimed in the direction of the massive vagueness that had to be the dining room table. I wondered if it was still set for eight. Then I wondered more seriously if Vessey might be sitting at one of the places. That'd be cute, might even be decent camouflage. I tried hard to distinguish individual chairs, looked for an inappropriate rounded shape. No, not his sense of humor, I thought.

After a reasonable pause, I decided to move on. He wasn't in the dining room. There was no cover, too many sharp angles against which a human being would stand out. I took the empty carousel I'd held onto and set it gently in the center of the doorway to the hall. If he came at me from the rear, I'd know it. Then, very slowly, I edged my way along the walls, until I arrived at the living room door.

Now I had to think hard about what to do next. There were a lot of places to hide in there. If I was right, he'd chosen one of them.

I reviewed my mental picture of the room. There was a huge sofa and a couple of deep chairs grouped around a glass-topped coffee table. The arrangement faced the entertainment center, which was against the streetside wall. There were shelves and cabinets to hold the equipment, store records and tapes, etc.

In the far left-hand corner, near the door to the other wing, was the bar. There was a counter, several stools, an area behind with a cooler, a sink and space to mix drinks. The various bottles were racked up on wall shelves, in front of a mirror etched with an old Coca-Cola advertisement.

In the near left-hand corner was a large glass-fronted cabinet, filled with a collection of something or other, I couldn't remember.

The poolside wall, between the bar and the glass cabinet, was all windows. Draped now.

There was a lot of cover. He could be anywhere. One approach would be to run through the living room, hoping to attract a shot. There wasn't much chance he'd hit me. Then again, there was the remote chance that he would. I didn't like that idea.

Next I considered making a diversionary noise. That had its advantages. But if he was as patient as I thought he was, he wouldn't stir. And he'd know that I was nearby.

I opted for plan three, to try to find him in the dark. That way, if I could maintain silence, he'd never know I was in the room with him until I tripped over him. All the while, the tension screws would be tightening. I'd be on the offensive and would be ready to strike when I found him. He'd be cramped, his reaction time slowed.

Of course, if he'd booby trapped the place. . . . Best not to think about that.

One last time, I reviewed my map of the room. I really didn't want to trip over something that I *knew* was there. Then, satisfied, I went in.

He'd expect me to come around the corner, so I went straight. Rather than crawling or going on hands and knees, I duckwalked on the tips of my toes, commanding my bum knee not to crack. The fewer the points of contact with the carpet, the less noise I was likely to make. I didn't make any.

I moved until I could feel in front of me the big furniture grouping in the center of the room. I reached out a hand. There it was. I snugged up next to it.

He was in the room. I hadn't heard him yet, but I could sense his presence. And now it was my turn to wait. I counted on him not having prepared as thoroughly as I had. He might be able to breathe softly enough not to give himself away. But sooner or later I'd hear one of the sounds clothing makes when you shift your weight.

It was sooner. Just the whisper of fabric, but to my concentrated attention almost like a gunshot. He was somewhere on the other side of the furniture. Where? I looked at the mental map again. He wouldn't be huddled like I was. It was a very poor defensive position. He wouldn't be in the doorway, where he might stand out. He wouldn't be behind the bar. Another trap.

Then I knew. He'd be in the space at the end of the bar that you passed through in order to get behind it. It was a good choice. The wall protected you on one side, the bar on another. No one could come from the rear unless they had been behind the bar to begin with. Anyone coming around the furniture would be an easy target. *If* you could hear or see them.

I would be best neither seen nor heard.

The one blind spot for him would be along the outside edge of the bar, where the stools were. To get there I'd have to cross his field of vision, so far as he had one. I'd have to go from the furniture group all the way to the draperied poolside wall, at which point the corner of the bar should shield me. For a while, I'd be completely exposed.

The key would be to move so slowly as to almost not move at all. I'd practiced the technique, during my combat training, but never had occasion to use it. I took a silent deep breath and tiptoed away from the furniture.

I was nearly halfway back to the door before I changed direction. My hope was that when I entered the exposed space my shape, if it were visible, would blend with the glass cabinet behind it. I crept forward until I knew I was about to enter the danger zone. I turned so that I presented my side to the other end of the room. Keep the target as small as possible.

Then I began to move. Slowly, ever so slowly, but constantly. One foot forward, plant and lean, bring the other around. Never stop. Never a jerky motion. Flow, and make no sound.

The whisper of cloth again. I froze. Was he turning to shoot me? No, nothing. A mistake to freeze. So hard to start up without jerking. It's why you never pause. Concentrate.

There was sweat trickling from my underarms down my ribs. I got going again, fought the desire to run, to get it over with. And then my elbow just nudged the drape. My heart slowed. I should be in the blind spot.

Now I moved carefully along the edge of the drapery, again on tiptoe, making sure I didn't brush against the fabric. As a precaution, I kept my free hand, the one without the gun, in front of me. That, perhaps, saved my life.

By good fortune, or fate, my hand just brushed the booby trap, without setting it off. It was a string, stretched taut in front of me at chest height, perpendicular to the drapes. I had no idea what it was attached to. Undoubtedly something that would make a lot of noise if I'd bumbled into the trap.

So Vessey had decided to supplement his own extra-sensory awareness with some good old-fashioned hardware. That suggested vulnerability, that he wasn't confident he could track me inside his mind. It made me feel in command of the situation.

There might be more than one string, of course. I felt upward. Nothing there. Then down. There was another string, about the level of my ankles.

This was going to be tough.

I got down on all fours, praying again that my knees not crack. They didn't. Then I raised my right leg, making it parallel to the floor. I moved it until I felt it was well clear of the lower string. I shifted my weight and dropped my knee, arching my back. It worked. I was straddling the string.

Some sweat beaded up on my forehead and dropped to the carpet. I froze. Had it made any sound? I couldn't tell, but Vessey stirred once more.

I couldn't wait. As quickly as possible, I completed my maneuver. I got my right arm between the strings, positioned it on the floor, then pulled the remainder of my body through. I made it without touching either of the strings.

The rest was relatively easy. I made my way forward until I could sense the near end of the bar. With my outstretched hand, I felt one of the stools. I slid my hand down its leg. Concentrating my strength, I grasped the stool and lifted it. I brought it away from the bar, and then I threw it toward the place where Vessey had to be crouching.

His gun went off, I think accidentally. Under cover of the noise of that and the stool crashing as he fought it off, not knowing what it was, I vaulted onto one of the other stools and went from there to the bar itself. He came lurching out from behind the end of the bar. I could just barely make him out. I timed it as best I could and leaped for his back, bringing my gun down hard on his skull.

He screamed. I'd only managed a glancing blow and he didn't go down. That was a bad break. He was a lot stronger than I was. He leaned forward and threw me over his head. I somersaulted in the air and hit hard, but on my feet, and I was able to dive sideways, toward the furniture grouping. He fired at where I should have been.

I whirled and returned fire, then scrabbled around to the

front of the couch. There was a muffled grunt, followed by silence. I believed that I'd hit him.

The silence stretched out, then he moved. I didn't dare raise my head. He ran along the other side of the couch, not more than three feet from me. He fired a blind shot that buried itself in the floor next to me.

He blundered through the dining room, banging chairs. I was after him by then. I made it to the door between the rooms, hugged the wall next to it. He hit the implement carousel on the run and went down hard. The impact shook the floor, I'd swear it. I heard the breath go out of him.

"Vessey!" I yelled. "It's no good. I know exactly where you are. I put that thing in the door. Throw your gun back this way or I'll shoot!"

I hardly knew whether I meant it or not. I heard him get up, but he didn't go anywhere.

Instead, he said, "All right, go ahead. Shoot. Avenge your brother, Swift."

"It *was* you," I said. "Wasn't it?"

"I didn't want to kill your brother. You're the one that was supposed to come out to the car."

He stood there in the hall, his vague outline framed by the dining room door. I was clear across the room, but it wouldn't have been a difficult shot. He moved a little, perhaps aiming his gun my way.

I don't know whether I would have been able to shoot. His last remark had hit me like a Clemens fastball. What was he saying, that he had been consciously screwing with my head when Ashley went rushing out to get me that drink? My mind teetered on the edge of chaos again. I began to lose my sense of where I was. The supporting wall was turning soft as cottage cheese. Another minute and I might have fallen to the floor and begun babbling in tongues.

And then the hall lights came on.

Nothing else, just that series of lights in the ceiling. Someone must have returned power to the house and that hall switch was still on, from when I'd flipped it earlier.

I don't know which of us was more surprised. Neither of us moved. He was an impossibly easy target now. I was still back in the shadows, halfway protected by the doorframe. His gun hand was slightly raised. There was a large blood-stain on his shirt, up under the other shoulder. I'd hit him.

The light jolted me back to my senses.

"Come on, Vessey," I said calmly. "Put it down."

I heard the outside door open, then close. He turned, faced whoever was in the hall with him. The person was out of my sight.

"You sonofabitch." It was Morgan Vessey's voice, and it was filled with hatred. Goddamn her. She just hadn't been able to stay put. "Where's Swift, did you kill him too?"

Drake was riveted to the spot. I could imagine her working her power on him. He wouldn't have a chance.

"I'm all right, Morgan," I called. "It's over now."

"You were never anything," she said to him. "You just couldn't bear either one of us, could you?"

When Drake finally spoke, he sounded like a machine.

"Eric was wrong," he said. "It was my gold, I found out about it. He told me I could never get it without his help. He said, 'I'll give you a ten percent finder's fee.' That's what he said." Vessey made that eerie chuckle again. Maybe she *couldn't* control him. "He deserved to die."

"You're right, Drake," I said. "He's dead. Put the gun down now." I sounded lame even to me.

"You *did* kill him." Her voice was ice. "Damn you, Drake, they've got the electric chair in this state and I'm going to see that you get it."

He stared at her, just stared for a long frozen moment with absolutely no expression on his face. Then there was the ghost of a smile.

"I killed him," he said mechanically. "Of course I killed him. And you know *why*, don't you, my sister? It wasn't for the money, you know that. It was for you. *You*. You're the one who lay with him."

He said the words slowly, pronouncing each one clearly and distinctly.

"Don't you *dare* try and make it dirty," she whispered, her voice cracking.

"If only it had been me," he said.

He raised his hand and pointed the gun at her. Then, just like that, he pulled the trigger.

CHAPTER
20

"**E**ric Vessey's buried secret," I said. "The one Grover Jordan had felt was tormenting him. It must have been eating away at Drake, as well."

I shook my head slowly, trying to clear away things that couldn't be cleared, and said, "After he shot her he dropped to his knees. He just rocked there, back and forth, back and forth, staring down at her. It didn't look as if his mind was still in this world, and I didn't want to go near him just then. I sprinted back to the office and used the phone there to call the rescue squad."

I'd come to the end of the story. I wanted to tell it, had to tell it, had told it to the cops, and now Patricia. She needed to hear it, but after her no one else. I never wanted to have to tell it again.

"Jesus," Patricia said. "How . . . how is she?"

"They think she'll live. One shot in the gut. It was bad, but it wasn't in the heart."

We sat in silence for a minute, wondering how you deal with such acts of madness.

Then I continued. "When I got back to the hall, he was still there, still doing the rocking thing. I decided to approach him. I asked him to give me the gun. I didn't know then if she was alive or not, but I didn't want him shooting her again if I could prevent it.

"At first, he didn't respond. He rocked there, speaking her name. Then he looked up at me. His face was like a death mask. I suppose he was in deep shock. There was just no expression, nothing. He stared at me for quite a while before there was any sign of recognition.

"I wasn't sure I *wanted* him to recognize me. He'd been trying to kill me, after all. I still had my gun in my hand and I was ready to use it if I had to. But then he *chuckled*. That same little chuckle, one last time. It absolutely immobilized me. And *then* he looked at Morgan, shook his head, looked back at me and said, 'And I didn't even kill him.'"

"But—" Patricia said. "But that's impossible, isn't it? He *confessed*."

"He confessed to *Morgan*," I said. "Whatever their twisted history was, all three of them, that's what he wanted *her* to believe before she died."

"But he *had* to. Dr. Slate saw his car at the quarry that night."

"He had to," I said. "That's what I thought, too. But at that point, what the hell did it matter if he'd killed Eric or the man had accidentally drowned. So I just asked him again to give me the gun.

"Instead, he told me his story. I guess there was some part of him that couldn't bear to die with anyone else thinking he'd murdered his brother. I don't know. He'd tried to kill me, had just shot his sister and would have done who knows what to Danny Jordan. Why should he care?" I shrugged. Brothers are strange things. "All I know is that he did.

"'I would have,' is what he said. 'I wanted to. We'd already had one fight that day. I went there and if I found him I would have strangled him and thrown him in the water. He had no right to do what he was doing without me. I even went there to kill him. But there was another car, already there.' He looked down at his sister and said, 'There was another car there, Morgan. I didn't do it. I turned around and I came home.'

"Of course I said immediately, 'Whose car, Drake?' But he

was through. He shook his head one more time, reached out and briefly touched her lips with his finger. There were tears on his face and he looked like he couldn't harm a soul. Then he put the barrel of the gun in his mouth. I tried to grab his arm, but . . . I just wasn't quick enough."

Patricia stared down at the tabletop. It was a scene we'd played before, me telling a story like this and she trying to come to terms with it. Each time it happened, there was the fear, fear of that one time too many, the one that made her realize she could no longer be involved with someone like me. My fear of that day was greater than of all the Drake Vesseys in the world.

I sipped at the coffee I'd laced liberally with John Jameson's fine Irish whiskey.

In a way, it was easier for her. She only had to deal with *me*, the kind of work I did, the kind of horrible things that sometimes happened around me. But *I* had to deal with the things themselves.

Once again, she pulled herself together, as I'd prayed she would. She is sickened by violence, frightened by it. I guess we all are, to some degree. There's so much of it. Personal violence, corporate violence, governmental violence, random terrorist violence. We each find our own way to cope and go on.

At the same time, Patricia has a true detective's mind. She is attracted to the ins and outs of intricate cases. In spite of all the blood, she'd want the final answers as much as I did.

"Did you believe him?" she asked.

"I don't know," I said honestly. I'd stared at that blank mask of a face and I hadn't known what to believe. No one would have.

"It was so implausible," I went on. "And yet. . . . Why would he bother lying when he was about to take his own life? And then there was that other time, on the phone, when he'd said he didn't kill Eric, and I'd felt so strongly that he was telling the truth. One thing that's come out of this case is that I put a lot more stock in my gut feelings.

"On top of that, there's something that's been stuck in the back of my mind ever since I first suspected Drake: There's just no evidence that he had the kind of technical expertise necessary to tamper with Eric's equipment, and do it so cleverly that everyone but a psychic twin sister would think accident.

"And finally, I had to consider that he'd originally come to me. We'll never know why now. Maybe he thought I'd help him locate the gold, be his partner or something. He *knew* Morgan had hired me from the moment he discovered I was a detective who'd been given the keys to the house, so maybe he wanted to keep tabs on my investigation. Whatever was going on in that strange mind of his, the important fact is that he did come to *me*, supposedly to have me look into Eric's death. It just didn't make sense that he'd have done that if he was involved in that death.

"Anyway, it looked like one of those questions that'd remain unanswered. Eric Vessey was dead and Drake Vessey was dead. Danny had been back at the house when Eric dived and the only car Paula had seen was Drake's. So how could we ever know?"

"I guess we can't," she said, then she saw my face. "Oh no. There *is* something."

"Uh huh. It came to me later on, when I was telling Campbell the story for about the third time. I suddenly thought: Drake Vessey's air tank. It's probably still in his car.

"I kind of casually asked Ridley if they'd found the car, and they had, parked about a block away. What of it? he wanted to know. I still hadn't told him Drake's last words. If they'd been lies, it didn't matter. And it they hadn't, well, something was holding me back. Another of those *feelings*, I guess. I don't know. But if I was ever going to tell him my suspicions, that was the moment. Again, I just couldn't do it.

"So I made up a story. I told him that Danny had lost a hat when he'd been kidnapped and that he'd asked me to try and get it back for him. He thought it might be in Vessey's car. I asked if I could take a look.

"I think Rid was suspicious, and he was still irritated with me for having gone to Eric Vessey's house alone. Though he admitted that if I'd called him he probably wouldn't have gone chasing phantoms in the middle of the night with me, just on the basis of some intuition of mine. But I played innocent and it was a harmless enough request on the surface of it. He said okay.

"After I'd finally finished making my statement, one of Campbell's men took me down and let me poke around in

Drake's car. I made a big show of looking everywhere for that elusive hat. But actually, all I wanted was to see if the diving gear was still in there. It was. So I very casually looked at his tank pressure gauge. Fifteen hundred psi. Half-empty."

She looked at me with a puzzled expression. Then, as she thought it over, she understood.

"One dive," she said.

I nodded. "He would have used the half tank yesterday afternoon, when he went in after me. That doesn't leave him enough for another dive, especially not for as long as it would have taken. He couldn't have been in the quarry the night Eric died."

"Unless he got a fresh tank."

"He didn't. We know he hadn't by Tuesday, the last time I checked Jonathan's records. And he didn't on Wednesday, because I asked Jon that night whether any of the principals had been in and he said no. And yesterday he was out at the quarry long before Underwater Charlottesville opens in the afternoon. It had to be the same tank."

There was a pause, then she said, "Now what?"

"I don't know," I said. "If Drake didn't kill his brother, maybe no one did. But there *was* someone else at the quarry that night. I feel like I owe it to Morgan to try and find out who."

"How?"

That was the question. I turned it over and over in my head, searching for possibilities. Nothing came to me.

Saturday arrived. For lack of anything better to do, I dug out the list of divers I'd made and talked to them all. I even drove to Richmond, talked to the dive shop owners there and anyone they could think of who might have been approached.

The weekend passed and I drew a blank. If Eric Vessey's equipment had been tampered with, it had been done without the cooperation of anyone within a hundred miles.

Monday morning. Morgan Vessey was finally able to have visitors. She was going to live. I went to see her and apologized. Somehow what had happened felt like my fault.

On my way out, I suddenly stopped in my tracks. The file, of course. Where was the file? With a rising sense of excitement, I drove out to Drake Vessey's house.

It was locked, silent, empty looking. No cops around. There was no reason to guard the house now. The whole thing would be sorted out in good time.

I broke in. Was it a crime to break into a dead man's house? As I expected, he had a room devoted to the tools of his trade. There were half a dozen filing cabinets, stacks of books and folders, papers strewn everywhere. But I had as long as it took.

The Jordan file from Eric Vessey's office had not been alphabetized. It was stuffed in the back of one of the drawers in one of the overflowing cabinets. I opened it on Drake's desk and went through it.

The first thing I saw was the coin book. Eric Vessey had made a couple of notes in it that I hadn't seen the night I found it in his desk. Notes about the potential value of the St.-Gaudens gold pieces. No wonder Drake had taken it from the room.

Then there were the other three items I'd seen a week earlier. There were also more photocopied pages from Henry's diaries; details about the corporate structure of the Institute; tax information about the property. And a lot of other stuff that I didn't bother with, because I found what I was looking for. As soon as I saw it, I knew exactly what had happened to Eric Vessey.

It was a photocopy of a hospital lab test. How Eric had gotten hold of it I'd never know. Probably bribed a records clerk. It didn't matter now. He'd been an extraordinarily resourceful man, that was clear. He'd also been vile, contemptible, cruel, anything else along that line you'd care to name.

I put the sheet of paper in my pocket, checked the file to make sure there were no other references to it, and left Drake Vessey's house.

I waited until late in the day, until closing time. I wanted to see him in the shop. I didn't want Benjy to be there.

As soon as Jonathan Searle saw my face, he said, "You know."

I just stood there, surrounded by the racks and shelves full of diving paraphernalia. Tanks and wetsuits, masks and weights and fins and snorkels, hoses and gauges and knives. Life-preserving B.C.s. Underwater Charlottesville felt like a museum.

"Uh huh," I said. "I know."

He sighed, sat down on a stool behind the big glass display case.

"I'm not surprised," he said. "After all that's happened. But how?"

"Eric Vessey kept a file. In it I found the lab report where you tested positive for AIDS."

"I'm not a homosexual." He laughed bitterly, shaking his head. "Isn't that weird, that that's the first thing I'd think of to say. As if that's what's important."

"The auto accident?" I guessed.

He nodded. "I needed blood. This was before they started routine testing of donations for the virus, so I picked it up. But that was four years ago. I don't have AIDS, Swift. I'm carrying the virus, but I don't *have* the disease. The vast majority of carriers are like that. They never get it. And they never give it to anyone, either. You can't get it except through unsafe sex or the transfer of infected blood. People don't understand *anything* about AIDS."

"The fact that it isn't active wouldn't have stopped Vessey."

"Of course not. He was an evil man," he said as though he met evil men every day. "When Grover refused to sell the property, he tried to get it through manipulation of the Board. Paula he already had on his side, I think. So first he offered to cut me in. When I didn't go for that, he blackmailed me."

"He threatened to go public with the lab report."

"Yes. You know what would have happened. The hysteria there is around here. I haven't even been able to sustain a relationship with a woman. As soon as I tell them, they're gone. If my employers found out I'd lose my job. I love working with children, Swift, but I think I might have survived that. The thing I couldn't have survived was losing Benjy. Vessey threatened to make sure I'd be declared an unfit guardian. You've met Benjy. If they put him in an institution, it'd kill him. And he doesn't have anyone else. I'd do anything before I let them take him from me."

"Including. . . ."

"Including ridding the world of someone like Eric Vessey," he said. "For what it's worth, it was as painless as possible. I gave him a fill that was heavy on carbon dioxide. Over time, he would have gotten drowsy and disoriented, then drowned. He would never have known what was happening. I went in after him to make sure the tank emptied out, so that it'd look like he ran out of air. Which is what he did, really.

"When I found his body, I didn't feel a thing except relief that it had worked. Don't expect any regrets at this point."

We looked at each other for a long moment. I felt a terrible sadness. Whatever friendship had been growing between us, there was no hope for it now.

Finally he said, "That first day, when you came into the shop, somehow I knew what you were working on. That's why I invited you to the house. I wanted you to know me better. I wanted you to meet Benjy. Then, if you ever did figure out what had happened. . . ."

There was another pause before he said, "What are you going to do?"

"Well," I said, "the cops are convinced Drake Vessey killed his brother. Unless you confess, they're not going to be looking for someone else. You're obviously not about to confess. I don't have any real evidence against you. So what *can* I do?"

"You can ruin me."

I took the photocopy of the lab report from my pocket. "So can anyone who gets their hands on this," I said, and I laid it on the display case.

Then I turned and walked out of the shop.

CHAPTER
21

I thought about it. I thought about it a lot.

Jonathan Searle had killed a man. A very nasty man, but a human being nevertheless. And he might well go unpunished.

Or would he? Searle had AIDS. Inactive, yes, but with this disease no one was really sure what might happen. He lived with the knowledge that he could come down with it at any time. The virus was there. It was in his blood.

And he lived with the possibility that someone else could always come along. Someone like Vessey, looking for personal gain. Or someone with a grudge. Or someone simply in the grip of AIDS hysteria. That someone, with one little sheet of paper, could destroy Searle's life, and probably that of his nephew as well. Any hour, any day.

How much punishment is enough?

On the other side of the coin, there was Morgan. Did she deserve to know the truth? What good would it do if she did? If I told her everything, would she then feel compelled to avenge Eric, whatever the cost? Eric her brother, Eric her lover.

I didn't feel competent to sit in judgment by myself. When I sat down to dinner that night, I intended to ask for help.

Patricia was there. Her brother Patrick. And Ashley, who'd been released into our care. If there was an answer, I'd find it around this table.

I told them all what I'd been doing for the previous two days. How I'd canvassed divers and dive shops and come up with nothing.

"Then I broke into Drake Vessey's house," I said.

"Loren!" Patrick said.

"Drake won't care," I said. "I wanted to see if he'd kept the Jordan file. Thought there might be something in it."

"And?" a couple of them said.

"It was there."

"And?"

I hadn't planned how I was going to tell it. I expected that I'd get some sort of inspiration at the last minute. And maybe I did. In my mind, I saw Benjy. He was laying his hand against my cheek. Then, as I had so often, I saw the face of Grover Jordan. The old man was smiling the way he did, like you could do no wrong.

"Nothing," I said without hesitation. "Nothing I didn't already know."

"Too bad," Patrick said. "Any other ideas?"

"I'm fresh out," I said.

There was a pause, then Patricia said, "Well, I guess that takes care of that, doesn't it?"

I guess it did. For everyone but me. I'd always know what I knew.

Patricia went to the kitchen for coffee.

When she did, Ashley said to me, "That's a fine lady you got there, little bro'."

"Goddamn it, Ash," I said. "Don't you dare be—"

"Calm down, Lor," he said. "Calm down. You know, I had a lot of time to think in that lumpy hospital bed. I figure I haven't been the best brother you could have. Okay, I admit it. And then I figured, well, I believe that everything eventually comes around. So maybe getting shot like that, maybe there you have an example of the powers that be balancing the scales. You suppose we're even now?"

He was grinning at me but it was a serious question and I knew it.

"Yeah," I said. "I reckon we're at least even."

He reached over and put his hand on my shoulder.

"Other thing I figured," he said, "is that it's never too late to start over. We're brothers, that's the important part."

"Okay, Ash," I said. "Okay. You're right. It starts again, from right here."

Patrick looked at us like he didn't understand but really did.

I smiled, reached over and clasped Ashley's shoulder warmly as Patricia came back in with the coffee.